CELTIC TREASURE

CELTIC TREASURE

A MICK SCOTT ADVENTURE

DC JOHNSTON

ACKNOWLEDGEMENTS

Over the last year, as I wrote Celtic Treasure, A Mick Scott Adventure, I enjoyed an exciting and rewarding journey. In this fast-paced, action adventure novel, Mick Scott makes his debut and brings his wife Joelle along for the ride. I hope you enjoy this first book of the series.

I give special thanks to my mother, Ruth Johnston, who passed in 2011. As a grade school teacher of English grammar for thirty seven years, she was instrumental in developing my love of reading and writing. My family, especially my wife Mary, our children, my sister Linda, and mother-in-law Becky, were incredibly supportive throughout the writing process. Without them and their encouragement, creative ideas and patience, Celtic Treasure would not have been completed.

PROLOGUE

Northern Gaul, 56 BC

IT WAS JUST a matter of time until the Romans would complete their expansion across Gaul and into the northwestern regions of Armorica. The Roman legion had become so powerful that the senate was almost a slave to their whims. In order for an ambitious man like Caesar to gain absolute political dominance over his rivals, a successful military campaign was the surest way to force his political rivals to bow to his power. Romans loved power. Caesar was cunning and saw a victory across Europe as the perfect means of gaining absolute control.

Caesar played Celtic tribe against Celtic tribe, even employing Celtic horsemen as mercenaries and winning weaker chieftains over to his side. It was only after he'd marched into the heart of the country that the Celts began to rally themselves.

Arios, a muscular, dark-haired warrior, was finally returning to his tribe, the Coriosolite. Riding the black Arabian horse that had served him well during many bloody mêlées, Arios still sat tall in the four horned leather saddle. He was alone, the sole Coriosolite survivor of the last Roman campaign taking place in the Loire River valley. It was little more than a week's ride from his home near the Atlantic Ocean. He was adorned with bronze armlets and a large golden tork around his neck that signified his many courageous acts. His Agen helmet had a broad brim, was made of iron and topped with a horse hair plumb. Arios was a Coriosolite warrior of great wealth and rank.

He wondered how well his family had survived during his long time away. Several months had passed as he fought Caesar's armies near the Loire. He had seen thousands of Roman soldiers brutally defeat his fellow Celtic tribesman. Many villages were burned to the ground and riches plundered by Caesar. Those who were not killed were captured and now had to live under strict Roman law. Although he had not seen any signs of fighting for the last few days of riding, Arios continued looking cautiously from side to side as he rode slowly towards his village, scanning the path for signs of the enemy. This simple habit had saved his life on many occasions. Covered in scars from many bloody skirmishes that he had endured, he was now close to his village and he hoped he would soon be walking among his family and friends.

As Arios finally emerged from the heavily treed forest, he saw the outline of his village in the distance. The ground level fog made it difficult for him to see any details ahead and he could not tell if Caesar's troops had yet arrived. His village sat along the coast of the Atlantic Ocean near the mouth of the Rance River, controlling not only the estuary, but the open sea beyond. The promontory fort of Aleth, a defensive structure located above the steep cliff, commanded all approaches to the Rance and used area topography to reduce the ramparts needed.

Nearing the village, Arios began to see movement of his fellow tribesmen among the structures. He was finally home. His village and family were still safe from Caesar's outstretched arm of war.

Arios dismounted from his black Arabian, tied the reins to a short wooden post and walked towards his home. Not knowing what he would find inside, he opened the large wooden door with apprehension. Everything appeared as it did when he left. Suddenly, his wife and son emerged from a side room and ran to greet him shouting with happiness. He quickly set down his long, wooden body shield and iron spear to accept their embraces. They were both overjoyed to see that he was not only alive, but not seriously wounded.

After spending a short time talking with his beautiful wife and handsome son, Arios walked away to bathe and tend to his most recent wounds of war. His wife, Ciara, was a beautiful woman with long dark silky hair styled in plaits. She wore a brightly colored cloak and a golden tork around her neck. Her makeup accentuated her strong facial features. Celts took great care in their appearance and frowned on those who let their bodies get soft. Arios later joined his wife and son for a meal and to give them an account of the many battles that had been fought to stop Caesar's approaching armies.

"Father, how much longer will we be safe to stay in our village?" asked Morica.

"I'm not sure my son, Caesar's vast armies are growing nearer every moment. We lost many brave men in the Loire River valley. There was much bloodshed and looting in every village. His armies are slowing moving west with plans to occupy all of Gaul to the Atlantic Ocean."

Jumping to his feet and grabbing his father's weapons by the door, Morica shouted, "I'm ready to fight for my village and to slay every one of them with my sword. LET THEM COME!"

"Brave words coming from such a young boy," said his father Arios with a smile. He was nearly as tall as his father and resembled his muscular build. He wore bronze armlets and had long dark hair, the color of his mother's. A sling hung from his woolen trousers. But at just twelve years old, Morica had never seen war and his father hoped he never would. "The king of our tribe has announced a meeting for later today to unveil his plan for securing our village against Caesar's approaching armies," said Arios. "I have been asked to attend."

King Brennus, leader of the Coriosolite tribe, had been named after one of his great ancestors that had sacked Rome in the 4th century BC. He had at one time been a mighty Celtic warrior with many victories to his name. He stood nearly six feet tall, with long blond hair and broad muscular shoulders. But time had passed, and Brennus was now an old man. At nearly forty five years old, he was the eldest in the village, but was highly regarded by everyone in the tribe for his wisdom.

As the nobles and warriors listened intently to Brennus's plan to secure the village and its treasures from the inevitable invasion by Caesar's vast armies, they realized how quickly they must act. Although the plan would not save all of their three hundred fellow tribesmen from capture or death, some would survive and their plan would preserve the wealth and knowledge they had acquired over four hundred years for future Coriosolite generations. The overall plan was composed of four key parts, three of which would occur simultaneously over the next few days.

Twelve Coriosolite warriors would flee to Andion, the big island off shore to hide a cargo of treasure in two specified locations; then return to the village to fight against Caesar

Twelve Coriosolite warriors would travel by chariot, wagon and horseback to hide three wagon loads of artwork, statues, jewelry, amber, coins, and weaponry, in two separate locations within a day's ride from the village; then return to fight against Caesar

Two equal-sized groups of nearly one hundred Coriosolite men, women and children, would each be led by a warrior to join forces with the Osismii tribe to the west and the Redones tribe to the south for protection and in hopes of helping them defeat Caesar

King Brennus, his six nobles and two dozen warriors would remain in the village

King Brennus then announced, "I have selected each of you for a specific phase of my plan based upon your skills as trained warriors. It is my sincerest hope that someday in the near future, you will all return safely to our village." He handed each of the four selected men a leather document with written instructions. "Arios and Cunous, you are to return to the village immediately upon completing your assignments. Ansgar and Kailen, may the gods be with you and your charges as you help to defend our nearby fellow tribesmen."

Arios, the most decorated Coriosolite warrior of his tribe, was selected to lead his twelve men in their voyage to Andion, the large nearby island. Cunous, a trusted warrior and eldest son of King Brennus, was selected to lead his group of twelve to hide the treasures of the village. Ansgar and Kailen, two legendary Coriosolite warriors, were chosen to each take nearly one hundred villagers to the nearby Osismii and Redones tribes. The six nobles remaining in the village with King

Brennus were Casnar, Airell, Nolan, Brice, Padrig and Druce along with two dozen warriors.

It was 57 BC and Caesar's armies had completed their march against the Belgae, who inhabited the area north of Aleth along the Atlantic coast. The Belgae had suffered heavy losses and eventually surrendered when faced with the destruction of their villages. A few months later, Caesar turned his attention to the remaining tribes of the Atlantic seaboard, notably the Veneti and Coriosolite tribes in Armorica, who had assembled a confederacy of anti-Roman tribes. They were both a seafaring people and had built sailing fleets in the Gulf of Morbihan, requiring the Romans to build galleys and under-take an unconventional land and sea campaign. In less than a week, the Roman Empire would extend across Gaul to the Atlantic Ocean.

The single-sail cargo boat selected by Arios for the voyage to Andion was constructed according to native Celtic tradition. Shipwrights constructed the wooden skeleton of a vessel first, and then attached the hull planking to that frame. It measured sixteen meters long and eight meters wide at its broadest point; and with a depth of just under three meters, it would set low in the water when laden. The curved bottom of the boat was built of multiple planks attached to a frame of slender skeleton timbers. Built of oak, it was capable of carrying up to four tons of cargo.

Arios knew the boat had spent many hard years of life at sea, but it still was capable of making this short voyage. It would securely transport the wealth of his village in its cargo hold and have room for all twelve warriors. Although the boat would have a speed of three to five knots with its large square-design leather sail, the sixty one kilometer voyage to Andion would take nearly two full days. It was now time to load the precious cargo and make final preparations before setting sail.

As the sun was rising on the second day, Arios' boat neared the largely uninhabited island of Andion. They had been given favorable winds and were well ahead of schedule. He and his fellow warriors scanned the shore and tree line for movement. There appeared to be no one in this area. Certain that he could put his boat ashore in safety, he made landfall on the southeast corner of the island in a small natural cove per the King's written instructions. Arios was charged with securing the Coriosolite treasures in two separate locations. The first site would contain artwork, golden statues, inlaid jewelry, amber and coins. The second site would be strictly a large horde of Celtic and Roman coins, nearly one quarter of the wealth of the village.

King Brennus had instructed Arios to seek out a long, bottle-shaped passage grave (dolmen) a short walk northwest from the shore. This would mark the first treasure site. He organized his men into four groups; Arios and one warrior to act as scouts ahead of the treasure and to find the stone dolmen, six warriors working together to move the treasures to the site, three warriors to carry cut timbers and two warriors to guard the boat and remaining coins. Although the distance to the dolmen was short, the treasures were quite heavy and slowed their pace.

Arios was the first to sight the bottle-shaped passage grave a short distance ahead. The Neolithic structure built around 3300 BC, had been constructed of rock and measured approximately five meters long by two meters wide with large flat stones forming the roof. He and two of his warriors quickly formed a circle of protection around the dolmen's perimeter to stand watch for approaching tribes. Three warriors were ordered to return to the ship to retrieve the remaining cut timbers. Next, he instructed a warrior to carve the tribe's symbol into the side of the largest stone. The engraved symbol would signify that treasures of the Coriosolite tribe lay nearby. He began chiseling a small section of stone slightly larger than the size of his open palm. The familiar lyre image quickly took shape. Next, he carved a letter 'C' at its base.

Meanwhile, Arios ordered three other men to dig out a deep pit near the dolmen and then reinforce it with cut oak timbers using wood that had been transported on the boat and covered in pine pitch. Timbers were placed along all four sides and the floor. Dozens of woolen bags filled with treasure were lowered into place. Arios removed the golden torc from around his neck and placed it inside a specially designed wooden box, then secured it inside a thick woolen bag and sat it in the vault. With all of the treasures in place, additional oak timbers were lowered across the top of the area as a lid. A deep layer of dirt was then shoveled on top and tamped flat. Satisfied with the secure location of the treasure, Arios ordered his men to return to the boat.

It was now nightfall and the full moon was brightly lighting the sky. Arios knew all of his men needed a night of rest before their long journey the next day. He selected two warriors to take the first watch and then went below decks. He had given instructions that they would all rise at first light.

Using the same tactics as the day before, Arios and one warrior took a scout position ahead of the other men. Walking due north from their boat, each of the six largest men carried two heavy woolen bags full of coins balanced across their shoulders. Three warriors carried cut timbers and two warriors remained to guard the boat. As instructed, they were headed for another ancient burial site and would arrive by mid-day.

When they were less than half way to their destination, Arios and his scouts noticed smoke on the horizon. Sensing that they were no longer alone in this area of the island, he raised his fist to command his warriors to stop. They dropped in place and readied their weapons. A short distance away was a small village, and Arios could see the faint trail of black smoke from a fire. If they proceeded to the menhir, they would most certainly be attacked and possibly killed. The Coriosolite treasure would be lost.

Weighing his options, Arios believed it best to bury the treasure where they stood. He ordered six of his warriors to form a tight circle around the area to guard their position. Four men dug hastily to form a deep pit in the soft soil. Cut oak timbers were placed along the bottom of the pit, but there was no time to line the walls or create a top. Quickly, they lowered all six woolen bags full of coins into the pit and replaced the soil. Arios could not properly mark the spot, but he knew that he was an hour's walk, due north of the boat. Still unseen by anyone in the nearby village, Arios and his warriors retreated to the shore and began the voyage home.

Back on the mainland, Ansgar and Kailen, two legendary Coriosolite warriors, had been directed by King Brennus to take two hundred villagers to the nearby tribes of Osismii and Redones to strengthen their numbers against Caesar. At the same time Arios was departing for the island of Andion, two large groups of villagers set off on their quest to neighboring tribes.

Ansgar and his charge of villagers covered the short distance to the village of Osismii along the coast without encountering any of Caesar's armies. Riders on horseback, wagons loaded with supplies and villagers, some walking, made the trek. Upon arrival, they were warmly embraced by their fellow tribesman. The Osismii appreciated their gifts of livestock and grains. The one hundred Coriosolite men, women and children were safe for now.

Leaving the Coriosolite village at the same time as Ansgar, Kailen and one hundred of his fellow villagers headed south toward the Redones tribe. After two days of travel, the Coriosolites entered the village with their wagons, chariots, and livestock. Like the Osismii tribe, the Redones were appreciative of the gifts of livestock and grains, but more importantly, there were now one hundred more tribesmen to help defend against Caesar's approaching armies.

Three days had passed since King Brennus had presented his plan to the nobles and warriors of his tribe. His eldest son, Cunous and his band of warriors left early on the second day and had completed their slow trek aside the Rance River. Three wagons were filled to the top of their wooden sideboards with a cargo of solid gold statues, fine jewelry, amber, art work, coins and armaments. A fourth wagon was filled with oak timbers, cut into equal lengths and stacked high. These would be used to reinforce the walls and floor of the treasure's hiding place.

Turning inland, they now headed due east to locate the stone menhir (long stone). It was after mid-day and the sun shone brightly. Cunous and two of his warriors acted as scouts traveling slightly ahead of the wagons loaded with Coriosolite treasure. Two warriors were ordered to guard the procession from the rear and provide an early warning signal to their tribesmen in case of attack. Although Cunous knew that Caesar's army would soon be approaching this area, there were no signs of Roman soldiers in the distance. The nearly treeless landscape was mostly flat with rolling hills of dark green grass in each direction. The large stone menhir would be easy for them to spot.

Without warning, it rose up from the green countryside like a bright, white beacon. Standing as tall as the combined height of three grown men, the menhir's quartz surface reflected the sunlight in a way that made it look ghostly. Cunous and his men approached the sight with caution. Commanding his warriors to establish a perimeter guard, six warriors formed a circle around the stone. At the same time, the other six warriors moved the wagons into place and began to dig the pit. They worked furiously until nightfall to prepare the site. Below the surface on the south side of the menhir now lay a room measuring ten by ten square. It was three times as deep as a man was tall. The walls and floor were lined with flat rough-hewed oak timbers so that the Coriosolite treasure would be secure. Cunous ordered three warriors to stand guard throughout the night and instructed one man to begin carving the tribe's symbol into the side of the stone. The engraved symbol was placed at knee height and would signify that treasures of the Coriosolite tribe lay nearby. He worked for several hours chiseling a small section of stone slightly larger than the size of his open palm. The familiar lyre image finally took shape in the hard surfaced stone. With that complete, he carved a letter 'C' at its base. At first light, his fellow tribesmen would return to unload the wagons.

Daybreak came quickly and there was still no sign of the enemy. As a precaution, Cunous ordered his men to stand guard. Six war-hardened soldiers armed with shields, spears and short swords stood evenly spaced around the perimeter. As the sun was still rising, four warriors carefully unloaded two small wagons filled with treasure. Woolen bags had been used to protect many of the smaller items from damage. Once the last piece was in place, Cunous sat a special woolen bag containing a wooden box with his father's torc into the vault. His men sealed the area by placing oak timbers close together across the top. Dirt taken out of the ground was shoveled on top of the timbers and tamped down. They had completed their task and it was not yet noon. Cunous ordered his warriors to mount and begin their journey southeast in hopes they would reach the next site by sundown.

More rolling hills of dark green grass filled the horizon. Their luck had held and they had not yet come across Caesar's legions. With the sun at their backs, they could easily make out the outline of tall trees on the horizon. Cunous and his two scouts were riding in advance of the wagons searching for the menhir location. The stone was rumored to be as tall as six men and as big around as an ox. Shortly before nightfall, they glimpsed a tall white granite stone in the distance. They had found the location as instructed by King Brennus.

Cunous ordered three of his warriors to stand watch through the night. The full moon that had been with them since the beginning of their journey was now dark. Without the light of the moon for his warriors to see, he decided to let them sleep until daybreak. His plan was to have the pit completed and treasure buried by early afternoon. He and his men would then turn toward their village. If they traveled throughout the night and all went well, they would return home by dawn.

It was barely first light and already five of the Coriosolite warriors were working doggedly to dig the ten by ten sized pit. Through hard packed soil and an impasse of large rocks, they toiled. With iron determination, they completed digging the pit and secured oak timbers around the walls and floor. The vault was not as deep as planned, only the height of a young boy. About the same time, the sixth warrior finished carving the tribe's lyre symbol into the white granite stone. With that complete, he carved a letter 'C' at its base.

It was mid-day and the wagon of treasures was not yet unloaded. One of the six perimeter guards facing the southeast shouted to Cunous to get his attention. "I see dust in the air and movement on the far horizon!" His commander quickly joined him to evaluate the situation.

"Men, it appears Caesar's armies are approaching from the southeast," said Cunous. "They could be upon us before we complete our task and escape. In honor of our King and our village we are duty bound to complete our task before we can flee." Cunous then ordered his guards to leave their posts and assist with securing the treasure. With haste, they unloaded the wagon of its precious cargo. After removing the golden torc from around his neck, Cunous placed it in a specially designed wooden box, then inside a woolen bag and sat it next to the other treasures. His men placed oak timbers on top of the vault as a covering and then using their hands, feet and shovels, the dirt was hurriedly scattered over the timbers. As they were tamping down the dirt and covering it with brush, they realized the possibility of escaping the Roman soldiers was bleak.

An army of one hundred thousand well trained Roman soldiers, moved decidedly across the southeast horizon towards Cunous and his men. If all of Caesar's troops stayed together in a slow moving battle line, he and his warriors would have a chance to escape. "MOUNT UP," shouted Cunous to his men. "We will ride northwest at once in hopes of distancing ourselves from the Roman soldiers." As their empty wagons, chariots and horses made their way across the rolling fields of deep green grass, Cunous continued to monitor the approaching armies' progress. He ordered his men to abandon the wagons and chariots so that they could escape more quickly on horse-back. They gained some distance, but it was not enough.

Cunous looked back and saw that Caesar had dispatched a unit of fifty well-armed cavalrymen to capture him and his men. The Romans were in close pursuit. Cunous could no longer avoid the obvious. He ordered his warriors to stop and boldly face their enemy. They would now most likely be captured or die in the skirmish. As the Coriosolite warriors' horses came about, each man prepared for fighting with a raised shield and sword drawn. The Roman soldiers advanced quickly and began consuming the Coriosolites. Men and their horses, both Coriosolite and Roman were soon lying dead across a wide area of the field. Only a handful of Roman cavalrymen had survived the mighty Coriosolite warriors, but Cunous and his men had perished. Caesar's legion would be upon the Coriosolite village near the coast in a matter of days.

Only six days after King Brennus enacted his plan to secure the village, Caesar sprang his attack. The twenty four Coriosolite warriors were no match for the thousands of well-trained Roman soldiers. Out manned, one by one, the brave men died protecting their King. As the Roman Legion searched the village for survivors, they were surprised that it was empty except for five noblemen and the King. All of the other villagers; men, women and children, had fled before the attack. King Brennus' plan had worked.

Each of the five noblemen and King Brennus were extensively questioned by the Roman leader. Slowly and painfully the Romans attempted to extract information from the nobles about the missing villagers and Coriosolite riches. After Casnar refused to speak, he was struck with the razor sharp edge of a Pompeii gladius sword across his neck. His body instantly collapsed to the ground as his severed head rolled away. Thinking the other nobles would begin to talk for fear of receiving the same fate, the Romans continued their questioning. One by one each of the remaining four nobles, Airell, Nolan, Brice, and Druce, refused to talk and were slain. Now they turned to the King to begin his questioning. When he would not speak either, several Roman soldiers secured his arms and legs and began beating him. As King Brennus neared death, they dragged his badly broken body to a locked room.

A short time later, Padrig, the sixth noble who had hidden from the Romans, appeared to the King through a small window. "King Brennus, you are still alive," he said. "I have come to help you escape."

"No, I do not have the strength to walk. My time is short," Brennus wheezed. "Before I die, I must provide you, the only remaining Coriosolite noble, with information about the location of our village treasures. Take this leather scroll, it contains my written instructions to Arios and my son Cunous. Safeguard it with your life." Although Padrig believed that he could still rescue the King, reluctantly, he agreed to accept the scroll and went into hiding.

During the first day back at sea, Arios updated his captain's log and included entries about their limited success at hiding the Coriosolite treasure. Although they had successfully hidden many valuable works of art, gold and jewels at the first menhir as planned, the bags of coins had been hastily buried in a field less than half way to the selected dolmen. He would need to make King Brennus aware of the location of the coins upon his return to the village.

After two days at sea, upon nearing the shoreline of their Coriosolite village, Arios saw dark black smoke billowing into the grey sky. He quickly realized that his King and village had been attacked. "Make preparations to go ashore," he barked at his warriors. "Our homeland is under siege by Caesar."

Arios divided his men into four groups of three warriors each to broaden the face of their attack upon the rocky cliff. As they ran up the steep, sandy embankment with shields up and gladius swords in hand, they were met with a volley of arrows and javelins from a multitude of Roman soldiers. Nine of his twelve warriors now lay dead on the cliffs covered in blood from their wounds. Arios let out a screeching battle cry as he and his two remaining warriors made their way toward the smoky, war torn village.

They had survived the arrows and javelins of the first attack, but were now on top of the cliff fighting hand to hand with the seasoned Roman soldiers. One Coriosolite warrior was run clean through by a Roman soldier thrusting his razor edged gladius, the other lay in a pool of his own blood clutching at his neck where he had been stabbed. It was a short and bloody fight to the end with Arios struggling as the last Coriosolite warrior standing. He too, had been mortally wounded and was feeling his life slip away. Stabbed multiple times in the chest with a leaf-shaped blade, he was bleeding uncontrollably and fell to the ground. As he took his last breath, his thoughts were of his beautiful wife Ciara and his son Morica. He reminisced about the aroma of her raven black hair the last time he held her in his arms and pulled her tight to his chest. A smile filled his face as he thought of his young son's heroic banter just a few days earlier. He prayed that Ciara and his son were still safe with the nearby Osismii tribe where they had traveled just a few days ago. Sadly, he would never know.

CHAPTER 1

Phoenix, Arizona — Present Day

ENJOYING ANOTHER WARM, relaxing morning around their tropically landscaped pool, it was hard for Mick and Joelle to believe that it was already Thanksgiving in Phoenix. Temperatures had finally fallen from nearly one hundred degrees Fahrenheit into the mid-eighties. All around them the sky was a deep turquoise blue without a cloud in sight.

"When do you think Kenzie will be getting home from ASU today?" asked Mick.

"Not sure," replied Joelle. "I know that she was taking her World History exam this morning and starting Thanksgiving break around noon. She should be here by 2:00 p.m., I believe. I really miss her."

Although this was her daughter's third year at Arizona State University in Tempe, Joelle was still getting used to her youngest child being away from home. This was the first time she had seen Kenzie since she started school in August and had a lot of catching up to do. Kenzie, a twenty one year old junior, had her mother's natural good looks and feisty personality. Standing five feet four inches tall, with long brown hair and hazel eyes, she kept fit by playing on the ASU women's soccer team.

Kenzie sang along to Katie Perry's *Fireworks* on the radio as she drove home towards south Phoenix in her bright blue 2009 Camaro convertible. With the top down and the warm wind blowing through her hair, she was thinking of seeing her friends back at home and enjoying her mom's home cooking. As she pulled onto I-10 heading east, she shifted her thoughts to the World History exam she had just completed. Her answers to the multiple choice questions were not a concern, those were quite easy. But the essay question, that was a different matter entirely. Would she be the only one in her class with such an unusual point of view? Was the recent Celtic coin discovery on the island of Jersey near Saint Malo, France a one-time event or just the beginning of many two thousand year old Celtic treasures to be found? Kenzie was anxious to discuss her theory with her mom and Mick during the break.

As Joelle finished her phone call to Mark and Donna, her real estate partners in Phoenix, Mick was in his office deeply involved in reviewing video and underwater photographs from a recent consulting project. Mick, fifty four and Joelle, forty, had relocated just four years earlier from Orlando after making a fortune together in the commercial real estate business. Mick, a man of English and Irish heritage, stood six feet three inches tall with steel blue eyes and light brown hair, worn short with grey around the temples. At fifty four, he was still in excellent physical shape due to his love of rowing, cycling and his two tours of duty as a Lieutenant in the U.S. Navy during his twenties. Following his years of military service, he had attended Purdue University and earned his undergraduate degree and MBA from the Krannert School of Business. He had then relocated to Florida and entered into the commercial real estate business.

Joelle, Mick's wife, stood five feet three inches tall, with long auburn hair and blue/grey eyes. Her figure, toned and fit, had just the right curves and complimented her feisty personality. Twenty years earlier, she had studied at Ohio State and received her MBA in finance. A few years later, she had moved to Orlando and met Mick at a real estate seminar. She was fluent in both French and Italian and listening to her speak in those languages was always fascinating to Mick. Joelle stayed in shape by practicing yoga and enjoying her favorite Zumba routines. She was also an active volunteer at the local community college, an accomplished scuba diver and part time treasure hunter.

Earlier in the year, Mick and Joelle had assisted a deep-sea exploration company out of Tampa, Florida in finding a sunken treasure. Odyssey, the world leader in deep-ocean shipwreck exploration, specialized in searching the vast oceans for sunken ships with intriguing stories, extraordinary treasure and precious artifacts spanning centuries of maritime travel. Mick and Joelle had assisted them on many previous shipwreck explorations and were renowned for their expertise in using the MAK-1M, a deep-tow low frequency sonar system. This approach enabled them to locate the target quickly without spending weeks utilizing a typical crisscrossing grid pattern. Once the shipwreck was discovered, a visual inspection of the site was then conducted with a Remotely Operated Vehicle (ROV) from the *Odyssey Explorer*.

The ship, heavy with silver, lay nearly two thousand five hundred meters beneath the surface of the North Atlantic Ocean. It was the remains of the *SS Mantola*, a four hundred and fifty feet long British-flagged steamer which set sail from

London on February 4, 1917, carrying passengers and cargo - including a shipment of six hundred thousand ounces of silver - to Calcutta, India. It sank on February 9, 1917, after being torpedoed by a German U-81 submarine during World War I. The one hundred sixty five crew members and eighteen passengers abandoned the ship and all but seven crew members were rescued by the *HMS Laburnum*. An unsuccessful attempt was made to tow the *Mantola* before she sank – less than a year after she was launched.

Mick and Joelle were not part of the original team who planned the exploration and recovery, but were called in for their expertise with towed-array sonar during the final phase of the operation. In September 2011, the UK Government Department for Transport awarded Odyssey a salvage contract for the cargo of the *SS Mantola*. Under the agreement, Odyssey would retain eighty percent of the net salvaged silver value recovered. Mick and Joelle, for their part, would enjoy a one percent fee, approximately one hundred fifty two thousand dollars for their participation in the final weeks of the salvage operation. In addition, they had been retained by Odyssey to review the video, still images and additional data from the expedition. It would be used to evaluate the condition of the shipwreck and to plan for future recovery operations, which would be conducted in conjunction with recovery operations on the *SS Gairsoppa* shipwreck. Mick and Joelle looked forward to returning to the area in the summer of 2013 to continue with the project. For now, they were quite busy analyzing the video and photos.

CHAPTER 2

AFTER A DAY of eating all of the delicious Thanksgiving fare and watching multiple football games, Joelle and Kenzie embarked early Friday morning on their annual Black Friday shopping spree. It was now Friday afternoon and the Scotts were ready to spend the rest of the day at home relaxing.

"So Kenzie, tell us more about how school is going and the World History exam you took this week. You seemed really excited about something that you had discovered," remarked Joelle.

"It's probably just my imagination at work," said Kenzie, "but it was a story about lost treasure and that always gets my mind going." The entire Scott family was well known for their success at finding lost treasure and solving ancient mysteries. In just the last year, they had assisted in the recovery of a shipload of silver on the *SS Mantola* and the discovery of a Roman-era commercial vessel buried in mud off Liguria province in northwest Italy. Kenzie had both Mick and Joelle's attention and continued her story.

"The first week of the fall semester, my World History teacher, Professor Brinkerman, presented a very interesting video news report from ABC to the class. It was a story about two men finding a large cache of old coins on an island near the coast of France." As Kenzie gave her summary of the news report, both Mick and Joelle listened intently.

"According to the ABC Report, the coins were about twenty one hundred years old. Sometime around 56 BC, the Roman armies of Julius Caesar made their way across France, pushing the local Celtic tribes toward the coast. The treasure was discovered on Jersey, one of the British Channel Islands off the coast of Northern France. It is thought that the coins were probably the wealth of an entire village in France, somewhere near modern Saint Malo. As the Roman conquerors progressed westward, the villagers may have sailed across to the island of Jersey and hastily buried their wealth. The trove was found under a hedge in a field."

"No one knows why they never got back to claim their buried treasure," continued Kenzie. "Perhaps they were killed by the Romans, or sold into slavery. Or maybe they just forgot where they put it. The exact quantity of coins in the find hasn't been determined, but authorities think it will probably be between five million and sixteen million dollars."

Mick and Joelle exchanged glances and a slight smile formed on each of their faces. "That's an interesting story Kenzie, but you mentioned something about a discovery that you had made," said Joelle. "We assume it has something to do with the gold coins, but what do you think you have found"?

"Well, I'm not sure that the treasure they found on Jersey Island is the only treasure left by the ancient Celtics," remarked Kenzie. "In my World History class this fall, I studied about the Romans conquering France. I noted that in most instances, Caesar's troops returned to their encampments with relics and valuables from the villages they had seized. During their final advances along the western coast of France in 56 BC, there were very few accounts of valuable riches found in the villages. I think that it is possible that the Celtic tribes in those areas knew that Caesar's armies would eventually reach their lands so they tried to protect their wealth and culture. My theory is that not only did the Celtic tribes travel to nearby islands to escape, but they also may have hidden the riches of their villages across the coast of France before they departed." Kenzie sat back and watched her parents' expressions, and then asked. "Do you think I made a good persuasive argument on my exam? Do you think it is possible that more treasures will be found?"

"Kenzie," said Mick, "I suspect you did very well on your World History exam. Very, very well. In fact, both your mother and I have studied the ancient Celtic civilization and would agree with you that your theory is worth investigating. Who knows, you may have just found one of our next great treasure hunts. I think I will give your Uncle B a call this weekend in Dublin. I can call him to wish him a happy holiday and run your idea past him since he is an authority on Irish and Celtic history."

Joelle smiled at Kenzie and said, "And I can get in touch with your stepbrother Clay, to begin researching your idea."

In a modest apartment a few miles west of the ASU campus, Paul Brinkerman was trying to control his excitement about one of his student's exam papers. He had read Kenzie's paper over and over to understand her discovery. With his extensive knowledge of ancient Celtic tribes and Roman history, Professor Brinkerman believed that Kenzie had made an important find. He also knew that Kenzie's parents, Mick and Joelle Scott, had been successful treasure hunters all over the world. If Brinkerman was ever going to retire from teaching and travel the globe as he desired, he needed to take a chance.

He had decided to contact a childhood friend about the potential treasure yet to be found near Saint Malo, France.

Paul Brinkerman had not seen Mario Sargusi in many, many years, but they kept in touch and he knew that if he asked Mario to come to Arizona for a discussion, he would come. He dialed Mario's private number and waited for him to pick up. "This is Mario, sorry I missed ya, leave a message."

"Mario, this is Paul Brinkerman in Tempe. I hope you are having a happy Thanksgiving with your family. I have some information that I need to discuss with you ASAP, but it must be in person. This could change both of our lives forever. I need you to meet with me this Saturday at 2:00 p.m. in Tempe. Here's the address. Thanks Mario, see you soon." Paul finished his voicemail and pressed the end button on his phone. He was nervous to ask Mario to fly across the country on such short notice, but he knew he would come.

Clay Scott, Mick's eldest son, worked as a technical analyst and software designer for a small startup company in the Orlando, Florida area. Standing six feet two inches tall, Clay had a lean build and his mother's dark brown hair and eyes; but his smile was pure Mick Scott. The twenty six year old summa cum laude graduate of the University of Central Florida wore high fashion Ray-Ban glasses and had a full face beard. He had a sixth sense about finding information on the web and often assisted Mick and Joelle with their cases. His wife Rachel, was expecting their first child in January and they were both busy preparing for her arrival.

CHAPTER 3

"CLAY, THIS IS Joelle. How have you and Rachel been?"

"We are all doing fine," remarked Clay. "Just enjoying lots of food and football this weekend."

"Did you prepare a fried turkey again this year?" asked Joelle.

"Of course, and I think it's better than my dad ever made," boasted Clay.

"Your father and I skipped the fried turkey this year and settled for a more traditional baked meal. We didn't need another turkey fryer fire out of control in our backyard," she laughed. "By the way, your stepsister Kenzie is home from ASU this week and has been sharing some very interesting ideas about possible treasure sites in western France."

"That's intriguing," exclaimed Clay, "tell me more."

Back in Orlando, Clay listened with growing enthusiasm as Joelle retold the story of the Celtic coin discovery on the Island of Jersey. She explained how Kenzie had proposed that the recent find was only a small fraction of the possible treasures still waiting to be discovered along the western coast of France near Saint Malo and on the island of Jersey. "So why have no other treasure hunters searched this area for Celtic coins and artifacts?" asked Clay.

"They have," said Joelle, "Kenzie just thinks they were looking in the wrong places. That's where you come in. We need you to research the Celtic tribes that lived along the western coast of France and specifically near Saint Malo around 56 BC. Anything that you find could be helpful. In the meantime, your father is calling Uncle B in Dublin this weekend to see if he can provide some assistance. We will touch base with you in a few days to compare notes. Make sure you are taking care of Rachel," said Joelle.

"I will," responded Clay. "Talk to you soon." Joelle ended the call on her iPhone and turned to speak with Mick, but he had left the room.

The next day, just an hour north of the Scott's home, in a sports pub near the ASU campus, Professor Brinkerman was looking forward to enjoying a very different type of holiday celebration. He had contacted an old friend of his to meet him Saturday at 2:00 p.m. for a drink. Paul Brinkerman had an interesting look about him with his small, dark beady eyes, dark hair slicked back into a short ponytail, and a distinctive limp in his right leg. He had received the wound as a boy on the tough streets of New York City and still walked with a cane. As he drove towards the Mill Street Pub in his silver 1994 Volvo 240DL sedan, he wondered if the man he invited would show up for a meeting. It was Thanksgiving weekend, but Paul hoped Mario would be pleased by the voicemail message he had left for him. Brinkerman parked his car at a meter in front of the pub just a few minutes before 2:00 p.m. and slowly walked inside. Looking around and not seeing many other customers or his friend, he took a seat at a small table in the rear so that he would have some privacy.

Just shortly past 2:00 p.m., a couple of well-dressed men in dark Italian suits entered the bar and scanned the room as if deciding to come in or not. From the way they dressed, they were definitely not from Phoenix, but more than likely from the East coast. As they spotted Brinkerman, they made their way to his table along the side wall at the back of the pub. Only four other patrons were in the bar. It was a dingy place that smelled of stale beer and fried foods. Most of the tables and chairs appeared to be a collection of odds and ends and were sticky from the endless use by local college students.

The smaller of the two men, Mario Sargusi, sat down across from Paul, but said nothing. He didn't need to. The hardness of his dark eyes, slicked back salt and pepper hair and his face heavily pock marked with scars could tell the story of a life involved with organized crime without him uttering a word. The larger man, who just went by the name Eddie, stood nearly six foot six inches tall and weighed about two hundred forty pounds. He was obviously the hired muscle, and stood at attention nearby.

Paul began to fidget nervously and began wondering if he had made a huge mistake contacting Mario. No words were exchanged, but Mario continued to look sternly at Brinkerman and the muscle slid his jacket aside to reveal a shiny hand gun. At that moment, Mario threw himself across the table towards Brinkerman and gripped him in a bear hug. "Paulie, how the hell have you been?" said Mario in a thick, Brooklyn accent. The bodyguard relaxed and closed his suit jacket to hide the gun. "I haven't seen you since the neighborhood." Mario was referring to an area of Brooklyn where the two had grown up together in row houses and played stickball in the streets. "How many years has it been Paulie, fifteen, twenty?" Still gathering his nerves from the strange encounter, Brinkerman began to breath normally again and a smile crossed his face.

"It's been close to thirty years, Mario. A lot has changed

since the days we were kids growing up in Brooklyn." The two had talked on the phone about business many times over the years, but this was their first face-to-face meeting since Brinkerman had left New York City and they had a lot of catching up to do.

"Paulie, you said you had something I would be interested in. Something big. What gives? What did I fly across the country on Thanksgiving weekend, none the less, to see? What has you so worked up that you asked me to come see you in person after thirty years? I know I owe you my life, but what is it that has you so excited?"

Holding out a stack of papers in his right hand, Brinkerman said in a meek voice, "It's an exam paper from one of my students."

Mario let out a short laugh. "Are you jerking my chain?" screamed Mario as he stood to his feet. "This better be good Paulie, or our little reunion here is not going to end so happily. Capisci?" A few customers across the room looked over towards the men, but chose not to get involved. Brinkerman, with sweat dripping from his forehead, began to stutter out the reason for asking his friend with Mafia connections to come to Phoenix. He knew that Mario would do nearly anything for him since he had saved his life during a gang fight when they were teens. Brinkerman had helped Mario escape with only a few scares to his face, but he; however, was left with a permanent limp in his right leg from the broken bones inflicted by a large wooden bat.

"Mario, I teach a world history class at Arizona State University here in Tempe and we study about lost civilizations and how they relate to current events. In my class this fall, we studied about a pair of treasure hunters living on an island off the coast of Western France who found a hoard of coins valued at nearly sixteen million dollars," explained Brinkerman. "The coins belonged to a people called the Coriosolites who had lived in that area." He paused to see Mario's response. Mario's face was staring blankly at Brinkerman and he didn't look happy.

"And so why should this interest me?" asked Mario.

Brinkerman again held out a copy of the exam paper that his student, Kenzie Scott, had written and a map of western France. He placed them both on the table. "This is why I called you and asked for a face to face meeting. I believe that this student is on to something important," said Brinkerman.

"And why is that?" asked Mario sarcastically.

"Don't you see?" asked Brinkerman excitedly. "The Celtic treasures are still hidden and they could be worth hundreds of millions of dollars."

Mario raised an eyebrow and cracked a thin smile. "Paulie, you may be on to somethin."

Seeing that he had captured Mario's interest, Brinkerman said, "A few years ago you mentioned a business acquaintance that collects Roman artifacts. I was thinking that if he is interested and locates the treasures, maybe you and I could get a cut of the find. I would be able to quit teaching and retire."

"Paulie, I don't know nothin about Roman history or their treasures, but I trust you. I always have since we were kids. If you say that this treasure exists and that it has value, I am sure it does. Let me think this over and I will give my friend Marcus Demetrius a call." With that said, the long-time friends exchanged hugs and the two men in dark Italian suits exited the pub as quietly as they entered. Paul Brinkerman had no understanding of the sequence of events that he had unknowingly set into motion or how his life would be changed forever.

It was a sunny Saturday afternoon in south Phoenix and

Mick was enjoying one of his favorite cigars, a Punch Grand Cru, as he relaxed by the pool. "Uncle B," shouted Mick into the phone with excitement. "Happy holidays! How have you been this fall?"

"I've been great, Mickey my boy," responded Uncle B in his usual Irish brogue. "It's great to hear from you. How is Joelle"?

"We are both well and have been enjoying the weekend with Kenzie, she is home from school," said Mick.

"Aah, tell her hi from her Uncle B, I miss seeing her."

Uncle B, was not his actual name nor was he a relative, but Brian O'Shanahan, a.k.a. Uncle B, had been given that title by Kenzie as she was growing up in Florida. Two years ago, Uncle B, the father of Kenzie's best friend, Danielle, decided to move to his homeland of Ireland when his daughter left for college.

Danielle attended ASU with Kenzie and was studying psychology in anticipation of becoming a psychiatrist. Although Kenzie and Danielle remained best friends in college, they rarely saw each other except for a few classes that they shared. This weekend, Danielle was with her boyfriend's family in Scottsdale.

"We are planning a trip to Dublin and wanted to see if you would be in town," said Mick.

"When do you plan on travelling?" asked Uncle B.

"Probably in the next few weeks," remarked Mick.

"Well, I'm glad you called me before you finalized your plans. I have a holiday scheduled for this Sunday, December 2nd through Sunday, December 16th," said Uncle B. "I will be traveling to Africa to study some of the indigenous peoples of Zimbabwe. Did you know that the white Zimbabweans are of European ethnic origin and are divided between the English-speaking Anglo-African descendants of British and Irish settlers, the Afrikaans-speaking descendants of Afrikaners from

South Africa, and those descended from Greek and Portuguese settlers?" questioned Uncle B.

"No, I didn't realize that," said Mick. "I see that you have not yet stopped expanding your firsthand knowledge of the world. Do you have time to meet with us before you leave?"

"Yes," said Uncle B, "I am available until Sunday."

"Well, then we will adjust our plans and see you later this week. I will make arrangements to fly out of Phoenix on Thursday which should have us arriving in Dublin on Friday morning," said Mick.

"Should I pick you and Joelle up at the airport?" asked Uncle B.

"No, we will be renting a car and should arrive at your home before noon."

"Ok, see you then," said Uncle B. "Have a safe trip." Ending the call, Mick sat his phone down, took a long draw on his cigar and resumed reading.

CHAPTER 4

A S JOELLE WALKED out onto the patio early Sunday morning, Mick was finishing up a phone call with a real estate colleague in Florida. Seeing concern on Mick's face as he ended the call on his iPhone, Joelle asked, "Is everything alright Mick"?

"Yeah, sure, just a small complication with the sale of the Ocean Coast strip center in Boca Raton."

"What's the problem, financing?" inquired Joelle

"No, just multiple partners that can't seem to agree on price with their money source overseas," said Mick. "We should be able to get everyone on the same page and close the deal in the next few weeks." Although their vast real estate holdings consumed less of their day to day activities now than in the past, both Mick and Joelle still enjoyed the excitement of making the deal and those deals funded their hobby of searching for lost treasure.

"I talked with Clay on Friday and asked him to start looking into the history of Celtic tribes in ancient France," said Joelle. "He thought that Kenzie's idea had some merit and was excited about digging into the Celtic history."

"When do you anticipate he will get back to us with the information?" asked Mick.

"Probably by early next week. His schedule at work is quite

hectic and he typically concentrates on our assignments in the evenings at home," responded Joelle. "Do you think we should give him a call"?

"No," said Mick, "let's give him a few days and get back to him mid-week."

The next morning, over sixty one hundred miles east of Phoenix, near the grounds of a two thousand year old villa located north east of Rome, Marcus Demetrius was meeting with his advisors to discuss acquiring his latest obsession in Roman artifacts when his cell phone sounded. "Please excuse me for a few moments," said Marcus to the room filled with his closest advisors. "I will notify you when I am available to continue this discussion." Everyone rose from their chairs and left the conference room quickly.

Looking at his phone's caller ID, Marcus was surprised to see the name Mario Sargusi on the screen. The two men had met many years earlier and formed some very lucrative business arrangements. "Mario, to what do I owe the pleasure of your call"?

"Marcus, how have you been? We haven't spoken in nearly a year," recalled Mario.

"I have been well, enjoying life and making more money than I will be able to spend in many lifetimes," said Marcus.

"Do you still have an interest in Roman artifacts?" asked Mario. "I know that collecting them has been a life-long passion of yours and I think I may have something of interest to you."

Marcus paused for a second and recalled his excitement of obtaining some of his most cherished pieces of antiquity over the years. "I may have some interest in hearing what you have to say. What is it concerning?"

"Not on the phone," cautioned Mario, "I would like to meet you in person to show you the information."

"Your timing is quite good," said Marcus. "I will be in New York City later this week on business. We should plan to meet. I will contact you when I arrive in the city and we can firm up our plans." Marcus ended the call and placed his cell phone on the large mahogany conference room table, exited the room and summoned his advisors to return.

His estate sprawled over two hundred fifty acres and contained thousands of museum quality artifacts gathered from all across the world. However, not all of the golden statues, priceless artifacts and symbols of ancient history were on display for Demetrius's guests to view. As his collection grew larger, Marcus had many specially designed secret rooms and galleries constructed to hold his most treasured acquisitions. Only he or his very special and trusted guests were able to enjoy viewing these rare treasures.

Protected by a nearly impenetrable security system, designed and installed by the same security firm which protects Le Louvre in Paris, Marcus had no concern of losing his treasures. Nearly his entire collection was from the period 500 BC to 56 BC and of Roman origin. As the last living ancestor of Julius Caesar and Cleopatra, Marcus felt he had a birthright to acquire all Roman artifacts and treasures he desired. His obsession with believing his ancestral connection with Caesar was strictly a figment of his imagination and had no basis in fact. But to Marcus, it was real and it was the driving force of his passion to acquire those treasures by any means and at whatever cost.

"As we were discussing before the interruption of my telephone call, I am interested in securing the Celtic coins on display at the museum on the island of Jersey," stated Marcus.

"The coins were placed on display earlier this fall and will be moving to the Smithsonian in Washington DC before year end. Once they are in transit to the United States, it will be much more difficult to make the acquisition. We will need to act quickly to take advantage of this window of opportunity."

Marcus's most trusted advisor and head of his security team was the first to speak. "I have acquired the floor plans and security installation specifications for the museum as you directed," stated Giorgio. "I have good news and bad news after reviewing the materials."

"Please explain," commanded Marcus with sternness in his voice.

"The good news is that we can bypass the security system and retrieve the coins."

"And the bad news?" prodded Marcus.

Giorgio continued, "We must wait three more weeks to act."

"And why is that?" Marcus challenged.

"The Museum officials are installing a new security system which is identical to what is used at the Smithsonian Institute. They currently are working around the clock to get the new system installed and there is a heightened state of alert. We will not be able to easily beat the new system and we cannot currently access the museum without being noticed by the additional security. Our best window of opportunity is actually while they are transferring from the old system to the new. That will occur the third week of December on a Tuesday evening after the museum closes."

Giorgio had made his case and Marcus was in agreement. He had learned years ago to trust his closest advisors to help him make the best choices. "Giorgio, I will be out of town for a few days, but when I return I expect you to have the plans for this acquisition ready for my review," said Marcus.

"Yes sir, you will not be disappointed," responded Giorgio. With the meeting complete, Marcus left the conference room and headed towards the indoor pool for a morning swim with his wife, Sabina.

Marcus had met his wife Sabina eighteen years earlier at a social event in Rome. Their romance developed quickly and they were married less than one year later. Sabina came from money, very, very old money. Marcus did not. Her family had been in the shipping business since the late seventeen hundreds and controlled most of the port traffic serving Rome. Nearly every cargo ship entering or leaving the port of Civitavecchia bore the family logo. The Sostos family name was recognized throughout Italy and the family played an active role in the most prestigious social circles.

Although Sabina's father had run a thorough background check on Marcus, he did not find the checkered past of a boy that grew up on the back streets of Italy with associations to organized crime. Instead, the report indicated that Marcus Demetrius was a very astute young businessman with many important political alliances throughout Europe. Marcus's clean identity had been carefully crafted by one of his closest associates and would pass the most stringent scrutiny.

As a young boy living in southern Italy, Marcus had a tumultuous life and rarely saw either of his parents due to their work schedules and carousing. On many nights, he was tossed out of the house like a bag of garbage so that the house could be used for another drunken party. He grew up on the streets and learned how to take care of himself. The friendships he made were not always with the most upstanding citizens, but they gave Marcus a sense of family and support. Some of his acquaintances helped him to supplement his income by acting as a local courier transporting packages that he dare not ask about.

At sixteen, he made the decision to live on his own and got a job at a small store in a seedy neighborhood across town. He had convinced the shop owner to rent him a small room above the store for his living quarters and began saving every dime he made. He used the location as a drop off point for his customers with special package arrangements. He never asked what he was delivering, but he knew that by the amount he was being paid, they were most certainly illegal drugs or contraband of some kind. This realization did not bother Marcus, in fact, it gave him a sense of satisfaction that he was being trusted with such important transactions. Two years later, just after Marcus turned eighteen, he had saved nearly one hundred twenty five thousand dollars and was ready to move on with his life.

During his years working as a courier, he had become very familiar with the port of Civitavecchia northwest of Rome and the cargo container business. He saw an investment opportunity in the business as a way to begin a legitimate career and to develop more connections. Knowing that the Sostos family controlled most of the ports on the western coast of Rome and owned the largest fleet of container ships, Marcus realized he somehow needed to meet Theophilos Sostos, the chairman and CEO of Sostos Industries. He not only met the chairman, he began working for him shortly thereafter and three years later, married his eldest daughter.

Sabina moved effortlessly through the crystal clear water as she approached the shallow end of the pool where Marcus was standing. She rose out of the water and walked slowly toward Marcus, wearing only a smile. They embraced and fell back into the pool. Their relationship had always been sexually supercharged and this morning was no exception.

CHAPTER 5

WITH NO HINT of the November sun yet making its way into the sky and early morning desert temperatures still hovering in the fifties, Mick and Joelle were enjoying a lazy morning of sleeping in after their four day holiday with Kenzie. She had gone back to campus Sunday evening to complete the fall semester. At 6:00 a.m., Joelle's cell phone rang waking them from their deep sleep. It was Mick's son Clay, calling with an update on the research he had found about the history of the Celts. Joelle picked up the phone and put it to her ear, fighting back a stream of yawns.

"Joelle, did I wake you?" asked Clay.

"Well, it is a three hour time difference, so it is only 6:00 a.m. here," she mumbled. "We were planning to get up at 6:30 a.m. this morning. We are really anxious to hear what you have found so quickly. Can you give us a few minutes to get down to our office and we will call you back?"

Clay said, "Talk to you soon," and pressed end on his phone.

Mick turned to face Joelle and enjoyed the sight of waking up next to his beautiful wife. They were still very much in love with each other after many years and enjoyed spending every day together whether working on real estate deals, hunting treasure or just enjoying the spectacular Arizona sky above their pool. "Let's grab a quick shower," suggested Mick, "and get down to the office to call Clay back. He really jumped on our request and I'm interested in listening to what he has found." With that said, they both sprang from bed and raced each other to the shower. Thirty minutes later, they were sitting in their office.

"Calm down Clay," said Joelle, "and take us through this slowly. We want to understand exactly what you have found."

Clay took a deep breath and said, "I began studying the recent find of Celtic coins on Jersey Island that Kenzie referred to in her paper. It seems that the group that located the coins had been searching the area for nearly thirty years."

"Had they ever found any other treasure?" asked Mick.

"Only a few coins here and there around Grouville, just enough to keep their interest," replied Clay. "The Celtic tribe of Coriosolites apparently used these coins and the area near Grouville has long attracted local treasure hunters. This recent find of coins is currently on display at the Jersey Museum and is valued at over sixteen million dollars."

"That's great Clay, what else did you find?" asked Joelle.

"Well, as Kenzie suggested, there may be other treasures that the Coriosolites left behind. Some may be located on the island of Jersey, but I believe there are other, more important finds in the coastal area surrounding Saint Malo."

"What led you to that conclusion Clay?" asked Mick.

"In studying their history, I learned that Coriosolites practiced the ceremony of object burial with the dead. The Celts' belief in an afterlife was so strong that they would put off the payment of debts until they met on the other side. So, the idea of burying objects that would be of help on the other side wasn't so unusual. Swords, chariots, jewelry, and even wine flagons were sent on the journey with the deceased. It was also common practice to hide treasures if an attack by another tribe was expected."

"So, if I'm understanding you correctly," said Mick, "it's not a matter of whether any Coriosolite treasures were buried, it's more a matter of where they were buried."

"Exactly," confirmed Clay.

"Mick and I plan to visit Uncle B in Dublin later this week and will visit the Jersey Museum as well," said Joelle. "We want to view the recent Coriosolite coin find that is on exhibit. Do you have some suggestions of other places that we should explore while we are in the area?"

"Certainly," quipped Clay, "I would suggest spending some time in the Grouville area on the island and talking with the locals. It has long been the favorite site of treasure hunters. There are several sites you should explore near Saint Malo, including Solidar Tower, Saint Malo castle, Municipal Museum and the Cathedral Saint-Vincent of Saint-Malo."

"By the way," said Clay, "I also came across some interesting articles regarding a large private collection of Roman artifacts. A business man, named Marcus Demetrius, living outside of Rome seems to have one of the largest private collections in the world of Roman artifacts from this period. That's all I know about him so far, but my intuition tells me that there is a lot more to this man than meets the eye."

"Interesting," said Mick. "It's probably a dead end, but anything that you can find out about this Demetrius fellow would probably be helpful."

"Thanks for all of your help on this Clay," said Joelle, "we really appreciate all that you do. We plan to return home later next week and will touch base with you on what we found."

"Talk to you in a week," added Mick.

"What did you and Uncle B work out for travel plans?" asked Joelle.

"We are booked on a flight to Dublin this Thursday morning and have a short layover at JFK in New York City. With the time change, we should touch down in Dublin at 8:30 a.m., just before breakfast."

"Oh Mick," said Joelle, "Let's eat at that small café just outside of the airport. What's the name of it? You know, we found it on our last trip to Dublin. It's the Coach or Coachman or something like that."

CHAPTER 6

EARLY THURSDAY MORNING, Marcus touched down on a private runway at JFK in his white Gulfstream G550 jet. Accompanied by his two bodyguards, he moved quickly down the gangway and into his armored, black Mercedes limousine. "To the warehouse on 107th Ave., just east of the Van Wyck Expressway," said Marcus to his driver. As they drove away from the tarmac, Marcus hit speed dial on his phone and said, "I will be at the warehouse within the next thirty minutes. Make sure that everything is prepared for my review." His next call was to Mario Sargusi to firm up plans for their morning meeting. "I will arrive at your office before noon and our meeting will be limited to one hour. I hope that my time is not being wasted," warned Marcus. He didn't wait for Mario to respond, he simply ended the call.

Shortly before Marcus's arrival at the warehouse, a white Range Rover had entered through the wide warehouse doors. Two men quickly jumped out and unloaded the SUV's contents of wooden crates. As the large steel warehouse doors opened for the Mercedes to enter, Marcus's security detail armed with Heckler and Koch MP5 machine pistols could be seen in every direction. He had installed a sophisticated security system including CCTV, motion detection and twenty four hour monitoring. Not your typical warehouse security, but Marcus did not have typical inventory stored in his warehouse.

"I want to inspect this shipment before it leaves the warehouse," commanded Marcus. Standing next to a large wooden crate embossed with a Columbian coffee logo, Marcus grabbed a pry bar and opened the lid. Moving layers of coffee beans aside, Marcus removed a small plastic bag of white powder and began to test the contents. Satisfied with the results, he selected another crate to inspect. Again the results were positive.

Marcus turned to the men standing next to the Range Rover and said, "We agreed on a price of two million five hundred thousand dollars. Your money is in this case." Marcus handed the briefcase to the taller of the two men. After checking the contents, they re-entered their Range Rover without saying a word and exited the warehouse. Marcus turned toward the man who ran his New York City operation and stated, "This is a very high quality product, I expect you to get at least five million from our distributors and I want it out of this warehouse in twenty four hours. The money must be deposited into the numbered account in the Caymans that I provided you. Understood?"

"Yes sir, I will not disappoint you," said his lieutenant.

"I would hope not or your fate will be the same as your predecessor's. Driver, let's go." Marcus got into his limousine, departed the warehouse and headed toward the sixteen hundred block of Flatbush Avenue in Brooklyn.

He had not seen Mario in nearly a year, but had enjoyed how lucrative their past projects had been. Marcus was not quite sure what Mario wanted to discuss with him, but he was still very interested in acquiring Roman artifacts and hoped that his detour to the Flatbush area of Brooklyn would be worth the effort.

"Driver, this is the place, let me out here," said Marcus. "I will return in exactly one hour. I expect you to be waiting here for my return." Mario's office was secluded in the back of a Gentlemen's VIP club and there were only a few patrons in the bar at this early hour. As Marcus and his bodyguards entered the club, they were greeted by a doorman and escorted in. Next, they were met by a very shapely young woman wearing see through lingerie. Her name was Victoria and she assisted Mario in running the club.

After walking them to Mario's office, Victoria knocked gently on her boss's door and waited for his response. "Yeah, what do ya want?" shouted Mario.

"I have a very handsome gentleman and his friends that would like to see you," responded Victoria.

"Who is he?" inquired Mario.

"He claims he is Marcus Demetrius, a friend of yours."

"Marcus, my friend," said Mario as he opened the door, "please come in." The three men entered Mario's office and Marcus took a seat across from Mario in front of his old, hardwood executive desk. The two body guards stood at attention on both sides of the office door and pushed it closed. Scanning the room for any threat to their boss's life, they continued to keep a watchful eye and a hand on their shoulder holsters as Mario began to speak.

Mario opened his desk drawer and slowly withdrew a stack of papers and a map. He spread them out on the table in front of his guest. "Marcus, you said on the phone that you still have an interest in Roman artifacts."

"Yes, I do. What do you have for me?" asked Marcus.

Mario continued, "I recently spoke with a childhood friend of mine that is a World History professor at Arizona State University in Tempe, Arizona."

Marcus was already beginning to feel that this was a waste of his time and said, "So why should that interest me?" Mario continued.

"My friend, Professor Brinkerman, came across an interesting exam paper that one of his students prepared regarding Celtic treasure in what is now western France. The student's name is Kenzie Scott, daughter of the famous Scott family that travels the globe searching for lost treasure," stated Mario.

"Ok, and what did Miss Scott find that was so intriguing that you requested a meeting with me?" asked Marcus a second time. Mario recounted the story that Brinkerman had told him just a few weeks earlier.

"As I am sure you already know," said Mario, "ABC recently reported on a large cache of twenty one hundred year old coins found on Jersey Island by a team of treasure hunters."

"Yes, Mario, I am aware of that. In fact, I have already visited the Jersey Museum to see the coin exhibit." Marcus began to stand up and said, "Mario, you have greatly disappointed me. This meeting was a colossal waste of my time."

As Marcus turned toward the office door, Mario rose to his feet as well and said, "Marcus, you are missing the point here, please take a look at this map that was submitted with the exam paper." Marcus moved towards the desk and Mario continued his sales pitch.

"Miss Scott thinks that there are at least three other large treasure sites yet to be discovered along the western coast of France and Professor Brinkerman believes that she is right. If the Celtic treasures are still hidden, they could be worth hundreds of millions of dollars," said Mario. Completely exhausted by his performance and with rivers of sweat rolling off his forehead, Mario sat back down in his chair and waited for Marcus's response.

Marcus Demetrius continued to review the map and exam paper carefully, then folded them and placed them in his coat pocket. "I will get back to you Mario," said Marcus without any sign of emotion in his voice. He then turned and walked out of the office. Both of his body guards followed closely behind until they reached the VIP Club entrance. Seeing that their limousine was waiting at the curb as instructed, they escorted Marcus to the car and secured his door. Once inside, Marcus pulled out his cell phone and dialed his first lieutenant, Giorgio.

CHAPTER 7

"GIORGIO, THIS IS urgent. I need you to find some information for me very quickly," requested Marcus. "I need to know everything that you can find on a pair of treasure hunters known as the Scotts. They have a daughter named Kenzie that attends Arizona State University. Find out who they are, where they live, what they are working on, their finances, etc. I expect that you will be back to me in less than one hour with an executive summary." Marcus hung up the phone and took out the exam paper and map from his pocket. He had not let Mario see his enthusiasm, but he was excited about the possibilities that Miss Scott had proposed.

It had been a very long day for Mick and Joelle flying from Phoenix to JFK, changing planes and then continuing to Dublin, Ireland. Although they always flew first class when using a commercial carrier, it was still a long trip. At 7:30 a.m. in Dublin, they deplaned, claimed their two pieces of luggage and made their way to the rental car counter. Thirty minutes later, Joelle was scanning the streets near Dublin International for the Coachman café where they had eaten on their last trip. "There it is," shouted Joelle, "just up ahead on the left." Mick parked the rental car along the curb and they walked inside the café not noticing the two men in a silver Mercedes parked just down the block.

Nearly twelve hours earlier, while Marcus Demetrius was still on his jet returning to Rome, he received a call from Giorgio to report his findings on the Scotts. "They are quite an interesting family," stated Giorgio. "Mick and Joelle Scott have been very successful amateur treasure hunters for the last five years. Their last project was assisting with the recovery of six hundred thousand ounces of silver valued at over sixteen million dollars from the *SS Mantola*. In previous years, they successfully recovered treasure in the amazon region of South America, from a King's lost tomb near Cairo and made some interesting discoveries on Easter Island."

"I see," said Marcus. "Tell me more about their background." Giorgio continued.

"Mick is fifty four and Joelle is forty. They relocated just four years ago from Orlando, Florida to the Phoenix area after making a fortune together in the commercial real estate business. Mick is six feet three inches tall and in excellent physical shape," said Giorgio. "He completed two tours of duty as a Lieutenant in the U.S. Navy during his twenties and then attended Purdue University earning his undergraduate degree and his MBA from the Krannert School of Business. Joelle, is five feet three inches tall with long auburn hair and blue/grey eyes. She studied at Ohio State and received her MBA in finance. She is fluent in both French and Italian and from her photo, she appears to be in excellent physical shape."

"What about their daughter, the one who wrote the paper?" asked Marcus.

"She is a twenty one year old junior attending Arizona State University in Tempe, Arizona. She is studying world history and business. She and her roommate live in an apartment near campus. Mick has an older son named Clay that lives in Orlando, Florida and provides him with research for his projects."

"Ok Giorgio, that's enough for now. I want to keep an eye on the Scotts. Do you know where they are currently?"

"Yes," responded Giorgio, "they are in route to Dublin, Ireland and will land early Friday morning. They may be planning to meet with an old family friend by the name of Brian O'Shanahan. He turned up in our research and they call him Uncle B."

"I've worked on some projects in the past with a Brian O'Shanahan," said Marcus. "It could prove quite helpful to us if he is one in the same. I will make a few calls."

Marcus thought for a second and then spoke. "Make sure that our contacts in Dublin keep a close eye on the Scotts when they arrive and then report to us on their activities. It appears that the Scotts believe that their daughter's idea of undiscovered Celtic treasure has some merit and are beginning to do their field research. I also want you to have two of our best men touch base with a man named Professor Paul Brinkerman. He teaches at Arizona State University. I want them to find out everything he knows about Kenzie Scott and her proposed treasure locations. Get this done in the next week."

"Excellent job Giorgio! I will be landing in a few hours. Have my car at the airport and set up a meeting with my advisors for 9:00 a.m. Saturday morning." Without waiting for an affirmative response from Giorgio, Marcus ended the call and sat back to relax for the first time that day. With the information from Mario fresh in his mind, he was even more determined to claim the large cache of ancient Celtic coins on display in the Jersey Museum when he returned. But for the next few hours, he was more interested in enjoying the company of his most recent flying companion, Samantha.

After experiencing a full Irish breakfast with eggs, bacon, sausages, potatoes and tomatoes, both Mick and Joelle left the café very content with the start of their day. Their first stop would be at Uncle B's house about a thirty minute drive southwest of the airport. As they traveled on the E01 and then merged onto the M50 towards Castleknock, neither Mick nor Joelle noticed the silver Mercedes sedan travelling close behind them. After exiting on the N3, Mick steered their car southward on Auburn Avenue and began looking for Castleknock Park. Uncle B's house was the third house on the right. They pulled into the long narrow driveway and parked.

Before Mick and Joelle could get out of the car, Uncle B had walked out of his house and was halfway down the stone walkway. "Welcome to my home," said Uncle B, "it has been far too long since we were all together." They embraced warmly and then grabbed their bags from the car. "Please let me help you with your luggage," offered Uncle B. As they all entered the house, the same silver Mercedes carrying the two tough-looking men turned onto Castleknock Park and pulled along the curb keeping Uncle B's house in their sight.

After getting settled into the guest room, Joelle and Mick sat down in the living room with Uncle B to catch up on their lives. "I am so excited that you have come to visit me. Tell me about Kenzie, how is she doing these days"?

"Well, she is a junior at ASU this year and still very interested in world history and ancient civilizations," said Joelle. "Danielle is doing great too. As you know, she and Kenzie have a few classes together and we see her as often as we can."

"This fall, Kenzie made a discovery in her World History class that prompted us to visit you," explained Mick.

"It must be really important, tell me what she found," implored Uncle B.

CHAPTER 8

A S MARCUS WALKED down the jet's stairway, he paused to kiss Samantha goodbye before getting into his awaiting limo. It was possible he would see her again, but unlikely. His flying companions were provided through a service and he rarely saw the same women twice. A short distance away from the airport, he arrived at his estate and went directly to the master suite to freshen up.

Marcus's extensive wardrobe reflected his incredibly good taste and resources. As he walked into his conference room at 9:00 a.m. sharp wearing a charcoal grey Hugo Boss suit, black Armani shirt, white Versace tie, and black Ferragamo loafers he looked like a model for GQ magazine. His obedient advisors sprang from their seats and applauded to welcome him back from a successful trip. Marcus took his seat at the head of the thirty foot long conference room table and began to review financial reports each advisor had prepared on their individual operations.

Marcus controlled a wide range of both legal and illegal operations throughout Europe and the United States. His legitimate businesses included import and export of coffee, wine and other agricultural products. He also owned a ten percent share of Sostos Enterprises, his father-in-law's shipping business and had exclusive use of a small fleet of cargo ships.

Although he was a millionaire many times over from his legal operations, his real wealth had come from his involvement in drugs, racketeering and prostitution.

Each of his six advisors was responsible for one area of business. They took turns providing Marcus with a summary of their financial results since last quarter. "It appears we have done quite well in every area of our enterprise this year, except for prostitution," remarked Marcus. "Edward, you have allowed your operation to be compromised multiple times by vice squad stings costing the corporation millions of dollars. That is unacceptable. We have discussed this before and you knew the possible consequences. It seems I need to make an adjustment in the leadership."

Everyone in the room knew what that could mean. Pleading for his life, Edward jumped up from his chair and begged Marcus for another chance. Marcus rose as well, while carefully removing a Heckler & Koch P8 handgun attached to the underside of the conference room table. Leveling the gun at Edward, Marcus placed a single 9mm bullet in his advisor's forehead. Placing the gun on the table in front of him, Marcus sat down and turned toward Giorgio, saying, "Exceptional performance should be rewarded, just as dismal failure must be eliminated. See that one hundred thousand euros are transferred into each of these men's accounts for their achievements this year. And please dispose of that body cluttering my conference room as soon as we finish."

"Now, for new business," said Marcus. He recounted his meeting with Mario Sargusi in New York City. "It has come to my attention that the coin heist that we are planning on Jersey Island may be more important than we once knew. Possibly, the horde of coins found earlier this year is only the first of many treasures hidden by the Celts over two thousand years ago. Many more treasures could be waiting for us to discover, but for now, we are going to concentrate on obtaining the coins from the museum. Giorgio, I asked you to prepare a detailed plan for my review. Do you have it ready?"

"Yes sir, absolutely. Here is my plan," explained Giorgio as he distributed detailed maps of the Jersey Island Museum and escape route to the other advisors and Marcus. "Museum officials have temporarily relocated the coin display to Gallery E at the rear of the museum while the new security system is installed; therefore, I have altered my plan accordingly." Giorgio continued.

"We will arrange for an electrical outage near the museum that prompts the city to undergo some emergency work the day before our heist. With the heavy equipment still near the museum on Tuesday evening, it will allow our team to borrow their front bucket loader to crash through the museum wall on the alley side. The coin display, located near the rear exterior wall, weighs about seventeen hundred pounds and will be transported using the front loader into a stolen tilt bed truck waiting in the alley."

"Hmmm, simple enough," Marcus remarked, "go on." Giorgio continued his explanation.

"Our team will drive the truck approximately seven hundred fifty meters north of the museum to the site where we are currently constructing an office building. They will dump the coins into a large metal storage container sunken into the ground. Then the truck will be driven about one point five kilometers north and pushed into the lake on Westmont Road to make identification more difficult. Our construction crew, which will be working late that night on the new building, will secure the container and cover the hole with construction debris. The coins will remain hidden underground until our team can return to claim the gold later in the week," said Giorgio.

"Our men will use daily construction activity to conceal loading the storage container onto one of our commercial delivery trucks. Once loaded, the truck will be driven approximately ten kilometers northeast toward Mont Orgueil Castle and the container offloaded to our boat moored in the marina. It's a short trip across the channel to Créances. The boat will meet another one of our commercial trucks to accept the cargo. Two days later, the gold coins will arrive at the estate here in Rome." Giorgio waited for a response.

Marcus thought about Giorgio's plan for a few minutes and then asked. "How do we deal with the guards around the display"?

"Not a problem, we bribed two of the three guards assigned to the treasure display," said Giorgio. "They will simply make sure that the other guard is standing between the exterior wall and the gold. The bucket loader will take care of the rest. Our remaining two guards will sound the alarm and appear to fire shots to stop the break in, but their shots will go astray. Since loading the gold will take only a few minutes, no other guards will have time to respond before the team is down the alley and transferring the gold onto the truck. The CCTV camera on the exterior of the building will be disabled as the bucket loader destroys the wall, so no one will be able to record our team's escape. Next, they will abandon the borrowed front loader and drive the truck loaded with gold to our nearby construction site. The rest, I already covered." Giorgio sat back in his high backed, black Italian leather chair and waited for Marcus' response.

Marcus stared intently at Giorgio and then appraised each of his advisor's visual reactions. "Any questions for Giorgio?"

asked Marcus. Not a single advisor spoke. "Well then Giorgio, it seems you have everything covered. Arrange for the men and supplies that you will need and plan to execute the heist on the night of my annual holiday gala. Let me know when everything is in place and when I will have the coins in my possession." Giorgio rose from his chair and approached Marcus.

"Sir, you have my word that the coins will be yours by the end of this calendar year," promised Giorgio.

"I should hope so," taunted Marcus. "Further, I want to conduct final interviews of your selected candidates to replace Edward. Our prostitution operation is far too important to go more than a few weeks without adequate leadership."

"Yes sir," responded Giorgio. "I will have my three top choices ready to meet with you before your holiday gala."

"Well enough," said Marcus. "You are all dismissed."

CHAPTER 9

NEARLY TWENTY FIVE hundred kilometers due west near Dublin, Mick continued to summarize the recent discovery of Celtic coins on Jersey Island for Uncle B. He explained that Kenzie believed that there could be other treasures hidden on the western coast of France.

"Hmm," sighed Uncle B. "Kenzie may be onto something, but it is going to take extensive field research and hours of ancient document review to determine possible treasure locations. You are in luck. The National Maritime Museum of Ireland is just south of Dublin and has a vast collection of Celtic maritime history that would help you to understand more about their culture."

"That sounds like a good place to start," said Mick. "Let's go there tomorrow morning. Until then, can you tell us what you know about Celtic history and their migration westward out of France?"

Uncle B began, "They called themselves Celts. One suggestion is that the word is derived from the Indo-European root 'kel,' which means 'hidden'. The Celts were the hidden people and were made up of a diverse group of tribal societies in Iron Age Europe."

For the next several hours, they discussed ideas presented in many of the history books stored in Uncle B's extensive library. Joelle stated, "So we know that a horde of two thousand year old coins was found earlier this year on the island. By identifying the coins, we also know that the ancient Celts traveled to Jersey Island by boat to escape the Roman advance. Whether they traveled there to live permanently or just to hide treasure and then return home, we do not know."

"Uncle B, what else can you tell us about the ancient Celts that may help us to locate their treasures?" asked Mick.

"I don't know if this will lead you to any treasures," explained Uncle B, "but the Celtic people practiced the ceremony of object burial with the dead. They believed in an afterlife and would put off the payment of debts until they met on the other side. Swords, chariots, jewelry, coins and other valuables were sent on the journey with the deceased. It was also common practice to hide treasure if an attack by another tribe was expected."

"Did they mark their graves like we do today to honor the deceased?" asked Joelle.

"Not exactly," replied Uncle B, "but like other ancient civilizations before them, the Celts used a variation of the menhir and dolmen called a passage grave."

"Aren't all of those similar to stone megaliths like Stonehenge in the English country of Wiltshire"?

"Yes, similar, just much smaller." Uncle B continued to explain everything he knew about menhirs, dolmens and passage graves to Mick and Joelle until well after dinner.

"I think we are going to turn in," said Mick. "We have to get an early start tomorrow and we are both exhausted from the travel." All three rose from their chairs and wearily climbed the creaky wooden staircase to their second floor bedrooms.

"Goodnight Uncle B," said Joelle. "Thank you again for letting us stay here with you. See you in the morning."

It was mid-Saturday morning when Mick and Joelle arrived at the National Museum of Ireland. During their drive, Joelle called Clay for some research assistance. They wanted to understand more about the megalithic structures that Uncle B had described and had many questions. Did any of those exist around 56 BC in the northwest coastal area of France? If so, do any of the megaliths still exist today? Which ones are they? They also wanted to hear any additional information that Clay had found on Marcus Demetrius. Mick knew that Clay would find the information quickly and expected to hear back from him later in the day.

"What an incredible museum," said Joelle. "I can't believe that we never came here before when we were in Dublin. You can really see the local craftsmanship in the intricate stone and woodwork. I wonder when it was built."

"I saw on a tarnished placard attached to the stone wall by the main entrance that it had opened to the public in 1890," replied Mick. "What exhibits would you like to see first"?

"Uncle B's history lesson yesterday has raised my interest in passage graves," said Joelle. "Let's go to the Duma na nGiall exhibit. It's the oldest visible monument on the Hill of Tara and the best known complex of archaeological monuments in Ireland."

Outside the Museum, two men exited a silver Mercedes and briskly walked into the main entrance a few minutes behind the Scotts. Keeping both Mick and Joelle in their sights, but not revealing their presence, the two men continued to observe. So far, their assignment had been less than exciting, but orders are orders. They had been directed to follow the Scott's 24/7 and report on their activities. Watching Mick and Joelle climb a winding stone staircase at the far end of the entrance lobby, they moved slowly, but kept the Scotts in sight. The passage grave exhibit was quite interesting and provided a good visual to add to Uncle B's description of their construction. Next, Mick and Joelle moved on to the Treasury area.

The first gallery was arranged chronologically, and explored the development of Irish art from the Iron Age to the twelfth century AD. "Some of these artifacts are breathtakingly beautiful," exclaimed Joelle. "Look at this crescent-shaped gold collar called a lunula. It says here that it dates back to the Early Bronze Age circa 2300-1800 BC."

"I agree, that is quite beautiful, Joelle, and it would look stunning around your neck," remarked Mick. Joelle smiled and gave him a wink. Watching them from an adjacent gallery, the two light-haired men made note of the Scott's interest in the gold collar and passage graves. They would report this later in the day to their contact in Dublin.

"I think we should move on to the Maritime Museum that Uncle B suggested we visit," said Mick. "We can finish up by 5:00 p.m. and then meet Uncle B at the restaurant where he made reservations for this evening."

"Sounds like a plan," quipped Joelle. "How far is it from here"?

"It's only thirty minutes or so depending upon traffic," replied Mick. "Do you have any information about the museum on your iPad"? Joelle turned the device on and quickly swiped the screen. Moments later she had found the site she was looking for. Reading from her screen, Joelle gave some history on the museum.

"The National Maritime Museum of Ireland is located in the former Mariners' Church in Haigh Terrace, Dún Laoghaire. This historic Church was built in 1837. The Church was designed to meet the needs of the seafarers whose vessels sought shelter in the asylum harbor of Kingstown. The church could accommodate fourteen hundred people and the Deed of Trust stated that one third of the seating was to accommodate the families of those in the seafaring, coastguard and revenue services."

"Ok," said Mick. "That was pretty boring. Do you see any exhibits that we should visit?"

"Yes, an exhibit on ancient ships on level three and the archive section located in the basement," replied Joelle.

Driving their way through the light afternoon rush, Mick and Joelle passed through Donnybrook, Blackrock and Monkstown before finally arriving at the Maritime Museum on seventeen South Great Georges Street. Following a short distance behind their rental car, was the same silver Mercedes sedan that had been shadowing them since their arrival in Dublin. Mick and Joelle walked into the museum and began looking for directions to an exhibit on ancient sailing vessels. As they climbed the staircase to the third level, Mick's cell phone rang. "Dad, did I catch you at a good time?" asked Clay. "I have the information that you wanted."

"Sure Clay, we just arrived at the National Maritime Museum and are free to talk for a few minutes."

For the next fifteen minutes, Clay explained to Mick what he had discovered about megalithic structures. "I found a lot of information Dad, but I will try to limit this call to the high points." Clay excelled at internet research and was a valuable resource to Mick and Joelle; however, he tended to ramble on at times with infinite and unnecessary detail about a subject.

"Here's what I found. Until recently, menhirs were associated with the Beaker people, who inhabited Europe during the early Bronze Age, about 300 BC. However, recent research into the age of megaliths in Brittany strongly suggests a far older origin, perhaps back to six to seven thousand years ago. Many menhirs are carved with megalithic art, images of objects such as stone axes, ploughs, shepherd crooks and yokes were common. Some menhirs were broken up and incorporated into later passage graves, where they had new megalithic art carved with little regard for the previous pictures."

"Clay, Stop," interrupted Mick. "Son, that is way too much detail. Can you fast forward to the point, please?" Clay cleared his throat and continued.

"Passage graves were often found in large clusters and were constructed at the tops of hills or mountains, indicating that their builders intended them to be seen from a great distance."

"Are any of the megaliths still visible today in northwest France or on Jersey Island?" asked Mick.

"I'm still researching that," replied Clay, "I should have more information for you early tomorrow. I gotta go."

Mick and Joelle walked slowly down the museum corridor observing many artifacts from the earliest mariners in Ireland. "What did Clay have to say?" asked Joelle.

"He had some background on menhirs and passage graves. He said he would call us again in a day or two with more information." A short distance away, their two observers hid from view behind a large exhibit. Watching the Scott's interest in the ancient ship exhibits, the men took several photos of the couple to send to their contact. Finished with the maritime exhibits, Mick and Joelle decided to visit the archive area of the museum to review ship's maps and captain's logs. As they entered the dimly lit old fashioned wood paneled elevator cab and pushed the button to descend, the walls rattled and creaked around them as they were lowered slowly to the basement level.

Although the church was converted to a museum in the 1890's, the archive section was very up to date with the latest technology and contemporary furnishings. Mick and Joelle discussed their research needs with the young archive assistant and waited just a few minutes for her to produce the materials. "These are incredibly well preserved," said Mick as he looked through digital copies of ancient shipping maps.

"The ship log books seem to be in excellent condition as well," remarked Joelle.

"Judging from what I have seen so far," stated Mick, "it is entirely possible that Celtic tribes along the western coastal region of France fled the area and sailed as far as Ireland."

Not able to follow the Scotts into the elevator, the two men split up and descended the staircase to the first and second floors. With the Scotts nowhere to be seen, they realized that Mick and Joelle were most likely in the basement archives. The men descended the final staircase and moved quietly through row after row of book shelves. They had the Scotts in sight and were now close enough to hear their conversation.

"So you think it is possible that the ancient Celts of 56 BC also had the capability of traveling those long distances by ship?" asked Joelle.

"I'm really not sure yet," said Mick, "the materials we are looking at here only date back to 500 AD. I'm only speculating at this point that the earlier Celts had similar capabilities. Hopefully, some of the sites we are going to visit on Saint Malo this week will provide additional information."

"Let's wrap up here and head back towards Dublin to meet Uncle B for dinner," suggested Joelle.

The Scott's left the Museum shortly before 5:00 p.m. and began driving back towards the city. The sky was cloudy and dark. A light rain had begun failing around them and lightening could be seen in the distance streaking through the evening sky. Driving through the countryside, they wound their way toward the lights of Dublin. Nearly five hundred meters behind them in the silver Mercedes, the two men continued to go unnoticed by the Scotts.

CHAPTER 10

PARKING THEIR BLACK Fiat rental car as close as possible to the Brazen Head, Mick and Joelle were excited to visit the oldest pub in Ireland. Established in 1198, it is unclear how much of the original 11th century coach house is still intact. "This place is simply amazing," remarked Joelle, "look at this stone wall and the parapets along the top." She ran her fingers over the rough stone and could almost feel the history that each one held.

"Let's get inside," said Mick, "I'm not used to this cold, rainy weather. I'm freezing."

"Me too, good idea," said Joelle.

The silver Mercedes pulled into a parking space near the Brazen Head just as the ancient wooden door closed behind the Scotts. "Do we follow them inside this time?" asked the man in the passenger seat.

"No, I have a better idea," said the driver. He opened his cell phone and began dialing. "Keira, this is McFadden, how have you been?"

"William, it's good to hear your voice. I'm good. Are you in Dublin?"

"Yes, I am," said McFadden, "I'm actually sitting outside of the pub where you used to work."

"I still work here," said Keira. "Why don't you come inside and we can catch up on old times"?

"Maybe another night, Keira, but right now I need a favor." McFadden described the Scotts to her and asked if she could get close enough to their table to listen to their conversation.

"Not, a problem," said Keira, "I will just make sure that I am their waitress."

"Excellent," responded McFadden, "I will contact you later tonight after the pub closes."

Finding Uncle B siting at a small wooden table near one of the three bar areas, Mick and Joelle sat down to join him for dinner. It was Saturday evening and the pub was crowded with both locals and tourists. In the far corner under dim lights, a young bearded man sat on a stool playing a familiar Irish ballad on his acoustic guitar. Guinness was the obvious drink of choice in this pub and Uncle B was already on his third pint of the evening.

"Welcome to the Brazen Head," said the cute, twenty-something waitress. "My name is Keira, and I am your server this evening. Is this your first time to visit our pub?" Mick and Joelle looked at each other's heavy clothing and realized that they did not blend in too well as locals.

"It's not our first time in Dublin," said Joelle, "but it is our first time at the Brazen Head. We're from Arizona and not quite used to your cold, rainy weather."

"Aah," said Keira, "then let's get you warmed up with a pint of Guinness."

"Make that two," said Mick.

"So, tell me how things went today at the museums," said Uncle B. "Did you find any information that would be helpful in locating the treasures?" Before Mick could answer the question, Keira had returned with their beers and a basket of warm, homemade bread. As Mick and Joelle were describing their day to Uncle B, Keira took her time serving each beer so that she could hear their conversation. Throughout the evening, Keira took every opportunity to spend time around the Scott's table. It appeared to Mick and Joelle that she was providing exceptional customer service, but actually, she had used her frequent visits to their table to hear considerable information about their Celtic treasure research. As the three continued talking, Keira waited on tables nearby.

"Both the National and Maritime museums were very interesting," said Mick. "The various exhibits helped us to understand more about the Celtic tribes, but our most productive time was spent in the maritime archives."

"The ship logs we found dated back as far as 500 AD," described Joelle. "The written accounts painted a clear picture of voyages from France to Ireland and the types of ships they used. We hope to find additional information when we visit Saint Malo."

"It sounds like your visit was very productive," said Uncle B. "I've really enjoyed seeing you both and having you stay with me. Anytime you are nearby, you always have a place to call home. What are your plans for tomorrow?"

"It's mostly a travel day," said Joelle. "We have a connecting flight in Paris, land in Rennes mid-afternoon, and then drive the remainder to Saint Malo."

"Well, it's getting late and you have an early flight," said Uncle B. "Let's finish up here and head back to my house."

Later that evening when the Brazen Head was about to close, McFadden and his associate walked in and took their seats at the bar. Keira saw McFadden and hurried across the pub to give him a kiss and a hug. "My, you are more beautiful than the last time I saw you," said McFadden.

"Thank you, William. And you are still just as handsome!" After they finished embracing, McFadden introduced her to his partner.

"So Keira, were you able to locate the Scott's and hear any of their conversation?" asked McFadden.

Keira recounted each of the Scott's conversations that she had overheard and provided details of their travel itinerary for Sunday. "Your help tonight has been exceptional," said McFadden. "I will make sure that you are paid well for your efforts. I will keep in touch." The two men exited the pub and drove to Castleknock Park so that they could keep Mick and Joelle in their sights until morning.

"That's right, we are keeping them under surveillance until they board their flight tomorrow morning," said McFadden to his contact in Rennes, France. "We have been watching them for several days now and have some current photos to send you."

"That will be most helpful," said the man on the phone. "I will need their flight arrival information as well."

"Of course," responded McFadden, "all of those details will be sent with the digital photos. Good luck."

Next, McFadden made a call to Giorgio to provide a summary of his surveillance on the Scotts. "So what do you have for me?" asked Giorgio impatiently.

"I'm sending you some current photos of the Scotts and a list of the museums that they visited. They seemed very interested in exhibits displaying ancient ships and burial sites related to the Celtic people. It does not appear that they discovered anything of major importance while in Dublin. Tomorrow they will fly to Rennes, France and will be visiting Saint Malo and Jersey Island over the next few days. I have asked our contact in Rennes to keep them under surveillance when they arrive."

"Good work McFadden," said Giorgio. "We will be in touch."

CHAPTER 11

A T SUNRISE ON Sunday morning, Mick and Joelle were saying their goodbyes to Uncle B before heading to the Dublin airport. Their flight on Air France, #1079, was scheduled to leave at 9:20 a.m. and would arrive in Rennes France by 2:35 p.m. Unfortunately, they had to change planes in Paris, but did not have time to enjoy any of their favorite spots. After arriving in Rennes, they would rent a car and make the short drive to Saint Malo.

Uncle B's insight into ancient Celtic civilizations had given Mick & Joelle some good starting points for their research. Both museums that the Scotts visited in Dublin had provided bits of information that was helpful, but they hoped to find even more in the next few days. That afternoon, while they were enjoying views of the rich green countryside, Joelle's phone rang.

"Hi Joelle, it's Clay. How is your trip so far?" Joelle activated her phone's speaker mode so that Mick could join the conversation.

"We're having a great time. Uncle B is always a terrific host and the two museums we visited were most helpful."

"Awesome," said Clay, "I'm glad you are enjoying Ireland. I have some more information for you on dolmens and also the Demetrius character I mentioned before."

"Ok," said both Mick and Joelle, "tell us what you found. But please keep it short."

"Well," said Clay, "a dolmen, also known as a portal tomb, is a type of single-chamber megalithic tomb, usually consisting of three or more upright stones supporting a large flat horizontal capstone. Dolmens were usually covered with earth or smaller stones to form a barrow, though in many cases that covering has weathered away, leaving only the stone 'skeleton' of the burial mound intact. I will email some photos so that you can better visualize the structures."

"That would be helpful," added Mick.

Clay continued, "Archaeologists still do not know who erected the dolmens, which makes it difficult to know why they did it. The most widely accepted theory is that dolmens were used as religious gathering places much like churches are today."

"Have you researched any specific locations where these megaliths still exist today?" asked Mick.

"No, that's my next task," replied Clay. "There are many passage graves, menhirs and dolmens still standing on the western coast of France and on Jersey Island. It's going to take some time to research each one thoroughly. When will you and Joelle be returning home?"

"Probably by next Friday, give or take a day," replied Mick. "Why do you ask"?

"I should have the research completed by then and we can review my findings. Do you have time to hear what I found out about our mysterious mister Demetrius?"

"Putting it like that, how can we resist?" said Joelle. For the remainder of their hour long drive to Saint Malo, Mick and Joelle listened to Clay give a detailed biography.

"Marcus Demetrius controls a wide range of both legal and

illegal business operations throughout Europe and the United States," stated Clay. "His legitimate businesses include import and export of coffee, wine and other agricultural products. He also owns a ten percent share of Sostos Enterprises, his father-in-law's shipping business. Although he is a multi-millionaire many times over from his legal operations, his real wealth is rumored to come from his involvement in drugs, racketeering and prostitution."

"Sounds like a real quality guy," quipped Joelle. "How has he evaded arrest with involvement in so many illegal operations"?

"He appears to be a very shrewd businessman," said Clay. "I have found layer upon layer of shell corporations, but nothing definitive that ties him to anything illegal."

"Ok," said Mick, "so he is rich and probably very dangerous. But why should that concern us?"

"Remember when I first mentioned Marcus Demetrius a week ago? He is reported to have one of the largest private collections in the world of Roman artifacts and admits to being obsessed with collecting. Here's where it gets really interesting," said Clay. "Marcus has been interviewed many times and this is what he revealed about his childhood in a recent article." With both Mick and Joelle listening intently, Clay continued.

"Marcus says that he enjoyed reading about history since the days when he was a little boy spending most nights by himself in a small apartment located near Rome. He was fascinated by the stories of ancient warriors, their bravery and their wealth. Most of his books recounted battles that were between the Celts and Romans throughout Gaul," said Clay. "Julius Caesar had become his hero. Marcus was extremely bright and began studying Latin so that he could better understand Roman history in its original text. As the years passed,

Marcus's interest in Roman history turned into an obsession that filled the gap of his absentee parents. He studied their government structure, strategies of war, discipline, politics and ancestral linages. By his early teens, Marcus had convinced himself that he was a direct descendent of Julius Caesar and was destined for greatness," finished Clay.

"Sounds like he suffers from delusions of grandeur and may be certifiable," said Mick. "Clay, do think there is really any possibility that Marcus is related to Caesar"?

"No, there isn't anyone who can realistically trace their ancestry back two thousand years. Reliable records, even in the most aristocratic families don't exist before the Renaissance. Even if reliable records did exist, the amount of formal and informal adoption and passing off one man's children as another's, means that after many generations, all people are descended from someone different to the official version of their bloodline."

"So what does all that mean?" questioned Joelle.

"It means that any of us with European ancestry might be descended from Caesar," said Clay, "but nobody will ever know for sure because proving it is impossible. Even if we had a sample of Julius Caesar's DNA, the amount of genetic drift that happens over two thousand years means that there is no possible way to definitively connect anyone from 2013 AD to any individual person from that era. The best I could say is that I can't rule out the possibility that Marcus might be descended from the Julian clan."

Mick and Joelle looked at each other with raised eyebrows and a look of concern on their faces. "I would suggest that you watch your backs," said Clay, "Marcus might be very inter-ested in your research into the Celtic treasures."

"We will," said Mick. "We just arrived in Saint Malo and

plan on getting a good night of rest. Thanks for all of your help on this research. We will call you in a few days before we head back to Arizona."

As Mick and Joelle walked through the hotel's front entrance, they were immediately greeted by an outwardly friendly man behind the desk. "Good evening, welcome to the La Rance. My name is Henri," said the desk clerk. He spoke in perfect English, but with a heavy French accent.

"Bonsoir. Comment vas-tu?" said Joelle.

"Je suis tout à fait bien," responded the clerk. "Comment puis-je être de service"?

Joelle exchanged glances with Mick indicating that she preferred that he take over. "We are Mick and Joelle Scott and have reservations for tonight through next Thursday," said Mick. "We would like to check in."

"We've been expecting you this evening," responded Henri. "Thank you for selecting us. I am sure you will enjoy your stay." A few minutes later with the help of a bellman, the Scotts settled into their quaint room in one of Saint Malo's most famous hotels.

On the narrow cobblestone road in front of La Rance, a white Peugeot sedan pulled to a stop. "Our contact in Dublin indicated that the Scotts will be staying here during their time in Saint Malo," said Malet to his partner. "You take first watch while I catch up on some sleep. If you see either of the Scotts leaving the hotel, wake me. We need to follow them."

Shortly after 7:00 p.m., following a refreshing shower and a change of clothes, both Mick and Joelle were ready for a relaxing dinner. They made their way to the hotel lobby and approached Henri for a restaurant recommendation. "That sounds perfect," said Mick, "Delaunay it is."

"Would you like for me to call you a cab, sir?" said Henri.

"Yes, thank you," responded Mick. Mick and Joelle exited the La Rance a few minutes later to wait for their cab.

Enjoying a gaze at the beautiful scenery and historic buildings, Joelle took notice of a white Peugeot with two men sitting in it parked down the street. "I'm probably being paranoid after our conversation with Clay, but does that Peugeot seem out of place?" asked Joelle.

"What do you mean?" responded Mick.

"No other businesses on this street are open at this hour except our hotel. Look at all the empty parking spaces here. Why did the Peugeot park nearly two blocks away in front of a vacant storefront?" said Joelle. "And why are two men sitting inside"

"It's probably nothing," said Mick. "But I agree, let's keep our eyes open."

As their cab slowly approached and pulled to the curb, Mick and Joelle got inside and instructed the cabbie to take them to Delaunay just three kilometers north. "Malet, wake up, the Scotts are leaving. Malet, now," yelled his partner! He started the car and a few minutes later began following the Scott's cab at a safe distance. Both cars negotiated through the narrow cobblestone streets of Saint Malo. As the Scotts arrived in front of the Delaunay restaurant, the two men stopped their Peugeot along the curb a block away. "Do we follow them in or stay here?" asked the passenger.

"Not yet, let them get settled at their table," said Malet. Five minutes later the two men entered Delaunay and made their way to the bar area. Across the room at a romantic table for two, Mick and Joelle were enjoying a bottle of locally produced Merlot.

CHAPTER 12

"MICK, THIS RESTAURANT was an excellent choice," said Joelle, "I'm really enjoying tonight." The Delaunay was tucked inside the walls near Porte St-Vincent and was one of many local restaurants serving high quality French cuisine in refined surroundings. Great emphasis was placed on the freshest local produce with dishes such as sea bass tartare with oysters and nut oil, lamb sourced from Mont St-Michel and scallops foie gras marinated in chouchen. Delaunay also boosted an extensive wine list from their cellar.

"I'm glad to see that you are relaxing tonight Joelle. Do you like the wine?" asked Mick.

"Oh yes, but how did you know to select this bottle?" asked Joelle.

"Before we left Phoenix I did a little bit of research on wines produced in the southwest of France. It's known as the most diverse wine region. It is also one of the oldest. Many grape varieties grow only in this region: Tannat, Manseng, Servadou, Mérille and dozens of other varieties. The history and the diversity result in unfashionable wines with a lot of personality. I selected the Merlot since we both enjoy it so much."

"Well, aren't you the connoisseur. You made an excellent

choice as usual," Joelle complimented. "We should have a case or two of this shipped to Phoenix."

"I'm sure that our waitress would be happy to arrange that," said Mick.

The two tough-looking men with black hair were intently watching the Scotts and taking note of their mannerisms. Although they could not hear the conversation, it appeared that both Mick and Joelle were quite excited about the topic. "Do you think we can get a table near the Scotts so that we can hear their conversation?" asked Malet.

"Let's talk with the hostess and see if we can be seated at the empty table behind them," said his partner. After presenting the hostess with a large tip, the two men were escorted from the bar to a table behind the Scotts.

For the next twenty minutes, Mick and Joelle discussed all of the places that they wanted to visit during their days ahead on Saint Malo. The city was originally an island, becoming linked to the mainland by a sandy isthmus back in the 13th century and contained an old city called Intra Muros, meaning 'within the walls'. Some of the sites they wanted to visit included Solidar Tower, Saint Malo castle, Demeure de Corsaire, Municipal Museum and the Cathedral Saint-Vincent of Saint-Malo. They also planned to visit the Jersey Island museum to see the Celtic coin display and tour Grouville where the coins had been discovered. It was a lot of ground to cover in just four days, but Mick and Joelle needed to make every minute count. They were quite hopeful that with a little patience and solid research, clues about the whereabouts of ancient Celtic treasures would be revealed.

Satisfied that they had heard enough of the Scott's itinerary for the week, both men exited the Delaunay and waited in their Peugeot parked down the street. A short time later, Mick

and Joelle walked out of the restaurant and got into the awaiting cab. "Nous animent à la Rance Hotel, s'il vous plait," said
Mick. Although his command of the French language was mea-
ger compared to Joelle, it was passable and would get them
back to the hotel. Several cars behind the cab, their observers
followed inconspicuously. Upon arriving at the La Rance, they
parked the Peugeot and entered the hotel as closely behind the
Scott's as possible without being seen. Standing in the lobby
where they had a clear view of the elevators, Malet watched
the elevator floor indicator lights.

"It appears they have gotten off of the elevator on the third
floor," said Malet. "Let's go back out front of the hotel and
see which room lights up." A minute later, Malet exclaimed,
"Gotch ya," as the hotel room went from dark to light.

"Now that we know where their room is," added his partner, "we can search it for clues later this week."

"My plan exactly," said Malet as they headed back to their
car. "You are on first watch, I'm getting some sleep. Wake me if
they leave the hotel."

It was early afternoon in Tempe, Arizona, when the two
well-dressed men entered Professor Brinkerman's office and
took a seat in the reception area. "We have a 2:00 p.m. appoint-
ment with Mr. Brinkerman," said the roughly handsome man
to the office manager. The two men took a seat without further
conversation. A few hours earlier, Brinkerman had received a
text message from his assistant advising him of the meeting.
There wasn't a lot of detail provided in the message, just the
time and that it was critically important. He thought this was
odd, but had a strange feeling that he should not miss the
meeting.

Several minutes after 2:00 p.m., Professor Brinkerman
walked into the reception area and greeted the men. After

exchanging names and business cards, he escorted them to his office. "Please have a seat," said Brinkerman as he closed his office door. "Now, what is this meeting concerning"? The taller of the two men began speaking first.

"We have been asked to meet with you to discuss a certain document that was given to Mario Sargusi a few weeks ago. Are you familiar with that document?"

"I... I... I'm not sure what you are talking about," stammered Brinkerman. The taller man, not looking too happy with the Professor's response, exchanged glances with his partner, took a deep breath, and continued asking questions.

"Let's see if this jogs your memory. Do you recognize this?" He handed Brinkerman a copy of the exam paper from Kenzie Scott, and sat back down in his chair. "It's your student's World History exam paper from earlier this fall. That is the document that was given to Mario Sargusi. The document you gave to Mario and suggested he look into. We want to know everything you know about this student and the paper she wrote." Professor Brinkerman was dripping wet with sweat and was feeling light headed.

The two men realized that their scare tactic was working on the Professor. Now it was time to reel him in. "Our employer may be interested in pursuing the claims made in the paper. I'm sure he would be most generous if you could assist us in understanding where to find these lost items."

"That depends. Who is your employer and what is he offering?" asked Brinkerman.

"Who he is, does not matter. If we are successful in acquiring all of the items, your compensation will be one million dollars, cash; if we are not, you get nothing. The money would be placed in an offshore numbered account for privacy."

"I understand," said Brinkerman, "and I'm sorry for my

reaction. I do recognize the paper and I was the one who gave it to Mario. I really believe my student is onto something and I'm sure that the treasures exist. Let's get started."

"Kenzie Scott is a junior in my World History class and is the daughter of Mick and Joelle Scott. You have probably heard of them or seen them in the news. The couple are amateur treasure hunters and their daughter frequently assists them. They travel around the world searching for treasure and have assisted in the recovery of silver valued at over sixteen million dollars from the *SS Mantola*, treasure in the amazon region of South America and gold from a King's lost tomb near Cairo, just to name a few. Their daughter, Kenzie is in my class and was asked to write a persuasive paper about a current event. We had been studying a Celtic coin find valued at nearly sixteen million dollars that occurred last July on the Island of Jersey. Let me summarize the main points in her paper for you," offered Brinkerman.

Both of the men nodded their heads in agreement as Professor Brinkerman continued to explain Kenzie's paper to them. "Although no one knows for sure where these treasures are buried," said Brinkerman, "I believe that you will find them in one or more areas that I have circled on the map."

"So how are we supposed to find them? The areas you circled in northwestern France and on Jersey Island cover hundreds of square miles," said the tallest thug.

"I would suggest that you keep a close eye on the Scotts and let them lead the way," said Brinkerman. "Mick and Joelle Scott seem to have a knack for finding lost treasure, but I don't see them sharing it with you. That is a problem you will need to solve."

Both thugs cracked an evil smile and said, "Relieving the Scott's of the treasure will not be a problem for us."

"I hope I will be hearing from you soon," said Brinkerman. "I would love to retire and spend the rest of my days on an island in the Caribbean." Both men gave Brinkerman a smirkish look and the tallest man uttered a warning.

"I trust you will share our discussion with no one." Pointing at Brinkerman's bad leg, he continued. "I would hate to see you have another... accident." They turned and left his office as abruptly as they arrived, but this time with a treasure map in hand. Their boss would be pleased and they called him as they left the building.

"Giorgio, our meeting with Professor Brinkerman was very productive. He was quite interested in providing us with all of the information that he had about the exam paper and the Celtic treasures."

"Do you think the detail he gave you is reliable?" asked Giorgio.

"Absolutely, I mentioned the possibility of a one million dollar reward and he jumped at it. He provided us with a map of the locations where he believes the treasures are buried."

"So at this point, do we need him any longer?" asked Giorgio.

"Not really," said the thug. "Do you want us to arrange for him to have an accident"?

"Yes, that would be most helpful," responded Giorgio. "Wait until the fall semester is over and the students are gone so that his demise will attract less attention. I expect that you will handle this task with complete discretion."

"Yes sir, it will be handled professionally."

"Excellent," said Giorgio. "I will wire you the money for your services once the task is completed." Giorgio hung up the phone and began preparing an update for Marcus.

CHAPTER 13

MICK AND JOELLE were up at sunrise and ready to begin their tour of Saint Malo. After enjoying some fresh croissants and a small cup of espresso at Le Café de LOuest, they were ready to walk to Solidar Tower.

The ancient 'City of Corsairs' has one of the most turbulent histories of any town in France. Founded over two thousand years ago, Saint Malo was often caught between the conflicting interests of Brittany, England and France. The history of Saint Malo dates back to the former maritime center of Welsh people known as the Coriosolites.

"Mick, what do you know about our first stop this morning?" asked Joelle. Referring to the brochure that he had picked up in the lobby of the La Rance, Mick began to read.

"It says that the Solidar was built between 1369 and 1382 by John V, Duke of Brittany to control access to the Rance River at a time when the city of Saint Malo did not recognize his authority. Over the centuries the tower lost its military interest and became a jail. It is now a museum celebrating Breton sailors and also offers superb views from the top. It's located in the former city of Saint-Servan, which merged with Saint Malo in 1967."

"Hmmm, sounds interesting," said Joelle. "Do you think we will find anything there about the Coriosolites"?

"I'm not sure," said Mick, "but we will find out shortly. There it is, just down the street."

The white Peugeot sedan that had been following the Scotts since they landed in Rennes, France was moving slowing behind them, but had not drawn their attention. Mick and Joelle turned right at the next corner, but were not sure that they had turned the correct direction. As Joelle spun around to look at the last cross-street, she took notice of a white Peugeot sedan similar to the one she had seen parked near their hotel the night they arrived in Saint Malo. Joelle whipped back around and looked directly into Mick's eyes. "I'm not sure Mick, but I think that the white Peugeot sedan that is at the corner behind me is the same one that was parked by our hotel last evening."

"Joelle, there are a lot of white Peugeots in France. How can you be sure that is the same car?" asked Mick.

"I don't know for sure. I just have a feeling," said Joelle.

"I will keep an eye on it," said Mick reassuringly. "Let's continue walking in this direction, the Solidar Tower should only be two blocks away at this point."

As it was described in the brochure, the museum was a testament to the courage and resourcefulness of the ancient sailors who lived in this area of northwest France. Mick and Joelle moved through the maritime exhibits on each floor rather quickly, but one object common to nearly every display caught Mick's attention.

"Joelle, have you noticed that in most every exhibit we have seen this morning, there is mention of a captain's log? In some cases, the actual log is still intact and mounted in a display case. They are in incredibly good shape for their age and prolonged exposure to the salty sea air."

"Not until you mentioned it," said Joelle. "Why has that piqued your interest so much"? Mick began to explain.

"If it was customary practice for a ship's captain to maintain a written log and guard it from harm, it is possible that whoever sailed from the Saint Malo area to Jersey Island in 56 BC may have possibly done the same thing. It's a long shot to think that it may still exist and even more remote that we could find it."

"Crazier things have happened to us in the past," said Joelle. "Don't you remember how we stumbled onto the treasure in the amazon region of South America two years ago"?

"That's true," said Mick. "If we hadn't come across that small statue in the antique shop in Santarem, we would never have discovered the location of the golden cave."

It was shortly before noon as Mick and Joelle exited the museum and walked toward the restaurant they selected for lunch. "Wasn't that an incredible view of the city from the top of the tower?" asked Joelle.

"Yeah, getting that bird's eye view helped me to understand the layout of the city and the importance of controlling access to the Rance River. I can see why the fort was built on this location."

"Did you also see the white Peugeot sedan parked along the street one block from the museum?" asked Joelle.

"Yes, I did," said Mick. "I think we are being tailed."

The white Peugeot and its two occupants continued to keep Mick and Joelle in their sights and did not know that they had been spotted. "So who do you think is having us followed and why?" asked Joelle.

"I'm not sure, but it could be connected to the Demetrius fellow that Clay told us about or it could just be some local crooks that think we look like wealthy American tourists and would be an easy mark."

"Why do you think that nasty criminal that Clay mentioned would want to follow us? How would he know what we look like or that we are here?" asked Joelle. Mick glanced behind him and noticed the same white Peugeot in the distance.

"I don't know the answers to any of those questions, Joelle, but I do know that we are still being followed. That same car is a block behind us. Let's duck into this café and decide what to do." Mick and Joelle opened the door and quickly walked into the Le Bistro De Solidor.

Looking thru the front windows, they saw the Peugeot parked across the street with a clear view of the entrance. The men in the car appeared to have a camera and were taking pictures of the bistro. After Mick and Joelle were seated at a small table for two, they ordered a bottle of local merlot to calm their nerves and began discussing the situation.

Mick took a sip of the merlot and let out a deep sigh. While keeping one eye on the Peugeot he began to summarize the situation to Joelle. "Ok," said Mick, "it's pretty apparent that we are being followed. I'm just not sure who they are or why they are so interested in us. If they were planning to rob us, why would they be taking pictures of the Bistro?"

"We should notify the police," offered Joelle.

"And say what?" asked Mick. "All we know at this point is that the same car with two men inside seems to be tailing us. We need more information."

After discussing many different courses of action, Mick and Joelle decided to exit the Bistro through the kitchen and into the rear alleyway. Their plan was to walk to the corner and then around the building to the front. From that vantage point they would be able to see the Peugeot's license plate number, but would not be spotted by the two men. Once they had the number, Clay would be able to run a computer search and hopefully shed some light on the two men's identity.

Satisfied with their plan, Mick and Joelle passed quickly through the small kitchen of the bistro and opened a door to the alleyway. Walking around the building only took a few minutes and they were soon standing at the front corner of the building about one half block away. "The plate number is AA 517 NS," said Mick to Joelle. She typed a short message including the number and description of the car into her cell phone and then sent the text to Clay. "Do you think he will get back to us quickly?" asked Mick.

"I asked for it ASAP," said Joelle, "I'm sure he will." Satisfied with their actions, Mick and Joelle began making their way to the next planned stop, Saint Malo Castle.

CHAPTER 14

RISING UP LIKE a medieval giant along the shore, Saint Malo castle loomed in the distance. On the east side of the square is the massive bulk of the castle with four towers. In one of the towers at the northwest corner is the Galerie Quic-en-Groigne, which has interesting displays with wax figures, illustrating events in the history of the town. In the southwest wing of the castle is the Municipal Museum, that covers a number of themes including the long maritime history of Saint Malo with a collection numbering over eighty five hundred items. The impressive Castle of Saint Malo also acts as the town hall.

Mick and Joelle began their museum tour in the northwest tower to get a sense of the town's history. Although they both found the history of Saint Malo interesting, none of the exhibits really provided any insight into the Celtic history they sought. Satisfied that they had seen everything, they moved into the southwest wing to explore the area's maritime history. Grabbing Mick's arm, Joelle said, "Mick, hold on a second, Clay is calling. Hi Clay, thanks for getting back to us so fast. What were you able to find out from the license plate information I sent you?"

"It was much more difficult than I anticipated to track this one down," said Clay. "The license plate belongs to a vehicle that is registered to a holding corporation named Jacques, Inc., located in Rennes, France. Jacques is a subsidiary of Romano, LLC operating in both the US and Europe, headquartered in New York City."

"What type of operation is Romano?" asked Mick.

"It appears to be an import-export business, but I don't know any other details. The search didn't end there. Romano, LLC is a subsidiary of Sostos Shipping Enterprises, operated out of Rome, Italy. Here's where it gets interesting. Sostos is owned and operated by Theophilos Sostos, the father-in-law to Marcus Demetrius. The same Marcus Demetrius that is rumored to own the largest privately held collection of Roman artifacts in the world. Coincidently, he also has a ten percent ownership in Sostos Shipping Enterprises. I can't say that he is behind the men following you, but it's certainly possible."

"So you think that the men in the Peugeot work for Demetrius or are somehow connected?" asked Joelle.

"It appears, that way," confirmed Clay. "Just keep an eye out for them and be careful." Joelle thanked Clay and ended the call.

"Mick, did you hear all of that"?

"Yes, I did. It appears that our hunch was right and our observers may be interested in the same treasure we are. I haven't seen the Peugeot since we got their plate number this morning. Maybe we lost them," said Mick.

"Maybe," agreed Joelle. "I guess we will find out when we leave the museum. Let's take a look at the maritime exhibits first."

Entering the southwest tower of Castle of Saint-Malo, Mick and Joelle spent the next hour examining various maritime exhibits. Most of the ship displays represented the mid 1800's through 1900's, with only a few from earlier than 1799. "We've reached the last exhibit, Mick. What do you want to do next?" asked Joelle.

"Let's head back to the hotel and get cleaned up for the evening. There are many excellent restaurants in the area to choose from, your choice. We can enjoy a romantic candlelit dinner, a bottle of local wine and then... who knows?"

"Ooooh, I like how you think," said Joelle with a knowing smile on her face.

CHAPTER 15

TUESDAY, MICK AND Joelle continued to play tourist in Saint Malo by first visiting the Demeure de Corsaire. Walking through the grand foyer, they quickly joined a tour in progress of the famous house.

"Welcome to the home of François-Auguste Magon de la Lande, privateer and merchant," stated the elderly male tour director. "François-Auguste Magon was one of the most powerful ship owners in the heyday of Saint Malo and a director of the French East India Company." He continued his monotone delivery.

"Built in 1725, this house is listed as a Historic Monument to protect its authenticity and guarantee that the restoration process respects historical accuracy," said the director. "Demeure de Corsaire is a house that explains life in the time of the corsairs. As you walk, you will discover several hidden staircases and stately salons with walls covered in wood. The cellars were used as a prison during the French Revolution and in the underground gallery we have a vast collection of weapons, chests, documents and coins from the early eighteenth century and before." Although the entire presentation was spoken in French, Joelle understood every word and Mick most.

"After we visit the rooms of the mansion, let's walk through the special underground gallery," said Mick. "We might find something of interest there in the document section." Joelle nodded her head in agreement as they continued exploring and taking note of the many magnificent antiques.

A few minutes later, Joelle asked, "ready for the underground gallery?"

"Sure," replied Mick, "let's spend some time there and then we can find a café for lunch on our way to the Saint Malo Library."

The gallery was impressive with its collection of eighteenth century weapons and coins, but the document section provided the most interesting surprise. Buried in one of two antique chests filled with various shipping documents, Mick saw something rolled tightly around a wooden dowel. Curious, he unrolled it completely and found it was the size of a magazine. It depicted the coastal area near Saint Malo and contained many handwritten notes. The parchment map was in surprisingly good condition and was still legible.

"Joelle, take a look at this. I think I found a captain's map and log for a ship that sailed to Ireland in 1129. Help me get a picture of this so that we can study it further." Joelle snapped several shots of the map making sure to get all of the details. Next, with great care, Mick rolled the map around the dowel and returned it to the chest. "Did you see any other documents of interest?" asked Mick.

"No," responded Joelle, "just lots of correspondence and none earlier than the 1600's. Let's continue our document search at the Librairie du Môle and find a cozy café for lunch on the way."

Sitting at a small wooden table for two along the Rue de la Fosse, Mick and Joelle enjoyed a delicious lunch of freshly made crepes. Their meal began with a bottle of Baron Philippe Rothschild Merlot and warm, homemade bread. Next, they enjoyed a selection of crepes including ginger beef, crepe cordon bleu and asparagus ratatouille. "Mick, I'm really enjoying our time together this week and at a more relaxed pace today. It also helps that we haven't seen the white Peugeot," Joelle quipped. "Why do you think they were following us"?

"I've enjoyed today with you as well," said Mick. "As for our persistent observers, we probably haven't seen the last of them. I agree with Clay. I think our research may have piqued the interest of Marcus Demetrius and we need to watch our backs." Pushing himself back from the table and gesturing with his hands, Mick indicated that he was done eating.

"No dessert crepes for my big eater?" questioned Joelle with a smile.

"Not right now," said Mick. "I'm anxious to get moving to the library to see if we can find any other leads."

Librairie du Môle was a short walk away located on Rue de Dinan, a narrow, cobble stone street. The library was housed in a non-descript, stone faced, three story building. As Mick and Joelle arrived at the entrance, they were surprised by the small size of the library. "This may be a complete waste of time," remarked Mick, "but let's go inside and see."

Starting on the third floor in the reference section, neither Mick nor Joelle found anything of interest and decided to walk down the stairs to the second level. Searching row by row, Joelle stopped in front of a section of books identified as Celtic Fiction. After thumbing through over two dozen books and finding nothing, a very interesting title caught her attention. Joelle picked up a book entitled, *Disappearance of the Coriosolites*, and began reading the inside cover. The book was written entirely in French, but she was fluent in the language and quickly read the inside cover and prologue. What was labeled a fictional account of the last days of the Coriosolite tribes, seemed to Joelle to be part fact and part fiction. She had read enough that she knew she wanted to get Mick's opinion about the book.

Mick was sitting in a small reading area with various books scattered around his chair. Looking up as Joelle approached, Mick said. "Although I have enjoyed looking through some of these texts, I haven't found anything that would get us closer to the treasure."

"Well, I may have," remarked Joelle. "Take a look at this book." She handed the book to Mick and waited for his comments. Seeing only a look of confusion on his face, Joelle realized the problem. Mick could speak conversational French, but he was not able to read it as easily. Snatching the book out of his hands, Joelle said. "Here, let me read some of it to you." She continued reading for a few minutes and then paused to look at Mick's reaction.

"Well, so what do you think Mick"? Without waiting for his response, Joelle continued. "It says here on the back cover that *Disappearance of the Coriosolites*, written in the early 1900's by Frederick Momont, was based upon an original text written in 1135. It was originally penned in Latin by Galfridus Monemutensis also known as Geoffrey of Monmouth."

"I never heard of either of them, Joelle, have you"?

"No, I haven't. Seems like we have some more research ahead of us and for Clay. Let's see what we can find in the library's census information on Saint Malo in the late 1880's," said Joelle. "Maybe we can locate records on Monsieur Momont or a relative."

Hours later after tirelessly searching through stacks of census records, Mick and Joelle had found the tattered birth record of Frederick Momont. Now came the tough part. They would need to piece together his ancestry back to current day to see if there were any distant relatives still living in the area. Just moments before Librairie du Môle's closing time, Joelle came across the missing piece of the puzzle that they had been feverously seeking.

"Mick, take a look at my notes," said Joelle. "If you start with the birth of Frederick Momont in Dinard, France and follow each of his ancestors that we have identified through various marriages, it appears that a great grandson of the writer actually lives here in Saint Malo. When I ran an internet search on his name, Geoffrey Torche, I found that he owns and operates a small antique and book shop located in the center of town. Strangely enough, he was named Geoffrey after his famous ancestor who lived in the 1100's."

Excited about the many pieces of information that they had uncovered throughout the day, Mick and Joelle wrapped up their research and headed back to the La Rance. A trip to Geoffrey's antique shop would need to wait until the next morning. "When we get back to the hotel," said Joelle, "let's assemble the information we found today and email Clay. Hopefully, by the time we return to Phoenix and get settled in, he will have completed most of his research."

"Sounds like a good plan," agreed Mick. "We can follow up with him on Sunday."

Malet and his partner were sitting in their white Peugeot parked a block away from the La Rance. "There they are," said his partner. "Do you want to follow them inside this time"?

"No, let them go to their room and get ready for dinner," said Malet. "When they leave the hotel later this evening, we can search their room. Hold it, the Scotts aren't going into the La Rance. They appear to be walking toward the market a few doors away."

At the same time, Mick turned to Joelle and said, "Before

we go upstairs, let's pick up some fresh fruit, cheeses, warm baguettes and a few bottles of that incredible local merlot."

"Ooooo... I like how you think," said Joelle. "We can have a romantic dinner on the balcony of our room."

"My thoughts exactly," said Mick.

As Mick and Joelle exited the small market with a bag full of groceries, it became evident to Malet and his partner that the Scott's would probably not be leaving the La Rance again this evening. "We will continue our surveillance from the car tonight, but I don't think we are going to get an opportunity to search their room," said Malet. "You get the first watch again. I'm getting some much needed sleep."

CHAPTER 16

MICK AND JOELLE got an early start on their final
day in Saint Malo. After speaking with Henry,
the proprietor of La Rance about antique shops
in the area, they began walking down Quai Sebastopol as he
directed. According to Henry, Geoffrey Torche's antique shop
was located just a few blocks away on Rue Mesle. Malet and
his partner were awake and alert as the Scott's appeared from
the Hotel. "I'm going to stay a few blocks back, but I want to
see where they are going so early this morning," said Malet to
his partner. As Henry had described, Mick and Joelle found the
shop next to a pub on Rue Mesle.

"It seems he doesn't open until 10:00 a.m.," said Joelle.
"That's only fifteen minutes from now, but we have time to
check out some of the other shops while we wait." As they
approached the corner of Rue Mesle and La Rue de la Corbière,
Mick noticed a white Peugeot parked down the street.

"Don't look now, Joelle, but our friends in the white car are
back."

"Do you think they know where we are headed this morning or why?" asked Joelle.

"I doubt it," replied Mick, "but let's be as discreet as possible and head back to the store. Maybe they didn't see us yet."

Mick and Joelle were immediately greeted as they entered

the antique shop. "Bonjour Monsieur et Madame. Mon nom est Geoffrey Torche," said Geoffrey. "Bienvenue dans ma boutique. Comment puis-je vous aider ce matin?" Joelle being the most comfortable with the French language answered for both herself and Mick.

"Good morning, Geoffrey. Je suis Joelle, et c'est mon mari, Mick. We were told that you have one of the most interesting antique and book stores in Saint Malo. We are primarily looking for items representing the early history of this area. Could you assist us with that?"

"Most certainly," answered Geoffrey. He was equally versed in English and decided it would be most helpful and appropriate to continue conversing in his guest's native tongue. "Do you have a specific time period or antiquity in mind?" asked Geoffrey. Deciding it was his turn to join the conversation, Mick began describing what they were looking for, but in somewhat general terms.

"We are quite interested in the Celts during the first century BC and how they lived. In fact, we found a book at the library entitled, *Disappearance of the Coriosolites*. We haven't finished it yet; however, what we have read so far is very fascinating."

Geoffrey began grinning broadly and asked, "Do you happen to have the book with you?"

"Why yes," said Joelle. "I have it in my backpack. Are you familiar with the book?" She pulled the book out and handed it to him.

"Very much so," answered Geoffrey. "It is so odd that you chose that book. You see, I'm actually related to the author." Trying to look shocked, both Mick and Joelle gave their best impressions of surprise.

"You're related to Frederick Momont, the author?" said Joelle with astonishment in her voice.

"I am. In fact, our family has never moved from this area. That connection to my past is the main reason I own an antique and book shop that celebrates the history of this region of France."

"Would you mind if we ask you a few questions about events described in the book?" asked Mick.

"Not at all," responded Geoffrey.

For the balance of the morning, Mick, Joelle and Geoffrey sat at a small antique table near the back of his store conversing at length about the ancient Celts. As they ask him questions about his ancestor's book, Geoffrey revealed that it may contain more fact than fiction. "So you agree that this book was based upon the original text written in 1135?" asked Joelle.

"Yes, I do," responded Geoffrey. "The original was penned in Latin by Galfridus Monemutensis also known as Geoffrey of Monmouth. My parents actually named me after him to help carry on the historic lineage. Our family believes that the history of this region was passed down verbally from generation to generation until Galfridus captured it in written form in the early 1100's. The events he wrote about are true to the best of our knowledge. What else can I answer for you?"

Both Mick and Joelle were elated by their good fortune in locating Geoffrey and his openness to discuss his heritage. However, neither of them wanted to reveal that the root of their interest lay in finding a lost treasure. Joelle worded her next question very carefully, but Geoffrey saw through the deception. He didn't mind. They were a nice couple and not the first treasure hunters he had encountered, and certainly not the last. "Do you think the account Galfridus gave of the battle of the Coriosolites and the Roman army in 56 BC was mostly conjecture?" asked Joelle.

"Well, no one knows for sure," stated Geoffrey; "however,

by all historical accounts, the events he described are certainly possible. Since the Coriosolites lived along the northwestern coast and had more advanced warning of the impending invasion by Romans than tribes to the east, they could have taken steps to prepare. It was common practice for a tribe to gather their riches and bury them for safe keeping if they knew that an invasion was eminent."

"Are you familiar with the recent find of Celtic coins on Jersey Island near Grouville?" asked Mick.

"Of course," said Geoffrey. "That discovery has increased the number of novice treasure hunters on the island ten-fold over the last six months. Everyone with a metal detector thinks they are going to find the next horde of coins."

"What do you think, Geoffrey?" asked Mick.

"I think it was a lucky find. If the Coriosolite tribes buried the treasures of their village to avoid Roman seizure, I believe that they would have taken greater care than to place them in the middle of a field. Further, the wealth of their village was not solely coins. It would have also contained artwork, golden jewelry, statues, amber, weaponry, valuable utensils and other items important to preserving their history."

Mick interrupted and said, "But nothing like that has yet been found."

"Not yet," answered Geoffrey. "Of course, that does not mean it does not exist." After a short pause, he continued. "I hope I have been of some help to you both today. If you like, please continue to browse throughout the shop. You may find some other books or maps of interest. If you need further assistance, I will be available." Both Mick and Joelle shook Geoffrey's hand and thanked him for all of his help.

The antique shop was quite interesting and contained collectables that ranged in age from the late 1700's to current day.

Along one wall of the shop, wooden bookcases rose from floor to ceiling and were jammed with a diverse collection of literature. The books seemed to be in topical order and covered a wide variety of subjects including seafaring, geography, maps, Celtic and Roman history, diaries and a collection of short stories from well know authors. Mick was drawn to the map section while Joelle found several books on Celtic and Roman history that were of interest to her. Thumbing through the pages of a tattered book written in the late 1990's, she came across several photos of ancient relics. The treasures had been discovered in the area of Saint Malo at various sites over the last one hundred years. She took pictures of each item with her iPhone and then sent them via email to Clay.

"Mick, have you found anything else that you would like to purchase here?" asked Joelle.

"Yes, I believe so. I found a book that I thought was about gold near Saint Malo, entitled *Thunder God's Gold*, but it is actually a book written in 1945 about the Lost Dutchman's Mine."

"Ok, I'll bite," said Joelle. "What and where is the Lost Dutchman's Mine"?

Mick cracked a thin smile. "Right in our own back yard. In the Superstition Mountains to be exact. What makes this so intriguing is the old newspaper article I found folded between the pages. It was written in 1895 by a reporter named Bicknell and published in the San Francisco Chronicle. There are handwritten notes on the edges of the article and a small map has been drawn at the bottom. The initials are hard to make out, but it looks like B.G."

Joelle took a quick look at the book and newspaper article before handing it all back to Mick with a smirk on her face. "Did you find anything else of interest?" asked Joelle. "Maybe a little more pertinent to our current project"?

"Yes," said Mick, "I have learned a lot from studying these old maps. Most of them were attached to copies of captains' logs with detailed descriptions of their voyages. It's amazing what those seafarers were able to accomplish with the simplest technology so many years ago. The captains were very specific in their descriptions and I'm quite certain that the Celtic captain who sailed the boat to Jersey Island nearly two thousand years ago, maintained a similar captain's log."

"Do you really think there is any chance that we will find a captain's log from over two thousand years ago?" asked Joelle.

"I have no idea," said Mick, "but the book we found, *Disappearance of the Coriosolites*, was very specific about the tribe's final days in 56 BC. We just need more insight on how they would select a hiding place for their village's treasures. When we get back to Phoenix we can discuss all of this with Clay. Hopefully, he will provide a new point of view to solve this riddle."

Looking down at her watch, Joelle realized why she felt so hungry. It was nearly 2:00 p.m. and her stomach was beginning to protest being ignored for so many hours. "Mick, we seem to be finished here. Let's head back towards the hotel and stop to get a bite to eat on the way."

"I completely lost track of time this morning," replied Mick. "I'm pretty hungry too. Hopefully our friends in the white Peugeot parked down the street will have grown tired of waiting for us to reappear and are no longer around."

Mick and Joelle exited the antique shop and began their short walk towards the La Rance. Not seeing the white Peugeot again was comforting. Stopping at the first café they saw, Mick opened the door for Joelle and they were immediately seated at a small white table by the window. After enjoying freshly made crepes and a bottle of local cabernet, the Scotts began to unwind.

"When we get back to the hotel, I would like to spend the rest of today relaxing with you in the room and discussing the various materials we have found so far," said Mick. "Later this evening I have a surprise for you. We have reservations at 8:00 p.m. at La Chalut."

"Oh Mick, I have read the reviews on that restaurant. They are usually booked one year in advance," said Joelle. "How did you get us a table"?

"I have my connections," replied Mick with a smile.

CHAPTER 17

EARLY THURSDAY MORNING Mick and Joelle checked out of the La Rance hotel and caught a taxi to the busy Saint Malo ferry port. It was Market Days and all of the cobblestone streets were filled with people carrying bags and moving to and fro. Mick and Joelle exited the taxi and made their way through the crowds and onto the Condor fast ferry. In less than thirty minutes, they would be docking in Saint Helier on Jersey Island. Walking a short distance behind them, Malet and his partner boarded the same ferry. Although Mick and Joelle had confirmed that they were being followed the day before they left Saint Malo, they had no idea what their pursuers looked like nor did they realize that the same two men were sitting directly behind them.

Before leaving the ferry, Mick made arrangements for their baggage to be transported to the Eulah Country House Hotel in Saint Helier. They would check in and unpack later in the day after seeing the Celtic coin exhibit. Following a quick breakfast at the terminal coffee shop, Mick and Joelle set their course for the Jersey Museum.

"I know it's cool out this morning," said Joelle, "but it's beautiful here and I would enjoy walking through the walled city to the museum."

"Sounds good, it's only about ten minutes away and we

can get a feel for the history of the island. What do want to see first at the museum?" asked Mick.

"Let's head to the Celtic coin exhibit first and then see the rest of the museum."

The Jersey Museum and Art Gallery recreates history from two hundred fifty thousand years ago and continues through the centuries to explore factors that have shaped the unique island and the people who live there. Mick and Joelle entered the museum and walked across the highly polished wooden floor to scan the exhibit directory. Their footsteps echoed loudly since they were the first patrons to arrive on Thursday morning. Looking down the list, they found that the Celtic coin display was on display in Gallery E located at the back of the museum. As they approached, Mick and Joelle saw the gold and silver antique coins protected behind a two inch thick bulletproof glass display case.

"That mass of coins must weigh close to one ton," said Mick. "What an incredible find! There must be tens of thousands of coins."

"Look what this placard says," said Joelle as she began reading.

"In early 2012, amateur archaeologists Reg Mead and Richard Miles initially found sixty silver and one gold Iron Age coins, possibly minted by the Curiosolitae tribe near Saint Malo, France. Further metal detecting by Mead and Miles in the area of the initial find led them to discover a huge mass of Iron Age and Roman coins embedded in clay. The horde measured 140×80×20 cm (55×31×8 in) and weighed approximately 750 kg (1,700 lb.). The Grouville Hoard is estimated to contain over seventy thousand late Iron Age and Roman coins. With assistance of archaeologists from the Société Jersiaise and Jersey Heritage, together with Celtic coin expert Philip de

Jersey, they worked to remove the mass and put in on display. Philip de Jersey has suggested that the coins could be valued at between £100 and £200 each, in which case the entire hoard may be worth between £7m and £14m."

"What an amazing find," said Mick. "This is why Kenzie got so excited and began to dig into the history of the Celts."

"Ha, ha, ha. Nice 'dig' joke Mick," said Joelle.

"No pun intended. I'm serious," said Mick. "If this is any indication of the type or size of treasures that the Celts hid throughout northwest France and on Jersey Island, we have exciting times ahead. Let's continue walking through the museum and see what else we can find."

Several hours later after finishing up their research, Mick and Joelle exited the museum and walked to a small street side café for lunch. Malet and his partner had followed the Scotts all morning after getting off the ferry. Standing in the shadows across the cobblestone street, they were able to click photos of the Scotts, but they could not hear their conversation. "After lunch, let's check into the Eulah Country House Hotel and then we can rent a car to Grouville," said Mick. "We may not be able to meet with the men that found the stash of Celtic coins, but we can at least explore the area."

After a short drive from Saint Helier northeast to the small village of Grouville, Mick and Joelle parked their rental car along the curb of La Grande Route Des Sablons and entered O'Brian's Pub. "You never know what you might learn at the local watering hole," said Mick. "Hopefully, we will find some locals inside that want to talk about the big coin discovery last summer. Let's take a seat at the bar." It was only a few moments before one of the locals approached Joelle and offered to buy her and Mick a pint.

"You two are not from around here. Are you reporters or treasure hunters?" asked the local.

"Neither," responded Mick. "We are antiquity collectors and wanted to talk to Reg and Richard about their find."

"Well, you won't find them here any longer. There have been so many pesky amateur treasure hunters on the island since the discovery was publicized, Reg and Richard have quit coming in."

"Well we appreciate you buying us a beer," said Mick. "Where do you think we might find them"?

"Not really sure, but this time of day you may want to try the farm field just north of La Rue du Moulin a Vent near La Rue du Champ. It's a short drive from here and it seems to be Reg's latest area of interest."

"We appreciate your help," said Joelle, "and your hospitality."

After a short drive south of O'Brian's Pub, Mick and Joelle arrived at the location. It wasn't difficult to spot the slow moving infamous treasure hunters using their metal detecting equipment in the barren farm field. As they approached Reg and Richard, the treasure hunters ignored the Scott's approach. They had gotten all too familiar with amateur treasure hunters and their constant questions. Both men just wanted to be left alone to pursue their dream of finding more lost Celtic treasures. Joelle was the first to speak to the men.

"Excuse me, excuse me," shouted Joelle. "Can we speak to you for a few moments? My name is Joelle and this is my husband Mick." Reg and Richard exchanged glances, shut off their metal detectors and removed their headphones.

"I'm sorry, I didn't hear your names. How can we help you?" asked Reg. The couple introduced themselves again and then began to explain their interest in the area.

"So you believe that the horde of coins we found may just be a small amount of the Celtic treasures buried in this area?" questioned Richard.

"We are not sure," answered Mick. "We have studied the Coriosolite's history extensively and believe that it is possible that the tribe chose Jersey Island and the northwest coast of France as hiding places for their treasures prior to Roman attack. Have you extended your search to any other areas of the island?" Neither Reg nor Richard were comfortable discussing their search areas or patterns with strangers, but they had not strayed from Grouville for over thirty years. They had no interest in expanding their search area and didn't think that the Scott's posed any threat to their operation.

"No, we are quite content to continue our search in this area. We have been successful in the past and believe that there is more to be discovered," responded Richard.

"We appreciate you taking the time to speak with us," said Joelle. "We hope that you are successful in your continued search of this area." Mick and Joelle walked back to their car and decided to begin visiting the menhirs that Clay had suggested as possible treasure sites. They began driving southwest toward the La Rue au Blancq with specific longitude and latitude coordinates provided by Clay. The menhir was thought to be located in a field on the south side of the road and easily accessible on foot. Mick parked their rental car on the edge of the road in the grass and the two began walking south across the open field.

La Rue au Blancq Menhir was situated about one hundred feet south of the road and was unremarkable at best. "I think we can mark this site off of our list of possible treasure sites," said Mick. "Although there is a small arrangement of stones, I don't believe that it would have been large enough to be a significant site in 56 BC."

"I agree," said Joelle, "let's take a few photos and then continue on to the Ponterson Lane Menhir while we still have good daylight."

The Ponterson Menhir was located in a field about five hundred feet west of La Rue du Pontlietau. The block of porphyritic dolerite had a flat base and stood on top of the property foundations. It is unlikely to have been transported and used in the construction of the building and is more likely to have been utilized by the builders because it was in the vicinity. Mick and Joelle returned to their car and headed for their last destination.

The final stop of the day, just before sunset, was at La Dame Blanche. A three point five meter high pointed menhir on the south side of La Rue de la Croix. "This menhir is tall and should have been quite visible from a distance," said Joelle. "Do you think this is a possible treasure site"? Mick rubbed his chin and thought about why this menhir may have been selected by the Coriosolites.

"I'm not sure," said Mick, "I think we may want to return to this site with some equipment to study it further. Let's take some photos and head back to our hotel. I'm looking forward to a relaxing dinner with you and a chance to wind down before our plane flight tomorrow morning."

Malet and his partner shadowed the Scotts all day long in their Peugeot as they drove to Grouville and then across the Jersey Island country side. Keeping a safe distance back to remain unseen had been challenging given the flat terrain. Each time the Scotts exited their car and walked across a farm field or through heavily treed areas, they were out of Malet's sight. Shortly before sunset, Mick and Joelle returned to their car and began driving back towards their hotel in Saint Helier.

Later that evening while the Scotts were out enjoying a romantic dinner during their last night on the island, Malet and his partner were busy at work in the Scott's hotel room. "What exactly are we looking for?" asked Malet's partner.

"Anything that refers to the Celts, Romans, treasure, coins, or maps," replied Malet. "Make sure you put everything back the way you found it. I don't want them to know that we were here." Searching through the Scott's backpacks, Malet came across a book that caught his attention. *"Disappearance of the Coriosolites* sounds like a book we should copy," said Malet. "We can't do that, but let's take a picture of the front and back cover."

Over the next thirty minutes, they came across everything that Mick and Joelle had discovered during the last week. It included a photo of a captain's map and log for a ship that sailed to Ireland in 1129, various notes on Celtic ships and photos of large rock formations. "I don't know if any of this information will satisfy Giorgio," said Malet, "but we need to take photos of everything."

A lite knocking was heard at the door and then, "maid service, I'm here to turn down your bed for the evening." Malet and his partner froze in place and exchanged glances. As the maid attempted to enter the room, the door's security chain held and she could not enter. Surprised, the maid said, "I'm sorry, I didn't know the room was occupied. I will come back later."

"Let's wrap up and get out of here before she or the Scotts come back," said Malet.

Mick and Joelle returned from dinner later that evening and began to pack for their trip back to Phoenix. "Mick, I can't seem to find the book we got at the Librairie du Môle. Have you seen it?"

"Sure, it's in our backpack," said Mick. "I put it in there this afternoon when we finished summarizing all of our data."

"Well, it's not in there. Oh, here it is, on the coffee table."

"That's odd," said Mick. "I distinctly remember putting it into the backpack. Look around our room. Does anything else seem out of place to you?"

"Yes, now that you mention it, not all of the drawers are closed on our dresser. Both of us are really anal about that. There are also more clothes on the floor than I remember. Do you think someone has been in our room?" asked Joelle.

"I'm not sure, but it does appear that someone has gone through all of our things," said Mick.

"Should we call the hotel manager?" asked Joelle.

"We could, but it doesn't seem as if anything is missing, just rearranged. Let's finish packing and get some sleep," said Mick. "We can discuss this further in the morning."

Shortly before 5:00 a.m., Mick and Joelle had finally fallen asleep, only to be startled by the ringing hotel phone. "Good Morning, it's 5:00 a.m., this is your wakeup call," said the desk clerk with a chipper voice. Mick hung up the phone and both he and Joelle sighed deeply. They had tossed and turned all night without sleeping more than a few minutes at a time and were completely exhausted. Knowing that their flight was leaving for Phoenix in just two hours, Mick and Joelle begrudgingly rose out of bed and began preparing to leave for the airport.

Although they had not been able to determine that anything was stolen from their room the night before, Mick and Joelle believed that someone had been in their room. They had an unsettled feeling from finding their dresser drawers left open, some research materials out of order and various pieces of clothing tossed about the room. Obviously, someone had broken into their room looking for something of value and left when it was not found. Their passports and most of their research materials were in a neat stack on the table, just as Joelle had left them. Nothing seemed to be missing and contacting the police would be pointless.

The long commercial flight back to Phoenix provided an opportunity for Mick and Joelle to catch up on lost sleep and still have time to review what they had discovered over the last several days. "I think Clay will be excited and surprised by some of the materials that we emailed and shipped overnight to him," said Joelle.

"I agree," said Mick. "Hopefully he will have completed his research and be ready to discuss his recommendations with us early next week. But for the next few days, all I want to do is relax with you by our pool and soak up some Arizona sunshine."

"Sounds like a plan," responded Joelle with a smile.

CHAPTER 18

FOR SEVERAL DAYS after receiving materials sent from Mick and Joelle, Clay studied the items intently. Stacks of various sized books on Celtic history covered Clay's work table. Hundreds of small yellow Post-it notes stuck out from their pages. Each note indicated passages that provided Clay with a small clue to the location of lost treasure. Although he had not determined the exact treasure sites, he had narrowed down the list and prepared a map of possible locations for Mick and Joelle to review. Clay was excited to discuss the results of his research and hoped that they would be able to catch a flight to Orlando to meet with him later in the week.

"Clay," this is Joelle. "Your dad and I have booked a flight arriving in Orlando this Wednesday around 4:00 p.m. Can you or Rachel pick us up at MCO? We are flying in on US Air 567."

"Sure Joelle," said Clay, "I will see you and Dad at 4:30 p.m. outside of baggage claim. Have a safe flight." Wednesday came quickly and as promised, Clay was waiting in his car as Mick and Joelle exited US Air's baggage claim area. "Welcome back to Orlando," said Clay as he hugged Joelle and his dad. "I've really missed seeing you two." All three enjoyed catching up on family news in the car as they drove towards Clay's house on the southwest side of Orlando.

"You two take some time to get settled into the guest

room," said Clay, "and then we can meet in my office to review the materials you sent."

"When will Rachel be getting home from work?" asked Joelle.

"She is working late today," said Clay, "she won't be home until 11:00 p.m."

Fifteen minutes later, Mick and Joelle were sitting with Clay and anxious to get started. "I have studied the books, maps, photos, ship's logs and all the other materials you sent to me while you were in France," said Clay. "The book, *Disappearance of the Coriosolites,* was especially helpful in determining possible treasure locations. The original text that it was based upon, was written in 1135 and penned in Latin. Many of the events described in the text helped me form a better picture in my mind of ancient Celtic society. Here is a list of the things that we know for sure from all the materials." Clay pushed a piece of paper listing the facts across the table so that it was easier for both Mick and Joelle to read.

Skimming down the list with her eyes, Joelle studied all of the information and then began reading aloud. "Number one, the Celts buried treasures with their dead to take into the afterlife. Number two, dolmens and menhirs are believed to have been used as places of worship and often as cemetery plots. Number three, the Coriosolites hid village treasures when facing an attack. Number four, the Coriosolites sailed to Jersey Island from the area near Saint Malo. Number five, the Coriosolites hid a large horde of coins near Grouville that was discovered in July, 2012. Number six, Celtic tribes along the western coast built seaworthy boats capable of carrying heavy cargo. Number seven, Celtic ship captains kept detailed logs of their voyages."

"Clay, you have outdone yourself," said Mick with a smile

on his face. "You mentioned that you prepared a map of possible locations."

"I did," said Clay. "Let me explain how I was able to specify the areas where I believe you should first concentrate your search."

"It's likely that there are treasure sites scattered across the coastal areas of northwestern France; however, I suggest starting on Jersey Island since we know the location where the horde of coins was found. Although these coins were discovered in an open field without any visible marker," said Clay, "it's probable that other treasure locations were well marked. It was common for the Coriosolites to select ancient menhirs and dolmens as reference points in their travels. I believe that additional treasure could be buried near some of the menhirs or dolmens in the Grouville area. The megaliths have existed since 3,000 BC and their location would have been common knowledge to the tribes."

Mick and Joelle were captivated as Clay continued to explain his thoughts. "I've researched all of the possible sites they could have reached during a day's travel by foot on the island," continued Clay. "I don't believe that the Celts would have brought horses and wagons on their trip across the channel due to the extra weight. In addition, I estimated their landing point by studying ancient maps of the shoreline and calculating the shortest sailing distance from Saint Malo. Give or take one half mile, I believe that they landed here." Clay pointed to a place on the Jersey Island map that was near a quiet cove southwest of Grouville. "Now it's just a matter of narrowing the search locations," he added.

"From this mooring site, the Celts would have been able to travel inland to five separate megalith sites within a day's walk," reasoned Clay. "I've indicated each of the sites on this map with a star and labeled with their longitude and latitude. The sites I believe that you should research on Jersey Island are, Le Dolmen du Mont Ubé, La Rue Laurens Stones, Ponterson Lane Menhir, La Rue au Blancq Menhir, and La Dame Blanche."

"Well," said Mick, "we can shorten that list by three. On our last day on Jersey Island, Joelle and I visited Ponterson, La Rue au Blancq and La Dame Blanche. So three of the sites can be eliminated. If we are lucky, one of the two remaining sites you targeted will be the treasure site."

"We've only talked about Jersey Island so far. What about the possibility of the Coriosolites hiding treasures along their own coastal area?" asked Joelle. "Have you prepared a list of sites we should visit in that area as well"? Clay was happy that she asked this question because he had discovered five highly probably sites located south of Saint Malo and was excited to share the news.

"Yes, my research has uncovered several sites that I believe could have been the burial vaults for the Coriosolite treasures."

"What makes you so sure about these sites?" asked Mick.

"There are more than a dozen notable sites within one to two day's horseback ride from the Saint Malo area," said Clay. "I have studied each of the ancient menhirs and believe that these five may have been chosen as burial sites by the Coriosolites." As Clay pointed to each location on the map, Mick and Joelle took extensive notes about the sites' longitude & latitude, physical descriptions of the menhirs and the best access points by road. The sites to be visited would include Chablé Menhir, Champ Dolent, Saint-Pétreux Menhir, Menhir Christianisé Lande Rosse and Pierre Longue de Saint-Jouan.

"It's getting pretty late," said Clay. "I know you two are tired from traveling. Why don't we start again tomorrow morning? I took a few vacation days so we can spend the rest of the week planning your return visit to the sites."

"That sounds like a great plan," said Joelle as she yawned. "See you in the morning, and tell Rachel we are sorry we couldn't wait up. Thanks again Clay."

The next two days went by very quickly as Mick and Joelle worked to determine the most likely sites to search. "According to common Celtic tribal practices," explained Clay, "if they knew that an invasion was eminent, their Chief or King would gather the wealth of the village and hide it until the threat passed. Prior to 56 BC, the Roman armies had conquered most of Gaul, but had not yet advanced to the western coast. My research has led me to believe that the Coriosolites living near the area of Saint Malo were very well organized and took steps necessary to protect the entire wealth of their village. That is why the large horde of coins was recently found near Grouville."

"It sounds like your research has validated Kenzie's exam theory," said Mick. "And you think that there could be multiple treasure sites"?

Clay sat a current map of Jersey Island on the table and pointed to two areas that he had circled in red. "When you return to the Island, I suggest that you concentrate your efforts on Le Dolmen du Mont Ubé and La Rue Laurens Stones," said Clay. "To assist you in scanning the underground areas with accuracy, I am ordering you a Minelab GPX 5000 metal detector with a 15" DD deep seeking search coil. It will arrive at your home in Phoenix shortly after you return." Clay removed the map from the table and replaced it with a larger one.

"Now let's talk about the sites I have targeted in western France," said Clay. "I have selected five possible locations where I believe you may find Coriosolite treasure. Each of these sites have a few things in common. First, each site boasts a large menhir that has been in the same location for thousands of years. Second, each of these sites are easily visible from a distance. Third, all of the sites are within a day or two's horseback ride from the Saint Malo area." Both Mick and Joelle were pleased with Clay's extensive research and the detail of his findings.

"Since some of the sites you are recommending we visit could be quite large, is there other equipment besides the handheld Minelab GPX 5000 that would be helpful? If I recall correctly, a group of archeologists in South America have been using a ground penetrating radar system to map underground areas very accurately," said Mick. Clay smiled and pulled out a specification sheet on a device that looked like an electric lawn mower.

"I believe this is what you have in mind," said Clay. He handed the glossy specification sheet to Mick.

"Hmmm," said Mick. "It says here that this GPR (Ground Penetrating Radar) system is optimal for surveys where large areas need to be covered quickly and systematically. The embedded software provides an easy to use 'survey & map' operation which logs data in a structured format enabling quick creation of plan maps. The bi-directional odometer triggers data acquisition when moved in one direction and provides back-up arrow positioning enabling 'locate and mark' real-time target mapping. Further, it's designed for manual movement over smooth to moderately rough terrain." Joelle had been listening to their conversation and was amused by the men's excitement over their latest electronic gadget.

"Clay, can you make arrangements to have one of these GPR units delivered with the metal detector?" asked Mick.

"Sure, I should be able to have it delivered to your home in

Phoenix before you leave for the holidays," said Clay. "If I run into timing problems, I can always have it delivered to your hotel on Jersey Island or Saint Malo. I'll let you know what I find out within a few days."

Their visit with Clay and Rachel passed all too quickly and they hated to leave. The return flight to Phoenix was scheduled to depart in a few hours, but Mick and Joelle knew that they would be returning to Orlando in January to see the birth of their first granddaughter. "We appreciate everything that you did for us and really enjoyed our visit," said Joelle.

"Clay, the information that you provided was exceptional," said Mick. "I think you and Kenzie are both onto something."

The next week passed by quickly as Mick and Joelle made preparations for their return to Dublin. Although they were excited to make the trip with their daughter Kenzie and her best friend Danielle, the Scotts had no idea how their lives would change over the next few days.

CHAPTER 19

FALL SEMESTER HAD ended at ASU and Christmas break was just beginning. Most of the campus was deserted except for a handful of students that would remain in Tempe to work at their part time jobs during the holidays. Kenzie had completed her last final exam that morning, finished packing and was now driving to pick up her best friend, Danielle. The two girls would soon be driving down I-10 toward south Phoenix, anxious to start their two week vacation from school.

"So, are you excited to see your dad in Dublin?" asked Kenzie.

"Of course I'm happy to see him," said Danielle. "I miss him a lot. I haven't seen him since he dropped me off when school started this fall. But I'm also really excited that you and I are going to have nearly two weeks in Ireland with your parents. The countryside is awesome. There are so many things to see. You are really going to love it."

"I know I will," agreed Kenzie. "I can't wait until we leave tomorrow morning."

"So, are Mick and Joelle going to stay in Dublin with us the whole time?" asked Danielle.

"No, they are going to continue their research of possible Celtic treasure locations around Saint Malo and on Jersey

Island," said Kenzie. "I hope we can get to the Jersey Museum as well. I want to see that huge coin exhibit."

"You never told me how you did on that exam paper you wrote for World History before Thanksgiving break. What did the Professor say about your theory?" asked Danielle.

"I got an 'A' on the paper, but Professor Brinkerman didn't seem to have much to say about my idea. In fact, he seemed to avoid me the rest of the semester."

"That's odd," said Danielle.

Five-thirty a.m. came more quickly than either of the two girls or Mick and Joelle liked. Scurrying around the house to finish up every last minute detail, they soon drove to Sky Harbor airport to catch their 10:15 a.m. United flight to Dublin, Ireland. Fifteen hours, two plane changes and multiple time zones later, all four weary passengers slowly disembarked the plane and made their way towards baggage claim. After such a long trip, they all hoped that their luggage had arrived as well.

Sitting in a 2011 silver Mercedes sedan parked near the rental car terminal, McFadden and his partner waited for the Scott's to pass by. A few minutes earlier they had received a call from the rental car agent assisting the Scotts. A fifty euro bribe was all it had taken for the agent to call McFadden and let him know that the Scotts were on their way. "Here they come," said McFadden, "they are in the black BMW 525 sedan." McFadden let them pass by and then pulled into traffic a few cars behind. This time, he knew where the Scotts were headed and proceeded to drive towards Castleknock.

Uncle B's home was the third house on the right after turning off of Auburn Avenue. Mick pulled the BMW into the long narrow driveway and came to a stop. Danielle was the first to jump out of the car and run up to meet her father. It had only taken thirty minutes from the airport to Castleknock, but

Danielle couldn't wait any longer. It had been six long months at school in Arizona and she wanted to be in her father's arms again. Mick and Joelle exited the car and began to unload their luggage from the trunk. After warmly embracing his daughter for several minutes, Uncle B turned toward the car and shouted, "Welcome to my home again. It's good to see you in Dublin for the holidays." Before he could say another word, Kenzie sprinted up the driveway and began hugging her adopted uncle, Uncle B. "Wow, you have grown up since the last time I saw you," he said. "But it has been over two years. I'm so glad that you came to visit with Danielle. Let's get you all inside out of the cold weather and enjoy an early lunch."

As they all entered the house, the silver Mercedes sedan carrying McFadden and his partner turned onto Castleknock Park and pulled along the curb to keep Uncle B's house in their sight. "Now we watch and wait," said McFadden. Several hours later, the Scotts and O'Shanahans left the house in Uncle B's Range Rover and headed towards town. McFadden and his partner followed closely behind.

After a short drive, they arrived at The Brazen Head for dinner. As they drove towards the pub, McFadden called Keira and asked her wait on the Scotts again. "I need you to make friends with Kenzie and Danielle and offer to show them around Dublin. You need to stay close to the girls and report their activities back to me," said McFadden. Keira agreed to do what was asked and began watching for the Scotts. Keira was tall and thin with dark black hair, a fair complexion and was only a few years older than Kenzie.

"Welcome back to The Brazen Head," said Keira, to Mick, Joelle and Uncle B. "I see that your party has grown. Who do you have joining you tonight?"

"Keira, this is our daughter Kenzie and her friend Danielle," said Mick. "The girls came back with us for the holidays."

"I'm sure both of you will enjoy your time in Dublin. If you have any questions about fun places to see or things to do, just let me know."

Throughout the evening both Kenzie and Danielle spoke at length with Keira and began to build a friendship. "I have lived here all of my life," said Keira. "I'd be happy to be your tour guide and show you all of the sights of Dublin. I have to work tomorrow, but I could meet with you both on Monday if you like."

"That sounds great," said Kenzie. "Danielle and I will be here at 10:00 a.m. Monday morning and you can show us around."

"See you then," said Keira.

Early Sunday morning Mick and Joelle began reviewing all of the information that they had found in Dublin, Saint Malo and on Jersey Island with Uncle B. "So far our research indicates that Kenzie's theory could be true," said Mick. "The book we found, *Disappearance of the Coriosolites*, has proven very useful and corroborates her idea."

"Did you find any other information that would narrow the search?" asked Uncle B.

"We found evidence of ancient maritime voyages that proves it possible that a ship of treasures could have been sailed from Saint Malo to Jersey Island around 56 BC," responded Mick. "When we gave this information to Clay he was able to determine an approximate landing site along the southern coast of the island. Using that as a starting point and assuming that the Coriosolites walked to their destination, Clay found five possible burial sites. Each of them are near an existing menhir or dolmen."

"During our last day on Jersey Island, Mick and I visited Ponterson Lane Menhir, La Rue au Blancq and La Dame Blanche," said Joelle. "But none of those sites seemed to reveal any clues about the treasure. Mick and I still need to investigate the sites of Le Dolmen du Mont Ubé and La Rue Laurens Stones."

"This time, we will have the appropriate equipment," said Mick. "Before we left Phoenix, Clay provided us with the latest in commercial metal detecting equipment. We will be using the Minelab GPX 5000 metal detector with a 15" DD deep seeking search coil. It should enable us to see relics or gold buried under ten feet of soil and rock."

"So tomorrow morning you are heading back to Jersey Island to continue your research?" asked Uncle B.

"Yes, we fly out at 8:35 a.m. on Flybe and will spend Monday on Jersey Island," said Mick. "Late tomorrow afternoon we will take the ferry to Saint Malo and continue our investigation of the five menhir sites that Clay recommended. We will probably spend the remainder of the week in Saint Malo and return to your house on Friday evening."

"That plan sounds great," said Uncle B. "I wish you both good luck and a safe trip. We will need to leave around 6:00 a.m. to get you to the airport on time. See you in the morning."

After bidding farewell to Mick and Joelle at Dublin Airport, Uncle B picked up his cell phone and dialed McFadden. "You probably already know this since you have been tailing me, but I just dropped off the Scott's at Dublin Airport. They are flying to Jersey Island today."

"I appreciate the heads up, O'Shanahan. I will contact our man in Saint Helier," said McFadden. "Do know what their plans are for the rest of week"?

"Yes, they are going to visit several menhirs on the island

today and then five more around Saint Malo this week. They believe that the menhirs are a key to finding the Celtic treasure. I will send you a text listing all of the sites."

"That would be most helpful," said McFadden.

"I promised Marcus that I would help him follow the Scotts," said O'Shanahan, "but I did not agree to put them in any danger."

"They will only be watched," said McFadden. "Our instructions from Giorgio are to take pictures and report their movements to him. That's all." Uncle B finished the call and turned into his driveway.

Later that morning, Kenzie and Danielle drove with Uncle B into Dublin. As his car came to a stop in front of The Brazen Head, Keira was outside waiting for the girls. "Ready to see the exciting sights of Dublin?" asked Keira.

"Absolutely," said Kenzie and Danielle in unison as they exited Uncle B's car.

"Let's go inside and plan out the day," said Keira.

After leaving the pub, Uncle B placed a call to Giorgio to report on the Scott's plans to find the treasure. "Giorgio, this is O'Shanahan. The Scotts are getting closer to the treasure. They left my house this morning and will be narrowing their search of sites on both Jersey Island and around Saint Malo. If all goes as planned, they could begin excavating in early January. I called McFadden and gave him a quick brief on their schedule. He is coordinating with his contact on Jersey Island."

"I appreciate your follow up O'Shanahan. Your assistance is going to make you a very rich man," said Giorgio. "If you hear any news from the Scott's, contact me immediately."

CHAPTER 20

L ATER THAT SAME morning, all three young women arrived at the Old Jameson Distillery in Dublin and spent several hours enjoying the tour. The distillery was founded in 1780 and was Ireland's most famous distillery for nearly two hundred years. The comparative whiskey tasting was their favorite part of the tour and set the mood for the rest of their day. After enjoying lunch at the 3rd Still Restaurant, Kenzie, Danielle and Keira began their whirlwind tour of Dublin.

Mick and Joelle's first site to visit on Jersey Island was La Rue Laurens Stones located east of Saint Helier. Mick picked up the rental car and then stopped to get Joelle in the baggage area. "I hope this metal detector is as good as Clay claimed," said Joelle. "It was really a pain getting it through security." Once everything was stowed in the trunk, Mick pulled away from the curb and headed toward Victoria Road.

La Rue Laurens Stones was only a twenty minute drive and they were anxious to see if it presented any clues. "Mick, take the next road left. It should be Rue Laurens and the menhir should be up ahead a kilometer or so." They stopped the car and pulled to the side near the megalith's longitude and latitude. "According to the information Clay gave us, the stone should be about thirty feet to our east in this field," said Joelle.

"It must be well hidden in the trees," said Mick, "I don't see it anywhere in the distance." As they walked directly towards the coordinates, a small stone appeared. It was approximately three feet in diameter and nearly flush with the surface.

"This isn't what I was expecting," said Joelle. "Do you think it was much larger two thousand years ago"?

"I don't know, but it won't take long to search around it with the metal detector. I'll be right back." After making multiple passes across a fifty by fifty foot area without a single hit, Mick decided to call it quits. "It appears that we need to move on to the next site," he said. "Hopefully, it will be a little more exciting."

Parked a short distance away, two men in a white Peugeot quietly observed the Scott's. "It appears they have found something of interest in the field," said Malet. "He's getting a metal detector out of the trunk and returning to the field." A short time later, both Scotts returned to the car and headed north.

"Their next stop is listed as Le Dolmen du Mont Ubé," said Malet's partner. "If we head back the way we came, we will beat them to the site."

"Take the next turn onto La Rue de la Blinerie," said Joelle. "We can park along the side of the road. According to Clay's information, Le Dolmen du Mont Ubé is located in trees approximately one hundred meters to the east."

"Let's hope this site is more productive than the last," said Mick. "I'll grab the metal detector."

"Listen to this," said Joelle as she read from Clay's extensive notes. "This passage grave was discovered in 1848 by workmen quarrying for stone. It leads into a bottle shaped chamber that originally had four internal compartments, each blocked with low stone slabs. The capstones have been removed. Within the passage, stands three stones that may also have had a low sill at some time. Items previously recovered here include pots, a Jersey bowl, vase supports, flint and stone tools, stone axes, polished stone pendants and a grape cup. Human remains were noted in the cists."

"This site is so unique," said Mick, "I could see it being referenced thousands of years ago as a marker. I'm going to start a search grid with the Minelab GPX 5000. Clay said that this model is equipped with a 15" DD deep seeking search coil that will enable us to see relics or gold buried under ten feet of soil and rock."

"Quite impressive," quipped Joelle. "While you are doing that, I will begin looking at each individual stone to see if I can find any markings."

With over two dozen different stones to inspect, Joelle had a lot of work ahead of her. The stones appeared to be sunken several feet into the soil and were each about waist high. Using a magnifying glass to study the stone's surface, she inspected each and every inch before moving on to the next stone. Joelle had completed one side of the passage grave and was now working on the largest stone placed at the enclosed end of the u-shaped area.

It was hard to distinguish from the rest of the surface, but it appeared to Joelle that there was some design etched near the base of the stone. Rubbing her finger over it she could feel a slight curved indentation. Using her camera's macro lens, Joelle zoomed in on the area and took several photos from different angles. Next, she downloaded the photos to her iPad and began viewing the images. One by one she saw the same curved lines. Was it a harp? She couldn't believe her eyes. Waving her arms and yelling her loudest, she was able to get Mick to look up and remove his headphones. "Come take a look at this Mick. I think I found a clue at the base of this stone."

Mick quickly set the detector and headphones on the ground and ran to Joelle's side. "What has you so excited?" asked Mick.

"Here, take a look at these photos. What do you see?" said Joelle.

"It's very faint, but it appears to be the carved image of a small stringed instrument. What do think it is?" asked Mick.

"I see the same thing. It looks like a harp to me. Could it just be two thousand years of weathering that produced this image?" said Joelle.

"Not sure. Have you seen anything else on the stones?" asked Mick.

"No, not a single clue until this."

"Let's send the images via email to Clay and have him do some research. With his computer system's extensive power and graphics capabilities he should be able to discern if this is a man-made image or just weathering," said Mick.

"He also needs to research the imagery used by Celtic tribes during the 1st century BC," added Joelle. "If this is a carved image, he may be able to pinpoint the tribe that used it. I'm going to continue removing soil around the base of this stone to see if there are any other markings. How is the search pattern going? Any hits yet?"

"No, nothing yet," said Mick. "But I've only covered about twenty five percent of the grid pattern. Hopefully something shows up soon."

It was late afternoon when Mick began getting some interesting readings on his metal detector's screen. Working in a very narrow back and forth search pattern, Mick was able to identify the outline of a large object buried five to six feet below the surface. It appeared to cover an area approximately ten by ten square. "Joelle, I believe that we have found a site that needs additional research," said Mick.

"I do too," added Joelle. "A few inches below the harp image I discovered a large letter 'C'. It was partially filled in with dirt and when I cleaned the surface it became quite clear. It was carved much deeper than the image above it. I need to get some more photos and then I am done with this stone."

"I think we have found enough at this site to warrant a return visit," said Mick. "Let's get packed up and head back to the car."

Their activities at the ancient passage site had been observed all afternoon by Malet and his partner from the edge of the field. It was obvious that the Scotts had found something of interest and would most likely be returning to this site. Keeping out of view, Malet and his partner returned to their car and waited for the Scotts to leave. They followed Mick and Joelle back towards Saint Helier, but kept them in view from a safe distance. As the Scotts boarded the fast ferry to Saint Malo, Malet and his partner decided to follow. "Once we get checked in at our hotel in Saint Malo," said Joelle, "I want to call the girls to hear about their day of sightseeing."

"And to tell Kenzie what we found today?" asked Mick.

"Of course, she will be so excited," said Joelle.

About the same time Joelle was thinking of calling Kenzie, the three young, but exhausted women, returned to Keira's apartment to relax. In less than eight hours they had visited the Dublin Castle, Christ Church Cathedral, Grafton Street, Kilmainham Gaol, Phoenix Park and St. Patrick's Cathedral. It was time for a shower, dinner and some sleep. Unfortunately, their slumber was interrupted by Kenzie's cell phone ringing. "Hi Mom. No, I wasn't asleep," said Kenzie as she fought back the urge to yawn. "Are you and Mick ok"?

"We are," said Joelle. "We are at our hotel in Saint Malo. How was your sightseeing today?"

"We had a great day. Keira is a terrific tour guide and we are staying at her flat tonight. Tomorrow we are flying to Jersey Island to see the coin display at the museum."

"How are you doing that?" asked Joelle.

"A good friend of Keira's is a pilot and has his own plane. He offered to take us all there if we could help out with the cost of the fuel," said Kenzie. "We are staying near the downtown port overnight and then returning to Uncle B's on Wednesday."

"Well, have a good time and please be careful. Are you sure he's a good pilot?" asked Joelle.

"Yes, Mom. Keira has flown with him many times." Kenzie decided to change the subject.

"So, how is your research of sites on Jersey Island going?" asked Kenzie.

"The first site was a bust, but the second site seems extremely promising," said Joelle. "Mick used the metal detector Clay recommended and located objects covering a ten by ten area. But the most exciting news is that I discovered some ancient carvings on one of the stones. We have emailed photos of the carvings to Clay for analysis. We should have some feedback from him tomorrow."

"Let me know what he says. Maybe you found a treasure site. Are you still in Saint Helier?" asked Kenzie.

"No, we took the ferry earlier this evening and are staying at the La Rance again in Saint Malo. Have fun in Saint Helier tomorrow," said Joelle. "Give me a call when you get back to Uncle B's on Wednesday."

"I will Mom. I'm going to get some sleep now."

At 8:00 a.m. the next morning after enjoying a home cooked Irish breakfast made by Keira, the three young women drove together to a small private airport south of Dublin. Two hours later, Keira, Danielle, Kenzie and the pilot touched down at the Saint Helier airport. "Let's grab some quick lunch in town and then head to the Jersey Museum," said Keira. "So what is so important at the museum that you wanted to fly from Dublin to see"?

"The coins that are on display were discovered by a pair of men that had been searching the Grouville area for nearly thirty years," explained Kenzie. "The coins that they found were used by the Coriosolites in the year 56 BC. I think there are many other treasures in the area that the Corisolite tribe buried before they were invaded by the Romans. I need to see the coins they found and learn everything I can about their history."

"Wow, do you really think you can find the other treasures?" asked Keira.

"I don't know yet," said Kenzie, "but I will know more after I see the exhibits at the Jersey Museum."

Just prior to 2:00 p.m., all three young women walked into the museum. Wanting to see the coin display first, they scanned the exhibit directory to find its location. Looking down the list, they found that the Celtic coin display was on display in Gallery E located at the back of the museum. Although it was a Tuesday afternoon, there were many patrons in the museum due to the holidays and the exhibit lines moved slowly. As they got nearer to the display, they saw the gold and silver antique coins protected behind a two inch thick bulletproof glass display case.

"Wow, what a huge pile of coins," said Danielle.

"It's called a horde," said Kenzie. "What an incredible find! There must be tens of thousands of coins."

"Look what this placard says," said Keira. All three women looked down at the writing and began reading.

"Can you imagine if this is just one of many Celtic treasure sites that could exist?" asked Kenzie. "This is why I got so excited when I learned about their find this fall. Let's look at the Celtic ship exhibit next. I want to learn more about how they traveled to this island from their tribe's home near Saint Malo." Both Danielle and Keira forced a smile and rolled their eyes, but continued following Kenzie through the museum. Although they really didn't have much interest in the museum, it was fun being together and taking pictures of each other in silly poses that would be posted on Twitter later in the day.

CHAPTER 21

FTER SEVERAL HOURS of wondering past boring exhibits, Danielle and Keira pleaded with Kenzie to leave the museum. "Let's head back to our hotel, freshen up and then hit some of the clubs in Saint Malo," suggested Keira.

"I'm up for that," said Danielle. "We'll take the ferry across."

"Ok, ok," said Kenzie, "we can go. Danielle, can you get one last picture of us by this ship exhibit before we leave?" As the young women left the museum a few minutes later, Kenzie wondered what her mom and Mick's site research had revealed earlier in the day.

Although Mick and Joelle believed the site on Jersey Island was very promising, they still wanted to visit all of the possible treasure sites Clay identified near Saint Malo. Leaving their hotel in Saint Malo shortly after 8:00 a.m., they headed south-east following the Rance river along D137, exited to the D117 and then turned south onto D7. "The Chablé Menhir should be just ahead on the right," said Joelle. "It shouldn't be too hard to find since it is composed of white quartz and is nearly five meters tall. Clay's notes indicate that it is very close to the road, but seeing it through the hedges which surround it is not easy."

"I'll pull over and park here," said Mick. "The coordinates indicate that it is just a few hundred meters from the road in those trees." Neither Mick nor Joelle took notice of a white Peugeot sedan with two male occupants parked one quarter mile behind them.

Mick and Joelle exited the rental car and made sure to have all of the necessary surveying equipment in hand. As they had done the day earlier at a similar site, Joelle began studying the surface of the stone and Mick used the Minelab GPX 5000 metal detector in a crisscrossing grid pattern across the ground. Mick was the first to register a hit. "Joelle, I've detected something buried at about eight feet below the surface. The detector indicates that it could be gold."

"Keep working your search grid," said Joelle. "Maybe you will get additional hits." Another forty five minutes passed without either Mick or Joelle discovering any clues. As Joelle worked her way around the gigantic stone menhir with a magnifying glass, she stopped at each indentation to evaluate its shape. Approximately eighteen inches from the ground on the south side of the menhir she came across a shape that was very similar to the harp carving she found on the stone on Jersey Island. Using her camera and macro lens, she photographed the area and sent the images to her laptop.

"Mick, I think I found the same harp image on this stone as we found yesterday on Jersey Island. The outline of the instrument and its strings are still very well defined."

"Did you find a letter 'C' on this stone underneath the harp?" asked Mick.

"Yes," confirmed Joelle, "the same harp and letter 'C' are carved into this stone as they were into the stone on Jersey Island."

"I suggest we finish up here and move onto the next site,"

said Mick. "We will need to come back to this menhir later in the week after the ground penetrating radar unit arrives."

"I agree," said Joelle. "When we get back to the car, I want to call Clay about the photos we sent to him earlier this week. He may be able to shed some light on the engravings we are finding."

Heading south on D137 toward the Saint-Petreux Menhir, Mick and Joelle hoped they would find more markings on the next stone. "Clay, this is Joelle. We're doing great, just touring the countryside and digging in the dirt. I was hoping that you had found some information for us on the photos we sent you."

"I just finished up my research earlier this morning," said Clay. "After scanning all of the images into my pc, I ran a software program that can pinpoint a match between your photos and known works of art. The search revealed several possibilities. The image you took that appeared to be a stringed instrument is an ancient lyre. That's a small, handheld stringed instrument much like the harp used in ..."

"We know what a lyre is," interrupted Joelle. "Did any of the tribes around 56 BC use that type of symbol on their buildings?" Joelle activated her cell's speaker so that Mick could hear the conversation too.

"When I ran a search on ancient lyre type symbols engraved into stone, I found a few examples located in northwestern France. An area near the Rance River, which is known today as Saint Malo," said Clay.

"Did your research indicate which tribe used the lyre symbol?" asked Mick.

"Yes, it did," affirmed Clay. "I found that the Coriosolites used the lyre symbol extensively in their buildings and artwork. They also regularly used the letter 'C' in combination with the lyre and on its own."

"Wow, I think you found exactly what we were looking for," said Joelle. "We have already identified one site on Jersey Island and one south of Saint Malo that bear those engravings."

"It seems that Kenzie's hunch was correct," said Mick. "Thanks Clay, we really appreciate your help on this. We'll talk to you again in a few days. Take care."

Turning east onto the D676, they were now only a few miles from their destination. "We are looking for a granite menhir that is located to the west of the road around the east side of Beaufort Lake," said Joelle. "It's a bit to the north of the Abbey at latitude 48.509100 north, longitude 1.8139 west. You can pull over and park on the side of the road anytime. We will need to walk through this field of wheat to find it." Mick parked the car and they both grabbed their search tools from the trunk.

As the Scotts moved across the rolling field, a tall granite menhir quickly became visible. Standing nearly four meters tall, it was easy to imagine this ancient megalith being used as a marker by the Coriosolites. Mick placed grid markers ten feet away from the menhir at the twelve, three, six and nine o'clock positions to define his search area. Working methodically from top to bottom of the circle, Mick watched the Minelab GPX 5000's screen with dismay. He had completed one half of the search area and not seen a single movement of the needle or heard a faint beep in his headphones. He hoped that Joelle was having more positive results.

Since she had found engraved images near the base of two menhirs, she thought it best to work from the bottom up. The stone's surface was fairly smooth, worn from thousands of years of exposure to wind, sun and rain. Joelle had finished scanning the first three feet of the stone and had not seen any sign of manmade engravings. She put her tools down and turned to speak with Mick.

"We seem to be coming up empty at this site," said Joelle. "Have you had any hits on the metal detector?"

"Not a single one," remarked Mick. "But I do want to complete the search grid before we discount this site. I should finish up in about thirty minutes." Joelle returned to scanning the stone, but did not find markings anywhere on the menhir. As they exited the field discussing their next stop, Mick noticed the faint outline of a white car parked a short distance down the road. "It seems our two friends are still keeping tabs on our movements," said Mick. "Take a look down the road behind our car."

"Why do you think they keep following us, but never make any contact?" asked Joelle. "Do you think we should confront them?"

"No," said Mick, "as long as they are keeping their distance and not interfering with our work, we should just keep an eye on them. Let's get moving to the next site."

On their way to the next menhir, Mick and Joelle drove through Dol De Bretagne and stopped to eat at Le Table Ronde. The cafe was decorated in a medieval theme and resembled a section of King Arthur's castle. After enjoying some excellent crepes and a bottle of local wine, Mick and Joelle returned to their car and began driving south on D795 toward the Champ Dolent.

"Mick, the background information Clay provided to us says that the menhir, or upright standing stone, of Champ Dolent is the largest standing stone in Brittany. It is located in a field outside the town of Dol-de-Bretagne, and is nearly nine meters high. It stands high on a little hillock overlooking the ancient city of Dol adjacent to the road. We should be able to see the top of it once we exit D795."

As Joelle had indicated, the Champ Dolent was easy to

spot and within a few minutes Mick was pulling their car into a parking spot along the curb. This menhir was different in many ways from the previous sites, especially its easy access from the road and the number of tourists walking around the site. It would be most difficult to thoroughly research this menhir site during the daytime. They would have to return at night to gather more information; but for now, they could study the surface of the stone.

This menhir was much larger than any other site they had visited, standing nine meters high and twenty three meters around its base. Joelle knew that even a cursory inspection of the first meter of the stone's surface could take over an hour. She decided to divide the task in half between herself and Mick. "You work to the left and I will work to the right," Joelle said to Mick. "That way, we should reach the other side of the stone in less than an hour." As they kneeled down to inspect the stone, tourists approached them asking questions.

"We are amateur archeologists and are working to determine the origin of this stone," explained Joelle. "My partner and I take notes and photos only. We will not deface or harm the stone in any way." In between interruptions, Mick and Joelle continued their study of the surface.

"Joelle, I may have found something. This faint image near the ground appears to be similar to what you found on the other menhirs. Can you take a look at this?" Joelle worked her way around to the other side of the stone's base and joined Mick.

"Where did you see the image, Mick?" asked Joelle. He pointed to several vertical lines that seemed man-made. "I agree, it looks similar to the engravings I found. Let's take some macro shots of that area and send them to Clay. Maybe he can enhance the photos for us." Completing their study of the remainder of the base, Mick and Joelle gathered their tools and returned to the car.

Their next stop would be the Menhir Christianisé Lande Rosse about one half hour south and one kilometer or so to the west of Bazouges-la-Pérouse. As they slowed their car along D796, they could see the top of a dark stone with a cross on top near the right side of the road. Mick and Joelle parked their car and walked the remaining distance. The stone was similar to the prior menhirs they had studied, only darker in color. It was approximately five meters tall and leaned markedly to the south. Another difference was the cross mounted on top.

After clearing the low lying brush away from the stone, Joelle began examining its surface. Mick made preparations to repeat the same ground scanning routine he had already performed at the other locations earlier in the day. Since the stone was located so close to the road, he could only effectively search one half of the area. He set grid markers and began scanning the ground around him.

"Mick, I have searched the perimeter of the stone to its mid-point and have not yet seen anything resembling a man-made mark," said Joelle. "I even dug around the base to insure I captured images that may have disappeared over time. Any strikes yet with the metal detector?"

"I've had a few faint beeps, but nothing significant. I marked those with orange cones, but I imagine I will only find scrap metal or nails when I dig," replied Mick.

Both Mick and Joelle continued their search for another hour until they had exhausted the possibility of the menhir serving as a treasure marker. "Let's pack our gear and head to the last menhir on our list. Maybe we will end the afternoon with discovering another engraved image," said Mick.

The next site was just four kilometers to the west on south

D285; however, it was not near the road or even in sight. Pierre Longue de Saint-Joan Menhir was located about one kilometer south of the crossroads. Mick and Joelle continued along the gravel lane turning to the left a couple of times until it ended at a farm. "Looks like we walk from here," said Mick. Joelle hoped this menhir would be as easy to access as the last one, but that wasn't the case. After grabbing their gear, Mick and Joelle walked along a dirt farm track to the south and found a homemade sign pointing to the menhir. It directed them to walk between two fields of maize, then turn west along a chestnut tree lined avenue for a hundred yards or so.

"I can't believe how well hidden this menhir is," said Joelle. "It seems to actually hide behind the trees which are shorter than it. And that's not easy considering it's over six meters tall and composed of solid grey granite."

It was mid-afternoon and Mick and Joelle would soon be running out of daylight. In surveying the area, they found that only one half of the stone's perimeter was easily accessible. On the east side of the menhir there stood a tall cornfield and barbed wire fence, on the south side a large chestnut tree. If they stood a chance of finding engravings on the stone, Mick and Joelle hoped to find them on the accessible side.

Beginning at the base of the menhir, Joelle brushed away the surface dirt and examined a small area of the stone's surface. As she continued around the base, the surface appeared completely smooth under magnification. Working in an upward spiral rotation around the perimeter of the stone, Joelle hoped to find some indication of an engraving. "Mick, I'm nearly finished examining the lower third of the menhir, have you had any hits with your detector?" asked Joelle.

Mick was walking slowly back and forth in a grid pattern about five feet from the stone. With headphones over his ears and concentrating on the ground he hadn't heard Joelle's question, but he did notice her waving her arms at him. "I'm sorry, I didn't hear you. Did you find something on the stone?" asked Mick.

"No, nothing at all yet," said Joelle. "I was just wondering if you had any hits with the metal detector."

"Not yet, but I have a few more passes to complete. It's unfortunate that we can't get access to the other side of the stone. Although unlikely, it's possible that is where we would find what we are both looking for," said Mick. He placed the headphones back over both ears and continued his back and forth search pattern.

Over the next thirty minutes both Mick and Joelle anxiously anticipated finding a clue about the lost Celtic treasure, but without any luck. "I'm done here, Mick. Every square inch of the menhir was smooth without any trace of engraving. Unless you have found something of interest with the metal detector, I vote for heading back to Saint Malo," said Joelle.

Driving north on the D137 towards their hotel, Joelle finished emailing the remainder of her research photos to Clay for his review. They had finished their preliminary research of each of the five menhir sites recommend by Clay and believed they had found some good leads. "After we have had a chance to enjoy dinner and relax, let's call Clay tonight," suggested Joelle. "It would be great to hear his input on the photos."

Since the minute the Scotts arrived in Saint Malo, Malet and his partner had followed them in a white Peugeot and documented their stops. It appeared to them that the Scotts were most interested in two menhirs; Chablé and Champs Dolent. Mick and Joelle had spent the longest times at those two sites and seemed animated as they returned to their car. "We need to get this latest information to Giorgio," said Malet. "Send him all of the photos we have taken today and a brief recap of the Scott's activities."

"I'm working on it as we drive," said his partner. "By the time we get back into town, I will be finished."

"Good," said Malet, "we can follow up with Giorgio first thing in the morning to answer his questions. The Scotts seem to be heading back to their hotel for the day."

Mick and Joelle arrived back at the hotel La Rance around 5:00 p.m., went to their room and began getting ready for dinner. "Thank you Mick for getting us into Le Chalut again," said Joelle. "I enjoyed it so much on our last trip, but I did not expect to go there again so soon. What a great way to end our trip in Saint Malo." Joelle paused and looked out the hotel window and across the Channel. "I hope the girls had a good time today on Jersey Island," said Joelle.

"I'm sure they did," responded Mick.

Just a short distance across the Channel from Saint Malo, three young women entered their hotel lobby on 9 Rue de la Corne de Cerf. Danielle reached for her cell phone to check in with her dad. "I can't find my phone," said Danielle. "I've looked through my purse and in my pockets. I must have left it at the museum. That was the last time I remember using it." Keira and Kenzie exchanged glances and rolled their eyes. Losing or forgetting things was typical of Danielle.

"If we hurry back to the museum before it closes at 6:00 p.m.," said Keira, "maybe we can find it."

"Let's try calling them first," suggested Kenzie. "Maybe someone found it and will answer." Kenzie dialed the number and waited. Danielle's phone rang and rang, then went to voice mail. "Nope, no luck," said Kenzie. "We need to hurry if we are going to make it back there by 6:00 p.m."

CHAPTER 22

A S THE WINTER sun was setting, guests arrived for the 4th Annual Black Tie Children's Charity Ball held at the Demetrius estate north of Rome. Marcus and Sabina Demetrius greeted every couple with a smile and embrace as they welcomed them into their lavish home. Each year, the event was held the week prior to Christmas and was well attended by nearly five hundred of the most wealthy and influential Europeans.

The villa was decorated throughout with trees adorned in twinkling white lights, banisters wrapped with fresh garland, hallways lined with ruby red poinsettias and a massive Christmas tree in the main foyer. Marcus had spared no expense in creating the appropriate impression of an astute business man and philanthropist. He and Sabina were both well respected and appreciated for the many charity events they held each year. Their guests were treated to endless buffets of culinary delights prepared by Marcus's full time chef, Philippe. Champaign fountains placed in several locations in the villa helped to loosen up the crowd and their checkbooks.

When the final guests had arrived, Marcus and Sabina moved into the main reception area of their expansive home and addressed their guests. Marcus took the podium and said, "Sabina and I are both honored to see a large turnout this year for such a worthy charity as the Homeless Children's Fund. Last year, with your generous donations, we were able to raise nearly seven hundred fifty thousand euros for the children. Tonight, we celebrate again with a cornucopia of food, drink and entertainment. Please enjoy yourselves this evening as our special guests and make sure to review all of the incredible silent auction items that have been donated. At 9:00 p.m. we will announce the winners of the silent auction and our donation tally for the evening. We thank you again for attending and please, on behalf of the children, give generously." With that, the guests applauded and Marcus began working the crowd with Sabina at his side.

Eighteen hundred kilometers northeast of the Charity Ball, on the tiny Channel Island of Jersey, a different type of party was getting underway. Six of Marcus's best men were in final preparations for their latest heist. They had arranged for a power outage the day prior in the vicinity of Jersey Museum by shorting out the main transformer. Repair crews had responded quickly to the emergency, but due to parts availability, it was late Tuesday afternoon before power was restored. The workers had left the site; however, their heavy equipment would not be picked up until the following morning.

The alley was clear of any traffic as most everyone in town was at home preparing for the holidays. Under cover of darkness, two of Giorgio's men dressed in city worker uniforms, opened the cab on the Volvo L120E front loader and hotwired the engine. As it roared to life, a quad cab tilt bed truck that had been stolen earlier in the day by two other men working for Giorgio rolled into position down the alley. The last of the six man team took their positions at the back of the museum. Each man carried a Heckler and Koch MP5 machine pistol and wore body armor under their black clothes. With the museum closing time in less than ten minutes, the big Volvo machine began rolling into position.

The Celtic coin display, located near the museum's exterior wall adjacent to the alley, weighed about one thousand seven hundred pounds and was contained in a large clear display case made of two inch thick bullet proof glass attached to a stainless steel base. Weight and motion sensors monitored the interior of the enclosure and were programmed to activate the alarm system if any change was detected. Surrounding the display were three armed museum guards assigned the single task of protecting the sixteen million dollar exhibit.

It was nearly 6:00 p.m. and most patrons had exited the museum for the day. As the front desk guard walked back towards the entrance to secure it for the evening, he was greeted by three very excited young women asking to get back into the museum. "I'm sorry, the museum is closed for today," said the guard through the glass door.

"But you don't understand," pleaded Danielle, "I left my cell phone inside earlier today. I have to get it back." Opening the door so that he could better understand what Danielle was saying, the guard again informed the three women that they would have to return the next morning when the museum reopened. "Please, please, help me out," cried Danielle, "I just need a few minutes to get my phone. I know exactly where I left it." That wasn't entirely true, but Kenzie and Keira both believed that she had left it near the ship exhibit when she was taking their picture.

"Ok," agreed the guard as he let them in the door. "You have five minutes to retrieve the phone and be back at this door. Do you understand me?"

"Yes sir," they all agreed, and proceeded to move quickly towards Gallery E.

At exactly three minutes before 6:00 p.m., two of the guards began walking away from the coin display toward their office to clock out. The third guard, remained at the back of the display not knowing what was about to occur. "Hey, where do you two think you are going? It's not closing time yet," said the guard. As the two men turned to answer, they heard a loud roar and saw the wall behind the coin exhibit explode inward. With brick and concrete debris flying into the room, the Volvo front loader appeared out of the rising dust cloud and moved toward the coins. The unlucky guard standing between the rear wall and the exhibit had been crushed instantly during the assault. The other two guards fired shots wildly into the air around the front loader so that they appeared to be stopping the heist as Giorgio had instructed.

Giorgio had made an arrangement with the two security guards for ten thousand euros each. They were instructed to have the unsuspecting third guard rotate to the position along the wall for the last hour of his shift. With him out of the way, they would be able to assist the front loader with scooping up the coin display and exiting the museum.

All three girls continued walking towards Gallery E in the rear of the museum. "Kenzie, dial my phone so that we can hear the ring," suggested Danielle. Kenzie dialed the number and all three girls turned toward the music. The song Call Me Maybe, started blasting through the quiet museum. It was coming from behind the ancient Celtic ship exhibit where they had been taking pictures earlier that afternoon. As they walked toward the area, the deafening sound of a loud explosion filled the air around them and they saw a large machine crashing through the rear wall. Before they could understand what they were witnessing, the girls were spotted by guards near the coin display.

Armed with the latest in Taser technology, the X3 CEW, the guards shot Danielle, Kenzie and Keira with neuro-muscular incapacitation darts. The girls were instantly immobilized, fell to the ground and passed out from the intense pain. "No one was to be here. All of the patrons were to have exited the museum by this time," shouted one guard to the other. "We can't have any witnesses. These three girls need to be handed over to Giorgio's men." A moment later, two men dressed in black, wearing ski masks and carrying MP5s ran in behind the machine. As the front loader made easy work of loading the coins and display case into the large rectangular bucket, alarms sounded and lights flashed throughout the museum. Both guards fired shots past the enormous machine being careful as they were instructed not to hit the driver. When they saw the two men near the rear wall wearing ski masks, they pointed at the girls and shouted, "Witnesses, you need to take them with you." Nodding in agreement, but saying nothing, two of Giorgio's men worked to load the three girls into the cab of the Volvo L120E before it backed out of the museum and headed down the alley.

Security guards in every part of the building were now on alert and several began running towards Gallery E. Hearing gunshots, they approached the area cautiously. When they arrived, there was an enormous hole in the rear wall of the museum and the Celtic coin exhibit had vanished. The two museum guards covered in dust from the explosion continued to fire shots through the opening in the wall as they shouted, "they got the coins, they got the coins."

At the other end of the alley, Giorgio's men completed unloading the large front loader's bucket filled with coins into the rear of the awaiting tilt bed truck. As other security guards arrived in Gallery E, the two guards assisting the strike team ran through the hole in the wall and fired shots towards the tilt bed truck. Before any museum security ran into the alley, the tilt bed truck had driven away and the Volvo L120E front loader had been abandoned. The truck drove approximately seven hundred fifty meters north of the museum and dumped the coins in a hole prepared in advance on a vacant lot where Demetrius was constructing an office building. Then the truck was driven another one point five kilometers further north into a lake on Westmont Road to make identification more difficult. The office building construction crew was working late that night and had been instructed to cover the hole with construction debris so that the coins would remain hidden.

A black Mercedes van was parked along Westmont Road waiting for the strike team to arrive. When the driver saw the six men walking from the lake area, he was confused to see them carrying something on their shoulders. "We ran into a small complication at the museum," said the team leader. "These three young women witnessed the heist and were rendered unconscious by the guards. We need to take them with us and get instructions from Giorgio on what he wants done with them."

"You should have dumped them in the lake with the truck," suggested the driver.

"I would rather have Giorgio make that decision," said the team leader. "They may prove to be valuable hostages." The Mercedes van headed west on the A1 and began driving to the dock area near Saint Aubin.

"Yes, this is Giorgio. What is the status on the job you were to perform?"

"We were successful," stated the team leader proudly. "The package is safe at the drop site and we have left the area."

"Any complications?" Giorgio inquired. There was a long

pause on the other end and then the team leader explained what had occurred. "You were wise to take them with you, rather than the alternative," said Giorgio. "I suggest that once you reach the boat, the new cargo should be taken to the island for safe keeping. Do not harm the packages in any way. Do you understand me?"

"Yes, sir."

"You will receive further instructions after I discuss the situation with Marcus."

"Understood," responded the team leader, "we will proceed to the island and wait for your call."

Most of Demetrius's guests had departed the Charity Ball and housekeepers were seen everywhere busily cleaning up the party's aftermath. Marcus and Sabina were reclining in one of their many sitting rooms and enjoying a quiet moment in front of the fireplace. Suddenly, the serenity of the moment was interrupted by a loud buzzing sound coming from Marcus's cell phone. It was Giorgio. "Marcus, I need to give you an update on the project in Saint Helier. Can we meet in the conference room before you retire this evening?" Marcus hesitated to answer, then responded.

"Tonight? Are you serious?" Looking frustrated by the unexpected interruption, Marcus agreed to meet Giorgio and asked Sabina to meet him in their bedroom in fifteen minutes.

Walking into the conference room, Marcus found Giorgio anxiously sitting at the table. "I assume you have an update on the heist," said Marcus. "When will I have my coins?" Giorgio sat up taller in the seat and began to recount the events of the evening to Marcus.

"We have all of the coins from the exhibit and most everything went according to plan."

"Most everything," questioned Marcus. "What does

that mean? What didn't go as planned?" Giorgio began his explanation.

"While the heist was in progress, three young women unexpectedly re-entered the museum and were in Gallery E when the wall collapsed."

"Were they killed by the falling wall?" asked Marcus.

"No, nothing like that. They simply witnessed the robbery and our men didn't want to take the chance of them going to the authorities. Our team leader made the decision to stun the three women with Tasers and hold them hostage until given further instructions."

"Where are they being held?" asked Marcus.

"I directed our men to take the cabin cruiser docked in port at Saint Malo and hold the women on Cézembre Island. We have used the old vacant monastery for jobs in the past and it is in a very isolated and protected location," said Giorgio.

Giorgio looked down at the floor with uncertainty and then back up at Marcus's eyes. He was unsure of how Marcus would react to the direction that he had given the team. Hoping that he had done the right thing, Giorgio awaited Marcus's delayed response. "Have any of the women been hurt?" asked Marcus.

"No," responded Giorgio, "I gave specific instructions to our team leader to insure their well-being."

Marcus began to pace quickly back and forth across the conference room. He did not like surprises and he would not tolerate failure. Marcus stopped, then looked directly at Giorgio. "I wanted this to be a clean job, no complications, no added media attention. Do you understand me Giorgio?" Marcus shouted. "Get the team leader on the phone for me, NOW!" Stuttering to respond and grabbing for his cell phone, Giorgio tried to quickly appease Marcus.

"Sir, there is no answer. They must still be in transit to the island and don't have a cell signal."

"Keep trying to get ahold of him," said Marcus. "The moment you reach him, find me on the veranda. I want to speak with the team leader before this complication of yours gets any further out of control."

Marcus stormed out of the conference room and headed for the veranda. He needed some time to think through how best to handle this latest dilemma. A few moments later, Giorgio walked onto the veranda holding his cell phone out for Marcus to take. "I have the team leader on the phone for you."

"This is Marcus Demetrius. I understand that you are in possession of three hostages from the heist. Please proceed to the island as Giorgio directed you and begin interrogations immediately. I want to know who these women are and what they saw. Hopefully, we can minimize the damage. We will be in touch tomorrow morning." Marcus handed the cell phone to Giorgio and turned to exit the veranda. "I expect an update first thing in the morning."

"Yes, sir. First thing in the morning," said Giorgio.

CHAPTER 23

MICK AND JOELLE had enjoyed a fantastic dinner in a romantic restaurant and an evening of relaxation. It was much needed after several days of intense research and keeping tabs on the mysterious white Peugeot that was following them once again. Joelle enjoyed a perfectly grilled steak sitting atop a thick gorgonzola cheese sauce with a heaping side of scalloped potatoes. Mick enjoyed locally caught baked fish in a fantastic tomato marinara sauce, washed down with a great Gaillac Sauvignon. Later that evening in their hotel room, Mick and Joelle cuddled on the couch and sipped some locally produced dessert wine while catching up on the news.

"Mick, quick, turn up the sound," said Joelle as she pointed excitedly toward the flat screen television. "They are talking about the coins. The coins in the museum in Grouville that we saw a few weeks ago. They've been stolen." As Mick and Joelle listened intently to the breaking news, the reporter gave his account of what had happened just one hour earlier.

"Approximately four hours ago," stated the young female reporter, "just prior to closing time at the Jersey Museum, a large horde of two thousand year old Celtic coins were stolen from Gallery E. It is not certain yet how the coins were stolen. According to museum officials, three guards were stationed in that exhibit hall with responsibility for guarding the coins and other antiquities. One of the three guards has not yet been located for questioning and may be linked to the heist. In the exhibit room behind me located in Gallery E, you can see what is left of the exterior brick wall. All that remains is a cavity three meters square and a large pile of rubble. It appears that the thieves broke through the brick wall and somehow made their getaway with over eight hundred kilograms of gold coins with an estimated value of at least twelve million euros." The station took a quick commercial break and then returned to the reporter at the museum.

"We're back, broadcasting live from the Jersey Museum in Saint Helier where an exhibit containing nearly twelve million euros of gold coins is missing." Turning towards the Museum spokesman, the reporter began asking more in depth questions and received the following response.

"We are working with local authorities to determine how this crime took place and who was behind the heist. We do not have many details at this time; however, we do know the following. At approximately five minutes before 6:00 p.m. as the museum was closing for the day, a group of three young women asked our main entrance guard for permission to re-enter the museum," said the spokesperson. "The three claimed they needed to locate a lost cell phone and believed it was near the Celtic ship exhibit. They were granted access and instructed to hurry since it was closing time. At two minutes before 6:00 p.m., there was a noise similar to a small explosion and alarms began to sound in Gallery E. Our guards followed emergency protocol and began an immediate shut down of the museum. Several guards were dispatched to Gallery E and upon arrival found a room filled with dust, brick debris and a large hole in the exterior wall. No trace was found of the three young women or one of the three guards assigned to the exhibit. We will continue to work with local police to assist them in solving this case." The museum spokesperson held up his hand and said, "no more comments at this time, thank you."

Mick and Joelle exchanged worried looks and knew what each other was thinking. Joelle picked up her phone and hit her speed dial to call Kenzie. The cell phone rang a few times and then went to voice mail. Next, Joelle called the cell number for Danielle. Again, the phone rang and rang, then went to voice mail. At the same time, Mick was placing a call to Uncle B to inquire about the girl's location. "Uncle B, it's Mick. Are the girls still staying with you? Have you seen them today? Can I talk with Kenzie?"

"Hold on, hold on," said Uncle B, "slow down, what is wrong?"

"We are trying to find the girls," explained Mick. "Are they still in Dublin or did they travel to Jersey Island to see the coins?"

"Mick, the girls left here yesterday with a friend that they met at the pub. You may remember her, she was our waitress at The Brazen Head during your visit here right after Thanksgiving. Her name is Keira and she has been showing the girls all the sights around Dublin. She knew that the girls wanted to see the Celtic coin display at the Jersey Museum in Saint Helier and offered to fly with them to Jersey Island in a friend's plane if they would pay for the fuel. The girls jumped at the opportunity and planned to tour the island today and visit the museum. They promised to be back here in Dublin Thursday afternoon so that you could all return to the states on Friday."

Joelle saw how worried Mick was beginning to look and could hear the trembling tone in his voice. "Thanks for your help Uncle B. We think the girls could have been at the Museum during a robbery that occurred late this afternoon and they aren't answering their cell phones. We are very, very worried."

"Why do you think it's our girls?" asked Uncle B.

"I don't know that for sure," said Mick, "but I know this. First, you said they planned to visit the museum today. Second, there were three young women that entered the museum just prior to closing today. Third, the young women were looking for a lost cell phone which our daughters seem to do frequently and fourth, I can't reach either of the girls on their phones. I just have an unsettled feeling about this," said Mick. "Do you have a cell number for their new friend Keira?"

"I do," said Uncle B. "I will try to reach her on her cell phone and then I will call you back. Talk to you soon."

Mick and Joelle discussed their options and then began making plans to leave Saint Malo on the first ferry out the next morning to Jersey Island. Whether the girls were at the museum during the robbery or it was all just a strange coincidence, it didn't matter. Both Mick and Joelle wanted to insure that their daughter was ok and the best way to do that was to get to Jersey Island. A few minutes later the phone rang and it was Uncle B. "I couldn't reach Keira on her cell, but I did talk to the manager of The Brazen Head. He said that Keira had taken the day off and mentioned flying to Jersey Island with some friends. That's all he knew," said Uncle B.

"So we know that the girls planned to be on the island today and they could have been the three young women reported to enter the museum around closing time," stated Mick. "We are taking the fast ferry tomorrow morning and will arrive in Saint Helier around 11:00 a.m."

"I will be taking the first flight out as well," said Uncle B. "I should land around 10:30 a.m. and I can pick you up at the ferry terminal."

CHAPTER 24

THE BLACK FORTY one foot Sea Ray cabin cruiser slowed its wake as it approached the dark, sandy southern shore of Cézembre Island a few miles off the coast of Saint Malo. It was almost midnight and moonlight was the only illumination visible on the small, uninhabited island. The forty four acre island had been used during World War I by the Belgian Army and as a result of intense Allied bombardment, Cézembre's landscape was still barren and pitted with very little natural vegetation. The island had not yet been completely demined and most of the island other than the beach was surrounded with a barbed-wire fence and large warning notices. This was the perfect location for Marcus's clandestine operations.

Cézembre's barren landscape was crowned by a crumbling monastery built in the fifth century and five small chapels. As the sleek cabin cruiser approached shore, Giorgio's men made preparations for landing. There were no docks or other amenities for their boat, just a sandy beach with a gentle slope where the boat could be run aground and anchored securely.

All three young women had regained consciousness, but cloth blindfolds restricted their sight and ropes bound their wrists tightly. Each of the men took charge of one hostage and began leading them up the rocky trail towards the monastery.

Navigating the uneven surface and unable to see anything at all, Kenzie, Danielle and Keira did their best to remain upright and not get injured. They felt the surface under their feet begin to change. It seemed they were walking on a solid surface now instead of loose stones. The sound of their footsteps echoed off the walls and created a very eerie feeling. None of the girls knew where they were, but the place sounded large, and felt cold and empty.

Led by their captors down a winding stone staircase, they continued down, down, down until they were walking on a flat surface. "Stop here," shouted the guard. They heard a metallic clicking noise like a lock opening and then a loud high-pitched creaking sound filled the air as the steel door opened to reveal a dark stone chamber. Danielle and Kenzie were pushed forward by the guard into the secluded room and both fell to the ground. Not being able to see, neither woman realized what was going to happen next. At the same time, they both felt the shock of a Taser as the sharp needles penetrated their skin. Shaking violently from the high voltage electric charge, and screaming from the pain, they again fell into unconsciousness. "That should keep them quiet until morning," said the guard.

Keira started screaming, but there was no one to hear her cries. "What are you going to do to me?" Keira pleaded. But no one responded. She heard a second steel door unlock. Then she was pushed down the corridor and tossed into another dark chamber of the monastery. Hitting her head and shoulder as her body met the floor, Keira let out a scream from the intense pain. Just as they had done to both Danielle and Kenzie, Keira was Tasered to keep her quiet. The electric charge shook her body violently, but blackness soon clouded her thoughts and she lost consciousness. After both chamber doors were locked securely, Giorgio's men made their way upstairs to more comfortable surroundings and turned in for the night. They would have preferred to lock up each woman in a separate chamber for better control, but they only had two secure rooms to use. The next morning after checking in with Giorgio, they would realize the good fortune of their decision.

Eight hours to the west in Tempe, Arizona, Professor Brinkerman was enjoying an early dinner at home and watching CNN. He had just walked back into the room from the kitchen when he heard a reporter saying something about Celtic coins and a robbery. He sat down on the couch and continued listening to the story.

"I'm broadcasting live outside the Jersey Museum in Saint Helier," said the attractive reporter, "where a large cache of two-thousand year old gold coins worth nearly twelve million euros were stolen late this afternoon. The coins were part of a Celtic exhibit in Gallery E and were under heavy security. Museum officials and police believe that the thieves broke through the exterior wall of the museum with a piece of heavy machinery and simply scooped up the coins and exited the building without incident. None of the security guards assigned to the exhibit have yet been located for questioning and may possibly have been killed during the robbery. There is also an unsubstantiated report of three young women entering the museum just prior to closing and may have been involved in the heist. We will continue to bring you breaking news as this story develops."

Jumping to his feet and stumbling on his bad leg, Brinkerman began shouting at the television. "How could this have happened? I gave that information to Mario. I told him about the coins and the other treasures. I even cooperated with Marcus's thugs when they came to my office. Mario wouldn't have known anything about any of these treasures if it wasn't for me. He owes me!" Falling backwards onto the couch and grabbing his cell phone, Paul Brinkerman frantically dialed the number for Mario Sargusi. The phone rang and rang and rang, then went to voicemail.

"You have reached Mario, leave a message," said the automated voice.

"Mario, it's Paulie. I wanna know who stole the gold coins today? What the hell is going on, Mario? I want my cut, or else I start to talk. Call me!" Brinkerman knew that Mario had to be aware of the coin heist. It was just too much of a coincidence. A few weeks earlier he had shown Mario the history paper Kenzie Scott wrote about a Celtic coin discovery on Jersey Island. Then, two hired thugs paid him a visit to verify the story about additional Celtic treasures. The men didn't say that they represented Marcus Demetrius, but Brinkerman was pretty sure that Mario had passed on the information to his wealthy associate. Now, the very coins that started this adventure, were stolen and Brinkerman wanted his cut. He would call Mario again first thing in the morning.

CHAPTER 25

KENZIE'S BODY APPEARED lifeless and lay sprawled across the cold stone floor. Her long dark hair hid any signs of injury to her face and neck. A few feet away, Danielle lay in the same lifeless position. The ancient chamber was dead silent. Not a single window to provide sunlight or any hint of where they might be. Across the room, a steel door locked them inside. At its base, a small gap provided the only means of light from the outside.

Kenzie strained to move her arms in a stretching motion, but quickly realized her wrists were tied together. Danielle rolled onto her side. As they both began to regain consciousness, the room seemed a blur around them. "Danielle, are you ok? Are you hurt?" asked Kenzie.

Muttering faintly, Danielle responded, "Yes, I'm ok, just really dizzy and I think my vision is fuzzy. How about you Kenzie?"

"I have a headache from hell and can't see anything either. My head is pounding so hard I feel nauseated. I think I'm blindfolded. What happened to us?"

"Wow, I'm not sure," said Danielle. "I remember going back to the museum to find my phone. As we got close to Gallery E near the back of the building there was a loud crashing noise like a car wreck, I saw several men running towards us, but then everything went black until we arrived here. Do you have any idea where we are Kenzie?"

"No, none at all. Let's try to get our blindfolds off and our wrists untied."

As the two girls sat up to get better oriented, they worked to push blindfolds from their faces. With only a hint of light peaking under the steel doorway, Kenzie and Danielle could barely make out each other's silhouette. "Where's Keira?" whispered Danielle.

"She's not in here," said Kenzie, "maybe she got away or they could be keeping her in a different room."

"I'm sure she is ok," offered Danielle. "We should try to escape from this chamber and find her."

"Good idea," said Kenzie, "but first we need to get our wrists untied." Working patiently to loosen each other's bindings, they were able to get free and begin walking carefully around the ancient chamber.

"How long have we been here?" asked Danielle.

"I'm not sure, my watch and cell phone are gone. It feels like it should be morning, but without any windows, who knows?"

Keira was being held in a separate chamber just thirty feet down the dark hallway and had not yet regained consciousness. As the chamber door creaked open and the guard nudged Keira with the toe of his boot, she began to move. Seeing her movement, he helped her up and sat her in a metal chair. Shaking the fuzziness from her brain, Keira began to remember what had happened and began to scream against the gag in her mouth. "Stop! Stop now," commanded the guard. "That is why we gagged you last night. If you will quit screaming I'll remove your gag. It's your choice." Keira quieted down and the guard removed her gag as promised.

"You made a big mistake kidnapping me. My name is Keira O'Malley. I'm a friend of McFadden and I was just trying to help him. Call him… use my cell phone and call him. He can vouch for me."

"I don't know anybody named McFadden," snarled the guard. Keira continued to protest her confinement.

"Go get your boss, he'll know McFadden. Everyone in Saint Malo and Jersey Island knows him. He's a powerful man." The guard looked at Keira in disbelief. Could she really be connected? He didn't know, but it would only take a few minutes to check out her story. If she was lying, he would have some fun with her before he finished her interrogation. He reapplied the gag to Keira's mouth, abruptly left the room and headed back upstairs to talk with the team leader.

"Have you already finished interrogating all three prisoners?" asked the team leader.

"No sir," answered the guard.

"Then why have you returned? Go finish your job!" The guard hesitated to speak again, but then decided to continue.

"One of the prisoners claims that she is a friend of a man named McFadden and that we made a huge mistake kidnapping her."

The team leader stood up rapidly and asked, "What is her name?"

"She said her name is Keira, sir." Picking up his cell phone, the team leader scanned his contact names and selected McFadden. It was nearly 7:00 a.m. in the morning, but after a few rings, a man's voice came on the phone.

"Yeah, this is McFadden. Who is this?" The team leader answered.

"I was hired by Giorgio to complete a project on behalf of Marcus Demetrius last night. We ran into some complications and ended up with three young women prisoners. One of them claims to know you and her name is Keira."

"Keira O'Malley?" asked McFadden. "You kidnapped Keira? If you have hurt her, I will kill you. I will kill all of you. Let me talk to her, now."

The team leader turned to the guard, covered the phone with his hand and shouted, "Go get the woman in cell number two and bring her to me immediately. GO!" In a much calmer voice the Team Leader continued speaking on the phone. "McFadden, she will be here in a moment. I assure you that she is fine. We have not harmed her in any way."

With her gag, blindfold and hand restraints removed, Keira moved quickly up the stone staircase with the guard. They entered the team's sleeping quarters and she was handed a cell phone. "Keira, this is McFadden. Are you ok? Have they hurt you?"

"No William, I'm, a little shaken up and bruised, but fine. I really don't know why this happened."

"I don't either, put the team leader back on the phone so that I can make arrangements to pick you up."

"Thanks William, see you soon."

Twenty minutes later, just before sunrise, the black 41' Sea Ray cabin cruiser slowed its speed to dock at a small pier near Saint Malo. McFadden and his partner had been in the area on business for a few days and were staying at a hotel in town. They arrived at the pier before the Sea Ray docked and were waiting nearby in their black BMW rental. McFadden was relieved to see Keira being helped off of the boat. Before she reached the car, the cabin cruiser was already heading back across the channel towards Cézembre Island.

McFadden jumped out of his car and ran to embrace Keira. They hadn't been together as a couple in over three years, but they still had strong feelings for each other. "Are you ok? I mean, really ok? They didn't…, well you know?"

"No William, they didn't touch me. I will be fine."

"Let's get you back to our hotel so that you can clean up and get something to eat." After they got settled back into the car, McFadden began asking Keira questions about what had happened to her. "Where were you today?"

"I was at the Jersey Museum in Saint Helier this afternoon, but I need to explain what happened a few days ago," said Keira. "Remember the couple you had me spy on a few weeks ago at The Brazen Head?"

"You mean Mick and Joelle Scott?" asked McFadden.

"Yes, the Scotts. They returned to Dublin a few days ago, but this time they brought their daughter Kenzie and her friend Danielle. When they all stopped by The Brazen Head for dinner, I waited on their table. During the evening I made friends with the two girls and offered to show them around Dublin. I thought it would be a good idea to stay close to them. Yesterday we flew over to Jersey Island in a friend's plane and ended the day at the Jersey Museum. Kenzie was really interested in seeing some special Celtic coin display. She kept talking about a paper that she had written for school and how important this coin find was to her."

"Ok, so you had a nice day at the museum. How does that have anything to do with you being kidnapped?" asked McFadden.

"Everything," said Keira. "We left the museum about fifteen minutes before closing, but Danielle realized she had left her cell phone in the museum. We convinced the guards to let us back inside even though it was a few minutes before 6:00 p.m. We headed towards Gallery E to locate her phone and just as we neared the area, we heard a huge explosion. Some large machine had crashed through the rear wall and was scooping up the entire coin display. The air was filled with dust, alarms were sounding and before we realized we were witnessing a robbery in progress, two security guards hit us with Taser darts. The next thing I remember was waking up on the deck of a cabin cruiser."

"Ok, and then what happened?" asked McFadden.

"We were blindfolded and our wrists bound," said Keira. "When the boat landed, we were taken by the guards across an area of rough rocks and then down a steep winding stone staircase. I started screaming and they gagged me. Then they threw me into a cell and hit me with a Taser until I fell unconscious. I woke with a guard kicking me in the side and then setting me in a chair to interrogate me. When he removed my gag I was able to shout your name and get them to call you. You know the rest," said Keira.

"I'm just glad you are ok," said McFadden. "It could have been much worse."

As their car rolled to a stop in front of the Oceania hotel, McFadden said, "When we get upstairs to the room, why don't you take a long hot shower and get cleaned up. Then we can tend to those nasty cuts on your forehead and knees. Meanwhile, I will order you some breakfast from room service." Once he had Keira settled, McFadden decided to make a phone call to a business associate in Rome. He needed to find out a little more about what took place the night before at the Jersey Museum.

The phone rang several times, then Giorgio answered, "Hello?"

"Giorgio, this is McFadden. I just picked up a friend of mine at the Saint Malo docks. She was kidnapped by a team that was supposedly doing a job on Jersey Island for Marcus. My young friend and two of her girlfriends appear to have interrupted a heist at the Jersey Museum. Do you have any idea what this is all about?"

"Unfortunately, I do," said Giorgio. "I received a report last evening from my team that they had run into a complication. It seems that your friend and two other young women witnessed the job we were conducting. My team leader made a decision to take them hostage versus eliminating them on the spot."

"A wise choice," responded McFadden. "Do you know the identity of the other two women?"

"Not yet," said Giorgio. "I know that the team leader will have them interrogated this morning."

"I can save you the trouble," said McFadden. "One of the captives is named Kenzie Scott and the other is her best friend, Danielle O'Shanahan. Kenzie is the daughter of Mick and Joelle Scott. The treasure hunters that you hired me to follow a few weeks ago." Although McFadden could not see the surprise on Giorgio's face, he could hear it in his voice.

"Are you telling me that we have the Scott's daughter, the one that wrote the treasure paper, in our hands?" asked Giorgio.

"Yes, you do," confirmed McFadden, "and I don't believe that she has been hurt."

"That's good, I gave specific instructions to my men to handle the women with care. I had no idea of their identity, but I did not want to draw more attention to the heist than necessary. I think this could work in our favor."

"How is that?" asked McFadden.

"I'm not sure yet. I'll know more after the interrogation. She may provide some much needed leverage with her parents," said Giorgio.

CHAPTER 26

I T WAS A long sleepless night for Mick, Joelle and Uncle B as they all tossed and turned waiting for morning to arrive. As Mick and Joelle entered the taxi and headed for the ferry terminal, Malet and his partner followed closely behind in their white Peugeot. "I thought they were staying all week in Saint Malo," said Malet to his partner. "Now it seems they are rushing off to the port. I wonder what has caused this sudden change in their itinerary?"

When the Scotts arrived at the terminal, they jumped from their cab and made a dash to the loading area to board the fast ferry to Saint Helier, Jersey Island. A few cars behind their cab, the Peugeot pulled to the curb and Malet jumped out leaving his partner in amazement. "I'm following them to Saint Helier, I will touch base with you later today," said Malet. He ran to the ticketing agent and was able to board the ferry as the last passenger before the gang plank was raised. He did not see the Scotts, but was sure that they were elsewhere on the ferry. Malet took a seat and caught his breath. He would locate them again when they disembarked.

After a quick twenty minute ride across the rough, choppy waters of the English Channel, Mick and Joelle waited for Uncle B outside of the Saint Helier Ferry Terminal. They were more than anxious to get started looking for their daughter,

Kenzie. Shortly before 11:00 a.m., Uncle B drove into the terminal and stopped along the curb in his small Fiat rental car. Mick and Joelle jumped in and a few moments later they were all headed toward the Jersey Museum.

"Hi Uncle B, thanks so much for picking us up. Have you heard anything from Danielle or Kenzie?" asked Mick.

"No, I haven't. I've called both of them repeatedly since last night, but their phones just go to voice mail."

"Same for us," said Joelle. "I'm really getting worried."

"I hope we can get more specific information at the museum," said Uncle B. "This morning, while I was waiting on my rental car, I phoned the Jersey Museum and spoke with the general manager. He was most cooperative and agreed to see us around noon today. I explained that our daughters may be two of the three young women that reportedly re-entered the museum minutes before closing."

Armed with recent photographs and descriptions of Kenzie and Danielle, the Scotts and Uncle B headed quickly through town to the Jersey Museum. If the general manager would show them CCTV recordings of the entry doors taken at closing time the night prior, Mick and Joelle could possibly identify the girls. It was their best shot at getting a lead.

In a taxi a few hundred feet behind Uncle B's rental car, Malet was on the phone speaking with Giorgio about the recent developments. "Yes, yes. I'm sure it's the Scotts," said Malet. "They and their friend from Dublin are in front of me and it appears they are heading towards the Jersey Museum. Are you sure the woman the team captured is their daughter?"

"Yes, Malet," said Giorgio with anger in his voice. "I have it on good authority that it is her. I need you to keep a close eye on the Scotts and report back to me later this morning. They have most likely heard the news reports that three young women disappeared during the heist and are trying to find out if it was their daughter and her friends. Malet, do you understand me?" shouted Giorgio.

"Yes, sir. I will call you back in a few hours."

Giorgio left his office and began walking toward the covered veranda where Marcus was enjoying a quiet breakfast with his wife, Sabina. Their estate was beautiful and covered over fifty acres. It was surrounded by tree covered land on all four sides. Various buildings dotted the grounds, including multiple art galleries, both public and private. The complex included replicas of Roman fountains, an amphitheater, library and several large Romanesque buildings with state rooms for visitors and quarters for their staff. One of the most striking and accurately recreated parts of the estate were the Roman pool and artificial grotto, both visible from the veranda.

Although the coin heist had proceeded like clockwork at the museum, no one anticipated that there would be witnesses. Giorgio knew that Marcus was upset by the news about the kidnapping, but hopefully he could spin the story into a positive. Having the Scott's daughter in their hands could help persuade Mick and Joelle to be very open about their recent discoveries in Saint Malo. Marcus was driven to collect Roman antiquities and the Scotts seemed to be closing in on a gigantic find. Giorgio neared the veranda.

"Good morning Marcus..., Sabina. How are you this morning? I hate to interrupt your quiet breakfast here on the veranda, but I have an important update on the Saint Malo initiative."

Marcus turned to Sabina and said, "sweet heart, please give me a few moments with Giorgio to cover a minor business matter. I will join you in the pool shortly for our morning swim."

"Certainly, Marcus," agreed Sabina. "Don't take too long." She leaned towards him and whispered into his ear. "I will be waiting in the deep end, wearing only a smile. You had better hurry." Marcus enjoyed the vision of his topless wife walking toward the pool and dropping the rest of her bikini as she entered the water. He then turned towards Giorgio who was trying desperately to avoid looking in Sabina's direction.

"So Giorgio, I trust that the issues we discussed last evening are resolved and the Roman coins will be delivered to me shortly?"

"Yes sir," said Giorgio, "the heist went as planned. The coins are secure and awaiting shipment at our office building construction site near Saint Helier. They will be transported by various secure means and will arrive here at your estate by Monday, December 24th at the latest."

"Splendid," remarked Marcus. "I am looking forward to adding them to my collection." Giorgio cleared his throat and continued.

"I have an update on the three women that were detained and taken to the island. Sir, as I said, the operation went very well; however, there were three women who witnessed the heist in the museum. Two of the guards working for us subdued the witnesses with Tasers and our team transported them to a holding cell on Cézembre Island."

"I know that," said Marcus. "You made me aware of it last evening. Get to the point!"

"It seems that one of the young women is an acquaintance of our operative in Saint Malo and the other two young women are associated with the Scotts."

"Do you mean Mick and Joelle Scott, the treasure hunters I have you following?" asked Marcus.

"Yes," confirmed Giorgio. "To be specific, it is their daughter

Kenzie and her friend Danielle O'Shanahan." Marcus began to pace the room and rubbed his chin as he contemplated the possibilities of this fortunate turn of events.

"Have you begun interrogating Ms. Scott or her friend yet"?

"No," replied Giorgio, "they are awaiting our instructions."

"What do you mean?" shouted Marcus. "I gave specific instructions last night to begin the interrogations immediately. Make contact with the team and instruct them to proceed with the interrogations NOW. These young women are naive college students and shouldn't be very difficult for our skilled team to break. I want to know everything we can learn about their involvement in the treasure hunt and what they saw at the Jersey Museum. Find out what the Scott's have learned about possible treasure sights and get the Kenzie woman to explain where she thinks the Celtic relics are buried." Giorgio nodded in agreement, but did not utter a sound.

"Giorgio," cautioned Marcus, "do not, I repeat, do not let the team hurt either of these women in any way. They are both important bargaining chips, but only if they are unharmed. Do you understand me?"

"Yes sir," responded Giorgio, "I will instruct the team accordingly. How soon do you want the interrogations to begin?"

"Immediately," snapped Marcus. "You have forty eight hours to get me the information." Marcus made a sweeping gesture with his arm and dismissed Giorgio like a lowly servant. Marcus turned and left the veranda to join his wife at the pool. He was anxiously anticipating his morning swim with Sabina and the incredible sex that would follow. But first, he needed to make a phone call to the Castleknock area of Dublin.

CHAPTER 27

LATER THAT MORNING on Cézembre Island, the strike team leader was listening intently to Giorgio's instructions over the phone. "Yes, the two hostages are unharmed and we have given them food and water since we arrived here last evening. We have not made any other contact with them since you and I spoke earlier this morning. How would you like me to proceed?" Giorgio communicated Marcus' interrogation instructions and gave the team until dawn on Wednesday to attain the required information. "What should we say if they ask about their friend that we released to McFadden?" asked the team leader.

"Tell them that she escaped," answered Giorgio. "They will not know any different and it might make them more open to your questioning. We need them to cooperate fully and provide us with the answers Marcus demanded. Do you understand me?"

"Yes sir, we will get the information and contact you immediately."

Marcus dialed a cell number stored on his phone and waited impatiently for his contact to answer. "Hello, this is Brian," said the faraway voice with an Irish accent.

"O'Shanahan, this is Demetrius. I need to inform you of a slight change to our plan with the Scotts. It seems we ran into a complication at the Jersey Museum." Shocked to be receiving a call from Marcus while in the car with Mick & Joelle, O'Shanahan quickly gathered his thoughts and responded to the caller.

"I'm sorry I'm currently not in my office, I will call you back when I return, thank you. Just a very impatient client of mine," explained O'Shanahan. As Brian parked near the Jersey Museum, he suggested to Mick and Joelle that they go on inside while he enjoyed a cigarette. This would give him a few minutes to call back Marcus without anyone hearing the conversation.

"Marcus, I'm aware of what occurred," said O'Shanahan. "It's all over the news. I need to know that my daughter is ok. Is she?"

"Yes," answered Marcus. "She and the young Scott woman are both fine. They are being held in a safe place near Saint Malo."

"What the hell happened at the museum, Marcus? I thought this was a well-planned heist and that there would be no witnesses."

"That was the plan," responded Marcus, "but your daughter and her two friends came back into the museum at closing time to find their lost cell phone and witnessed the robbery. My men had two choices; kill the three women or take them captive. Fortunately, they chose the latter."

"What are you planning to do with Danielle and Kenzie," questioned O'Shanahan, "and who was the third young woman?"

"My men interrogated the other woman first and learned that she is a friend of one of our most trusted operatives. Her name is Keira and I believe that you and the Scotts met her at The Brazen Head. She was showing the two women around

Dublin and offered to take them to the museum on Jersey Island. Obviously, the timing of their visit was very poor. Her intention was to keep an eye on them for McFadden, our operative, and gain their trust. Once we discovered who she was, we released her to McFadden," added Marcus.

"So, what are your plans for my daughter and her friend?" asked O'Shanahan.

"They will be questioned about what they saw at the museum and your daughter will be released. I plan on keeping the Scott's daughter for a while longer. I want to learn everything she knows about the Celtic treasure locations. She also may prove be very valuable as leverage with her famous parents."

"When will my daughter be released?" asked O'Shanahan. "Where can I pick her up? You promised me nothing like this was going to happen if I helped you."

"Look O'Shanahan," said Marcus, "there were no guarantees. You knew the risks when you agreed to provide me information about the Scotts in exchange for a piece of the treasure they find. Your daughter was just in the wrong place at the wrong time. I will have my team release her tomorrow at the pier in Saint Malo. You can pick her up there around sunrise."

"I appreciate getting my daughter back, but what about Kenzie? How long do you think you are going to hold her?" asked O'Shanahan.

"That's not your concern," said Marcus, "I will keep her in captivity as long as necessary to get the cooperation I need from the Scotts. Further, I will have the coins in my possession in a few days and I want to focus on the remaining Celtic treasures."

At the same moment on Cézembre Island, Giorgio's team had moved Danielle to a separate cell and were busy interrogating her about what she had seen at the Jersey Museum. "We were just there to get my phone," pleaded Danielle. "I'm telling you the truth. We had visited the museum earlier in the day and were pretty sure that I left my cell phone in the Gallery E exhibit." As Danielle paused to collect her thoughts, the interrogator was called over to the cell door by another member of the team.

"We just received instructions from Giorgio to let the O'Shanahan woman go. You need to stop the interrogation immediately and leave her alone until she is released. We have orders to return her to the pier in Saint Malo by sunrise tomorrow. Understood?"

"Yes sir," said the guard. "Should I begin interrogating the Scott woman next"?

"Yes, it seems we may be holding her quite a while."

O'Shanahan ended his call to Marcus and then joined Mick and Joelle inside the museum. They had already begun their meeting with the museum's general manager and were busy reviewing CCTV images. "This section was recorded prior to 6:00 p.m. the night of the robbery. As you can see, it shows three young women speaking with our guard and entering the museum."

"Can you zoom in further so that we can see their faces clearly?" asked Joelle. The enlarged image came into focus and it became apparent that it was Kenzie, Danielle and Keira.

"Do you have any other images of them in the museum?" asked Mick. "We need to see what happened to them next."

"Yes, we do," said the guard. "Here they are walking into Gallery E, just prior to the robbery."

"Oh my," exclaimed Joelle as she witnessed the gallery filling with dust from an explosion. "I can barely see the girl's silhouettes. Why are all three women collapsing to the floor?

What is happening?" The general manager of the museum interjected his opinion about what had occurred.

"It seems that the three women entered Gallery E just as the Celtic Coin exhibit was being stolen. Our CCTV footage shows that the three women were Tasered and then taken hostage by three men in black. After that, the cameras went dark."

"Mick, we have to find our daughter!"

"We will Joelle, but we need more information," said Mick. Both Uncle B and Mick turned to the general manager and began firing questions at him. Although the museum had a state of the art security system and ample CCTV coverage to see every area of the museum, the technology provided few clues as to what had happened.

"When the exterior wall was breached, we lost most of our CCTV coverage in that area," said the manager. "We do; however, have an image of the vehicle they used to crash through our wall and steal the coins. Our exterior camera captured this image as the vehicle approached the rear of our museum. It seems they used a street maintenance vehicle that was parked in the area for utility work."

"Can we zoom in on the cab of the front loader to see the driver?" asked Mick.

"Our exterior cameras are not PTZ, they are fixed," said the manager, "so no, we cannot get a clearer image than what you see here."

"Is there anything else that you can tell us to help find our daughters?" asked Uncle B.

"Not here, but your best resource will be Chief Bowman with the Saint Helier Police Department. He was here yesterday investigating the robbery. His office is only a few blocks away."

"Thank you for all of your help," said Mick. "Please contact us if you learn anything that you think might help us find our daughters."

Less than ten minutes later, the Scotts and Uncle B walked into the Saint Helier Police Station and asked to speak with Chief Bowman. They were shown into his office and took a seat in front of his desk. "How may I assist you?" asked Bowman. Mick took the lead and began speaking.

"Both of our daughters were taken hostage during the coin heist at the Jersey Museum yesterday. We need your help in finding them and getting them home safely."

"I see," said Bowman without expressing much compassion. "What about the third woman? Is she one of your daughters too?" he said with sarcasm.

"No, her name is Keira and she is a friend of our daughters," answered Joelle. "She is from Dublin and has been showing our girls around the country the last few days." Joelle was losing her patience with the Chief and her face was turning bright red. "It's obvious from the CCTV coverage that all three women were taken by the robbers. What are you doing to locate them?"

"Calm down, Mrs. Scott," responded Bowman. "We have all of our resources working on this case and I believe that we will locate your daughters shortly. Our intelligence sources indicate that after the robbery, your daughters may have been taken by boat to one of the small Channel Islands just off our coast."

"So why haven't you rescued them yet?" shouted Mick.

"Mr. Scott," answered Chief Bowman, "it's not quite as easy as it sounds. We are still working with Interpol to verify the intelligence report. Many of the islands are nearly impossible to approach without being seen and we don't want to compromise the girl's lives."

"So are you suggesting that we just wait and do nothing?" shouted Uncle B.

"No," responded Bowman, "once we have verified their exact location, we will work with our contacts at Interpol to devise a rescue plan. I will keep you advised of our progress. At this point, I have nothing more to say and I would prefer if you allow me to get back to work. I will contact you immediately when I have more information to share."

CHAPTER 28

KENZIE BEGAN TO regain consciousness and realized that her captors had restrained her to a metal chair in the middle of the chamber. They must have hit me with the Taser again, she thought. Her hands were bound tightly behind her back and her ankles to the base of the chair legs. Although she could not see anything due to the blindfold over her eyes, Kenzie could hear the chamber door squeak open. Without her sight, her sense of hearing was very acute and she could sense someone approaching.

"Ms. Scott," said the guard, "one of your friends escaped before we could question her. Your other friend, Ms. O'Shanahan, well, she did not provide any useful information to us. In fact, she was quite troublesome. We see no reason to keep you alive either unless you can give us the information that we need."

Kenzie screamed, "No, not Danielle. You killed Danielle? You killed my best friend? You will pay for this!" The guard began laughing at her and then slapped her face to get her attention. Kenzie began to whimper.

"Now," said the guard, "are you ready to cooperate? I need to ask you some questions." The guard reached out and removed her blindfold. As her eyes adjusted to the dim light of the chamber, she could make out the guard's silhouette, but not his features. She glared at him. She hated him for what he had done to Danielle.

"We will start with you explaining to me what you saw occur in the museum," said the guard, "and be specific." Kenzie's lips were quivering and she found it hard to speak. She took a deep breath and began her story.

"We visited the Jersey Museum earlier in the day and my friend left her cell phone in one of the exhibits," explained Kenzie. "When we realized where it was, we hurried back to the museum and begged the guard to let us in just before closing. All three of us walked back towards Gallery E and then tried calling her phone. We heard it start to ring and then there was a loud explosion. The room around us filled with dust and smoke. We saw some large machine break through a wall and then head directly toward the Celtic coin exhibit. There were two guards standing nearby, but before we could yell for help, I passed out."

"Then what happened?" asked the guard.

"The next thing I remember is being carried off of a boat and locked in this chamber," said Kenzie. "Why are you holding me here? I don't know anything. I don't have anything to give you." The guard ignored her questions and placed the blindfold back over her eyes. Kenzie began screaming again hoping someone would hear her. She had no idea how useless that would be.

Several hours later the guard returned to Kenzie's holding chamber, but this time he brought company. Kenzie awoke at the sound of the door opening and heard several footsteps. "Stay away from me," she screamed. "I don't know anything. Just let me go!" As the second man neared her chair he removed a small vial and syringe from his medical bag.

"I hope you will be interested in telling us everything we

want to know," said the guard. "The doctor will be giving you a small injection." Pressing the syringe against her restrained arm, the older man administered a small amount of clear liquid. "You have been given a dose of Hyoscine-pentothal truth serum," said the guard. "It is one of our favorite methods to interrogate suspects because it also utilizes pain as an additional incentive. A small dose will produce agonizing chest pain. An overdose of the serum could cause you to have cardiac arrest. Hopefully, we have not given you too much."

Kenzie shrieked when the needle penetrated her skin. "What are you doing to me?" she screamed. "Leave me alone!" A few moments passed and she was nearly motionless. The guard removed her blindfold and threw a glass of ice cold water in her face. Kenzie snapped awake and tried to focus on her captors, but their image was blurred by the intense light illuminating the room.

"Now, Ms. Scott, let's talk about Celtic treasures," said the older man. "Tell me why you think there are caches of gold waiting to be discovered on Jersey Island and near Saint Malo." Kenzie was more awake now and able to gather her thoughts, but she seemed to be feeling a strange pressure in her chest. She hoped it was just anxiety.

"Go ahead, Ms. Scott," said the guard, "tell us about the treasure before the pain gets so intense you can't speak. We will administer an antidote once we have the information we want." He sat a small recording device on the ground next to her chair and turned it on. Without much hesitation, Kenzie began re-telling her story about the Celtic coin discovery and why she believed there were other treasures yet to be discovered. After listening to her for several minutes, the guard interrupted. "Enough!"

"We do not need all this detail. Where will we find the

treasures on Jersey Island? That is all we care to know at this time."

"If I tell you that information, you have to promise to let me go," said Kenzie.

"It is in your best interest to tell us what we need to know and to do it now," shouted the guard. "We are not promising you anything except increasing pain if you do not cooperate."

"I believe that the tribe buried their treasures near some of the most easily seen menhirs on the island," said Kenzie. "I have narrowed it down to five locations quite close to the southern shore of the island."

"What about your claim that there are treasure sites near Saint Malo?" asked the doctor.

"My research indicates that the Celtic tribe living near Saint Malo had significant riches and plenty of advance notice of the Roman invasion. I believe that there may be two or more significant treasures sites in the area. There are many ancient dolmens and menhirs within a day's horseback ride of Saint Malo that could have served as markers. I believe that the treasures are buried somewhere near them," stated Kenzie. "That's all I know." She began frantically wrestling to get out of the bindings that were holding her legs to the chair. "I've told you everything," she cried. "Just give me the antidote and let me go!"

The guard retrieved his recorder from the floor, switched it off and then reapplied the blindfold to Kenzie's face. She couldn't see them now, but she heard them starting to walk away. "Where are you going?" screamed Kenzie. "You can't leave me here to die. I told you everything. Please, please let me go. I need the antidote!" Kenzie began to cry hysterically as the two men exited the chamber. She was not sure if she would live to see them return.

CHAPTER 29

MICK PROVIDED CHIEF Bowman with all of their contact information and then exited the Police Station with Joelle and Uncle B at his side. Their next stop was the dock area near Saint Helier. Hopefully, they would find someone that saw the girls and might know where they were taken. It was a long shot, but he couldn't just sit and wait for the police to call with an update.

The docks were only a short cab ride away. The driver dropped them off at the end of the dock area and then drove away to pick up his next fare. "Well, where do you suggest we start?" asked Mick.

"We have current photos of both of the girls," responded Joelle. "Let's show them around and see if anyone saw the girls yesterday." Several hours passed by as they showed both girl's photos to every dock worker that they encountered.

"Either the girls didn't leave from this dock," said Mick, "or everyone is too scared to talk. We need to find a hotel for the evening so that we can start fresh again tomorrow."

Not far away, on Cézembre Island, Kenzie lay in a silent heap, collapsed on the cold stone floor of her cell. The interrogation was over. She had been most cooperative. The guards had completed their questioning and now were preparing their report for Giorgio, complete with an audio file so that Giorgio and Marcus could review her statements.

The guards had literally scared Kenzie into telling them everything they needed to know. What she didn't realize was that the syringe used on her simply contained a mild sedative. She had not actually been given truth serum or any other harmful drug. She was being manipulated psychologically so that she would cooperate. Although, if she hadn't talked, they were prepared to do whatever was necessary to get the information that Giorgio requested.

Mick and Joelle arrived at the Pomme d'Or Hotel with Uncle B late Wednesday afternoon and checked in. "If you like, you can stay in our suite tonight, we have plenty of extra room," offered Joelle.

"I appreciate that, but I don't want to impose. I'll just get my own room for tonight if they have one available," said Uncle B. "Why don't we all freshen up and then meet again in the lobby around 7:00 p.m. for dinner? We can discuss our search plans for tomorrow."

Not long after Uncle B entered his hotel room, he received a call on his cell phone. "O'Shanahan, this is Giorgio. We have made arrangements to release your daughter tomorrow. She will be dropped at the pier in Saint Malo just after sunrise. This is a good faith gesture and we expect that you will continue to work with us. Is that agreed?"

"Of course," responded O'Shanahan without thinking. "How is Danielle? Have your goons hurt her in any way?"

"No, as soon as my men discovered that she was your daughter, they stopped the interrogation," said Giorgio.

"Are you releasing the Scott's daughter as well?" asked O'Shanahan.

"No, we are not," said Giorgio; "however, we will be in contact with the Scotts shortly. Goodbye."

Brian O'Shanahan was excited to know that his daughter, Danielle, was being released. But now he had a new problem. How could he explain this to Mick and Joelle? How did her captors know how to reach him and why would they only release Danielle? As he showered and changed clothes for the evening, O'Shanahan pieced together a story in his mind that would explain Danielle's release and hopefully hide his association with Marcus. Maybe Mick and Joelle would believe it.

Exiting the lobby elevator, Uncle B found the Scotts waiting for him in the hotel lobby as agreed. "So, where do we want to have dinner this evening?" asked Joelle. "I'm so worried about Kenzie that I don't have much of an appetite, but I know that I need to eat. And a glass of wine sounds fantastic."

"We'll go to Le Bulot," said Mick. "It's just a short walk, has a casual atmosphere and boasts an extensive wine list." Joelle gave Mick a curious look and started to ask how he would know all that information. "Our friendly hotel manager made the recommendation," explained Mick. "Let's go."

As the three exited Pomme d'Or Hotel, they spotted a familiar white Peugeot parked down the street. Resisting an urge to confront the occupants of the car, Mick continued walking with Joelle and Uncle B to Le Bulot. After being seated at a secluded table near the rear of the restaurant, and each taking a sip of Chateau Noaillac Medoc Cru Bourgeois, they began to relax. Joelle was the first to speak. "This wine is exactly what I needed to unwind. What an excellent blend of Merlot and Cabernet-Sauvignon." Uncle B took a long drink and sat down his wine glass.

"Mick, Joelle, I have some news. As we expected, the girls

are being held captive. Their captors made contact with me on my cell about thirty minutes ago," said Uncle B.

"What are you saying?" asked Mick. "Why did they contact you"?

Uncle B begin delivering his well thought out explanation. "While I was in the hotel room freshening up, I received a phone call on my cell. The caller said that they had Danielle and would release her if I agreed to help them."

"What did they mean by, help them?" asked Mick. "And when will they release Kenzie"?

"And what about the girl's friend Keira?" asked Joelle.

"They said that I can pick up Danielle at sunrise tomorrow morning at the Saint Malo pier," explained Uncle B. "They promised me that she was ok."

"What about Kenzie?" demanded Joelle. "Is she ok? Why aren't they releasing her too?"

"They said that the third girl escaped and that Kenzie would not yet be released. They have other plans for her," said Uncle B.

"What sort of plans?" said Joelle.

"Please, let me explain," responded Uncle B.

Mick and Joelle exchanged glances and were curious what Uncle B would say next. "So how are you helping them?" asked Joelle. Uncle B took a deep breath.

"They released Danielle in exchange for me persuading you and Mick to lead them to the treasure on Jersey Island and they are holding onto Kenzie for leverage. Once we find the treasure and hand it over to them, Kenzie will be released."

"Why should we trust them?" asked Mick. "They're criminals."

"I don't think we have a choice," said Uncle B. "They told

me that they would contact you both tomorrow about the trade."

"Mick, we need to go to the police," cried Joelle.

"If you do that, they will not release Danielle tomorrow morning," said Uncle B. "They could even kill the girls. We just need to keep quiet and do what they say. We can pick up Danielle at sunrise tomorrow morning at the pier."

CHAPTER 30

AFTER ANOTHER SLEEPLESS night of worry, Uncle B, Mick and Joelle were up an hour before sunrise so that they could arrive by ferry before Danielle was dropped off at the pier. As their ferry approached the Saint Malo dock and was tied off, Uncle B spotted what looked like Danielle in the distance. "I think that's her," said Joelle.

"Danielle O'Shanahan," screamed Uncle B. He began wildly waving his arms in the air.

The Scotts and Uncle B quickly exited the ferry and began running down the pier. Danielle appeared unharmed, but was crying hysterically. She wrapped her arms around her father for comfort. "They, they still have Kenzie," Danielle sobbed. "And I'm not sure if Keira is dead or alive. I never saw her again after the museum." Uncle B continued to hold his daughter tightly.

"We know that Kenzie is ok," said Joelle. "We hope to get her back soon, but we haven't heard anything about Keira."

"Maybe she escaped," offered Mick.

"Let's get you back to the hotel so that you can get cleaned up and get something to eat," said Joelle. "You don't appear to have been hurt, but we've arranged for you to see a physician later this morning, just in case."

As the Scotts and O'Shanahans took their seats on the ferry

for a return trip to Jersey Island, Malet and his partner were observing their interaction. "It appears from the Scott's behavior that they have no idea yet that Brian O'Shanahan has been working for us," said Malet. "Actually, that's a good thing for everyone concerned." After the ferry left the dock, Malet and his partner approached the terminal and waited for the next boat to Jersey Island. They knew where the Scotts were staying and would stake out their hotel as instructed by Giorgio.

It was a short trip to the island and Uncle B was relieved to be sitting with his daughter again. They disembarked the ferry and walked a short distance to the Pomme d'Or Hotel. A few hours later, after Danielle had a chance to get cleaned up, eat and get thoroughly checked by a physician, it was time to talk about her abduction.

"We were walking through the museum toward Gallery E. That's where I thought I had left my cell phone," said Danielle. "Just as we entered the gallery, there was a huge explosion and thick smoke began to fill the air. I was really confused about what was happening. Before I could say anything to Kenzie or Keira, I felt a sharp pain in my chest."

"That must have been the Taser dart," said Mick. "Then what happened"?

"The pain grew very intense and I remember falling to the ground. The last thing I saw was Kenzie stumbling towards me. Then I blacked out."

"Do you know where they took you when they left the museum?" asked Joelle.

"Not really. The next thing I remember is waking up on a boat," said Danielle. "They placed a blindfold over my eyes and tied my wrists tightly with rope. I think it was still night when we got off the boat. Someone grabbed my arm and began leading me up a rocky trail. The ground was hard to walk on and I kept losing my footing and stepping into holes. Then we began walking up a steep set of stairs."

"Did you hear any sounds that would help us identify the location?" asked Uncle B.

"No, other than the sound of stones crunching under our feet, it was very quiet. I noticed that after we finished climbing the stairs, we walked a short distance on a solid floor. Our footsteps echoed around us and created a very eerie feeling. Wherever we were, the echoes made it sound like a huge cavern," said Danielle.

"There are a lot of caves on the surrounding islands," said Mick, "but your description sounds more like you were in a building. What happened next?"

"Our captors led us down a long winding stone staircase until we were walking on a flat surface again," said Danielle. "They told us to stop and then I heard a metallic clicking noise like a lock opening. A loud high-pitched creaking sound filled the air. It was the steel door to the room where I was held. I wasn't able to see anything and didn't realize what was going to happen next. They pushed me forward and I tripped and fell to the floor. Before I could push the blindfold off of my eyes to see what was happening, I felt the shock of a Taser again. It made my whole body shake and then I blacked out."

The Scotts and Uncle B saw the anguish on Danielle's face and told her to take a break. Even from the short descriptions she had provided them, they were beginning to narrow down the possible locations of her imprisonment. They hoped her clues would lead them to where Kenzie was still being held.

"Can you describe any of your captors?" asked Joelle. "Were they all men? Did they have any accents, tattoos or other things that might help us to identify them?"

"I didn't see any of them until they came to my cell to

question me, but I think that they were all men. They sounded like they were from somewhere in Europe," said Danielle. "The man that came to question me was probably in his mid-twenties. He had dark hair and spoke with the same accent as the other men. Maybe they were in some military group."

"Do you know if they still have Kenzie?" asked Mick.

"I believe so, but I didn't see her again after they placed us into separate chambers. I don't even know why they took us hostage," said Danielle. "None of this makes any sense to me." She lowered her head into her lap and placed her hands over her head. Danielle was done talking and just wanted to rest.

"Danielle," said Joelle. "Why don't you go lie down in the bedroom and get some sleep. We are not going anywhere today. We will all stay here until you wake up." So that they didn't have to leave Danielle alone, lunch was ordered from the hotel and delivered to the room. Later that afternoon, the silence was broken by Mick's ringing cell phone.

"Hello, I'm calling for Mr. Mick Scott," said Giorgio.

"This is Mick, who is this?"

"My name is Giorgio. I'm calling about your daughter, Kenzie. Your daughter has not been harmed. She is quite well currently and I am sure that you would like to see her returned to you in that condition. Do I have your attention?"

"Yes, of course," shouted Mick. "What do you want from us? We just want our daughter back." Both Joelle and Uncle B thought Mick had received a business call until they heard his response about Kenzie.

"Oh my, it's the kidnappers," said Joelle.

"I will make this brief," said Giorgio. "My men have been following you for several weeks. We know that you are successful treasure hunters and that you have been researching sites on Jersey Island and near Saint Malo. Recently, you visited a site on Jersey Island near Le Dolmen du Mont Ubé that may hold vast treasures of the Roman Empire. We want that treasure in exchange for your daughter's release. You have until Monday." Mick said nothing. He paused to control his rage, then began speaking slowly.

"We don't even know yet that any treasure exists at that site," said Mick. "We cannot trade something we do not have in our possession."

"Oh, I believe that you will find a way," quipped Giorgio. "Your daughter's life is counting on it. I will have trucks available at the site for transport of the treasure to my client. Once the treasure is in route, I will send word to release your daughter. It will be most unfortunate for your daughter if you do not comply. Do you understand me?"

"Yes," said Mick.

"Do not involve the police or Kenzie will die," warned Giorgio. "People who cross us tend to have unfortunate accidents. People like your daughter's professor Brinkerman. Do not test us."

Mick sat his cell phone down on the table and took a seat next to Joelle. "It was the kidnappers," said Mick. "They have Kenzie, but she is ok. They are willing to trade her."

"You said something to him about treasure and not having it in our possession," said Joelle. "What's all this about"?

"It's exactly as Uncle B explained to us last night," said Mick. "They want us to find the lost Celtic treasure near Le Dolmen du Mont Ubé and trade it for the release of Kenzie."

"We need to contact the police," said Joelle.

"They threatened to kill her if we do that," said Mick. "I'm not sure that is our best course of action, just yet. Let me explain."

"The man on the phone called himself Giorgio and said

that he was representing a client. He also mentioned that his men had been watching us the last few weeks on Jersey Island and around Saint Malo."

"The men in the white Peugeot?" asked Joelle. "Didn't Clay trace their car back to a shipping company based in Rome"?

"That's right," said Mick. "Here's the connection. The license plate belonged to a vehicle that is registered to a holding corporation named Jacques, Inc., located in Rennes, France. Jacques is a subsidiary of Romano, LLC operating in both the US and Europe, headquartered in New York City. Romano, LLC is a subsidiary of Sostos Shipping Enterprises, operated out of Rome, Italy. Here's where it gets interesting," continued Mick. "Sostos is owned and operated by Theophilos Sostos, the father-in-law to Marcus Demetrius. The same Marcus Demetrius that is rumored to own the largest privately held collection of Roman artifacts in the world." Both Joelle and Uncle B were nodding their heads in agreement as Mick continued to explain his theory.

"I believe that the man on the phone, Giorgio, works for Demetrius as his front man. They were responsible for the coin heist at the Jersey Museum a few days ago and Kenzie just happened to be in the wrong place at the wrong time," said Mick.

"When they discovered who she was, they realized they could hold her for leverage," added Joelle. "They had been following us and knew we were searching for the lost Celtic treasure." Uncle B had been listening intently to the conversation, but now felt he had something important to add.

"You should both realize, that if this chain of events is all connected to Marcus Demetrius, we are dealing with a very rich and powerful sociopath," said Uncle B. "Demetrius believes that he is directly related to Julius Caesar and that all Roman treasures are his birthright. If the ancient Coriosolites buried their treasures to hide them from the Romans as Kenzie speculated, Demetrius believes that they belong to him. Now, with Kenzie as a bargaining chip, he recognizes that he can persuade you to find the lost treasures and turn them over to him."

"I think we are all in agreement to hold off involving the police," said Mick. "In the meantime, let's contact Clay to bring him up to speed and find out when the ground penetrating radar unit will arrive." It was later that afternoon when Mick was able to get Clay on the phone. He made arrangements for the GPR to arrive at Saint Helier pier early Saturday morning. Clay also used his extensive network of contacts to secure portable lighting equipment, generators, an ATV and trailer, a Bobcat compact excavator and a crew to help with the excavation. Throughout the rest of the afternoon and evening, the Scotts and Uncle B worked diligently to craft a plan to locate and retrieve the treasure they believed still lay hidden near Le Dolmen du Mont Ubé.

"Marcus, this is Mario Sargusi, in New York."

"Hello Mario," said Marcus with a dry tone in his voice. "What is the nature of your call?"

"I want to congratulate you on completing your recent acquisition. I was surprised by the heist, but then again, I know that you have a real soft spot for Roman artifacts. Go figure. I'm calling you to touch base on a couple of points of business," said Mario. Marcus detested Mario's thick, Brooklyn accent and hoped their phone call would be very brief.

"Go ahead," said Marcus.

"When we met at my office, I showed you a map of some potential projects. I'm calling for an update. Also, the professor that provided the map, has become, sort of a problem."

"What sort of a problem?" asked Marcus. Mario continued to explain.

"It seems Professor Brinkerman watched CNN last Tuesday evening and saw coverage of the coin heist on Jersey Island," said Mario. "He thinks that we have the coins and now we owe him something in return."

"I really don't care about your Professor or what he thinks he deserves. The map he provided you has nothing to do with the coins in the museum," said Marcus. "Is that why you called me?" Mario was clearly getting agitated by Marcus's tone. He wasn't used to being talked to in that manner.

"Look," said Mario, "Brinkerman is threatening to talk with the police about the coin heist. He plans on implicating both of us in the robbery. I think he needs to be redirected, if you know what I mean?"

"Yes, Mario, I know what you mean. The problem will be handled. Anything else?"

Mario began asking a series of questions about the treasure map he had provided, but Marcus was not quick to divulge many details. "We have made some inquiries and believe that the Scotts could be helpful in locating the items of interest," said Marcus. "If and when we gain possession of the items, I would be happy to pay you a generous finder's fee. Was that your main concern?"

"Aah, yeah," stammered Mario. "Ya know, it's just business. If you find the treasure, I think I should get my cut." Marcus was done talking. He considered Mario an underling and was ready to move on to more pressing matters.

"We will be in touch," said Marcus.

CHAPTER 31

I T WAS THE Friday evening before Christmas and ASU was a ghost town. Most everyone had left for the holiday several days earlier, including all of Professor Brinkerman's students. Solitude was not his friend and he longed for companionship. His childhood pal, Mario Sargusi, had not yet returned his numerous phone calls and his attempt to the get the local media interested in a coin heist on Jersey Island had been fruitless. He hoped his meeting and complete cooperation with Marcus' thugs would pay off. Even if they stiffed him on the full one million dollars, they would probably throw him a smaller payout to keep him quiet. Frustrated by the turn of events, Paul Brinkerman thought enjoying dinner and a few drinks at one of his favorite restaurants in Scottsdale would provide some comfort.

He sat at the long granite bar with a few other patrons and enjoyed a tumbler of Jameson neat. The bartender was certainly attractive, but she was young enough to be his daughter and didn't seem to spend much time talking with her customers. Without any family or real friends to talk with, Brinkerman would have been happy to have anyone take an interest in him.

As he finished his fourth tumbler of Irish whiskey, an attractive, middle-aged woman approached the bar area and ask him if she could take the adjacent seat. "Well of course you can," said Brinkerman with a smile. "I'm here by myself tonight. Are you visiting Scottsdale? Your accent tells me that you are from somewhere in the New York area."

"You are very perceptive," she said. "I'm here visiting my daughter at ASU for Christmas break. The weather in New York City this time of year is awful, so here I am. Warm temperatures, sunshine and shopping with my daughter. Arizona Mills, here we come." She turned to the bartender and ordered a glass of white wine.

Paul extended his hand and said, "My name is Paul Brinkerman. I'm a professor at ASU. What's your name?"

"I'm Claudette," she said. "Very nice to meet you, Paul. So, why is such a handsome man here by himself the week before Christmas?"

"Well, I'm not from here originally, so I don't have any family in town. I grew up in Brooklyn, that's how I recognized your accent. Unfortunately, all of my family, except a few cousins, have all passed on." As Brinkerman took the last swig of his Jameson Irish Whiskey, Claudette offered to buy him another drink.

"Really, it's the least I can do," she said. "Consider it an early Christmas present. Bartender, another Jameson neat for my friend, and make it a double."

"I appreciate that, thank you," said Paul. After several more holiday cocktails followed by a delicious Angus steak dinner, Brinkerman was ready to return home and turn in for the evening. "I've really enjoyed meeting you tonight," Brinkerman slurred. "I hope you and your daughter have a very pleasant holiday."

"I'm sure we will. Can I walk with you out to your car?" said Claudette. Brinkerman gave her a funny look. "You've had a few cocktails tonight and I just want to make sure you get to your car safely."

"Certainly," said Brinkerman with a smile. "Let's go." Brinkerman nearly fell into his car as Claudette opened the door for him. "Thanks again," he muttered. "Have a nice holiday." After attempting for several minutes to find his seat belt and snap the buckle, he gave up and started the car. With slightly blurred vision and the cover of darkness, Brinkerman had not noticed Claudette stooped next to his car after she closed his door. In only a few moments, she had loosened the fitting on his brake line enough that brake fluid was starting to drip from the connection.

He left the restaurant and steered his silver Volvo down W. Westcourt Way towards 48th Street. As he approached the bottom of the hill and began breaking for the curve, his brakes were not very responsive. He pumped the brakes frantically, but with no results. As he reached for the emergency brake, his thoughts turned to the recent meeting in his office. The two tough looking men had threatened to arrange for him to have an accident if he didn't keep quiet about the treasure. Did his call to Mario about the coins push them to take action? He pulled up hard on the emergency brake lever, but the car continued to gain speed. Brinkerman swerved the car from lane to lane trying to slow its speed. He was running out of options.

At nearly sixty five miles per hour, Brinkerman lost control of his car as it entered the sharp curve. It began to cross the gravel median, missing small ornamental trees and boulders. Just a hundred yards away, families enjoying themselves in the park took notice of the out of control car and began to run in every direction. A young woman pushing her baby's stroller was wearing ear buds and didn't hear the shouts or understand why everyone was starting to run. As she turned around, she saw the car bouncing over a curb and heading directly for her. Frozen in fear, she couldn't react fast enough. Brinkerman desperately tried to slow the car by shifting it into park, but the car didn't respond. Moments before the Volvo reached her and her baby, a young man pushed them both out of harm's way as the car crashed into two large mesquite trees lining the baseball field. The 1994 Volvo was in disrepair and did not have working airbags. On impact, Brinkerman, without a seatbelt fastened, was catapulted over his steering wheel and through the windshield. His world went dark.

When the EMTs arrived fifteen minutes later, Brinkerman was pronounced dead at the scene. He reeked of alcohol and the police reported it as a DUI accident. Fortunately, there were no other victims. The young woman and her baby were shaken up by the ordeal, but were not harmed. As a local TV correspondent interviewed the young man responsible for saving two lives, police worked the accident scene.

Paul Brinkerman would no longer pose a threat to the illicit operations of Mario Sargusi or Marcus Demetrius. Nor would he realize his dream of retiring to the Caribbean with his share of the treasures. News of the fatal crash and heroic act to save a young woman and her baby was carried that evening by a Phoenix news affiliate and then picked up by CNN. It was a heart-warming story for the network to run just prior to the holidays. Within a few hours Giorgio was apprised of the news. His only reaction was a thin, satisfied smile. Marcus would be pleased that he had tied up a loose end.

Eighteen hundred kilometers to the west, the Scotts had turned in for the night and were watching the news and reading before they fell asleep. "So," asked Joelle. "Were you able to arrange for a policeman to watch our hotel tomorrow while we are away?"

"Yes," said Mick, "Chief Bowman was quite helpful when I called him this afternoon. He was relieved that Danielle had not been harmed and was back in our care. I didn't even ask him for an officer to watch over her, he suggested it. Hopefully, we will only be gone for two days and return with Kenzie on Monday."

"I can't wait to see her Mick," said Joelle. "Do you think she is ok"? Before Mick could respond, Joelle sat up and shouted.

"Mick, that CNN story is about a fatal car crash in Scottsdale," said Joelle. "Can you turn up the volume"? As they both watched the report, the name, Brinkerman, didn't register in their minds. Then it hit both of them. "That was Kenzie's professor at ASU," said Joelle. "The one she wrote the exam paper for last fall."

"And the same Brinkerman that Giorgio referred to earlier today," said Mick. "He said that people like Brinkerman who cross him have unfortunate accidents."

"This wasn't an accident, Mick. They killed him. Giorgio knew earlier today that this would happen tonight," said Joelle. "We made the right decision to not get the police involved. We need to do whatever Giorgio says to get our daughter back alive."

"I agree," said Mick. "Let's get some rest so that we can be at the pier first thing tomorrow morning."

CHAPTER 32

E ARLY SATURDAY MORNING, Mick, Joelle and Uncle B were anxiously waiting at the pier with their rental truck as the first wooden crates were unloaded off of the freighter. If all went as planned, the Noggin 1000 MHz ground penetrating radar unit mounted on a Smart Cart would soon be sitting on the pier. Clay had arranged for the GPR, two generators, various excavation tools, and a portable lighting system. He had also hired a crew of six men to assist with the excavation through a contact in Saint Malo. They would arrive on site after sundown Sunday evening. Other equipment needed for the job would be picked up by the Scotts and Uncle B from a local rental firm once they left the pier.

Shortly after 9:00 a.m., all of the equipment had been uncrated and loaded onto the rental truck. Their next stop was Saint Helier Heavy Equipment Rental. Arriving at the shop, the Scotts and Uncle B found that their equipment was already loaded on a trailer and hitched to a white, Ford F350. The Bobcat compact excavator and ATV were securely attached with chains to the trailer. Uncle B would be driving the Ford F350 and following Mick and Joelle in their rental truck. After paying for the rentals, the group headed northeast out of Saint Helier. Their plan was to make a quick stop for lunch and then travel to the treasure sight arriving shortly after noon.

It was a short distance from the pier to the White Horse Inn, a small pub on A4. The Scotts and Uncle B entered the pub and were shown to a table where they could have a working lunch. "So Mick, can you explain how this ground penetrating radar unit is going to help us find the treasure?" asked Uncle B. "It looks more like an electric lawn mower than a sophisticated radar device." Mick laughed at the comparison and began to explain how the device works.

"I will give you a quick overview of the equipment, my surveying plan and then we can discuss the specifics. A ground penetrating radar unit like the Noggin can be used to detect and map subsurface archaeological artifacts, features and patterning," said Mick. "With ground penetrating radar, the radar signal, an electromagnetic pulse, is directed into the ground. Subsurface objects and stratigraphy (layering) will cause reflections that are picked up by a receiver. The travel time of the reflected signal indicates the depth. Data may be plotted as profiles, as plan view maps isolating specific depths, or as 3-dimensional models."

"I see where Clay gets his attention to detail," quipped Uncle B. Mick ignored his sarcastic comment and continued with his explanation.

"The plan view maps can show subsurface structures at different depths. As we crisscross the survey area, lines of data, individually representing vertical profiles, will be collected and assembled as a 3-dimensional data array that can be horizontally 'sliced' at different depths. The Noggin will in essence, draw a picture for us of where to dig and give us an idea of what we will find."

"Wow," exclaimed Uncle B. "That really does sound incredible. Will it take long to survey the area?" Mick went on to explain his surveying plan.

"Once we get everything unloaded from the truck, we will need to transport our equipment to the site and then begin laying out the survey area," explained Mick. "Joelle, I will need your help as well to measure and mark off the area. Once we complete a section, we will define another grid area and begin surveying. Depending upon the information our Noggin provides, this could be a very quick or very long process."

"Mick, do you think the men that have been following us will be watching us at the site?" asked Joelle.

"I expect Giorgio will have his men in the area to keep an eye on us and to ensure that every piece of treasure we find is loaded onto their truck," said Mick. "After seeing how they murdered Professor Brinkerman in Scottsdale, I don't believe it would be wise to cross them."

The Scotts and Uncle B finished their lunch and began driving towards Le Dolmen du Mont Ubé. Once they arrived, unloading the GPR unit, ATV and trailer of equipment took less than an hour. Although the site was only one hundred meters to the east of the tree line, it took another hour to move all of the equipment into position and begin surveying. Mick was accustomed to using radar of various types including handheld detectors like the Minelab GPX 5000, but he had only used a large scale ground penetrating radar unit a few times.

The Noggin 1000MHz was mounted onto a Smart Cart and as Uncle B observed, looked much like an electric lawnmower. Before Mick could begin surveying the area, he and Uncle B set marker stakes. They began with a small search area measuring roughly thirty by thirty feet square. Setting markers every two feet on each side produced the outline of a grid. Next, Joelle, Mick and Uncle B, using bags of white chalk, walked across the grid from marker to marker, spreading the dust. The result was a white checkerboard pattern with two foot by two foot squares outlined in white. It was now time to begin the tedious job of searching each square for signs of metal below the surface.

The Noggin GPR was equipped with a digital video logger (DVL) display screen to translate the data it received into a meaningful picture. Mick had finished surveying the first thirty by thirty foot area without anything of interest appearing on the display. After marking another checkerboard area of similar size with the help of Joelle and Uncle B, Mick resumed his back and forth scanning of the ground. It was a tedious process, but moving the Noggin too fast could provide erroneous results. On the last pass across the grid, Mick began seeing a different stream of data on the screen. He stopped at the end of the row. "Joelle, take a look at this last data stream," said Mick. "Do you see the same thing I do?" Both Joelle and Uncle B studied the images on the screen.

"It seems that there is a faint outline of metallic objects about seven feet below the surface," remarked Joelle. "And the image appears denser toward the edge of the grid. Should we extend the survey area another ten feet to see if the image continues?"

"I think so," replied Mick. "We may be on to something."

Hurriedly, Mick and Uncle B set markers every two feet until they had extended the survey area to the new size. Joelle grabbed the bag of white chalk and began laying out the checkerboard pattern from marker to marker. When she finished, Mick continued his methodical scanning of the new survey area. Almost immediately, the Noggin began registering metallic objects laying six to seven feet under the surface. As he progressed across the grid, images continued to fill the screen. At midpoint he stopped and asked Joelle and Uncle B to extend the search area another five feet while he continued scanning. "Most everything I'm seeing is about six feet below the surface and seems to extend down to a level of nearly twenty feet," said Mick. "This appears to be a very large treasure site."

Another hour passed as Mick completed scanning the remaining search area with the Noggin. As he neared the middle of the five foot extension grid, fewer images appeared on the display. On the next two passes, he found nothing metallic registering underground. "I've finished the scan," said Mick. "I think we should review the data and decide upon our excavation technique. If some of the objects indicated by the data are as small and fragile as they appear, we will need to proceed carefully to avoid damaging the artifacts."

"From the data I see, it appears to be about ten feet wide by ten feet long and possibly up to twenty feet deep," commented Uncle B. "How are we going to excavate this large of a site properly in the short time span we have"?

"The tribes of that time period often constructed rudimentary vaults when burying their valuables," said Joelle. "If we are lucky, the perimeter of the excavation area will be lined with timbers or some other strong material."

"Once we find that lining," explained Mick, "we will be able to enter the vault room from one side to exhume the artifacts."

"And if that is not the case?" asked Uncle B.

"Then it will be a painstakingly slow process and we may not complete the excavation for several days or longer," said Mick. "Let's hope for the best."

All afternoon, Malet and his partner watched the Scott's activity around Le Dolmen du Mont Ubé from the nearby tree line. Using a combination shotgun and parabolic laser microphone, they were able to hear bits of the Scott's conversation, but not enough to record. Although they could not hear the conversations, body language indicated that the Scotts had been successful in identifying an area to excavate. Malet took digital pictures of their activity with a telephoto lens and then wirelessly uploaded the photos to Giorgio for his review. Later that afternoon, Malet prepared a detailed report and transmitted it to Giorgio's office outside of Rome. Included in the report were the exact coordinates for delivery of the transport truck scheduled to arrive early Sunday evening. After seeing the Scott's and Uncle B secure their equipment and drive away from the site, Malet and his partner emerged from the tree line and headed for their vehicle parked nearly one-half mile away. Once they were back in Saint Helier, Malet parked his white Peugeot across from Pomme d'Or Hotel and began another night of keeping an eye on the Scotts. He hoped that this assignment would soon end.

In the Scott's hotel room everyone was busy recuperating from the day of processing information from the site. Joelle placed a call to Clay to insure that he received all of the data from the Noggin and the images of the site. Mick was grabbing a quick shower and Uncle B was enjoying some quiet time with Danielle in the front room of the suite. Room service knocked on the door and Uncle B was the one to answer. The bellhop was shown in and quickly removed each entrée from the cart and placed them on the dining table. There were many various sized and shaped dishes, but Uncle B was not sure what everyone ordered. He tipped the bellhop and announced to Mick, Joelle and Danielle that dinner was ready.

After everyone sat down and began lifting the covers on each of their plates, Mick realized that there was one dish that no one had claimed. "Does anyone know what this item is?" asked Mick. They all looked curiously at the plate. "Maybe the hotel sent us a desert, compliments of the house. Here goes." He lifted the lid while everyone looked on in complete shock.

Sitting on the plate was a severed human finger, a blood soaked knife and a folded note.

"Oh," gasped Joelle. "Is it real? Is that, is that... Kenzie's?" Danielle screamed and covered her mouth with both hands.

"It appears to be a man's pinky finger," said Mick with a calmness to his voice. "I suspect it's a warning from Giorgio."

"Mick, what does the note say?" asked Uncle B. Mick began reading as Joelle and Uncle B listened intently.

"DO NOT CROSS ME. LET THIS BE A WARNING OF WHAT WILL HAPPEN TO YOUR DAUGHTER IF YOU DO NOT FOLLOW MY ORDERS. YOU ARE BEING WATCHED. RETRIEVE THE TREASURE TOMORROW NIGHT AS PLANNED. A TRUCK WILL ARRIVE AT 3:00 A.M. FOR LOADING. DO NOT INVOLVE THE POLICE OR YOUR DAUGHTER DIES, VERY PAINFULLY. YOU WILL BE CONTACTED AGAIN AFTER THE TRUCK IS LOADED AND LEAVES THE SITE."

Mick sat the note down, covered the plate and looked around the table. "I don't see that we have a choice, but to follow Giorgio's orders," said Mick. "He doesn't seem to be bluffing." Uncle B and Joelle shook their heads in agreement.

"Should we go talk to the bellhop and see if he knows anything?" asked Joelle. "Maybe he saw who put the extra plate on his cart."

"We already know the answer to that," said Mick. "It was someone working for Giorgio. Probably one of the men assigned to watch us." Uncle B left the table and carried some food into Danielle's room to try to console her. She had been released from capture only a day ago and was still dealing with her emotions. Now she again feared for Kenzie's life. It was too much for her to grasp. She sat crying with her face in her pillow. Uncle B knew that Marcus would take whatever steps necessary to acquire the treasure, including murder. He needed to help Mick and Joelle find the treasure, turn it over to Marcus and put an end to this nightmare.

CHAPTER 33

EARLY SUNDAY MORNING, Giorgio met with Marcus in the grotto. Sabina had not yet awakened and was still in the main house, so the two men were able to openly discuss business. "I trust you have good news for me this morning," said Marcus. "How soon will my coins be delivered?"

"Yes sir, they are in route," said Giorgio, "and due to arrive tomorrow evening here at the estate."

"Splendid," said Marcus. "Have them placed in Building Four so that they can be properly cleaned and made ready for display. And what is the status of my treasure on Jersey Island? Will the Scott's follow your orders and turn it over to us?"

"I have taken many steps to insure their compliance," said Giorgio. "They know we are watching them and that we will kill their daughter if they disobey any of our instructions. My men on the island have observed the Scotts surveying the site around Le Dolmen du Mont Ubé and believe that they will be excavating tonight as planned. I have arranged for an unmarked delivery truck to arrive there at midnight."

"What about Brian O'Shanahan?" asked Marcus. "Do we still need him alive or is he a liability"?

"I would suggest that we continue to let him assist the Scotts in acquiring this treasure," responded Giorgio. "Of course, once we have the antiquities in our hands, it may be best if he is eliminated." Marcus looked at Giorgio with a thin smile on his face.

"Well done. I trust you will advise me if anything changes."

"Of course, sir," said Giorgio.

It was only 6:30 a.m., but Mick, Joelle and Uncle B were up and preparing for the long day ahead. They hoped Clay had finished analyzing the Noggin data and had not yet turned in for the evening. Getting his read on the site would be crucial to their successful excavation of the treasures. Without his insight and understanding of the vault, the project could fail. That was not an option if they hoped to see Kenzie alive again. Mick picked up his cell, put it on speakerphone and dialed the Orlando number.

"Clay, this is Dad. Clay, are you there?" asked Mick.

"Yeah," said Clay with a yawn.

"I know it's late there, but we need your help on the Noggin data. Were you able to complete the analysis?" asked Mick. Clay turned on a few lights so that he could see the site materials and took a seat at his desk. With radar images filling two computer screens in front of him, Clay was now ready to discuss his findings.

"The data you provided from the GPR unit was very helpful," said Clay. "I was able to create a three dimensional computer model of the vault and its contents. I don't know exactly what you will find, but some of the larger objects are identifiable and nearly everything in the room seems to be made of gold." After providing Mick and Joelle with descriptions of the items contained in the vault, he shifted his emphasis to the excavation.

"Getting everything out of the vault without a cave-in or requiring weeks of painstaking removal has been the challenge. I believe that the plan I devised will allow you to enter the vault and literally carry the treasures out," boasted Clay. Mick, Joelle and Uncle B exchanged glances. They hoped Clay's plan was as good as it sounded.

"Go ahead," said Mick. "We're all ears."

"I recommend that you start the excavation on the south end of the survey area. Use the compact excavator to start digging about six feet outside of the south marker line. Dig down to the six foot level and stop. Only dig across one half of the marked area."

"What next?" asked Mick. Clay continued.

"I would inspect the area for signs of a vault lining. It's possible that they used timbers or stones to line the sides of the vault. Even if the wooden timbers have decayed, you should see some trace in the soil. If you find nothing, continue to dig another three foot section. If nothing is found, I recommend moving three feet closer to the marker line and resume excavating."

"I thought the Noggin data would provide us with a more exacting road map," said Mick. "It seems we are proceeding very cautiously as if we don't really know what we may find. Am I understanding you correctly?" Clay realized he needed to provide a more detailed explanation of his strategy.

"Let me describe what I believe we are excavating at this site," said Clay. "That should help you better understand the method we are using."

"Ancient Celtic tribes typically buried valuables in vaults lined with cut timbers on each wall and the floor prior to an invasion," said Clay. "Once the vault was filled with treasure, a thatched timber cap was placed across the top of the vault and then covered with several feet of dirt. As you have found, they would mark the site with stones so that once the invading tribe was subdued, they could return to the vault and reclaim their treasure. The Noggin data indicates that there is a void in the soil in the marked area."

"So you think the vault cap is still intact?" said Mick.

"I do," said Clay. "The data indicates a void which I interpret as an air space. That is why I'm recommending excavating at one end of the survey area. If we are lucky, once the side is removed, the vault will be open." Clay continued with his recommendations.

"You should begin to see remains of the vault wall between the three and six foot level," said Clay. "Once you have identified the outlying vault wall, I suggest continuing your excavation all the way across the ten foot side. This area should be dug out to a minimum six foot depth. At this point you should have a work area that is six feet deep, ten feet long and six feet wide. Once the entire length of the vault wall is exposed, I would suggest expanding your work area out away from the site and provide a gradual slope. This will help you to remove artifacts from the site," Clay explained. "Continue excavating the area along the marker line until you reach the bottom of the vault. According to the DVL data, that should be about fifteen to eighteen feet below the surface. Then you can remove any of the timbers that remain so that you have access to the vault."

"I understand the process," said Mick, "but what about the cap of the vault caving in on us? This vault is over two thousand years old."

"I have included jack stands, two by fours and sheets of plywood in the equipment shipment," said Clay. "Those should be used to reinforce the ceiling so that you can work inside the vault."

"It seems you have thought of everything," said Joelle.

"When will the crew of men you hired to assist us arrive at the site"?

"They will arrive around midnight and will work with you until the truck is loaded," said Clay. "The crew's supervisor goes by the name, Ramon. Give all of your instructions to him and he will direct his men as necessary. You can trust him. He has been paid very well for his work and to keep an eye on his crew."

"Thanks Clay for all of your help," said Mick. "We will touch base with you later today."

"Hold on," said Clay, "there's one more thing. I'm sending you a text version of my excavation plan. Just in case you need it. I know you will be careful tonight, but don't forget who wants this treasure. Marcus is a sociopath and will stop at nothing to get what he wants."

"Clay, I appreciate your concern," said Mick. "We have taken some steps to insure our safety and to make sure that Kenzie is returned as promised. Talk to you soon."

Mick sat the cell phone down and turned toward Joelle and Uncle B. "What was that about?" Joelle asked. "What steps have we taken"?

"I've been working on a backup plan with Uncle B," said Mick. "He has a lot of connections in Dublin. Men who are happy to lend a hand and have the firepower to protect us if needed."

"Is that a wise move considering Giorgio's warning?" asked Joelle.

"The men will hide from view near the survey site and will only take action if needed," explained Uncle B. "No one will know they are present. I trust each of these men with my life."

"No," said Joelle, "you are trusting them will all of our lives."

CHAPTER 34

A S KENZIE'S DAILY allotment of food and plastic bottle of water were slid under her chamber's door, she was startled from a deep sleep. The sedative administered during her interrogation was just beginning to wear off. Her mind raced. She realized that she hadn't died and wondered if they had given her the antidote. As full consciousness returned, Kenzie wondered how many days had passed since she was taken hostage. It seemed like an eternity. She believed she was being fed once a day and had marked each time on the floor with a scratch from a small stone. There were four marks on the stone floor. She believed it was sometime Sunday.

Her captors had placed a two inch wide steel clasp around her left ankle and secured it with a chain to a hook in the floor. She could only move in a six foot circle around the center point and felt restrained like a rabid dog. Although she had fought furiously to remove the steel clasp, it was simply too tight to slide over her foot. Kenzie reached out to pull the food tray and water closer. It wasn't much, but it was all she had to look forward to each day. Taking a small stone in her hand, she put a fifth scratch on the floor indicating day five. She hoped the information that she had provided her captors about the treasures would earn her release. All she could do was wait.

Traffic was light along A4 as Mick, Joelle and Uncle B made

the short drive with their equipment to Le Dolmen du Mont Ubé. It was nearly sundown as they arrived at the survey site. Since it was a holiday weekend, the ancient site had received no visitors in several days. Most likely, it would be weeks before anyone discovered that the site had been excavated.

Mick and Joelle began by unloading all of the small equipment including the generator and portable lights. They would need to set up lights around the perimeter of the site since it was now past sundown. Uncle B had unfastened the Bobcat compact excavator and was driving it towards the survey site. He was glad he thought to get extra fuel for the Bobcat as finding gasoline in the middle of the country after midnight could be challenging if not impossible. With every piece of equipment unloaded from the trucks and portable lights in position, it was time to begin remarking the excavation area.

Using the Noggin GPR unit, Mick easily detected the south edge of the survey site so that Uncle B and Joelle could place the markers. A thick line of white chalk was applied to the ground to define the edge. Next, they set markers at three feet and six feet away from the white line. They would begin excavating six feet out from the vault edge to insure that it not collapse if their GPR readings were incorrect. "Uncle B, are you ready to begin the excavation?" asked Mick.

"Ready as I ever will be. It's been a few years since I last worked with a Bobcat," said Uncle B, "but I think I can handle it."

Brian O'Shanahan was actually quite adept at using the Bobcat after years of working on the docks of Dublin as a youth. Loading and unloading ships with a forklift was a far more precise exercise and O'Shanahan guided the Bobcat compact excavator like a pro. After digging all of the way across the plotted area to a depth of three feet, Uncle B stopped the machine. Mick and Joelle inspected the dirt and found no evidence of rotted timbers or a rock lining. Following Clay's instructions, Uncle B proceeded to remove another layer of soil. Now they had exposed an area roughly three feet wide, ten feet across and six feet deep. If no evidence of the vault lining was found here, they would begin excavating closer to the white chalk line.

Mick and Joelle sifted handfuls of the sandy soil through a separator looking for evidence of wood. Satisfied that they had not yet reached the vault lining, Mick gave Uncle B a signal to begin the next section. He moved the Bobcat into position and lowered the bucket into the soil just outside the white chalk line. "Here we go," said Uncle B as the compact excavator began moving forward.

Working carefully to remove the soil in small layers, Uncle B created another trough approximately three feet across and three feet deep, then he stopped. "Mick, do you and Joelle want to analyze this area before I go on?" said Uncle B.

"Yes, we do," said Mick. "This is where Clay believes we may find evidence of a vault lining." Again, they carefully sifted the soil through a separator and found nothing. "Ok Uncle B, let's remove another foot of soil." Their pace was painstakingly slow, but this method of excavation gave them the best chance of finding the vault without causing it harm.

Uncle B moved the Bobcat into position and again began to remove layers of soil in small amounts. On the third pass, the excavator seemed to hit some resistance in the ground. He moved the Bobcat back out of the trench and asked for Mick to take a look. "I seem to have hit a snag," said Uncle B. "Maybe a large rock is in the way." Inspecting the area, Mick used his hands to move away small sections of soil.

"It appears the excavator blade was stuck into a thick

timber," said Mick. "I believe that we have found the outer edge of the vault. And most amazing, it seems to be almost petrified." Using a small hand tool, Mick continued to expose the edge of the hardened timber. "Let's move the Bobcat excavating path about six inches away from this edge so that we do not damage it."

Uncle B positioned the Bobcat as Mick suggested and continued excavating soil all the way across the ten foot span. Mick and Joelle used shovels and small hand tools to remove the remaining soil and further expose the vault lining. "It seems we have found the edge of the vault, just like Clay predicted," said Joelle. "What are the next steps"?

"I suggest that we continue following his plan," said Uncle B, "and remove more soil."

Excited by their find, neither the Scotts nor Uncle B noticed several figures moving stealthily along the distant tree line. Carrying M-10 machine pistols, each of the men assumed a camouflaged position not too far from the survey area. Their guns effective range was only fifty meters. If needed, they would move closer for the kill.

Uncle B got back into the Bobcat and began excavating the remaining soil outside of the white chalk line all the way across the ten foot expanse. The trough was now six feet deep along the vault lining and most of the soil had fallen away from the timbers. He had created a work area that was six feet deep, ten feet long and six feet wide. As Clay had suggested, Uncle B continued excavating the site until the entire length of the vault wall was exposed, and then expanded the work area out away from the site providing a gradual slope.

Standing in front of the ancient wall of timbers nearly fifteen feet below the surface, Joelle, Mick and Uncle B were in awe. They had repositioned their portable lights so that the excavated area was well lit. "I have a feeling that was the easy part," quipped Mick. "Now all we have to do is saw through this wall of nearly petrified wood, shore up the ceiling so it doesn't collapse on us, remove the treasures and avoid being shot by Giorgio's men."

"Sounds like a walk in the park," replied Joelle. "Hey, it's nearly midnight. The men Clay hired to help us should be arriving soon."

"I'll go take a look," said Uncle B as he walked up the gradual slope of soil. As he reached the top, he did not see anyone from the crew Clay had hired. Instead, he noticed a small light along the tree line about fifty meters away.

Uncle B pulled out a flashlight, turned it on and began sending Morse code. The distant light responded and a smile formed on his face. They were here. The six men he had contacted in Dublin were all in place, sufficiently armed and ready to protect them from Giorgio's men if necessary. Now he needed to find the crew Clay had hired. Uncle B began walking toward the spot where he parked the equipment trailer. A short distance down the road, he saw six men approaching the area with one man leading the way.

"I am looking for Mick Scott," said the muscular stranger as he approached. "We were hired by his son, Clay. My name is Ramon, and these are my men." Uncle B extended his arm and shook the man's hand.

"Call me O'Shanahan. We've been expecting you. Mick is at the dig site with the equipment and his wife Joelle. All of the items that we are excavating must be loaded onto a truck no later than sunrise. Can your men work quickly?"

"Of course," said Ramon. "They do what I tell them and nothing less. We are ready to work. Lead the way."

Before O'Shanahan and the crew turned to walk toward the

survey site, they saw lights in the distance and then heard a large truck approaching. "Unexpected visitors?" asked Ramon.

"No, that is the group we hired to transport items from the excavation site," said O'Shanahan. "Let's keep moving. I'm sure they will find us." Uncle B didn't want to explain who was really driving the truck or that all of their lives were in danger. He hoped that the Scott's excavation plan would go smoothly, but just in case, he did have his friends from Dublin nearby.

CHAPTER 35

WITH ALL OF the soil removed from their work area and the timbers exposed, Mick was ready to begin cutting a passage into the vault. He began at the top of the wall on the left side of the vault. Using an electric Milwaukee reciprocating saw, or Sawzall, he was able to remove a small section of the top four timbers in just minutes. "Joelle, can you please get me a flashlight from the equipment truck?" asked Mick. "I've created a hole large enough that we should be able to see the vault's interior." As he waited for the light, thoughts of Kenzie filled his mind. Is she still ok? Will her captors release her as they promised? What if there is no treasure on the other side of these timbers? The noise of several footsteps approaching the dig site shook him from his thoughts.

"Mick," shouted Uncle B, "these are the men that Clay hired to help us with the excavation. And this is their supervisor, Ramon." Mick turned towards the crew and introduced himself. Reaching out to shake Ramon's hand, Mick noticed that Joelle was standing among the men as well.

"Ramon," said Mick, "this is my wife Joelle. We were just ready to take a look inside the vault. If all goes as planned, we will be taking the rest of this wall down shortly."

"My men will follow my orders," said Ramon. "Just let me know what you need done."

Mick reached out and took hold of the powerful flashlight that Joelle had brought him. Although the air on the inside of the vault was now filled with sawdust particles from cutting the timbers, Mick could still see the outline of objects inside the vault. As his flashlight beam shone back and forth across the room, glimmers of light reflected off of the larger golden objects. This was the place. Kenzie's research had been correct. Now it was time to remove the rest of the wall and begin the excavation process.

Mick stood up and walked toward Joelle and Uncle B with a big grin on his face. "I think we found the Celtic treasures," said Mick.

"What could you see?" asked Joelle excitedly.

"The vault appears to have a few large items that glimmered a golden color when the light hit them. The rest of the room appears to be filled with cloth bags of some kind. We really won't know much until we get this timber wall removed," said Mick.

After receiving specific instructions from Mick, Ramon spoke with his crew and explained what needed to be done. As Mick and Uncle B worked to saw timbers away from the soil holding them in place on each end, Ramon's crew members removed the sections and then carried them away. Foot by foot, the timber wall became shorter. Before Mick and Uncle B removed the last three rows of wood, they instructed Ramon to retrieve all of the two by fours, sheets of plywood and floor jacks from the truck. These would be used to shore up the vault ceiling as Clay had recommended.

As Ramon and his crew returned from the truck, they were accompanied by three other men. It was easy to distinguish

Giorgio's men from Ramon's. Each of Giorgio's men was dressed in black military style fatigues and carried a Heckler and Koch MP5 machine pistol. The largest of the three men looked directly into Mick's eyes and spoke. His tone was direct and uncompromising.

"We are here to transport the items. As you excavate the site, we will be watching. Every item is to be placed onto the truck. We will not be assisting you in any way. We will be observing only. If anyone here attempts to steal something from the site, he or she will be shot. No excuses. Do you have any questions?" Joelle looked with piercing blue eyes directly at the man speaking to her husband.

"Yes, I do," said Joelle. "When will our daughter be released"?

"I don't know anything about your daughter, nor do I care. I have been instructed to contact Giorgio once our truck is loaded and in route. Nothing more. I suggest you get busy. I have instructions to be on the road by sunrise."

Mick and Uncle B resumed sawing the last three rows of timbers while Ramon and his crew began placing floor jacks throughout the vault. As Clay had predicted, the vault still contained an air pocket and had not collapsed in any section. Once the roof of the underground room was stabilized and would resist collapse, Mick had Ramon placed portable lights in several locations to illuminate the room.

Joelle began at the back of the vault photographing and cataloging each antiquity. Although there were a few large golden statues and ornamental shields of war, most all of the smaller treasures had been placed into what appeared to be woolen bags. The passage of over two thousand years had dried out the bags and they turned to dust when touched. However, the beautiful items they contained looked untarnished by the passage of time.

As Joelle and Mick worked in each area of the vault, they found jewels, amber, coins, golden buckles with animal motifs, golden torcs of every size and design, golden helmets, bracelets, rings, small statues of gods and goddesses, Celtic crosses, gold covered mirrors, necklaces and pendants. The items were carefully placed into various sizes of storage containers and sealed. Once the containers were stacked at the vault opening, Ramon's crew loaded them onto the truck. One of Giorgio's men stood guard at the opening to the vault, one next to the truck and one man in-between the two locations. They watched the work crew carefully to assure that none of the precious artifacts were stolen.

"Mick, this is an incredible find," said Joelle. "The value of these antiquities is probably close to one hundred million dollars."

"Which of the smaller items do you think is the most valuable or would be most prized by Marcus?" asked Mick.

"I know what you are thinking," said Joelle with a smile. "But you heard their warning. Take something from the vault and they will shoot us."

"They have to catch us first," said Mick. "Besides, I want something to hold over Marcus's head if he doesn't release Kenzie as promised. We don't have to take it with us, we can simply bury it here and return later."

"In that case, yes, I did come across an item that I believe Marcus would crave for his collection," said Joelle. "Follow me."

Mick and Joelle walked about midway into the vault area and stopped next to a large golden statue. "Joelle," said Mick with a grin on his face, "I think that might be slightly too large for us to bury without being noticed." She looked at Mick and raised her left eyebrow.

"Really? Not the statue, Mick, look next to the base of the statue," said Joelle. "See the wooden box"? Mick crouched next to the statue and ran his hand across the finally crafted wooden box. As his hand passed across the lid brushing away a thin layer of dust, an image appeared. "I found this earlier and moved it here. I believe that whatever is inside this box belonged to a wealthy man. This is the same symbol I found chiseled into the marker stone. It's the lyre and a letter 'C'."

"Did you open it yet?" asked Mick.

"No, I wanted you to see it first," said Joelle. "The guard can't see us from this angle. I'll keep an eye on him while you open the lid."

Mick took out a small pocketknife and used it to pry along the box edge. "Hmmm," said Mick. "It doesn't seem to want to open. Let me look at it more carefully." As Mick turned the box over in his hands and carefully studied the surface on each side, he noticed a different color of wood near one corner. "I wonder," he said. Holding the box in his left hand and using the thumb on his right hand to push on the darkly colored area, Mick heard a faint click. The lid released and popped up enough that it could be opened. "Let's see what's inside," said Mick.

Raising the lid slowly as if something might jump out and scare him, Mick pushed it open and they both looked inside. All they saw was a woolen bag, much like the ones scattered around the vault. Joelle lifted the bag from its resting place and it disintegrated, revealing its contents. It was a solid golden torc neck piece nearly two inches thick. Intricate carvings adorned every surface. At each end of the U shaped neck piece, were large precious stones. In the middle, a capital 'A' and above it a sword.

"This is exactly what we need to guarantee Kenzie's safe return," said Mick. "Let's get it back in the box and buried for safe keeping. We can come back and get it later today." As Mick and Uncle B continued to carry sealed storage boxes to the vault's entrance, Joelle worked to bury the wooden box. She measured three feet diagonally across the floor from the right rear corner and dug a small hole. Once the box was placed underground, Joelle packed the soil tightly around it and covered it with loose rock and soil. Unless someone used a metal detector on the site, it would go unnoticed.

Most of the smaller contents of the vault had been removed and loaded onto the truck. A few storage containers remained, but would be loaded next. Each large golden statue was carried to the truck separately and secured. Before they were ready to leave, Giorgio's men made a sweep of the vault. The three men emerged and approached Mick. Again, the largest man was the only one to speak. "It seems you have followed my orders and have removed all of the treasures. But before we leave, each of you and your work crew will be scanned for metal. Have everyone line up behind you."

Mick, Joelle and Uncle B knew that they had not placed any of the treasures in their pockets, but they were unsure of Ramon or his men. Slowly, each man was scanned with a Garrett hand-held wand by Giorgio's thugs. Other than audible beeps as belt buckles and pocket change were detected, nothing else was found. No one had stolen any of the treasures. Satisfied with the results, Giorgio's men retreated toward the truck. Throughout the entire night, they had not noticed any of the well-armed men O'Shanahan had brought in from Dublin for back up. If the Scott's or O'Shanahan's lives would have been threatened, the men from Dublin would have opened fire.

"You have what you came for," said Mick. "When will you call Giorgio so that he releases our daughter"?

"As I explained before," said the largest man of the three, "I will make a phone call once this truck is on the road. Not sooner. We have one more task to accomplish." He looked at his two men and nodded. They began moving toward the vault with their weapons raised.

Pulling fragmentation grenades from their utility belts, each man tossed an explosive into the empty vault. The explosion immediately caused the vault ceiling to splinter and collapse. The treasure site was now just a deep hole with a pile of broken timbers and dirt covering it. Looking satisfied with their work, all three of Giorgio's men climbed into the truck and drove away. Mick and Joelle could only hope that a phone call would be made to Giorgio to release Kenzie.

Seeing that they could now emerge from the safety of tree cover, the six men from Dublin walked slowly towards the treasure site. No one but O'Shanahan and the Scotts knew that they had back up. Ramon's work crew starred at the men as they walked out of the trees. Uncle B turned towards Ramon and said, "I thought we might want some insurance just in case Giorgio's men decided to play rough."

"Probably a good idea," said Ramon. "But I'm glad we did not need them."

After the men from Dublin departed, Mick directed Ramon and his crew to assist him in clearing away debris caused by the explosion. Once all of the timbers and dirt were removed, Joelle worked quickly to find the wooden box she buried less than an hour earlier. Measuring out from the corner wall, she identified the location and removed the box and its ancient contents. Uncle B was not aware that she had hidden the treasure or why she and Mick had taken such a risk.

"Joelle, what is in the box?" asked Uncle B. "You obviously knew it was buried there. What treasure can be worth risking your lives?"

"Mick and I found this at the back of the vault and believe that it belonged to a very wealthy warrior," explained Joelle. As she depressed the secret latch allowing the lid to open, the beautiful golden Celtic torc came into view.

"Wow, that truly is beautiful," said Uncle B. "But I still don't know why you would risk your lives over it."

"Just like you," said Mick, "we wanted some insurance. If Marcus does not release Kenzie as he has promised, I think we can use this as a bargaining chip."

"That's a great idea," said Uncle B. "Hopefully, it will not be necessary, but I understand your motivation."

After Ramon and his men assisted with stowing all of the excavation gear on the truck and saying their goodbyes to the Scotts and Uncle B, they disappeared back the way they arrived. With the Bobcat compact excavator secured, Uncle B pulled his truck on to La Rue de la Blinerie and headed back toward Saint Helier. Mick and Joelle followed closely behind.

It was first light and the sun was making its way into the morning sky as Uncle B and the Scott's arrived at their hotel. Exhausted after a night of hard physical labor at the excavation site, they were all ready to get some rest.

CHAPTER 36

A T A SMALL airport near Saint Peter, Jersey Island, Giorgio's hired men completed loading the Sostos private jet with antiquities. Once the plane was safely airborne and headed towards Rome, a phone call was placed to Giorgio. "All of the treasure has been recovered and is on its way to the specified location," said the large man. "I trust our payment will be wired as previously agreed"?

"Yes, of course," said Giorgio. "As soon as the shipment arrives, I will make arrangements for the wire transfer. You should have your money later today."

Pleased with the news he had just received, Giorgio walked out of his office and across the estate, quickly heading for the garden grotto. He expected to find Marcus having breakfast with his wife, Sabina. As he approached the beautiful patio area, he was surprised to find Marcus by himself. "Sir, I have an update on our project on Jersey Island," said Giorgio. Marcus was reading the morning news and enjoying his coffee. He didn't quit reading or lift his head as Giorgio spoke.

"And what is your update?" said Marcus in a dry tone.

"All of the treasures have been recovered from Le Dolmen du Mont Ubé and transferred to our private plane," said Giorgio. "It is currently in flight and will arrive here late this afternoon. Do you want me to contact our men on Cézembre Island and release the Scott's daughter as we promised?"

"You are certain that the treasures are in route?" asked Marcus.

"Yes sir, I am certain," said Giorgio.

"Then proceed with returning her to her famous parents," said Marcus. "I'm feeling generous. It must be my gracious holiday spirit." Marcus gave Giorgio a dismissive look and went back to reading his newspaper.

It was mid-morning in Saint Helier when the phone began ringing in the Scott's hotel room. Only a few hours earlier they had arrived back at Pomme d'Or Hotel and were sound asleep. Mick was a light sleeper and rose quickly from the bed upon hearing the phone. When he saw that the call originated from outside of the area, he hoped it was a call about his daughter.

"Hello, Mick here."

"This is Giorgio. You were very wise to follow my instructions. Your daughter will be released later today near the ferry pier in Saint Helier. She will arrive around 4:00 p.m. Do not be late." Giorgio hung up his phone before could Mick could say a single word. Joelle was awakened by the phone ringing and was listening to the conversation.

"Who was that?" asked Joelle. "You didn't say a word."

"That was Giorgio," said Mick. "He called us to verify that Kenzie will be released this afternoon around 4:00 p.m. They are dropping her off near the ferry pier in Saint Helier."

"Did he say if she was ok?" said Joelle. "What else did he tell you"?

"That was it," said Mick. "That was all he told me, then he hung up." Mick started walking towards the bathroom, then spun back to face Joelle. "Hold it, he did say one other thing.

He said that we were wise to follow his instructions. He also warned me not to be late," said Mick.

"Sounds like we got away with keeping the wooden box containing the golden torc," said Joelle.

"I'm pleased that we have it, just in case something still goes wrong," agreed Mick. "It's not much, but it's the only leverage we have over Marcus."

CHAPTER 37

ICK, JOELLE, UNCLE B and Danielle were all waiting with the local police at the Jersey Island ferry pier expecting Kenzie to arrive by car. It was almost 4:00 p.m. on Christmas Eve and the streets of Saint Helier were nearly empty. As a black Mercedes sedan with darkened windows slowed along the curb near the pier, the Scotts looked inside expecting to see Kenzie. But it was not her, just a last minute passenger being dropped off for the ferry to Saint Malo. Mick had received a call from Giorgio earlier in the day instructing him to be at the pier around 4:00 p.m. He hoped Giorgio would keep his word and return Kenzie unharmed.

Another twenty minutes passed and not a single car approached the pier. Mick and Joelle were getting very worried about their daughter. About that same time, the Saint Malo ferry whistle sounded as it neared the dock. Ropes were thrown toward the pier and secured around large yellow bollards. Once the ferry shut down its engines, passengers were allowed to disembark. Mick and Joelle turned toward the ferry terminal and realized that their daughter Kenzie, was walking toward them.

"Mick, it's our little girl," cried Joelle. "She's ok." Both Mick and Joelle ran towards Kenzie with Uncle B, Danielle and the Saint Helier Police close behind. Moments later, Kenzie was embraced by her mom and dad and welcomed back by her best friend, Danielle.

"Did they hurt you?" asked Mick. "Are you ok"? Kenzie gave him a sarcastic look.

"Do you mean other than being taken hostage, tied up, Tasered multiple times, tossed into a nasty dark cell, barely fed and my life threatened for days? Nope, I'm good." Both Mick and Joelle grinned at their daughter's dry sense of humor and then tightly embraced her.

"We're so sorry this happened to you," said Joelle. "We can't undo what they did, but you are safe now. Let's go back to the hotel so that you can rest. I know you want to get cleaned up and eat as well. We are staying at Pomme d'Or Hotel. It's just around the corner, a short walk from here. Do you feel up to walking?"

"Yes, I'm fine," said Kenzie. Although she was completely exhausted, Kenzie did not want to admit it to her mom.

Before the Scotts and Danielle left the pier area, Uncle B ran to catch them. "I was just speaking with the police and they want to interview Kenzie about the coin heist and the men who kidnapped her," said Uncle B. "They said that they are willing to wait a few days since it's Christmas Eve."

"That's good, because no one is taking her from us today," said Mick. "Once she has rested and feels like traveling in a day or two, we are going to spend the rest of the holidays with you in Dublin as we had originally planned. We can all return here after the first of the year to meet with the Police."

"I agree," said Uncle B, "I will let them know. I'll meet you at the hotel shortly."

CHAPTER 38

MARCUS HAD BEEN anxiously awaiting the arrival of the ancient golden coins for nearly six months. Earlier in the year after reading a news article about two treasure hunters finding a large horde of two thousand year old Celtic coins on Jersey Island, he began making plans to acquire them. Marcus wanted the coins not for the sake of their sixteen million dollar value, but because he believed that they would have been captured as Roman property when Caesar's armies conquered France in 56 BC. As a direct descendant of Julius Caesar, Marcus was entitled to the coins, or so he believed.

It was quite the norm for a Sostos Delivery truck to visit the Demetrius estate each week. In fact, deliveries of various materials were made on almost a daily basis, but today was different. As the heavily loaded delivery truck approached the villa, it was obvious this was not a typical delivery. As the driver checked in at the well-guarded entrance gate, a phone call was placed to Giorgio.

"Sir," said the gate guard, "your special delivery has arrived."

"Excellent," said Giorgio. "They are right on time. Send them to Building Four." The guard opened the security gate and instructed the driver to continue down the main road and take the first left turn. The truck would be met by a work crew when it arrived at the building.

Giorgio was relieved that the golden coins had arrived before Christmas as he promised Marcus. However, before he alerted Marcus about their arrival, he preferred to check the truck's cargo himself. As Giorgio arrived at Building Four, the truck's rear doors were already open and a forklift was working to remove what appeared to be a large, steel waste container. Carefully, the forklift driver maneuvered the machine into position and began lifting the heavy load. Giorgio directed his men to move the container into the open garage area within Building Four and then close the doors.

The entire horde of coins was lowered into the container immediately after the heist and the lid welded shut. No one had seen what was inside the container since it was closed. Giorgio was hopeful that when the lid was cut open, everything inside would be as he expected. To assure that all of the coins were moved out of the steel container and into the cleaning area without coins disappearing, Giorgio had three of his most trusted men guarding the room. Each man was armed with a Heckler and Koch MP5 machine pistol and proficient in its use.

The lid was opened and Giorgio peered inside. "They are as magnificent as Marcus described," said Giorgio. "There must be tens of thousands of ancient golden coins melded together." Turning to the supervisor of the work crew, Giorgio began quickly issuing instructions. "These need to be lifted from the container and moved into the adjoining room for cleaning. I want to present these to Marcus later this evening. All of the loose soil must be removed and the coins made as clean as possible. You have three hours to prepare them for viewing. Get to work."

Giorgio left Building Four and headed for the main house. He was anxious to share the news with Marcus that his Celtic coins had arrived. Hopefully, the delivery truck carrying the Celtic treasure from Jersey Island would arrive tonight as well. He could only wish that everything arrived as planned.

As Giorgio entered the main house of the estate and made his way towards the conference room, he noticed Marcus sitting alone in the library. "Good evening sir. I have good news for you," said Giorgio.

"That's excellent," said Marcus, "but first I have a question for you. We have been associates for many years. You've supported me on every project and have always been loyal." Giorgio was surprised by Marcus's solemn tone and his appearance of vulnerability.

"Yes sir, how can I be of assistance?" asked Giorgio.

"You may have noticed that I was having breakfast by myself in the grotto this morning," said Marcus. "Sabina did not join me. Likewise, here I am sitting in the library enjoying a fine merlot by myself. She seems distant and uneasy being in my presence. Has she spoken to you about anything or have you noticed any odd behavior?" asked Marcus.

"I can't say that I have spoken to Sabina lately, but I have noticed her frequent absences from the estate," said Giorgio. "A few days ago I overheard her speaking with her father on the phone. She seemed very upset and I heard her mention Jersey Island and that she had overheard a closed door meeting with you and me. She told him that she only heard bits and pieces of information, but was troubled by the words and wanted to confide in her father. He seemed to agree to help."

"Go on, what happened next?" asked Marcus.

"Then the next day," said Giorgio, "Theophilos came to the villa to meet with her."

"Do you know the subject of their meeting?" asked Marcus.

"I don't know exactly what was discussed," replied Giorgio, "but she appeared very upset by whatever her father said to her. Before he left, they embraced and shook their heads as if in agreement."

"Hmmmm," said Marcus while rubbing his chin. "It seems they may know something about our project on Jersey Island. We will need to watch both of them very carefully."

"I agree sir, I will report anything I see or hear," said Giorgio.

"What was that good news you spoke of when you came into the library?" asked Marcus.

"The coins have arrived sir. Your Celtic coins from Jersey Island," said Giorgio. "They are still being cleaned and prepared for viewing. If you would like to join me in Building Four at 8:00 p.m., I think you will be quite pleased."

"Thank you Giorgio," said Marcus. "That is good news. What is the status on the larger shipment?"

"I spoke with the pilot and we are expecting delivery before midnight tonight," said Giorgio. "Once the plane lands, the cargo will be loaded into a Sostos delivery truck and driven here to the estate."

"Good, well done Giorgio," exclaimed Marcus. "I will see you in Building Four at 8:00 p.m. sharp."

Across the estate in a small, one level room that Marcus and Giorgio rarely visited, Sabina was enjoying a quiet conversation with her father. He had come to spend time with her on Christmas Eve, but also to apprise her of new information he had discovered about Marcus.

Theophilos Sostos had been very surprised by Sabina's accusations against Marcus. The young man that he took under his wing years earlier had been a natural in the shipping business and was creating a nice life for both himself and Sabina. Although he doubted Marcus was involved in any wrong doing, he loved and trusted his daughter completely. If she thought something was wrong, he should at least look into it.

Theophilos had agreed to investigate the issues and get back to Sabina as quickly as possible. Sostos made a few phone calls and instructed an associate to begin following Marcus. Two days later, Sostos had received a complete background profile that was much different than the one he pulled prior to Marcus marrying his daughter ten years earlier.

"Sabina," said her father, "I took the information that you gave me and had my associates begin watching Marcus closely. Your suspicions were correct, he is involved in many aspects of organized crime and has a history of doing whatever it takes to reach his goals. He has become quite wealthy and powerful aside from the money he has made through his legitimate interests in Sostos Shipping. I also have information that proves he has not be faithful to you, and on more than one occasion. Marcus is not the man he pretends to be," said Theophilos.

Sabina, although not entirely shocked by the news, was still visibly trembling. "I knew something was wrong," said Sabina, "but as we grew further apart over the years, I became accustomed to Marcus's frequent business trips and odd business associates. I expected that he bent the law on occasion to make deals, but I had no idea that he was a criminal. You said that you found he has ties to organized crime? Has he murdered anyone?" Sabina was sobbing at this point and her father did not want to torment her further.

"At this time Sabina," said Theophilos, "I don't have all of the details about Marcus's activities, but I would not underestimate him. I believe that he is entirely capable of murder. We need to be very careful. I think it would be best if you take an extended holiday and leave the estate as soon as possible."

"Father, tomorrow is Christmas day," said Sabina, "and next week we are hosting our annual New Year's Eve Masquerade Ball. It's a charity event and we have over two hundred guests that will be attending. The soonest I could possibly get away from here would be later next week."

"Then that should be our plan," said Theophilos. "But don't wait any later than January 10th before you leave on holiday. It will not be safe to stay here."

"What do have in mind father?" asked Sabina.

"I have several connections within Interpol," said Theophilos, "and I think they would be most interested hearing about the illegal businesses Marcus is running. In fact, they may already be watching him. Regardless, he needs to be stopped and I need to know that you are safe. For now, let's just keep this between us. Go about your typical daily routine and treat Marcus like nothing has happened. We can talk more and finalize your plans next week before New Year's Eve."

"Thank you father," said Sabina, "good night."

CHAPTER 39

U NCLE B HAD arrived at the Pomme d'Or Hotel about an hour after the Scotts and went to his room to freshen up. It was nearly 8:00 p.m. when he entered the Scott's suite. "Mick, I arranged everything with the Saint Helier Police," said Uncle B. "They understand that Kenzie went through a lot of anguish over the last few days and they agreed to conduct her and Danielle's interviews after the first of the year."

"So when do we need to be back on Jersey Island?" asked Mick.

"I agreed that we would have both of the girls back here on January 2nd," said Uncle B. "That should give all of us a chance to recover from the last few days."

Joelle had been listening to their conversation from the adjoining room and decided to join in. "So, I assume we are spending the night here, but are we flying out to Dublin tomorrow?" asked Joelle. "It's Christmas day and I would really prefer that we stay here and enjoy the holiday instead of sitting on a plane."

"You get your wish, Joelle," said Mick. "There are no flights out tomorrow. We will be leaving for Dublin on the 26th."

"Before it gets too late here, let's give Clay a call," said Joelle. "I'm sure that he's anxious to hear that Kenzie is ok and we can fill him in on the results of the excavation." Mick picked up his cell and dialed Clay's number, then put it on speaker phone so that Joelle could hear. It rang a few times and Clay answered.

"Merry Christmas Eve," said Mick to his son. "Are you still at work"?

"No, I actually I have the day off and I'm running some last minute errands," said Clay. "What's up? I hadn't heard from you or Joelle since we discussed the excavation a few days ago. I was beginning to get worried."

"We're all ok," said Mick. "They released Kenzie as promised and we are staying at the Pomme d'Or Hotel in Saint Helier. She's ok, she just needs a lot of rest. They were pretty hard on her."

"If I know her," said Clay, "she probably dished it back to them as well. She's a tough little sister. If they released her, the excavation of treasure must have been a success."

"It went extremely well," said Mick. "Joelle catalogued all of the items we found and we have photographs of each. We were able to retain one piece that could be a very important find. It's a large golden torc that was encased in a sealed wooden box. It bore the Coriosolite's lyre symbol and we believe it may have belonged to the King who ordered their treasures buried. I will email photos of it and the box to you tonight."

"Thanks, I'll begin my research," said Clay. "What are you and the O'Shanahans doing for the rest of the holidays"?

"We plan on celebrating Christmas here tomorrow and then flying back to Dublin the next day," answered Mick. "Uncle B has invited us to stay with him and Danielle through New Year's Day. After that, we agreed to return to Saint Helier so that the police can take both Kenzie's and Danielle's statements about the coin heist."

"Hey, Dad," said Clay. "I gotta run. I'll give you all a call tomorrow on Christmas Day. Gotta go, bye." Mick and Joelle had both gotten used to Clay's idiosyncrasies and quick phone exits.

"I guess he's done talking to us," said Mick with a chuckle. "He said he'd call us back tomorrow."

CHAPTER 40

I T WAS 8:00 p.m. sharp as Marcus walked into Building Four by himself. He rarely came to this building, but tonight was a special occasion. The building's primary purpose was to prepare collectables for presentation within the walls of the estate. Marcus had an extensive collection of Roman and pre-Roman artifacts that would rival many of the world's finest art museums. Tonight, he would be adding to that collection.

Giorgio emerged from a small office area and greeted Marcus upon his arrival. Building Four was comprised of one large two-story room for arrival and departure of goods, several small well lit cleaning and restoration rooms, a fully functional lab, a walk-in vault and Giorgio's office. Security cameras were visible throughout the entire building and were closely monitored 24/7 by staff in a secure room adjoining the main estate. Marcus did not take security of his prized possessions lightly.

"As you know," began Giorgio, "the coins on display in the Jersey Museum were left in their natural state, just as they were found. Most of the coins were melded into a large mass where they were buried over the last two thousand years. Only a few hundred coins were loose so that we can identify the artwork on the front and back of each."

"Will our restoration experts be able to separate more individual coins from the mass?" asked Marcus.

"They are hopeful," said Giorgio. "It will be a painstaking process, but they will preserve these antiquities with the upmost care. Would you like to see their progress?"

"Most certainly," said Marcus. "Please lead the way."

Several technicians were busy cleaning and sorting coins in the first restoration room. They would not be leaving to celebrate Christmas with their families or most likely New Year's Day. However, they were being paid very, very well and were willing to comply with the round-the-clock assignment. "Please select some of the fully restored coins for Mr. Demetrius to view," Giorgio instructed the technician. The thin, grey-haired technician instantly complied and presented a small tray of golden coins for Marcus to inspect.

"These are remarkable," exclaimed Marcus. "The condition of these coins is miraculous for their age." He picked up a coin and turned it over and over in his hands. "The artwork on this coin depicts a stylized head of Apollo facing right and on the reverse side an image of a charioteer and horse boar." Giorgio feigned an interest in the coin and gave Marcus his undivided attention as he continued his proud rant. "If these coins were not buried on Jersey Island over two thousand years ago, my ancestors would have possessed these as they completed their expansion across France. However, they are now finally in the hands of their rightful owner, a descendant of Julius Caesar. Giorgio, show me the rest of the horde."

As Marcus toured the rest of Building Four he saw the remainder of the coin horde in different phases of restoration. In each room he grew more and more excited over his recent acquisition. "Giorgio," shouted Marcus. "When will the Celtic treasure shipment arrive from Saint Helier? Seeing these ancient coins has rekindled my desire to own more of my ancestor's antiquities."

"It is expected before midnight tonight," said Giorgio. "I spoke with the pilot just before I came to Building Four. He is estimating his arrival around 10:00 p.m. Once the shipment is loaded onto our truck, it should arrive here at the estate before midnight. Do you want me to notify you when it arrives?"

"Yes, of course," said Marcus. "I would expect nothing less." As he left the building and walked towards the main house, Marcus continued to admire the ancient coin in his hand. His thoughts drifted forward in time and he began imagining the treasures he would see later that evening.

CHAPTER 41

WITH CHRISTMAS BEHIND him and New Year's Day less than a week away, Theophilos Sostos decided to make a phone call to an old friend working for Interpol. At this point, he believed he had enough evidence of Marcus's involvement in illegal activities that Interpol would be interested in beginning an investigation.

"I'm calling for agent Louis, Frederick Louis," said Theophilos into his phone.

"He is currently on his line, would you like to hold?" said the operator.

"Sure, I will wait," said Theophilos. A few minutes later a familiar voice came on the line.

"This is Frederick, who am I speaking to?"

"Frederick, this is Theophilos Sostos, how have you been?"

"It's good to hear your voice old friend," said Frederick. "How are you"?

"Very well," said Theophilos, "I have a wonderful life here in Rome."

"How can I help you?" asked Frederick.

"I have conducted some preliminary research into my son-in-law's business activities and I believe that he may be involved in organized crime," explained Theophilos. "Of course he has an active interest in Sostos Enterprises, but it seems he may have been using my legitimate company as a front for his illegal operations. His name is Marcus Demetrius. Do you have any information on him?"

"Theophilos, it's been a long time," said agent Louis. "Thank you for making contact about Demetrius. The short answer to your question is, yes. Actually we been working for the last two years compiling evidence of his activities so that we could pursue him. Whatever specific records or documents that you have concerning his organizations would be very beneficial."

"I understand," said Theophilos, "just give me your email address and I can send everything I have to you." The men exchanged contact information and agreed to touch base within the next seventy two hours. Theophilos believed that he had done the right thing. He had known his son-in-law, Marcus, for many years and he wanted to give him the benefit of the doubt. On the other hand, he would do anything to protect his daughter from harm.

Several days had passed since the treasure shipment arrived at the Demetrius estate. Unloaded into Building Four, the vast treasure trove took up much of the space in the main room. Marcus had seen the antiquities as they were delivered, but was more interested in seeing each of the items as they were restored. He made arrangements earlier that day with Giorgio to meet him in the restoration area at 4:00 p.m.

"I think you will be very happy with the progress we have made so far in restoring one of the largest golden statues in the collection," said Giorgio. "Considering the age of these items, most of them are quite well preserved and will require minimal restoration." Intricate patterns had been carved into the statue over most of its surface. Marcus ran his fingers across the design in awe of the incredible craftsmanship.

"Are the other antiquities as remarkable as this?" asked Marcus.

"Yes sir," answered Giorgio, "they are. I believe these are some of the finest examples of Celtic art that have been found to date."

"Any idea of the value of such a collection?" asked Marcus.

"That is hard to say sir," said Giorgio, "but considering the number of items and their condition, a museum would probably value this collection at seventy three million euros or more."

"That's an incredible sum," said Marcus. "However, their value to me is measured quite differently." Marcus began recounting his numerous acquisitions of Roman antiquities over the years and his ancestral connection to Julius Caesar. Demetrius had amassed one of the largest private collections of Roman treasures in the world. His estate was filled with hidden galleries of priceless antiquities. Galleries filled with weaponry, jewelry, artwork, coins, and various rare treasures. Only a few of the many galleries were available for public viewing. Most of them were hidden on subterranean levels or behind false walls. Only Giorgio and Marcus had access to every gallery.

"Giorgio, this is only the beginning," said Marcus. "We know that the Scott's have found evidence of other Celtic treasures buried in the area around Saint Malo. At least two other sites. I must acquire the rest of the antiquities. These could possibly be the remaining treasures of the Coriosolite tribe. We need to contact O'Shanahan and persuade him to help us with the Scotts again." Giorgio paused before he spoke.

"Do you think he will be willing to get involved again considering what just happened to his daughter and the Scott's daughter?" asked Giorgio.

"If the amount we offer him is substantial, he will do whatever we ask," answered Marcus. "Of course, if he refuses, we can always kidnap their daughters again until they comply. I really don't care which way they choose, just make it happen."

"Yes, sir," responded Giorgio hesitantly, "I will make the arrangements."

CHAPTER 42

THE HOLIDAYS WENT by very quickly for the Scotts and O'Shanahans, but now it was time to return to Jersey Island as they had promised Chief Bowman. Traveling by chartered plane from Dublin into Saint Helier airport was the most direct route and avoided all of the hassles of commercial travel. They landed just before noon, picked up their rental car and headed toward the Saint Helier Police Station. Both Danielle and Kenzie were very nervous about speaking with the police, but they hoped the information would help catch the thieves.

"It's good to see you all together again," said Chief Bowman. "I'm thankful that both young ladies were returned to you unharmed. Not all hostage situations turn out this well."

"We are aware of that," said Joelle. "I'm sure that the girls will be happy to answer any questions that you think will help you apprehend the kidnappers. How would you like to start?"

Chief Bowman selected one of his best detectives for the interrogation. He wanted someone with excellent communication skills and the ability to calmly obtain all of the details without further traumatizing the girls. "This will probably take a few hours," said Chief Bowman. "There are several excellent cafés nearby. You would most likely be more comfortable waiting there than sitting here at the station. Mr. Scott, I have your cell number. I will call you as soon as we finish with both of the girls." Mick, Joelle and Uncle B agreed that a café would be a more enjoyable place to wait and it would give them an opportunity to talk in private.

By mid-afternoon, both the Scotts and Uncle B were becoming frustrated by the long wait. They expected to hear from Chief Bowman around 2:00 p.m. and it was now 3:15 p.m. "I can't understand what is taking so long with the interviews," said Joelle. Before Mick could respond, his cell phone rang.

"Yes, I understand. Thank you," said Mick. "That was the Chief. They have finished with the girls and we can pick them up at the station."

"Your daughters have been extremely helpful," said Chief Bowman. "I am hopeful that with this additional information, we will be able to track down the thieves behind this crime. Thank you again for all of your support. We hope to see you again in Saint Helier. Of course, next time, under better circumstances."

It had been a long day for everyone and Joelle knew that the girls had to be hungry. "Mick and I would like to take all of you to our favorite restaurant here in Saint Helier," said Joelle. "We can enjoy a fantastic meal and watch the sunset over the Channel. It's our last evening together before Danielle and Kenzie fly back to ASU." Everyone agreed as they piled into the small rental car and drove toward the restaurant.

Although the holidays were over, nearly every table in the restaurant was occupied. "We are fortunate to get this table for five located next to a large window," said Uncle B. "Someone here must have a connection."

"The maître d' always takes very good care of us," said Mick. "I'm glad you are enjoying the view. Joelle, would you like some wine this evening?"

"Absolutely," responded Joelle. "We need to celebrate Danielle and Kenzie's safe return and our somewhat successful excavation."

After selecting several local wines for everyone to sample, Mick began talking about the extensive menu and his recommendations. It was a welcome change to be talking about something other than the kidnappings. "I've decided to have the Chilean Sea Bass with prawn and lemon butter tonight," said Mick. "Joelle, are you having your usual?"

"No, actually, I'm trying something new. I've decided to have the braised leg of lamb steak with garlic mashed potatoes and mixed vegetables. How about you Kenzie? What sounds good to you?" Both of the girls were so happy to be out of captivity and back in normal surroundings that they would be happy eating anything put in front of them.

The sun had set slowly over the Channel providing a spectacular dinner show for the Scotts and O'Shanahans. "We have made some really good and not so good memories on this trip," said Kenzie. "The time Danielle and I spent with Keira touring Dublin was a lot of fun. I really hope she is ok."

"I do too," said Danielle. "Do you think she escaped and went back to Dublin"?

"It's hard to say," said Uncle B. "I called the Braden Head Pub after all of you were reported missing. No one at the pub has heard from her since the day you all left for Jersey Island. We may never know what happened."

"I want to believe that she is ok," said Danielle. "And that's the way I'm going to remember her."

CHAPTER 43

EARLY THURSDAY MORNING, the Scotts and O'Shanahans boarded their chartered plane back to Dublin. Once they landed and disembarked at the Dublin Airport, they said their goodbyes. Mick, Joelle and Uncle B were driving back to his house in Castleknock while the girls were continuing on to Phoenix and returning to ASU.

Kenzie and Danielle had a long day of travel ahead of them. The girls walked across the airport terminal toward gate four to catch Aer Lingus Flight 105 to JFK. Later in the day, they would transfer to another plane headed to Phoenix. "We have plenty of time before our next flight," said Kenzie. "Why don't we stop for a light lunch"?

As the two young women entered the Shamrock Pub, they noticed a familiar face behind the bar. Danielle and Kenzie looked at each other and then back at the young woman bartending. Was it really Keira, they wondered? They moved closer to the bar and Danielle was the first to speak. "Omg, Keira, we thought you were dead." The bartender looked at both of them, puzzled about their odd comment.

"Are you talking to me?" she asked.

"Yes, Keira, we are talking to you," said Kenzie. "Why are you acting so strange, like you don't even know us."?

"I'm sorry I resemble someone you know, but my name is not Keira. I'm Elizabeth, Elizabeth Kelly."

"You look just like our friend Keira," said Kenzie. "We were traveling together and visiting Jersey Island a few weeks ago. We got separated and never heard from you, I mean Keira again."

"And we don't know if she is dead or alive," added Danielle. "It's so strange. You could be her identical twin." While they were talking, Kenzie continued to study Elizabeth's features and noticed a birth mark in the shape of a heart on her right ankle. Kenzie could also see the tip of a Celtic cross tattoo just below Elizabeth's neckline.

"We're sorry we bothered you," said Kenzie. "We were just excited that we found our friend. Have a good day." Danielle looked at Kenzie and understood that she wanted to leave.

"Nice meeting you, Elizabeth," said Danielle. The girls began slowly walking toward gate four, totally confused by the strange encounter.

"Let's stop here and have a cup of coffee," said Kenzie to Danielle. The girls took their seats at a table that offered an unobstructed view of the airport pub.

"Ok Kenzie, what's up?" asked Danielle. "You were acting very weird back there."

"She can call herself Elizabeth or whatever, but that was Keira," said Kenzie.

"How can you be so sure?" asked Danielle. "If she was our friend Keira, why the deception? Why wouldn't she be glad to see us?"

"I don't know," said Kenzie. "But I do know that Keira has a heart shaped birthmark on her right ankle just like Elizabeth. She also has a Celtic cross tattoo just below her neckline on her left side. I am sure that was Keira. She must be hiding here for some reason and working under a different name."

As Kenzie and Danielle watched Elizabeth from a distance, they could see her taking out her cell phone and making a call. About twenty minutes later, a tall dark-haired man walked into the pub and approached Elizabeth. They embraced, kissed and then sat down at a pub table to talk. It was obvious they were lovers from their body language. "Does that look like the man in the photographs that Chief Bowman showed us yesterday?" asked Kenzie.

"It does," said Danielle. "I think his name was McFadden."

"If that is Keira and he is McFadden, she had to be in on the heist and the kidnapping," said Kenzie. "That's why she is in hiding and going by a different name."

"We need to get ahold of our parents," said Danielle. "With this information, the police may be able to catch who orchestrated the coin heist and held us hostage."

Kenzie took out her cell phone and dialed her stepfather's number. "Mick, it's Kenzie. Yeah, I'm fine. We're still at the Dublin airport waiting to board our plane. Something really strange just happened. We saw Keira."

"That's great," said Mick. "Is she ok? Why hadn't she contacted us?"

"We saw her working at a pub here at the airport," said Kenzie. "When we approached her, she denied that she was Keira and insisted that we had mistaken her for someone else. She claims her name is Elizabeth."

"Well Kenzie, maybe you did mistake her for Keira," suggested Mick. Kenzie explained to Mick about Elizabeth's birthmark, Celtic cross tattoo and then the appearance of McFadden.

"Kenzie, keep your distance from them," said Mick. "These people are very dangerous. I appreciate you calling me and letting me know this information. First thing tomorrow morning I will make a call to Chief Bowman. For now, get to your gate and don't miss your flight to JFK. When you arrive at Sky Harbor in Phoenix, I have arranged for a driver to pick up both of you. He will be waiting in the baggage claim area holding up a placard with your name. Before you get into his car, make sure you ask him for the code word. It is jellybean." Kenzie laughed at the code word and remembered that jellybean had been her safety word since she was a toddler.

"Thanks Mick," chuckled Kenzie. "I'm sure that we will be fine. I'll call you when we get back on campus at ASU. Love you."

CHAPTER 44

MICK AND JOELLE were happy to have some time to relax after the hectic holidays and everything that had occurred. Their interest in learning more about the possible treasure sites near Saint Malo had not diminished, but they needed more information. "We haven't talked with Clay in a few days," said Mick. "Why don't we give him a call and update him on the latest developments"?

"That's a good idea," said Joelle. "And we can ask him some more questions about Chablé Menhir and Champ Dolent. I'd really like to study each site more thoroughly."

Clay's phone rang several times before he could pick it up. He had missed the call, but it showed his dad's picture and name on the screen. Pressing the number, his phone rang a few times and then he heard his dad's voice. "Hey, sorry I missed your call," said Clay. "I was on the other side of the house working on the baby's room and didn't pick it up in time. How are you both doing? Are you still in Dublin?"

"We're fine," said Mick. "We are staying with Uncle B at his house and plan on flying back to Phoenix in the next week or so. We wanted to give you an update on your sister and we have a couple of questions about two of the possible treasure sites in France. Do you have a few minutes?"

"Sure," said Clay. "How is Kenzie and her friend Danielle?

Are they going back to school or do you think that is safe?" Mick activated his phone's speaker and had Joelle join him on the call.

"They are both fine," said Joelle. "The girls recovered quickly from the ordeal without any serious injuries. We were able to spend the rest of the holidays with them here in Dublin."

"Will they be going back to school?" asked Clay again.

"Yes, in fact, their plane should be landing shortly in Phoenix. We made arrangements for a driver to pick them up at the airport and take them back to their apartment near campus."

"Do you think it's safe considering they were kidnapped less than two weeks ago?" asked Clay.

"I contacted an associate in Phoenix and he has assigned two highly trained body guards to watch over them until we return," said Mick. "Ex-military contacts can be quite helpful. But you do raise a good point. Something rather odd happened to them at the airport in Dublin before they caught their flight."

Mick went on to explain the mysterious appearance of Keira at the airport pub and her attempt to conceal her identity from Kenzie and Danielle. "Why did she do that?" asked Clay.

"We aren't sure," said Mick, "but shortly after the encounter, Keira made a phone call and one of Giorgio's men showed up at the pub. It was evident that she and the man are close friends from their body language. We are fairly certain that Keira was somehow connected to the heist and kidnapping."

"Do you want me to run a thorough background search on her and her friend?" asked Clay.

"That would be very helpful," said Mick. "I also need you to find out everything you can about Chablé Menhir and

Champ Dolent. We may be planning an excavation and I'm not sure which French agencies would need to be notified."

"I should have all of it back to you early tomorrow," said Clay. "I'll give you a call. Gotta go."

Later than afternoon Mick and Joelle were enjoying a nap in a hammock on the enclosed patio and O'Shanahan was in the family room reading. His phone rang and it was Giorgio. He had hoped that his association with Giorgio and his sociopath boss, Marcus, was over. Why is Giorgio calling me, he thought? "Good afternoon, this is O'Shanahan," he said dryly.

"Brian, this is Giorgio," he said in an upbeat voice. "I hope the remainder of your holidays were enjoyable and I must apologize for the error we made in holding your daughter. I hope that she is well."

"Yes, she is fine," said O'Shanahan. "Why are you calling me"?

Giorgio was tempted to explode in anger at O'Shanahan's disrespectful tone, but he needed to win him over. Giorgio would say anything necessary to achieve that goal and gain O'Shanahan's cooperation. "We appreciate how much you helped us in acquiring the treasures on Jersey Island. Marcus is in awe at the beauty of the collection. He has asked that I secure your assistance in excavating and recovering the treasures near Saint Malo."

"And why would I do that?" asked O'Shanahan.

"I have a proposition for you to consider," said Giorgio. "Here is what I have in mind."

Giorgio's offer was one million five hundred thousand dollars in advance and one million five hundred thousand dollars upon delivery of treasures from both Chablé Menhir and Champ Dolent. Although it was a solid offer, O'Shanahan countered with three million dollars in advance and three million dollars upon delivery. If Brian could make this score, he would be set for life. After much dickering back and forth, they arrived at a number they could both live with.

"Ok, so I will wire you two million dollars today and you will receive three million dollars upon delivery of the treasures," said Giorgio. "Do we have a deal"?

"Not just yet," answered O'Shanahan. "I need to talk with the Scotts and get their agreement. They really don't need or care about the money, so I will need to find another motivator."

"Maybe this will help," said Giorgio. "I would rather pay what we agreed rather than take other actions to reach my goal. Do you understand me? Maybe next time your daughter is not so fortunate. I need your commitment within twenty four hours or I will be forced to make other arrangements. Good bye."

Uncle B considered Giorgio's proposition, but knew that he and Marcus could not be trusted. They already kidnapped his daughter once and would do it again if necessary. This could be an excellent opportunity to double-cross Marcus. I need to think this through, he thought.

That evening, Mick's cell phone rang and it was Clay. "I was able to find information on treasure searches on French soil quite easily," said Clay. "They are very restrictive in their approach and it will require the authorities' complete cooperation to conduct a dig at either of the two sites you provided me."

"What are the restrictions?" asked Mick. He knew that Clay would have a very detailed response and prepared himself to listen without interrupting.

"This is what I found," said Clay. "No one may use metal detecting equipment for the purpose of searching for monuments and objects which could interest prehistory, history, art or archaeology without first having obtained administrative authorization issued according to the qualification of the applicant and also the nature and method of searching. When the searches are to be carried out on land which does not belong to the applicant, the written application must be accompanied by a document of consent written by the owner of the land and, if appropriate, anyone else who has the right." Clay paused to catch his breath.

"So," said Mick. "We need permission."

"It's a little more complicated than that," said Clay, "but yes, you need permission to carry out a search or excavation."

"Were you able to get any more information on Keira or the male friend that met with her at the pub?" asked Mick.

"No, not yet," said Clay. "I will keep working on that and get back to you as soon as I find anything. Do I need to make arrangements again for the excavation equipment?"

"No, hold off. If we need it, I will get back to you," said Mick.

Uncle B had come back down stairs when he heard Mick's cell phone ringing and listened to part of the conversation. "You don't look too pleased with the information that Clay provided," said Uncle B.

"It's not that," said Mick, "it seems that the French laws are very restrictive on treasure seekers. We will need to jump through a lot of hoops to retrieve the treasures at Chablé Menhir and Champ Dolent. And, even if we can get permission to dig, I am not sure of the government's policy on treasure rights. We could end up with nothing."

"I have another complication for you to consider," said Uncle B. Joelle was now in the room as well and was curious what the two men were discussing.

"You two seem so serious," said Joelle. "What is going on"?

"I received a phone call this afternoon from Giorgio when you were both outside on the patio taking a nap."

"Why would he contact you?" asked Mick. "What did he have to say"?

"He has a proposition," said Uncle B. "They want more treasure."

Mick's face turned bright red as he stood up from his seat. Joelle had rarely seen Mick this angry, but if Giorgio was threatening them or their daughter again, she knew he would not allow it. "And what is his proposition?" asked Mick. "They won't kidnap our daughters again if we go along with their demands"?

"Actually, they have offered quite a large sum of money to us if we help them get the treasures thought to be buried near Chablé Menhir and Champ Dolent," said Uncle B.

"We don't need his money," stated Mick, "and he knows that. What else did he say?"

"Giorgio said that his boss, Marcus Demetrius, has demanded that the treasure be brought to him at whatever cost. If that means holding our girls hostage again or even killing them, he would go that far. Marcus is delusional and believes these treasures belong to him due to his ancestry. He will stop at nothing to get them."

Although Uncle B was enticed by the incredible five million dollar payout for betraying his friends, he was not sure if he could play the game. "I have an idea," said Uncle B. "What if we tell Giorgio that we will do as he asks and retrieve the treasure"? Both Mick and Joelle looked at Uncle B with astonishment.

"Are you serious?" asked Mick and Joelle in unison.

"Let me finish my thought," said Uncle B. "That is just the beginning. We know that Marcus Demetrius is in receipt of the treasures we excavated from Le Dolmen du Mont Ubé. More than likely he was behind the coin heist from the museum on Jersey Island. According to Clay's research, Marcus has one of the largest privately held collections of Roman artifacts in the world."

"Ok," said Mick. "You are starting to sound like Clay. Can you get to the point"?

"I think we should double-cross Marcus and use his obsession with Roman artifacts against him," explained Uncle B. Mick cracked a knowing smile and began adding his input to the plan.

"I like the way that sounds," said Mick. "We need to contact the authorities and discuss this with them. More than likely, the French National Police and Interpol would be very interested in recovering all of the antiquities that Marcus has stolen over the years. In addition, we are going to need the government's support to allow our excavation."

"But if we involve the authorities wouldn't Giorgio or Demetrius find out?" asked Joelle.

"Our plan will have to be crafted very carefully," said Mick. "We are going to need some assistance in planning out the logistics. I think I know just the right person to call."

CHAPTER 45

UNCLE B WASTED no time contacting Giorgio the next morning. "This is O'Shanahan," he said. "I've spoken with the Scotts and persuaded them to continue excavating the treasures at Chablé Menhir and Champ Dolent. They are under the impression that all of the recovered treasure will be excavated under French National Police supervision and then delivered to the Louvre in Paris."

"How do we get the treasures out of the Louvre?" asked Giorgio. "That seems like a very bad plan."

"There is more," said O'Shanahan, "please let me continue. I said that the Scotts have the impression that all of the treasure will be driven to Paris. Actually, the trucks will be switched mid-route. The trucks carrying the Celtic treasure will be driven to the Demetrius estate in Rome. The decoy trucks will continue on to their destination in Paris. Not until the trucks arrive at the Louvre will anyone suspect a switch. By then, it will be too late."

"Your plan is brilliant," said Giorgio. "But are you willing to let your friends be accused of switching the trucks and stealing the treasure"?

"I have convinced both Mick and Joelle that we are double-crossing Marcus," said O'Shanahan. "They think that the decoy trucks will be going to the Demetrius estate and the trucks carrying the treasure will be bound for the Louvre. The Scotts will not realize that I've duped them until it's too late. By then, I will be out of the country and five million dollars richer. They have their wealth and now I will have mine."

"It seems you have developed a very well-thought-out plan," said Giorgio. "I commend you on your cunning. Once you provide me with your numbered account information in the Cayman's, I will make the wire transfer of two million dollars as agreed. Remember, you have two weeks to complete this task. Marcus is a very impatient man. I will be in touch."

Later that morning, Mick and Joelle placed a call to the Wilmington, Delaware area. "Hello, this is Richard Haroldson."

"Richard, it's Mick and Joelle. How have you and Claudia been?"

"We're doing great," said Richard. "Hang on, I'll get your sister on the phone too. She missed talking to you two over the holidays."

Richard Haroldson was a retried expert in biology and chemistry, but had a passion for studying history and logistical planning. He had married Mick's sister nearly thirty years prior and he and Mick had grown as close as brothers. "We're both on the phone now," said Richard.

"Hey little bro," said Claudia. Even though Mick was a grown man nearly fifty five years old and standing six feet three inches tall, his sister had always referred to him as her little brother. Claudia stood five feet one inches tall and was twelve years older than her baby brother. They had always been extremely close.

Claudia, like Richard, was retired. She had worked as an internationally known interior decorator most of her life. The two had traveled throughout the world including frequent jaunts to remote European and Asian destinations. She loved to shop and on most trips returned with spectacular new custom jewelry or apparel.

"Are you still in Dublin?" asked Claudia.

"Yes, we are still here enjoying the hospitality of Uncle B," said Mick. "We are having a great time." The four talked on and on for nearly an hour, catching up on the smallest detail in each of their lives.

"You mentioned earlier that you need Richard to help you on a current project," said Claudia. "I'll get off the line so you three can talk business. Love you little bro, and you too Joelle. Talk to you soon."

"So what's this project you need assistance with?" asked Richard. "I get the feeling it's not something you want me share with your sister."

"She worries too much," said Mick. "Let's just keep it between the three of us." As Mick and Joelle brought Richard up to speed on the events of the last few months, culminating with Kenzie's kidnapping and release, Richard had to agree that sparing Claudia the details was a very good idea.

"Now that I understand the background of this project," said Richard, "what specifically are you two planning to do next?"

Mick and Joelle took their time explaining the recent proposal from Giorgio and how they planned to double cross Demetrius. Nearly thirty minutes later, Richard had heard enough detail and believed that he could fashion a logistical plan that would deliver the desired results. "Give me a day or so to rough this out," said Richard. "I will call you to discuss it and then we can adjust the plan as needed. Sound good"? Both Mick and Joelle thanked Richard for his help and hung up the phone.

"You know, Mick; this just might work," said Joelle.

CHAPTER 46

I T WAS THE first Sunday of 2013 and Mick, Joelle and Uncle B were enjoying a leisurely breakfast at a street side café. They knew that their lives were going to become very hectic again, and quite soon. This quiet time was needed to plan the next two treasure excavations and decide upon how they were going to approach the police for assistance.

"Uncle B, were you able to find the number for your acquaintance at Interpol?" asked Mick.

"Yes, I did find it and I gave her a call," said Uncle B. "She provided me with the name of a field agent that should be able to provide some assistance. His name is Frederick Louis."

"I think we should give him a call first thing in the morning," suggested Joelle.

"I agree," said Mick. "Let's discuss how we are going to approach this with him."

For the remainder of Sunday morning, the Scotts and Uncle B began formulating their plan. The overall strategy needed to address several key elements; including, excavation of the treasures, capture of Marcus, return of the treasures to various national museums and getting through the whole ordeal, alive. They required a few more pieces of information before they could contact Agent Louis at Interpol Monday morning. Clay had not yet called them to discuss what he found out about

Keira and McFadden. Also, they needed Richard's information on handling the Marcus double cross. They decided to take a quick break and then call Clay.

As customary, Giorgio found Marcus having breakfast in the garden grotto and reading his morning paper. However, he was surprised to find Marcus sitting alone at the table, again. It appeared the tension between Marcus and Sabina had not yet eased.

"Good morning sir," said Giorgio. "How are you today"?

"Quite well actually," answered Marcus. "I would be even better if I knew I was going to be receiving the remaining Celtic treasures."

"Well, then I have very good news for you," said Giorgio. "I reached an agreement with O'Shanahan yesterday. He has convinced the Scotts to locate and excavate the treasures for you. Trucks will be delivering treasures from both sites to your estate within two weeks."

"That is excellent news," said Marcus. "I will be traveling extensively over the next week to attend to some urgent business matters, but I will return to the estate on Monday, January 15th. I expect to see the treasures shortly after my return."

"Yes sir, I will make sure they arrive by then," said Giorgio.

"I need you to make arrangements to have the corporate jet waiting for me later today," instructed Marcus. "I want to be wheels up at 4:00 p.m."

"Should I have the pilot file a flight plan?" asked Giorgio.

"No, that will not be necessary," said Marcus. "I will provide him with instructions upon my arrival. Make sure to arrange for my travel companion to arrive at the airport by 3:30 p.m., sharp."

"Yes sir, anything else?" asked Giorgio.

"No, that is all," said Marcus.

Clay answered his cell phone on the first ring. "Hello, this is Clay."

"Hi son," said Mick. "Both Joelle and Uncle B are sitting here with me. We're calling to hear what you found out about Keira and McFadden."

"Not much," admitted Clay. "However, I did find out that they have distanced themselves from the operation involved with the coin heist. They seem to be settling down in Dublin."

"It's good to know that Keira and McFadden are no longer a threat," said Mick. "We will, however, be providing their names to our contact at Interpol so that they can follow up."

"Hopefully, the police can connect them to the coin heist and Kenzie's kidnapping," said Clay. Mick and Joelle nodded their heads in agreement.

"Are you still planning the additional treasure excavations?" asked Clay.

"Absolutely," said Mick. "Why do you ask"?

"I will need to make arrangements with the equipment rental company and give them a specific day for you to pick it up," said Clay. "Will you be needing the same equipment as before"?

"Yes," said Uncle B. "It worked out quite well. The main difference on this excavation will be the involvement of Interpol and the local police. What can you tell us about the various law enforcement agencies where we will be excavating?"

Clay loved these kind of questions because they gave him an opportunity to demonstrate his vast resources of information. "You will more than likely be working with at least three agencies during the operation," said Clay. "They are Interpol, the French National Police and several branches of Italian Police. Let me give you some more back ground." Uncle B rolled his eyes and exchanged looks with Mick and Joelle.

They all knew they would be listening to Clay until well after lunch time.

"The National Police, formerly the Sûreté Nationale," said Clay, "is one of two national police forces and the main civil law enforcement agency of France, with primary jurisdiction in cities and large towns. The other main agency is the military Gendarmerie, with primary jurisdiction in smaller towns and rural and border areas. Most likely, your contacts will be with the National Police."

"What about Interpol?" asked Mick. "Shouldn't we contact them first"?

"Yes, I would suggest making contact with one of their agents," said Clay. "Interpol deals with the worst criminal elements on the globe. They track and hunt those guilty of capital crimes and white collar criminals involved in complex scams. The full name of Interpol is the International Criminal Police Organization, or the ICPO," added Clay. "It may also be abbreviated as OICP, for Organisation Internationale de Police Criminelle, the French version of the name. Usually, it is referred to as Interpol, a name first selected as the telegraph shorthand name for the agency. The theft and trafficking of stolen art is a favored international crime because there are dealers and collectors all over the world. Interpol maintains a database of stolen artworks and publishes documents showing clear photos of them so art dealers and collectors can better recognize stolen goods when they see them. Again, I would suggest you start by contacting an agent."

"Uncle B has a contact within Interpol and we plan to contact agent Fredrick Louis tomorrow morning," said Joelle.

"He probably offices in Lyon, France at the Command and Coordination Centre (CCC)," said Clay. "Once you have spoken to him, he will coordinate his agency's actions with the French National Police."

"You mentioned that there are several policing agencies in Italy," said Mick. "Do I need to make contact with them as well"?

"There are three main agencies," Clay began; "however, I imagine that Interpol will work with the Guardia di Finanza. They are an Italian Law Enforcement Agency under the authority of the Minister of Economy and Finance. They function as the Italian police force and would have jurisdiction in and around Rome. Let me explain," said Clay, and then continued his monologue.

"The Corps is in charge of financial, economic, judiciary and public safety, tax evasion, financial crimes, smuggling, money laundering, international drug trafficking, illegal immigration, customs and borders checks, copyright violations, anti-Mafia operations, and political and military defense of the borders," said Clay. "They have a strength of around sixty eight thousand soldiers working as agents. The Guardia di Finanza also maintains over six hundred boats and ships and more than one hundred aircraft to fulfill its mission of patrolling Italy's territorial waters."

"Will Interpol work with the Guardia di Finanza as well?" asked Joelle.

"Yes," answered Clay. "Since Interpol is an international police agency that helps other law-enforcement agencies track criminals who operate across national borders, they will coordinate their actions with both the French National Police and the Guardia di Finanza."

"Clay, we really appreciate all of your help on this," said Mick. "I think the three of us have a much better understanding now of how Interpol will provide us with assistance. Talk to you soon."

They decided to leave the house and grab some lunch. Their next phone call would be to Richard Haroldson when they returned. Hopefully, he had completed formulating a plan that would safeguard the treasures and facilitate Marcus's arrest.

About an hour later, while Uncle B was pulling his car into the drive way, Mick's cell phone rang. "Mick, this is Richard. I believe I have developed a plan to double-cross Marcus without him becoming suspicious."

"You pulled that together rather quickly," said Mick. "I'm anxious to hear the details. We are just returning from lunch, let me give you a call back in a few minutes once we get inside the house."

The Scotts and Uncle B hurried into his house and Mick began dialing. Richard answered the phone quickly and started talking again where he had left off. "Are you familiar with the movie, *The Thomas Crown Affair*?" asked Richard.

"I seem to remember it vaguely. Wasn't it about an art heist?" asked Mick.

"Exactly," said Richard. "Let me explain my thoughts."

"In the movie, when Pierce Brosnan was returning the one hundred million dollar painting he stole from the museum, he dressed in a dark suit, long overcoat and wore a bowler style hat. Knowing that he was being watched by the museum authorities on their CCTV system, he arranged for dozens of men dressed exactly the same as him to walk around the museum as decoys. The authorities began chasing the decoys walking in every direction. Brosnan simply removed his dark overcoat and hat, disposed of them in the trash and then exited the museum wearing a light brown jacket," explained Richard.

"So you want to use decoy trucks in some fashion, I presume?" asked Mick.

"Exactly," said Richard. "Here's how it will work."

Their conversation continued for over an hour until all of the Scott's and Uncle B's questions were answered. "You have outdone yourself again, Richard," said Mick. "Thanks for your help. We will begin making plans to create the diversion."

CHAPTER 47

I T WAS HER first day back in classes at ASU and Kenzie had nearly forgotten about the stress of her ordeal on Jersey Island. Just before she stopped for lunch, Kenzie received a text message from a friend that was in her World History class during the fall semester. "Did you know that Professor Brinkerman is no longer teaching here?" said her friend. They exchanged texts several times and Kenzie quickly learned that Professor Brinkerman had died a violent death over the holidays. The police had reported it as DUI accident, but Kenzie was uncertain if that was true. He just didn't seem the type.

Kenzie dialed Mick's number on her cell phone and a few seconds later, he answered the phone. "Hi Kenzie, are you doing ok on your first day back?" asked Mick.

"I am," said Kenzie. "I've only been to three classes so far, but I think I will like each of my Professors. I called to tell you about Professor Brinkerman. You remember him, he was my World History professor last fall. He died in a car crash over the holidays. They say it was a DUI accident." Mick paused to gather his thoughts.

"Kenzie, your mother and I found out about the accident while we were on Jersey Island," said Mick. "The man responsible for the coin heist and then holding you hostage was behind the accident. It was not simply a DUI related crash. Giorgio told us that people like Brinkerman can have unfortunate accidents. He said that to us on the phone twelve hours before the accident occurred. Now you can understand the need for you and Danielle to have bodyguards watching over you until this is over."

"We both appreciate you having the bodyguards here for us," said Kenzie. "I will give Danielle a call and explain about Brinkerman's death. I think that will put this all into perspective for her like it did for me. Thanks again Mick for taking care of me. I will call you later this week."

Uncle B logged onto the internet and began checking the balance of his account at Cayman National bank. He hoped that Giorgio kept his word and deposited two million dollars as agreed. That deposit and the remaining three million dollar fee would help him to live the life he believed he deserved. "Excellent," said Uncle B quietly to himself. "All of the money is there. Even if Giorgio never wires another dime, I will be able to retire a wealthy man." Mick happened to walk into the room as Uncle B was checking his account.

"What's all the excitement about?" asked Mick. "You seem very pleased about something."

"Aah, I just received a text from Danielle. She seems to be very happy with our choice of bodyguards," said Uncle B.

"Hopefully they will be as effective as handsome," said Mick with a smile. "By the way, we need to contact that agent at Interpol you suggested. Do you have a few minutes?"

"Sure," said Uncle B.

Mick asked Joelle to join them and the three sat down to place a call. Since Joelle was fluent in French, she initiated the call and asked to speak with Frederick Louis. When Agent Louis picked up his line, Joelle introduced herself and then placed Mick and Uncle B on speaker phone. After exchanging pleasantries, Mick provided a quick overview of his and Joelle's background as amateur treasure hunters.

"Agent Louis," said Mick. "We are calling you about a recent kidnapping and theft of over one hundred million dollars in antiquities."

"You certainly have my attention," said Agent Louis, "but please, call me Frederick." Mick continued to describe the recent heist of coins from the Jersey Museum, Kenzie and Danielle's kidnapping, recovery of the hidden Celtic treasure and the recent phone contact by Giorgio representing Marcus Demetrius. "Did you say the name, Marcus Demetrius?" asked Agent Louis.

"Yes, that is his name," said Mick. "Do you know him"?

"This is very strange," said Agent Louis. "I received another call concerning Mr. Demetrius just last week."

During the remainder of their conversation, the Scott's briefed Agent Louis on Giorgio's demands and their knowledge of the two possible treasure sites. Due to the fast timetable that Demetrius had established, it would be necessary to meet the Scotts in person as soon as possible. Agent Louis and Mick exchanged contact information and set a meeting in Dublin for Wednesday.

After finishing his conversation with the Scotts, Frederick Louis knew that he needed to follow up with his old friend, Theophilos Sostos. "Hello Theophilos," said Frederick, "I have some more information for you regarding your son-in-law. It appears that he may have been involved in the recent coin heist from the museum on Jersey Island and possibly linked to a kidnapping and one hundred million dollars of stolen antiquities."

"I cannot say that I am surprised by your findings," said

Theophilos. "After we last spoke, I began doing some investigative work of my own. I discovered that Marcus has integrated his illegal operations into my shipping company and used my ships for transportation."

"I came to the same conclusion after reviewing the documents you sent to me," said Frederick.

"And you believe that he may have been involved in a kidnapping?" asked Theophilos.

"Yes, let me explain," said Agent Louis.

Theophilos listened carefully as Frederick recounted the story he had heard from Mick Scott about the stolen coins, kidnapping and theft of ancient treasures worth nearly one hundred million dollars. Although he wanted to trust Agent Louis, it was hard to believe that they were talking about his son-in-law. He wondered what other crimes Marcus had been involved in over the years. His estate had many galleries filled with expensive art from around the world. It seemed extravagant, but Theophilos never thought that his son-in-law was a thief.

"Frederick, if what you say about Marcus is true, he must be stopped," said Theophilos. "How can I be of assistance"?

"It would be most helpful if you could provide me with blueprints of his estate outside of Rome," said Frederick. "Also, if you know anything about his security system, staffing levels, or other details that may be helpful, please send those to me."

"I can begin assembling that information today," said Theophilos. "I will have everything to you tomorrow via email and larger items sent overnight mail to you within a few days. How long do you think it will be before you arrest him?"

"That depends," said Frederick, "upon the quality of the information that you send to me and results of a meeting I have planned for this Wednesday."

"Let's hope that all goes well," said Theophilos. "I will speak with you in a few days."

"Sabina, this is your father. It's very important that you leave the estate as soon as possible. We were correct about Marcus and his involvement in organized crime."

"Father," said Sabina, "Marcus left the estate yesterday on a business trip and does not plan on returning until January 15th. I made plans to fly out of Rome today and stay with a friend in Paris."

"Thank you for taking this seriously, Sabina," said Theophilos. "You shouldn't return to the estate until this is over. I will call you when it is safe to return."

"Thank you father, I love you," said Sabina.

Mick knew that making the two week deadline to find and recover the treasure would be difficult at best. Although he had not yet spoken to the authorities to gain their permission to search for and excavate treasure on French soil, Mick decided to call Clay to make arrangements for all of the rental equipment needed. He had a tentative schedule worked out in his mind which had them surveying the two sites on Sunday, January 13th and excavating on the 14th. Hopefully, Clay could have the equipment ready for them in time.

"Clay, it's Dad again," said Mick.

"Hi Dad. What's up?" asked Clay. "I usually don't get to talk with you twice in one day."

"We are going forward with the site survey and excavation plans," said Mick. "I'm going to be using all of the equipment we have stored on the rental truck and will need you to line up some additional items for pick up."

"So," said Clay. "You basically need all of the same equipment as last time"?

"Yes, except we will need two Bobcat Compact Excavators,"

said Mick, "Have each one on a separate trailer and get two strong trucks to pull them. Do you think you can have everything ready for us to pick up in Saint Malo by Saturday?"

"I will start working on it right away," said Clay. "Anything else"?

"Yes, but you will be sorry you asked," said Mick.

"I need you to rent ten, twenty four feet long, white Renault delivery trucks," said Mick. "The trucks should have no labeling and be in good condition. You will be disguising them as Auchan Hypermarket delivery trucks. I would suggest that you get on their website and become familiar with the logo. Each truck must have Auchan graphics applied to the truck sides and cab doors identical to the actual Auchan trucks. Five should have rear gate identifier numbers of #019581 and five with #019582."

"I have a contact located in Rennes, France that is dependable," said Clay. "He will be able to secure the trucks, apply all of the graphics and deliver the trucks per our instructions."

"That's great," said Mick. "There is more. We will also need ten complete sets of Auchan uniforms and eight drivers. Two of the uniforms are for Giorgio's men that he will most likely provide to drive the trucks filled with treasure. Can he help you with that as well?" asked Mick.

"It shouldn't be a problem," said Clay. "When and where do you need these delivered"?

"Eight of the trucks need to be delivered near LeMans, France on Monday," said Mick. "They should be staged out of sight in a warehouse with easy access to D155 west of LeMans. The other two trucks must be delivered to Chablé Menhir and Champs Dolent. Make sure that there is an Auchan uniform in each of those two trucks for Giorgio's men."

"There's one more thing," added Mick. "Eight of the trucks

must be carrying at least five tons of scrap metal or some other cargo of equal weight. You can use your imagination. The trucks must appear loaded from the exterior. Once we finalize the plan, I will be able to provide you with more specific instructions."

"I think that's enough to keep me busy for a while," said Clay. "I will let you know my progress in a few days. Tell Joelle hi."

"Will do," said Mick.

CHAPTER 48

MICK, JOELLE AND Uncle B walked into the Brazen Head Pub and made their way to a large wooden table near the rear. It was still morning and other than pub staff, they were the only patrons. Promptly at 10:00 a.m., Agent Frederick Louis of Interpol entered the pub. He quickly scanned the room and found the Scotts and Uncle B sitting at a table in the back. As he approached them he removed his Interpol credentials from his jacket pocket and introduced himself.

"I'm Agent Louis, Frederick Louis," he said. "I presume that you are Mr. & Mrs. Scott and Brian O'Shanahan"?

"Yes, we are," said Mick. "This is my wife Joelle and our friend Brian O'Shanahan. We call him Uncle B for short. Please have a seat."

Mick and Joelle provided Agent Louis with a quick summary of their background and expertise in the area of treasure hunting. As they recounted the last two months, he began to grasp Demetrius's involvement and his connection to the treasures. "Help me understand why you are interested in excavating at the two sites and continuing your association with Demetrius," said Agent Louis. "It would seem to me that would be the last thing on your mind."

"We have several motives that are inspiring us to excavate

the treasures and continue communicating with Demetrius's associate," said Mick. "Let me explain." Agent Louis had been taking notes throughout the conversation to record the details, but now set his pen down to just listen.

"Demetrius and his associates have made this ordeal very personal to us by kidnapping our two daughters," said Mick as he gestured to himself and Uncle B. "Thankfully, both Kenzie and Danielle were returned to us unharmed. He has continued to threaten all of our lives over the last two months in his quest to obtain the Celtic treasures. We decided to use his obsession against him and to excavate the treasures as bait. If everything works out as we have planned, the antiquities that we excavate will be safeguarded and Demetrius will be arrested."

"That is very interesting," said Agent Louis. "And how do you propose we use the treasures as bait"?

For nearly an hour, the Scotts and Uncle B described their intricate plan to Agent Louis. He was quite impressed by the level of detail in their planning and yet its simplicity. "I believe I have everything that I need," said Agent Louis. "Considering the two week deadline that Demetrius set, we will need to coordinate our efforts immediately. Are you sure that all of your provisions will be in place by Sunday?" Mick looked at Joelle and Uncle B for their agreement.

"Yes, we will have everything ready so that we can survey the sites on Sunday and begin the excavation on Monday," said Mick.

"I will complete my report from the information you provided today and begin coordinating Interpol's resources with both the French National Police and the Italian Guardia di Finanza," said Agent Louis. "I will contact you by Friday so that we can discuss the final details of this operation. We have been monitoring the illegal operations run by Marcus

Demetrius for over two years. We would be most happy to put him behind bars. Thank you for your assistance."

Now that they had Interpol's cooperation, the Scotts and Uncle B would be able to survey and excavate both Chablé Menhir and Champs Dolent without violating French law. Agent Louis agreed to ensure that the French National Police supply officers at the dig sites to provide a measure of protection. They did not know if Giorgio would send an armed team to the site like at Le Dolmen du Mont Ubé, but it would not matter with the French National Police onsite.

Agent Louis was anxious to compile the information he gathered from his investigation of Demetrius, materials provided by Theophilos Sostos and his meeting with the Scotts. For the operation to be possible, he would need to finish his comprehensive report, send it to his peers at the French National Police and the Italian Guardia di Finanza, then finalize a plan within a few days. Difficult, but not impossible. Capturing Demetrius was worth the effort.

Using blueprints of the Demetrius estate provided by Theophilos, including his hand written notes, Agent Louis was able to better understand the expansive complex. He worked to assemble all of the case materials he had collected over the last two years and added information from his recent meeting with the Scotts. The result of his hours of effort was a cohesive report that he sent to his contacts at both agencies to review.

"This is agent Frederick Louis with Interpol. I'm calling for Captain Michael Russo." A few moments later, Russo answered his phone.

"Hello, this is Captain Russo."

"Michael, its Frederick Louis with Interpol. How have you been?"

"I'm well," said Michael. "And you?" The men were old

friends and spent a few minutes catching up. "I know you didn't call me just to chat, how can I be of assistance"?

"I just emailed you a report I compiled on Marcus Demetrius," said Agent Louis. "He is a resident of Rome, Italy, but frequently conducts illegal operations on French soil. I've also sent the report to Captain Alberto Augustino with the Italian Guardia di Finanza."

"It sounds like you are planning a large scale operation," said Captain Russo.

"Read the report," said Agent Louis, "and I will set up a conference call for the three of us to discuss it in a few days. Talk to you soon." Next, Agent Louis dialed Captain Augustino and had a similar conversation. In a few days they would formulate their plan to capture and arrest Marcus Demetrius.

Agent Louis's report was divided into three sections and included an overview of Demetrius's known illegal activities and personal background, his known accomplices and the layout and security of his estate. In addition, Agent Louis sent each Captain a full set of estate blueprints via overnight courier.

To charge and arrest someone as prominent and wealthy as Demetrius, it would be necessary for all police agencies to work together closely and have thorough knowledge of his estate. Both Captain Russo and Augustino focused primarily on studying the estate portion of the report so that they could coordinate their teams' actions.

Estate Diagram & Security

The Demetrius estate is located approximately sixteen kilometers northeast of Rome. The main grounds cover over fifty acres and the entire estate is nearly one kilometer in each direction. Surrounded by tree covered land on all four sides, the estate is a little over three hundred acres. There are many buildings on the grounds. They include: the Main House which is attached to the Business Office wing and Master Suite wing. Separate buildings include;

Building One - Library & Art Gallery, Building Two - Theatre & Art Gallery, Building Three - Rec Center, Building Four – Art Restoration Center, the Main Public Art Gallery, a Guest house, an Owner's Retreat, the Garage, Estate Services/ Staff Housing and a Stable. The Main House and Owner's Retreat are connected by an enclosed porte-cochere/art gallery. A diagram of the estate is attached for your reference.

The main grounds of the estate are surrounded on all four sides by a stone wall measuring three meters in height. Embedded in the wall cap are large shards of glass designed to repel intruders. Running parallel to the inside wall, an electrified fence, two meters high, encloses the perimeter. High resolution CCTV cameras are located throughout the grounds and inside of each building. An onsite security force of five armed guards patrol the grounds 24/7 and check on all of the buildings routinely. They are each equipped with a Heckler and Koch MP5 machine pistol. The business office wing adjacent to the main house is divided into several sections, including conference rooms, Marcus's office, Giorgio's office, a security control center, and a staff office.

Three heavily secured and gated entrances restrict access to the property. The main gate to the estate is monitored by CCTV cameras and can only be opened remotely by personnel in the security control center. A second secure entrance is located one hundred meters to the east and provides access for the estate staff. The third gate is located at the western rear of the property and provides access to the riding stable.

Blueprints of the estate indicate that there are multiple places that you will likely find stolen art, including Buildings One, Two, Four, and two galleries adjacent to the main house. We are aware that Marcus has built a safe room under the main house, but it is not shown on the blueprints. Access to the safe room is thought to be located in the main house library. It is quite possible that additional hidden galleries exist, but do not appear on the blueprints.

After reading the comprehensive report, both Captain Russo and Augustino understood that all three agencies would need to work cooperatively. They would need to obtain the necessary legal documents required for the Scotts to conduct an excavation and provide assistance in escorting the treasures. This would be a complex operation with many moving parts all occurring within a very short time-frame.

CHAPTER 49

O VER THE LAST week, the plan to arrest Marcus Demetrius at his estate in possession of stolen antiquities had taken shape. Interpol's Agent Louis, Captain Russo of the French National Police and Captain Augustino of the Italian Guardia di Finanza worked diligently to coordinate their manpower and resources. Now it was time for the Scott's and Uncle B to play their part in acquiring the treasures that Demetrius so desperately craved.

It was Saturday morning as Mick, Joelle and Uncle B boarded a flight to Saint Malo and checked into the La Rance hotel. All three were becoming familiar faces to the hotel manager and were able to stay in the same rooms as their last visit. Most of their day was spent reviewing plans to survey and excavate Chablé Menhir and Champs Dolent. If all went well, both of these sites would contain vaults very similarly constructed to the one at Le Dolmen du Mont Ubé. Adhering to the tight time schedule they had agreed to with Agent Louis was critical to the success of the mission.

Mick and Joelle called Clay to review each of the tasks he was assigned to complete. Meanwhile, Uncle B drove to an unmarked warehouse on the south side of Saint Malo to check on their equipment. After the Le Dolmen du Mont Ubé excavation, all of their survey and excavation tools were loaded onto a rental truck that was parked in a locked warehouse. Uncle B opened the truck's tail gate and inspected each piece of equipment thoroughly. Satisfied that all of the portable lights, generator, Noggin ground penetrating radar, floor jacks and other assorted tools were ready for use, he locked up the truck and exited the warehouse.

Driving back towards the La Rance Hotel, Uncle B's phone rang. Without looking at the screen, he had a gnawing feeling in his stomach that he knew who was calling. "O'Shanahan," said Giorgio. "Are you and the Scotts prepared to deliver the remaining Celtic treasure as promised"?

"Yes," answered O'Shanahan. "All of the plans are in place to excavate the treasure vaults on Monday. The trucks will be in route to the Demetrius estate by sun up Tuesday morning."

"And the decoy plan, is that in place?" asked Giorgio.

"Yes," affirmed Brian. "As I said, the Scotts have the impression that all of the treasure will be driven to Paris. Actually, the two trucks will be switched mid-route. The trucks carrying the Celtic treasure will be driven to the Demetrius estate in Rome. The decoy trucks will continue on to their destination in Paris. Not until the trucks arrive at the Louvre will anyone suspect a switch. By then, it will be too late."

"As I stated before, your plan is brilliant," said Giorgio. "However, as added insurance, I will be providing drivers for each of the two trucks. They will arrive in Saint Malo on Monday and be present at both sites as you excavate the treasures."

"How do I know that you will transfer the remaining three million dollars into my account when you receive the shipments?" asked O'Shanahan. "Perhaps I should hold onto one of the trucks as leverage"?

"Unless you are prepared to put yourself, your daughter

and the Scott's lives in jeopardy again," threatened Giorgio, "I would suggest you stick to the plan as agreed. If both truckloads of treasure arrive at the Demetrius estate as planned, wiring the money to you is of no consequence to me. Do not disappoint me and you will be a wealthy man."

Although he had expected a call from Giorgio sometime before they began excavating, talking with him always made O'Shanahan nervous. He didn't trust Giorgio and knew that he and his boss, Demetrius were cold-blooded killers. Although Brian's plan was risky, each piece was falling into place perfectly. Giorgio believed that he was betraying the Scotts for a five million dollar payoff, but Giorgio didn't have any idea that he himself was being double-crossed and that the Scotts and Interpol were involved. The two trucks loaded with treasure would arrive on schedule at the Demetrius estate as promised and with any luck, Interpol would capture Marcus red-handed. Giorgio was right; O'Shanahan's plan was brilliant in its simplicity. Giorgio just didn't know that he and Marcus were the ones being double-crossed.

CHAPTER 50

L EAVING THE LA Rance Hotel shortly after 7:00 a.m., they drove southeast following the Rance River along D137 to an area dotted with warehouses. Once inside the non-descript building, Mick opened the rental truck's tail gate. All of the equipment Clay had previous acquired for them was sitting on the truck, ready for use. It held the Noggin 1000 MHz ground penetrating radar unit, two generators, various excavation tools, and a portable lighting system. Uncle B got into the cab and started the engine. As they exited the warehouse, Mick led the way in his rental car with Uncle B following closely behind in the truck. Their next stop was Saint Helier Heavy Equipment Rental.

Arriving at the shop, the Scotts and Uncle B found that each Bobcat Compact Excavator was already loaded onto a trailer and each hitched to a white, Ford F350. Uncle B would be driving one Ford F350, Mick the second and Joelle leading the way in their equipment truck. After paying for the rentals, the group headed southwest out of Saint Malo. Their plan was to survey both sites by dark so that they could begin excavation on Monday. First stop, Chablé Menhir.

Driving slowing enough to keep each other in sight, Mick, Joelle and Uncle B exited to the D117 and then turned south onto D7. The Chablé Menhir should be just ahead on the left, thought Joelle. It shouldn't be too hard to find since we were just here a few weeks ago and it's nearly five meters tall. She pulled her truck to the side of the road as her cell phone began ringing. It was Mick calling. "This looks like the place," said Mick.

"What gave it away?" asked Joelle.

"I don't know," quipped Mick, "possibly the three French National Police vehicles parked alongside the road? I'll have Uncle B leave his truck here and he can ride with me to the site. We will follow you in when you are ready."

Joelle eased her truck off the road and began making her way slowly towards the Chablé Menhir site. Mick followed her in his Ford F350 with three police vehicles closely behind. The tourist attraction had been temporarily closed to the public for maintenance work by order of the French National Police. This would allow the Scotts time to survey the site and excavate the treasure without interruption or onlookers.

"Once we get everything unloaded from the truck," said Mick, "we will need to transport our equipment the rest of the way to the site and then begin laying out the survey area. Joelle, I will need your help again to measure the area and set markers."

They began with a small search area measuring roughly thirty by thirty feet square. Setting markers every two feet on each side produced the outline of a grid. Next, the Scotts and Uncle B, using bags of white chalk, walked across the grid from marker to marker, spreading the dust. The result was a white checkerboard pattern with two foot by two foot squares outlined in white.

Using the Noggin GPR unit, Mick easily detected the south edge of the survey site so that Uncle B and Joelle could place the markers. They applied a thick line of white chalk to the ground to define the edge. Next, they set markers at three feet and six feet away from the thick white line. Mick had finished surveying the first thirty foot by thirty foot area without anything of interest appearing on the display. After marking another checkerboard area of similar size with the help of Joelle and Uncle B, Mick resumed his back and forth scanning of the ground.

It was a tedious process. Again, nothing showed up on the screen. He stopped at the end of the row. "Joelle, take a look at this last data stream," said Mick. Both Joelle and Uncle B studied the images on the screen.

"Should we extend the survey area another ten feet to see if any images appear?" asked Joelle.

"I think so," replied Mick. "I still believe that there is treasure in this area."

Mick and Uncle B began setting markers until they had extended the survey area to the new size. Joelle grabbed the bag of white chalk and began laying out the checkerboard pattern from marker to marker. Mick continued his methodical scanning of the new survey area. This time faint images began to appear. The Noggin began registering metallic objects laying nine or more feet under the surface. As Mick progressed across the grid, more images filled the screen. At midpoint he stopped and asked Joelle and Uncle B to extend the search area another five feet while he continued scanning. "Most everything I'm seeing is at least nine feet below the surface and seems to extend down to a level of at least twenty feet," said Mick. "This site appears to be similar to Le Dolmen du Mont Ubé, just further from the surface."

Another two hours passed as Mick completed scanning several more search areas with the Noggin. As he neared the middle of the last grid, fewer images appeared on the display.

On the next two passes, he found nothing metallic registering underground. "I've finished the scan," said Mick. "I think
we should review the data and decide upon our excavation
technique."

"From the data I see, the vault appears to be eight feet wide
by ten feet long and possibly twenty feet deep," commented
Uncle B. "What are your thoughts on excavation"?

"If we are lucky," said Joelle, "the perimeter of the excavation area will be lined with timbers just like the last site. Mick,
is there anything else we need to complete before moving onto
the Champs Dolent?"

"No," said Mick. "Our next step here is to begin the excavation and that needs to wait until tomorrow. Let's pack up our
smaller gear and drive to the next site."

"What about the Bobcat, truck and trailer?" asked Uncle B.

"I made arrangements with one of the French National
Police vehicles to remain here overnight," said Mick. "They
will protect our equipment until we return in the morning."

Although the Champs Dolent was located just twenty eight
kilometers south east, it was over an hour later before the caravan of trucks and police vehicles arrived. The large standing
stone was easy to spot as they exited D795 and Mick pulled his
Ford F350 into a parking spot he created along the curb. This
menhir was different in many ways from the previous sites,
especially its easy access from the road.

"Once we get everything unloaded from the truck," said
Mick, "we can begin laying out the survey area. Joelle, Uncle
B, I will need your help again to measure and set markers. Are
you both ready to start?" They nodded in agreement and the
three began the process.

Mick used the same routine as on the previous sites and
began with a small search area measuring roughly thirty by

thirty feet square. The white checkerboard pattern was covered with two foot by two foot squares outlined in white. He began searching each square for signs of metal below the surface.

Using the Noggin GPR unit on the south side of the survey area, Mick found no images of buried material. Uncle B and Joelle applied a thick line of white chalk to the ground to define the edge. Next, they set markers at three feet and six feet away from the thick white line. It was the same process they had used very effectively at the previous sites. Mick had finished surveying the first thirty by thirty area and found a small image close to the surface. After marking another checkerboard area of similar size with the help of Joelle and Uncle B, Mick resumed his back and forth scanning of the ground. Immediately, distinct images filled the screen. Mick stopped at the end of the row.

"Joelle, Uncle B, take a look at this last data stream," said Mick. Both Joelle and Uncle B studied the images on the screen.

"These images indicate that some items are laying very close to the surface," observed Joelle. The Noggin was registering metallic objects buried only three to four feet below. Although this site was similar to the last in size, it appeared to be much shallower.

As Mick completed scanning several more defined search areas with the Noggin GPR, images continued filling the display. Then on the last two passes, he found nothing metallic registering underground. "I've finished the scan," said Mick.

"From the data I see, the vault appears to be similar to the Chablé Menhir," commented Uncle B, "but only three to four feet deep. Will we excavate this site using the same techniques?"

"If we are lucky," said Mick, "the perimeter of the excavation area will be lined with timbers just like the last site and with such a shallow depth we will not need to support the roof. This may be the easiest excavation of the three. I believe that finishes up our survey."

"So, we can wrap it up here?" asked Joelle.

"I believe so," said Mick. "We can leave the Bobcat compact excavator, trailer and truck filled with equipment here at the site. One of the French National Police officers will be securing this area until we return in the morning. We can take the Ford F350 back to Saint Malo."

"Is the other police officer staying here as well?" asked Uncle B.

"No, actually he will be following us back to Saint Malo and keeping an eye on us until morning," said Mick. "Agent Louis wants to make sure that we are protected from Demetrius until this is over."

"That reminds me," said Joelle, "weren't you supposed to call Agent Louis this afternoon with an update?"

"You're right," said Mick, "let's give him a call on the way back to Saint Malo." It had been a long, tiring day for the three and they appreciated the short drive back to Saint Malo.

"Agent Louis, this is Mick Scott."

"I was waiting for your call," said Louis. "Were you successful surveying the sites today"?

"We were." said Mick. "Everything is in place for us to start the excavation tomorrow morning. Will you be at either of the sites?"

"Actually, I plan to start the day with you at Chablé Menhir," said Agent Louis, "and then drive to the Champs Dolent site later in the day. See you tomorrow morning."

When Mick, Joelle and Uncle B returned to the La Rance, they spent a few minutes freshening up and then left for dinner. One of their favorite restaurants was only a short walk away. As they enjoyed a relaxing meal, the three discussed Clay's excavation strategy. "Our plan seems solid," said Mick. "We have finished surveying the sites and know where to begin digging. Uncle B, do you have any concerns?"

"No, I think we are ready to roll," said Uncle B, "but I could really use a good night's sleep."

On the walk back to their hotel, Mick gave Clay a quick call to review last minute details about the arrangements. Clay had hired a crew of twelve men to assist with the excavation through a contact in Saint Malo. Six of the men had assisted with the Le Dolmen du Mont Ubé dig and would be split equally between assisting Uncle B and Mick. They would arrive at both sites Monday morning by 8:00 a.m. The crew foreman, Ramon, that assisted at the dig in Saint Helier and his cousin, Edward signed up as foreman again. Ramon would assist Mick and Edward would assist Uncle B. Mick was happy to hear that all of the details were in place.

Upon returning to the La Rance, Uncle B remained outside to enjoy a cigarette and check in with Giorgio. "This is O'Shanahan. Everything is in place for the delivery Tuesday evening. The Scotts are still unaware of our plans."

"I hope you don't disappoint us," said Giorgio. "If the trucks arrive as you promise, you will be a wealthy man very shortly. If not, well, that could be most unpleasant for you."

Giorgio wanted to provide Marcus with an update on the treasure excavation, but since his return to the estate earlier in the day, Marcus had spent most of his time in seclusion. Their only conversation had been upon Marcus's arrival when he inquired about Sabina. His questions were short and to the point. He was obviously upset that she was not at the villa and she had not apprised him of her whereabouts. That was most unusual. Giorgio noticed that Marcus was incredibly tense and did not offer to discuss any details about his recent business trip. Possibly, they would talk more tomorrow, but now was not the time.

Marcus sat alone on a wooden bench near the grotto outside of his master suite. He was visibly upset and even a casual observer would note his odd demeanor. During his time away for the estate, Marcus was contacted by a close friend associated with Interpol. Although the contact did not have specifics to share with Marcus, he informed him of an ongoing investigation into his various business enterprises. Upon returning to the estate and finding his wife Sabina absent, Marcus became more suspicious that something was wrong. He could no longer trust Giorgio or anyone else for that matter. It was time to get his affairs in order and be prepared for a hasty departure, if needed.

CHAPTER 51

AS MICK AND Joelle arrived at Chablé Menhir, six men that Clay had hired to assist with the excavation were already on site and speaking with the French National Police officer. They also noticed an Auchan delivery truck parked at the site, compliments of Clay. "Good morning," said Ramon. "It is good to see you and Mrs. Scott again. My men are ready to work. Just give us our instructions." Storing all of the excavation equipment on site the night before made it much easier for Mick and Joelle to get started.

Ramon and his men unloaded all of the small equipment including the generator and portable lights from the truck. Since Uncle B was in charge of excavating at Champs Dolent, Mick had assigned Ramon the task of driving the Bobcat at this site. He unfastened the Bobcat compact excavator from the trailer and drove it towards the survey site. Mick was glad he thought to get extra fuel again for the Bobcat as finding gasoline nearby could be very time consuming. He was ready to begin remarking the excavation area.

With most of the white chalk markings from their survey still visible from the day prior, Mick began using the Noggin GPR unit to re-verify edges of the site before they began digging. He quickly found the south edge of the survey site and Joelle began placing the markers. A thick line of white chalk was applied to the ground to better define the edge. Next, they set markers at three feet and six feet away from the south edge. Ramon would begin excavating six feet out from the vault edge. "Ramon, are you ready to begin the excavation?" asked Mick.

"Yes sir," said Ramon. "I have operated this type of machine many times in my life."

Although Uncle B was actually quite adept at using the Bobcat on the Le Dolmen du Mont Ubé site, he did not compare to Ramon's expert handling of the equipment. It was like watching a surgeon operate on a patient. After he dug all of the way across the plotted area to a depth of three feet, Ramon stopped the machine. Mick and Joelle inspected the dirt and found no evidence of rotted timbers or a rock lining. Following Clay's instructions, Mick instructed Ramon to proceed with removing another layer of soil. Now he had exposed an area roughly three feet wide, ten feet across and six feet deep. If no evidence of the vault lining was found here, they would begin excavating closer to the white chalk line.

Satisfied that he had not yet reached the vault lining, Mick gave Ramon a signal to begin the next section of excavating. He moved the Bobcat into position and lowered the bucket into the soil. "Here we go," said Ramon as the compact excavator began moving forward. Mick wondered how Uncle B was progressing at the other excavation site.

Uncle B had arrived at the Champ Dolent site around 8:30 a.m. The men Clay hired to assist with the dig were arriving in a large truck at the same time. Uncle B walked toward the truck and was greeted by Edward. "Good morning, I am Edward," he said in broken English. "I am Ramon's cousin. Are you Brian O'Shanahan?"

"Yes I am," said Uncle B. "Please have your men began

unloading all of the small equipment including the generator and portable lights from my truck."

Uncle B returned to unfastening the Bobcat Compact Excavator from its trailer and drove it towards the survey site. "Edward, can you operate this piece of equipment?" asked Uncle B.

"Yes." said Edward. "Not as well as my cousin Ramon, but I will be able to dig out the area as you instruct."

Using the Minelab GPX 5000 metal detector with a 15" DD deep seeking search coil, Uncle B easily detected the south edge of the survey site so that Edward could place the markers and define the edge with a thick line of white chalk. Next, they set markers at three feet and six feet away. Excavation would begin six feet out from the vault edge. "Edward, are you ready to begin the excavation?" asked Uncle B.

"Yes, I'm ready," said Edward.

After digging all of the way across the plotted area to a depth of three feet, Edward stopped the machine. Uncle B inspected the dirt and found no evidence of rotted timbers or a rock lining. Following Uncle B's instructions, Edward proceeded to remove another layer of soil.

Uncle B sifted handfuls of the sandy soil through a separator looking for evidence of wood. Satisfied that they had not yet reached the vault lining, Uncle B gave Edward a signal to begin the next section. Working carefully to remove the soil in small layers, Edward created another trough approximately three feet across and three feet deep, then he stopped. Again, Uncle B carefully sifted the soil through a separator and found nothing. "Ok Edward, let's remove another foot of soil," said Uncle B. Their pace was painstakingly slow, but they wanted to find the vault without harming it and they knew that it was very shallow.

Agent Louis had arrived at Chablé Menhir as he promised and was intrigued by the activity. He watched as Mick and Joelle used a very well-planned digging technique to carefully reveal the ancient vault. Ramon created another furrow approximately three feet across and three feet deep, then he stopped. "Mick, do you and Joelle want to analyze this area too before I go on?" asked Ramon.

"Yes, we do," said Mick. "This is where Clay believes we may find evidence of a vault lining." Again, they carefully sifted the soil through a separator and found nothing. "Ok Ramon, let's remove another foot of soil."

Ramon moved the Bobcat into position and again began to remove layers of soil in small amounts. On the second pass, the excavator stopped. He moved the Bobcat back out of the trench and asked for Mick to take a look. "I seem to have hit a hard object," said Ramon. "Maybe the vault wall." Inspecting the area, Mick used his hands to move away small sections of soil.

"I believe that we have found the outer edge of the vault," said Joelle. "And most amazing, it seems to be almost petrified, just like at Le Dolmen du Mont Ubé." Using a small hand tool, Mick continued to expose the edge of the hardened timber.

"Let's move the Bobcat excavating path about six inches away from this edge so that we do not damage it," said Mick.

Ramon positioned the Bobcat as Mick suggested and continued excavating soil all the way across the ten foot span. Mick and Joelle using shovels and small hand tools removed the remaining soil to further expose the vault lining. "It seems we have found the edge of the vault, just like Clay predicted," said Joelle. "What are the next steps"?

"I suggest that we continue following his plan," said Mick, "and remove more soil."

Ramon entered the Bobcat cage and began excavating soil

remaining outside of the white chalk line all the way across the ten foot expanse. The trough was now six feet deep along the vault lining and most of the soil had fallen away from the timbers. He had created a work area that was six feet deep, ten feet long and six feet wide. As Clay had suggested, Ramon continued excavating the site until the entire length of the vault wall was exposed, and then expanded the work area out away from the site providing a gradual slope. Uncle B was making similar progress at the Champ Dolent.

Mick decided to check in on Uncle B and gave him a call. "We have made good progress today," said Mick. "Joelle and I have found the vault and should be able to remove the treasures using the same technique as we used at Le Dolmen du Mont Ubé. How are things progressing at Champs Dolent?"

"Edward and his men have been very helpful," said Uncle B. "This vault appears to be much shallower than the others. Unless we hit a snag, we should be loading the truck later this evening."

"Thanks for the update," said Mick. "I will call you back later when we are ready to begin loading our truck."

Standing in front of the ancient wall of timbers nearly twenty feet below the surface, Joelle, Mick, Ramon and Agent Louis were in awe. "I have a feeling that was the easy part again," quipped Mick. "Now all we have to do is saw through another wall of nearly petrified wood, keep the ceiling from collapsing and carefully remove the treasures."

"I think I have heard you say something like that before," said Joelle. "At least we don't have Giorgio's men aiming guns at us this time."

"That is a good point," said Mick. "But I have a feeling his men could still show up." Mick and Ramon continued working on the timbers as one of Giorgio's men assigned to drive the Auchan truck arrived.

"I'm here to transport the items," said the rough looking man. "As you excavate the site, I will be watching you. Every item is to be placed onto the truck and I must be in route by sunrise. Do you understand?" Mick, Joelle and Ramon didn't pay too much attention to his veiled threats since an officer with the French National Police and Agent Louis were standing nearby.

"Yes, we will be ready," said Mick.

Mick resumed sawing the last row of timbers while Ramon and his crew began placing floor jacks to support sheets of plywood against the ceiling throughout the vault. As Clay had predicted, the vault still contained an air pocket just like Le Dolmen du Mont Ubé and had not yet collapsed in any section. Once the roof of the underground room was stabilized, Mick had Ramon place portable lights in several locations to illuminate the room.

As before, Joelle began at the back of the vault photographing and cataloging each antiquity. Although there were a few large golden statues and ornamental shields, most all of the smaller treasures had been placed into what appeared to be woolen bags. Over time they had dried out and turned to dust when touched. However, the beautiful items they contained looked unharmed by the passage of time. "This is truly an amazing find," said Agent Louis. "I can see why Demetrius is so obsessed with these artifacts. Since everything is well underway, I'm going to drive to the Champs Dolent site and review Uncle B's progress. I will meet up with you later this morning in route to LeMans."

"See you soon," said Mick.

Joelle and Mick found jewels, amber, coins, golden buckles

with animal motifs, golden torcs of every size and design, golden helmets, bracelets, rings, small statues of gods and goddesses, Celtic crosses, gold covered mirrors, necklaces and pendants. It was nearly a mirror image of the Le Dolmen du Mont Ubé site, just deeper. The items were carefully placed into various sizes of storage containers and sealed. Once the containers were stacked at the vault opening, Ramon's crew loaded them onto the truck.

"Mick, this is an incredible find," said Joelle. "The value of these antiquities is far more than one hundred million dollars." Mick and Joelle walked about midway into the vault area and stopped. "See the wooden box?" asked Joelle.

"I wonder if it contains another golden torc?" asked Mick.

"Only one way to find out," said Joelle as she handed him the ancient box.

Mick turned the box over in his hands and carefully studied the surface on each side. As before, he noticed a different color of wood near one corner. "I'm curious," he said. Holding the box in his left hand and using the thumb on his right hand to push on the darkly colored area, Mick heard a faint click. The lid released and sprang up enough that it could be opened. "Let's see what's inside," said Mick.

Raising the lid slowly in anticipation, Mick pushed it open and they both looked inside. It was the remains of a woolen bag and peeking out from underneath, another solid golden torc. The neck piece was nearly three inches thick and covered with intricate carvings and jewels. At each end of the U shaped neck piece, were large precious stones. In the middle, a capital 'B' and above it a large crown.

"Let's put it back in the box and bury it for safe keeping," said Joelle. "We can come back and get it before we leave." As Mick and Ramon continued to carry sealed storage boxes to the vault's entrance, Joelle worked to bury the wooden box. Just as before, she measured three feet diagonally across the floor from the right rear corner and dug a small hole. Once the box was placed underground, Joelle packed the soil tightly around it and covered it with loose rock and soil.

Most of the smaller contents of the vault had been removed and loaded onto the Auchan truck. A few storage containers remained, but would be loaded next. Each large golden statue was carried to the truck separately and secured. Things were going well. Unfortunately, Uncle B was not experiencing the same success at Champs Dolent.

Standing in front of the ancient vault, Uncle B saw that the timbers only extended three to four feet below the surface. With this shallow of a structure, Edward would be positioning portable lights around its perimeter, not inside. All of the timbers covering the top would need to be removed. And with little to no air gap present, each antiquity would need to be excavated separately from the top.

As Uncle B and Edward discussed their next move, a rough looking man assigned to drive the Auchan truck by Giorgio, arrived on site. "I work for Giorgio," said the driver as if reading from a script. "I'm here to transport the treasures. As you excavate this site, I will be watching you. Every item is to be placed onto the truck. I have instructions to be on the road by sunrise, so I suggest you get busy." Uncle B and Edward ignored his empty threats and simply pointed him towards the Auchan truck Clay had delivered earlier to the site. A few moments later, they noticed Agent Louis arriving as promised.

"Welcome to Champs Dolent," said Uncle B. "Your timing is very good. We are just now preparing to extract treasures from the vault."

"Please proceed," said Agent Louis. "I'm just here to observe."

Enlisting the help of Edward's men, Uncle B instructed them to clear the soil covering the vault cap and then begin removing each of the top timbers one by one. It was a very slow process and took well past 2:00 a.m. Once the timbers were removed, Uncle B and Edward began removing treasures. Their luck had held and very little soil had fallen into the vault. Without Joelle on site and so much time spent removing the top cap, Uncle B had to forego photographing and cataloging each antiquity.

As they explored the shallow vault, Uncle B and Edward found jewels, amber, coins, golden torcs, bracelets, rings, small statues of gods and goddesses, necklaces and pendants. The items were carefully placed into various sized storage containers and sealed for transport, then loaded onto the truck. Giorgio's man stood guard next to the truck and watched the work crew carefully to assure that none of the precious artifacts were stolen.

Knowing that Joelle had found a wooden box containing a golden torc at both Le Dolmen du Mont Ubé and Chablé Menhir, Uncle B scoured the vault area for a similar item. Sitting next to a small golden statue, Uncle B spotted a wooden box. As his hand passed across the lid brushing away a thin layer of dust, an image appeared. He remembered that Mick had turned the box over for it to open. Carefully studying the surface on each side, he noticed a different color of wood near one corner. Holding the box in his left hand and using the thumb on his right hand to push on the darkly colored area, Uncle B heard a faint click. The lid had released and popped up enough that it could be opened.

Raising the lid slowly, he looked inside and saw a woolen

bag, much like the ones scattered around the vault. He attempted to lift the bag from its resting place, but it disintegrated, revealing its contents. It was another solid golden torc neck piece over two inches thick. Intricate carvings adorned every surface. At each end of the U shaped neck piece, were large precious stones. In the middle, a capital 'C' and above it a small crown.

Uncle B put the torc back into the box and buried it for safe keeping. He would retrieve it prior to leaving the site. Edward continued to carry sealed storage boxes to the truck where they were positioned by his men. The truck was nearly loaded and soon Uncle B would be giving Mick a call to confirm their ETA.

"Mick, we will be ready to meet you on the road in a few hours," said Uncle B. "We should arrive at the meeting site around 6:30 a.m."

"We are finishing up here too," said Mick. "We will see you soon."

CHAPTER 52

WITH ALL OF the work completed at the excavation site and the truck loaded, it was time to depart. Mick had prearranged for Ramon and Edward to remain at the sites with their men. They were responsible for loading all of the excavation gear, dropping off the equipment trucks at the warehouse and returning the rental equipment to Saint Malo. Clay had paid them all very well for their trouble. By making this arrangement, Mick and Joelle were free to follow the trucks filled with treasure.

The Auchan delivery truck was loaded with enough treasure from Chablé Menhir to completely fill its twenty-four foot compartment. The truck's tailgate had been closed and padlocked for safe keeping. Giorgio's driver had changed into an Auchan uniform and was sitting in the truck's cab waiting to depart. With everything wrapped up at the site, the Auchan truck and French National Police vehicle drove away with Mick and Joelle close behind in their Ford F350.

The plan was to drive the truck south on D137 and then east on E401 towards LeMans. If all went well, they would join the truck carrying treasure from Champs Dolent around 6:30 a.m. on the D155.

"Uncle B, this is Mick. We recently left the site and are driving east on the E401. What is your status?"

"We are loading the last few items on the truck now," said Uncle B. "I estimate that we will be finished and on the road in about fifteen minutes. See you shortly."

"You shouldn't have trouble spotting us," said Mick. "The white truck with its red Auchan logo really stands out."

Right on schedule, the truck carrying treasure from Champs Dolent entered the D4 heading south. A French National Police vehicle followed directly behind and then Uncle B in his Ford F350. They would be meeting up with the other Auchan truck on D155 in La Boussac. After 6:30 a.m., the caravan had doubled in size. It was now seven vehicles, including two Auchan trucks, two French National Police cars, two white Ford F350s and Agent Louis. Within ninety kilometers, they would all be turning onto D178 and then E50 towards LeMans where they were scheduled to arrive around 8:00 a.m.

Mick picked up his cell phone and set up a three-way conference call with his son and Uncle B. "Clay, this is Dad and Uncle B. We have both exited E50 and are on D357. Our ETA at the Auchan Distribution Center is 7:56 a.m. Is everything in place?"

"Yes, I have checked in with each of the drivers. They will be leaving the area within the next two to three minutes. I can see the GPS signal from both trucks you are following on my computer screen. "You should all be approaching the roundabout at 8:00 a.m. sharp," said Clay.

"Thanks," said Mick. "We will call you again after the switch."

Before the Auchan truck left the Champs Dolent excavation site, O'Shanahan took Giorgio's driver aside to brief him on the plan. Both men had been directed by Giorgio to drive their Auchan trucks to the Demetrius estate near Rome, Italy. With French National Police escort vehicles directing them toward Paris, neither driver knew how they would break free without being caught. After hearing the plan presented by O'Shanahan, Giorgio's driver understood that he should travel through LeMans and then exit on D357 heading southeast towards Rome. He agreed to notify the other driver of the plan once in route. O'Shanahan promised to call them with further instructions.

At 8:00 a.m., dozens of Auchan delivery trucks begin leaving the distribution center to service local hypermarkets. Eight decoy trucks with drivers hired by Clay, joined the real Auchan trucks exiting the center. Each of the decoy trucks was filled with scrape metal approximately the same weight as the treasure so that they would not outwardly appear different. To complete the ruse, drivers in each decoy truck were dressed in Auchan uniforms.

As all of the Auchan trucks approached the roundabout, it was impossible to discern the trucks filled with treasure from those with hypermarket supplies versus those filled with junk metal. Officers in both French National Police vehicles attempted to keep the truck they were escorting in their view. Once every vehicle entered the roundabout, that task became futile. It was chaos. All of the trucks looked identical. A few moments later, two Auchan trucks exited the large roundabout and drove toward Paris traveling northeast on A11. Those two Auchan trucks had numerical identifiers of #019581 and #019582 on their rear panels.

At the same time, two other trucks with Auchan logos and identifier numbers of #019581 and #019582 headed south on A28 toward an airport in Tours. Two other trucks with Auchan logos with identifier numbers of #019581 and #019582 headed southwest on A11 toward Nantes. A final pair of trucks with

Auchan logos with identifier numbers of #019581 and #019582 headed north on A28 toward Le Havre.

Both officers driving the French National Police escort vehicles were confused by the mass of Auchan trucks they were seeing on the road. The officers increased their speed and exited the roundabout heading northeast on the A11. A moment later, they found one of the trucks labeled #019582, but not truck #019581. Before the officers radioed for assistance, they spotted the missing truck up ahead on the right. Both trucks and police cars were now back in their original formation and headed towards Paris. But they noticed that neither of the white Ford F350s nor Agent Louis were still behind them. That was not their concern. Their assignment was to get both trucks carrying treasure safely to the Louvre in Paris.

Fifteen minutes later, two of the several Auchan trucks that departed the roundabout on D357 heading southeast began to slow down. Before they arrived at the small town of Bouloire, Giorgio's drivers stopped their trucks per O'Shanahan's instructions. They exited their truck cabs and quickly peeled off the Auchan graphics on the side panels and doors of their trucks. A new identifier number of #060872-M was placed on the rear of the first truck covering the original number. They removed the second truck's graphics and placed a new identifier number of #060872-J on the rear to cover the original number. Next, both drivers changed out of their Auchan uniforms so that they would not be spotted. Only ten minutes had passed before they were back in their unmarked trucks driving toward Rome, Italy. With the Auchan truck melee Clay created at the roundabout, the French National Police would spend hours searching for the original trucks. By then, Giorgio's men would be over half way to Rome. Their ETA at the Demetrius estate was 10:00 p.m.

An hour east of LeMans, at about the same time, both French National Police officers realized that something very odd had occurred near the Auchan Distribution Center. They wondered, what was the likelihood of so many Auchan delivery trucks leaving the distribution center at exactly the same time? It had made the task of keeping their assigned delivery trucks in sight very difficult. Each of the officers recognized that they may no longer be following the correct truck. The lead escort vehicle turned on his lights and siren and began directing his assigned truck to the roadside. The second officer did the same.

Several minutes passed before the Auchan truck drivers realized what the Police escorts were instructing them to do. Pulling to the side of A11, the trucks came to a stop. Officers from both police vehicles approached the trucks with caution and asked the drivers to get out. "What is this all about?" asked the driver. "We have to keep to our schedule." Although both drivers were wearing Auchan uniforms, something looked different about them to the police officers.

"We need you to open the back of your trucks," said the officer. Each driver returned to their cab and retrieved the keys that would open the padlock on their truck's lift door.

One truck's lift gate was opened at a time. As the door was raised, it quickly became evident to both officers that the first truck was not carrying any treasure. It had been filled with junk metal. Both officers drew their weapons and ordered the drivers to open the lift door on the second truck. Just like the previous one, this truck too was filled with junk metal. They realized that the Auchan delivery trucks had been switched, probably near the Auchan Distribution Center on the roundabout.

Both truck drivers were handcuffed and placed in the back of the police car so that they posed no threat. Next, the officers called headquarters in Paris and reported their situation. "We have been instructed to take both drivers into custody and bring them to our station in Paris for questioning," said the officer to his partner. "Central dispatch is broadcasting a BOLO for the original Auchan trucks carrying treasure. I described what occurred near the Auchan Distribution Center outside of LeMans. Officers throughout France will be on the lookout for two Auchan delivery trucks with identifiers #019581 and #019582."

It was nearly 10:00 a.m. before French National Police began searching for the missing Auchan delivery trucks. With each truck carrying an estimated one hundred million dollars in treasure, it was imperative that they locate the trucks quickly.

"Dad, this is Clay. I'm tracking the two Auchan trucks via GPS. They are approximately six kilometers ahead of you and Uncle B. The decoy trucks appeared to do the trick in LeMans. I've been monitoring the police radio frequencies and our two French National Police escort vehicles just stopped the decoy drivers outside of LeMans. They discovered the empty trucks and placed both drivers under arrest. I should have reports on the other six decoy trucks throughout the day."

"That's great work Clay," said Mick. "Talk to you soon."

Over the next six hours, French National Police and Interpol worked diligently to find the missing trucks. It was nearly 6:00 p.m. before all of the Auchan decoy trucks were located. One pair of trucks was abandoned in Nantes, two others at the port area along La Loire and one pair at the port in Le Havre. The final pair of trucks were found at the St. Symphorien Airport in a hanger. All of the trucks were abandoned, wiped clean of fingerprints and loaded with about five tons of scrap metal. The two Auchan delivery trucks carrying treasure from Chablé Menhir and Champs Dolent had vanished.

CHAPTER 53

G IORGIO'S MEN HAD been driving since 6:00 a.m.,
eluded the French National Police in France and a
few hours earlier crossed the border into Italy. As
they drove the two unmarked Auchan trucks across the border,
it was evident that Demetrius had made arrangements for
them to pass customs without an inspection or any questions.
Driving southeast, their next stop for petrol would be in Genoa.

"Giorgio, we are in Genoa," said the driver. "We should
arrive at the estate around 10:00 p.m. as planned."

"I assume there were no issues at the border crossing from
France," said Giorgio.

"That is correct," said the driver. "After reviewing our
passports, they allowed us to proceed without inspecting the
trucks."

"Very well," said Giorgio. "When you arrive at the estate's
main gate, show the guard the security passes I provided.
Proceed to Building Four, they are expecting you."

Only Agent Louis, Captain Russo, Captain Augustino, the
Scotts, Uncle B and Theophilos Sostos knew the entire plan to
trick and arrest Demetrius. It was imperative that Giorgio and
Demetrius believe that O'Shanahan had double-crossed the
Scotts and authorities for the plan to work. Once the round-
about decoy operation was complete, Agent Louis boarded a

plane in LeMans. He planned to fly directly to Rome and arrive early enough to meet Captain Augustino that evening.

"Thank you for picking me up at the airport," said Agent Louis. "Are all of your men in place around the Demetrius estate as planned"?

"Yes," responded Captain Augustino, "I have a squad of thirty heavily armed men ready for the assault. We also have six armored tactical vehicles on site to breach the estate perimeter wall."

"It seems that all of the pieces of this operation are coming together nicely," said Agent Louis. "What is our ETA at the Demetrius estate"?

"We will arrive around 9:30 p.m.," said the Captain. "That will give us ample time to review all of the squad's positioning and make any necessary adjustments."

"Excuse me," said Agent Louis. "I need to take this call."

"Agent Louis, this is Mick Scott. We are approximately six kilometers behind the Auchan trucks traveling southeast on A12. Our team has been tracking the two vehicle's GPS signals since they left the treasure sites earlier today."

"It appears they are driving directly to the estate outside of Rome as we predicted," said Agent Louis. "I have coordinated our breach of the estate with the Guardia di Finanza. All of our assets are in place and prepared for their 10:00 p.m. arrival."

"The three of us would be happy to lend a hand in capturing Demetrius," said Mick.

"Mr. Scott, we are well staffed and trained to handle this operation," said Agent Louis; "however, we would appreciate your expertise in recovering the stolen antiquities on his estate once it is secured."

"Roger that," said Mick, "we will park outside of the estate and await your call." Joelle heard what Mick said to Agent Louis, but gave him a bewildered look.

"Mick," said Joelle, "I know that you will not simply park our truck outside the estate and wait for Agent Louis's call. That's not like you. What crazy plan do you have in mind?"

Mick cracked his usual smile, looked over at Joelle and said, "Aah, just a little plot that Clay and I concocted to ensure that Demetrius is caught. Nothing extravagant." She hated that word. Mick's plans were always extravagant and this one would be a whopper.

By the time both Auchan trucks neared their final turn towards the estate, Mick and Uncle B had passed them and were about seven kilometers ahead on SS4. For the plan to work, the Scotts and Uncle B had to work quickly. Clay had carefully selected a vacant lot for the operation based upon its proximity to the estate. Setting up several road detour barricades with orange flashing lights on SS4 only took a few minutes for Mick and Uncle B. Next, they parked the two Ford F350s out of sight and Joelle remained in her passenger seat out of harm's way. The detour would direct both Auchan trucks to turn left into a roadway which quickly dead ended at a chain link fence.

Mick and Uncle B hid in the shadows, but still had a clear view of the roadway. A few minutes of silence passed and then Mick saw the headlights of two large vehicles approaching. Both trucks slowed and then without hesitation, followed the barricade's instruction to turn left. In moments, the first truck screeched to a halt before hitting the fence line. The second truck driver crushed his brake pedal to the floor hoping to avoid hitting the rear of the first truck. The dust settled and both drivers exited their cabs to discuss the situation. Before they realized they were not alone, Mick and Uncle B fired Taser darts into each driver. The men shook violently and then collapsed. With the drivers incapacitated and their wrists bound with zip ties, both Mick and Uncle B were able to quickly switch into their clothes. After removing the barricade signs and stowing them in the back of her Ford F350, Joelle followed closely behind the Auchan trucks. It would be hours before the two unconscious drivers awoke, and by then Demetrius would be in custody.

Agent Louis, Captain Augustino and the Guardia di Finanza were in position outside of the perimeter wall surrounding the Demetrius estate. It was a few minutes before 10:00 a.m. when one of the Guardia officers hidden along SS4 reported spotting two large trucks and then a white Ford F350.

"They are approaching the main gate," said the officer. "I will advise you when they are permitted through."

Mick slowed the large truck and stopped it just short of the estate's security gate. Uncle B followed closely in the second truck. As the guard approached the driver's door, Mick lowered his window and handed the guard a Demetrius Estate security pass that he found on the truck's console. The guard was expecting the special delivery at 10:00 p.m. and the pass was authentic. Without any further thought, he waved Mick through the gate and motioned for Uncle B to pull ahead. The entry process for Uncle B took even less time. As both men drove toward Building Four, they were unsure of what lay ahead. Hopefully, their plan would work.

Captain Augustino and his team were cautiously waiting for the right moment to advance towards Building Four. He had given his team instructions to stand down until the appropriate time. Since he had no one on the inside of the estate, neither he nor Agent Louis would know when Demetrius entered

Building Four to see the treasure. He would have to trust his gut. They would not be waiting much longer.

"Marcus, this is Giorgio. Both trucks have arrived and they will be unloading your treasure in Building Four. Do you want to wait until they are finished to view the items?"

"Absolutely not," said Marcus. "I am on my way." His response seemed typical, thought Giorgio. Perhaps whatever was bothering Marcus when he returned from his trip was resolved?

Once both trucks entered Building Four, they were instructed to pull all of the way forward so that the outer doors of the building could be closed. Mick and Uncle B were still sitting in the truck cabs. Anxious to notify Agent Louis that they were inside, both Mick and Uncle B hesitated to call until they knew that Marcus was in the building. Stepping out of the truck cabs, they approached one of the guards and ask for directions to the restroom. Keeping their heads down and hoping to go unnoticed, Mick and Uncle B hid from view behind a stack of wooden pallets and waited for Marcus to arrive.

Giorgio was very pleased that both trucks had arrived on schedule and were carrying a large load of treasure similar to the Le Dolmen du Mont Ubé excavation. He knew that Marcus would be quite pleased with the results. O'Shanahan had come through and for that he would be paid very well. Giorgio planned to wire the funds to him as agreed once all of the treasure was unloaded and authenticity verified.

Fifteen minutes later, Marcus entered Building Four and walked directly to the rear of the trucks. "I thought they would be unloaded by now," he snapped. "What is taking so long"?

"Sir," said Giorgio, "I have instructed the men to work very carefully with these antiquities. You must remember that these works of art are over two thousand years old."

"Yes, of course I understand that," said Marcus. "I do not need an antiquities lesson from you. Show me what has been unloaded."

CHAPTER 54

"I GUESS THAT'S OUR cue to call in the troops," said Mick. "Text Joelle for me and ask her to stay in the truck outside the gates until after the assault. I'll call Agent Louis." Mick picked up his cell phone and began speaking quietly. "Agent Louis, this is Mick Scott. We are in Building Four. We switched places with the drivers before they arrived at the estate. Demetrius just walked into Building Four and is looking at the treasures." Agent Louis could hardly believe what Mick was saying to him. He had instructed Mick to stay outside of the estate wall and wait for further instructions.

"Are you telling me that you are in Building Four right this moment and have Demetrius in sight?" clarified Agent Louis.

"Yes," said Mick. "We have hidden from view near the restrooms and are about thirty meters from the trucks."

"Stay put this time," commanded Agent Louis. He picked up his Motorola two-way radio and spoke to Captain Augustino. "Issue the command for your teams to advance. Demetrius is in Building Four."

Immediately, Mick and Uncle B heard automatic weapons' fire and then several loud explosions. They knew that Agent Louis had directed the Guardia di Finanza to enter the estate on the west side through a perimeter wall. It would only be seconds before they arrived at Building Four. Demetrius and

Giorgio were completely caught off guard by the loud explosions and gunfire. Not knowing what would happen next, Marcus sprinted towards the north door. If this attack was connected to the investigation that his friend at Interpol had warned him of, he would need to seek shelter in the safe room immediately. He ran towards the master retreat hoping to gain access to the safe room door. Both Uncle B and Mick chased Demetrius out of Building Four as the wide loading doors exploded inward and Guardia di Finanza troops began their assault.

At the same moment, another squad of Augustino's men breached the estate's east perimeter wall using armored tactical vehicles. They established a presence around the main house and each of the separate buildings. Giorgio's men put up little resistance against the trained officers and were quickly subdued. Still running after Demetrius, Mick and Uncle B arrived at the master retreat just as he disappeared from view. They split up and began searching the building. If Demetrius was hiding, they believed they could find him. Instead, they found an empty house and a very conspicuous metal door located in the library. Marcus had probably used this door, since the painting covering it had been removed and tossed on the floor. It was rumored that a safe house existed underground; however, it was not shown on the house blueprints. Mick and Uncle B decided to find Agent Louis or Captain Augustino so they could track Demetrius further.

The firefight between the troops of Guardia di Finanza and Giorgio's men in Building Four did not last long. Although Giorgio's men were all armed with Heckler and Koch MP5 machine pistols, they were out manned three to one. Seeing that they faced a losing battle, Giorgio ran toward the building's north exit. If he could make it to the safe room entrance in the master retreat, he could wait this out. He was sure Marcus had already reached the luxurious safe room under the house. Unfortunately for Giorgio, that was his last thought as a bullet entered the back of his skull and ended his life.

A few hundred feet away, Demetrius was watching his world fall apart, but from the comfort and security of his safe room. What had happened, he thought? His contact at Interpol had warned him of an investigation, but he did not expect an assault on his estate. Nearly forgetting that two truckloads of Celtic treasure remained in Building Four, Marcus turned to more pressing matters. Should he remain in the safe room and wait out the assault or use the escape route and leave the property?

Nervously, he watched the CCTV monitors. It appeared that all of his men in Building Four were dead, including Giorgio. As he continued checking cameras across his estate he saw men from the Italian Guardia di Finanza everywhere. Tactical assault vehicles, K-9 units and dozens of police were searching the grounds. Marcus saw flashes of light on the CCTV screen as his remaining men exchanged gunfire with the police. For now, he would wait. He knew it was only a matter of time before the trained officers realized that he had either left the estate undetected or was still hiding somewhere on the grounds, most likely in a safe room.

Several years earlier, Marcus had personally designed his safe room and its many connecting tunnels. He hoped that neither he nor Sabina would ever need to make use of the secure area; however, he was a realist. He had not become wealthy by making friends and many of his enemies would prefer to see him dead. Outside of himself, Sabina and Giorgio, he believed that no one knew of the safe room's existence, or at least, its location and design.

The safe room was located underground, ten feet below the main house of the estate and could be accessed through four different hidden entries. One access point was concealed in the main conference room, the second in the master suite, the third was located in the main house library and the fourth was located in the master retreat. After gaining access through the first door with a proximity card, it was necessary to descend a short flight of stairs and then enter a passcode at the next steel, mag-locked door. Behind this second door, lay a ten foot long angled hallway that ended at another secure door. The same proximity card and a second password were needed for final access to the safe room foyer. All four hidden safe room entrances converged at this point.

The final entrance was copied from a bank vault design and secured by three integrated password keypads. It was a class one door and would require at least thirty minutes to breach. The entire safe room area was surrounded by poured concrete walls, reinforced with sheets of Kevlar and steel. Measuring nearly three feet thick, the walls could withstand large explosive charges or armor piercing ammunition. This was the only way into the main safe room.

Once inside, occupants could choose to stay in the main living area or secure themselves in three separate safe rooms, each equipped with a filtered ventilation system and a hidden escape shaft. Located in the main living area, a bank of CCTV video monitors tracked external security cameras and intruder alarms. Designed for comfortable short or long-term stays, the main living area and each safe room was set up like a studio apartment with full kitchen and bathroom facilities. Electricity was provided by a remote, secure propane generator. Satellite TV, internet and phone were provided for complete connectivity to the outside world. Marcus had thought of everything in his design.

Not finding any other signs of Demetrius, Mick and Uncle B returned to Building Four and were met by Agent Louis. "I see you two have trouble with following instructions. Can you explain to me why you were in this building?" asked Agent Louis.

"We knew that without someone on the inside, the operation would have little luck of capturing Demetrius," said Mick.

"So where is he then?" demanded Louis.

"We followed him into the master retreat," replied Mick, "but then lost him. I think he used a secure door located in the library to access a safe room underground."

"Show me to the area," said Agent Louis. "Maybe we still have a chance of catching him." Agent Louis got on his two-way radio and requested that Captain Augustino's troops secure the exterior perimeter of the estate. He hoped that Demetrius had not yet escaped.

CHAPTER 55

O FFICERS WITH EXPERTISE in using cutting torches and directional explosives were brought to the master retreat to remove the secured door. Several attempts were made before the final blast sent the thick metal door hurling through the air. Walking down a narrow stairway, Agent Louis and Augustino's men came upon a second secure doorway. "It looks like we have another obstacle," said Louis. "Remove it!" This door was much harder to get through due to its location underground in a narrow corridor. Special cutting torches were brought to the area to remove the door. Ten minutes later, they were through the second doorway and walking toward the safe room.

Marcus had been monitoring his intruder's progress and decided to move to one of the internal safe rooms. If necessary, he could use the escape tunnel and leave the property. If they were able to breach the final door, he would have no choice but to flee.

"This must be the main safe room door," said Agent Louis. "It looks like the door to a bank vault. Can we get through this one?" Although no one on the team had forced open a door of this type, they believed it could be done.

"We will need to drill several deep holes in the door frame and fill them with C-4 to even have a chance of removing it," said one officer. "I am not sure if the tunnel ceiling can withstand the blast. We will need to shore it up before we proceed."

"Are there any other alternatives?" asked Agent Louis.

"Not that I am aware of sir."

"Then proceed," ordered Louis.

The horrific explosion rocked the entire master retreat and caused a partial collapse of the tunnel ceiling. It had made the air so thick with dust, Agent Louis could barely see what remained of the vault door. A small opening along one side of the door was created by the explosives. Not large enough to walk through, but ample for a man to squeeze through, one at a time.

With access to the safe room, Agent Louis quickly discovered that Demetrius was nowhere in sight. "Captain Augustino," said Louis. "We have breached the door to the main safe room and have not yet found Demetrius. It's possible that he is still else-where on the grounds. Keep your men at high alert. We have one final area to penetrate."

"Roger that," replied Captain Augustino. "I will instruct my men to extend their search to the outer perimeter of the estate."

The safe room contained one large seating area and three sep-arate secure rooms. Possibly, Demetrius was hiding in one of the three rooms, or possibly, he never came to the safe room at all. Reluctantly, Agent Louis ordered all three doors removed and hoped he would find Demetrius hiding in one of them.

Several minutes before the main safe room door was blown off its hinges, Marcus decided to use the escape tunnel and leave the property. Opening a hidden safe, Marcus removed several passports with different identities, a small bag with one hun-dred thousand euros and a Glock 19. It was nearly fifteen min-utes before Marcus reached the outer perimeter of his estate. Exiting the tunnel, Marcus climbed a wooden ladder leading into a small, barn-like building.

With all three interior safe room doors removed, Agent Louis was able to complete his search. At the rear of each safe room, he discovered a hidden doorway. All three of the doors led to a common corridor that appeared to run towards the west edge of the property. "An escape tunnel," Louis said to himself. "Demetrius could have left the property over an hour ago before we even penetrated the first door." He radioed Captain Augustino and confirmed that Demetrius may have left the estate. "Be on the lookout for evidence of a tunnel access point," said Louis. "I believe that Demetrius may have exited along the western edge of his estate."

As Agent Louis and Augustino's men returned to Building Four, they found Mick, Joelle and Uncle B working diligently to inventory the treasures already taken off the trucks. "Any luck finding Demetrius?" asked Mick.

"Not yet, but we found the safe room and escape tunnel. He could still be on the outer perimeter of the grounds," said Louis. His radio chirped.

"Sir, I think we have found something you need to see," said the officer. "We are on the far western edge of the property, near the road. We have found a small structure."

"I will be there momentarily," said Agent Louis.

The Scotts and Uncle B followed behind Agent Louis in their truck as he drove across the estate and through the large hole in the west perimeter wall. In the far distance, Joelle thought she noticed a car's tail lights as it disappeared into the night. They approached a small building, not much larger than a single car garage. On the ground, there were long muddy tracks from a vehicle. Evidence that someone had exited the shed in a hurry within the last few hours. Most likely, Marcus Demetrius had escaped.

CHAPTER 56

OVER THE NEXT few days, both the Scotts and Uncle B worked with Interpol to search the estate for additional treasures. All of the antiquities on display in the main galleries were inventoried, photographed and prepared for transport. Items in Building Four, including the horde of coins from Jersey Island, were collected and prepared for shipment to the Louvre for restoration. Mick and Joelle enjoyed hunting for and finding many hidden galleries throughout the estate. In all, they discovered six additional private galleries that no one but Demetrius and Giorgio knew existed. The estate contained one of the largest collections of Celtic treasures in the world. And now, it would all be distributed to the original countries of origin to be enjoyed by the public.

"Agent Louis, thank you for helping us to return all of these antiquities to their rightful owners," said Joelle. "We had hoped you would apprehend Marcus Demetrius as well, but he will most likely pop up again."

"We have taken his estate and all of his treasures," said Agent Louis, "but men like Demetrius tend to have money hidden elsewhere. I'm sure it is not the last we have seen of him."

"We have some items in our truck that we would like to send with you," said Joelle. "I'll let Mick explain."

"When we were excavating the Le Dolmen du Mont Ubé site and Demetrius still had our daughter held hostage," said Mick, "we found a very unique item in the vault." Uncle B had now returned from the truck and was holding all three wooden boxes in his arms. "When we discovered what was inside, we thought it could be used as leverage with Demetrius if he failed to release our daughter. Fortunately, that was unnecessary. When we excavated both Chablé Menhir and Champs Dolent earlier today, we kept an eye out for similar boxes. Uncle B is holding all three."

"So what is inside that would have been so important to Demetrius?" asked Agent Louis.

Mick, Joelle and Uncle B started opening the wooden boxes so that Agent Louis could see the contents. "Each of these golden torcs are adorned with jewels and we believe were owned by the last Celtic tribe living in the Saint Malo area. All three torcs have a letter and symbol engraved in the gold. There is a letter 'B' with a large crown above it, a letter 'C' with a small crown above it and a letter 'A' with a sword above it. After speaking with the head curator of the Louvre, we believe that these were worn by the Celtic King Brennus, his eldest son Cunous and their most decorated Celtic warrior, Arios. They are absolutely priceless."

"Speaking for all three countries including the UK, France and Italy," said Agent Louis, "I want to thank you on their behalf. Your role in this operation made it possible to return a vast amount of antiquities to their rightful homes. On behalf of the insurance carriers for the Louvre, Galleria Borghese, the British Museum and the Jersey Island Museum, I have been instructed to present you with a finder's fee of five million dollars."

"That is most generous," said Mick. "Thank you. We will

of course be splitting this with Uncle B. We are all glad that we could play a part in this recovery and the downfall of Demetrius. I'm sure that we will cross paths again someday, but for now, Joelle and I are returning to the U.S. for some much needed rest. Uncle B, are you headed home?"

"No, I'm going to the U.S. as well. I need to spend some quality time with my daughter at ASU. I won't be as good looking as her recent body guard, but I think she will be happy to see me."

CHAPTER 57

A FEW DAYS LATER, after wrapping things up in Saint Malo, Mick, Joelle and Uncle B boarded a flight back to Arizona. "I'll see you both in a few days," said Uncle B as he claimed his luggage. "I'm going to be staying at the Mission Palms in Tempe near Danielle for the next ten days." They all hugged and said their goodbyes.

Over the next week, Mick and Joelle enjoyed time together with Uncle B, Kenzie and Danielle on several occasions. With the treasure hunt and hostage situation well behind them, they were all ready to move forward. As they were enjoying dinner one night at a popular restaurant in Scottsdale, Uncle B turned to Mick and said, "I have a little surprise for you both."

"Before you go on," said Mick, "Joelle and I have something to announce to the girls. Kenzie, your mother and I would like to do something special for you as a thank you for leading us to the Celtic treasures. Without your insight, finding the antiquities would not have been possible." Kenzie had no idea what Mick and Joelle were going to say next.

"As soon as school is out this spring," said Joelle, "you will be leaving for Paris. We have arranged for you to spend the summer in France with Danielle, all expenses paid." Kenzie and Danielle exchanged looks of disbelief.

"Are you serious?" asked Kenzie. "Both of us are going to Paris, France"?

"I've never been to Paris," said Danielle.

"Neither have I," said Kenzie.

"I know that you girls are really excited to go," said Joelle. "Mick and I have worked out some of the details with Uncle B and the five of us can discuss the rest over the next few weeks."

Mick turned towards Uncle B and said, "I'm afraid to ask what your surprise might be."

"Is it a good surprise or a bad surprise?" asked Joelle.

"I believe that it is a good surprise," said Uncle B as he handed Mick and Joelle a check for one million dollars. Mick and Joelle were both stunned.

"What is this for?" asked Mick. "Why would you be giving us a check and especially for this large amount"?

"It's not from me," said Uncle B, "it's from Giorgio."

Completely baffled, Mick asked. "Why would Giorgio be sending us a check? He died in the assault on the estate."

"That's true, he did," said Uncle B. "As part of my agreement with Giorgio to persuade you to help excavate the treasures at Chablé Menhir and Champs Dolent, I negotiated a payout of five million dollars. That large amount made it believable to Giorgio that I would double-cross my best friends. What he didn't know, was that I was double-crossing him. He wired two million dollars into an account I have in the Cayman Islands as an advance. Obviously, the remaining three million dollars was never paid since Giorgio died and the treasure was recovered." Mick, Joelle and the girls sat with their mouths open in disbelief. "This check is your half of the advance," said Uncle B. "Not bad for a few day's work, enjoy."

"Oh we will," said Joelle as she snatched the check from Mick's hand.

Several weeks later Mick and Joelle were at home in Phoenix enjoying the warm February weather on their patio. Mick was on the phone with Clay wrapping up some details from the Celtic discovery and Joelle was researching an upcoming trip to Germany in the spring.

"Clay, we really appreciate everything you did on this last project," said Mick. "You outdid yourself! Joelle and I have wired you your usual consulting fee and a little extra. One hundred thousand dollars extra, to be exact." Clay was speechless. He just sat with the phone in his hand and a blank expression on his face.

"Did you say one hundred thousand dollars?" asked Clay.

"Yes," affirmed Joelle. "With a baby on the way, you and Rachel will have a lot of extra expenses. And as your dad said, we would not have been successful on this project without your help."

"Thank you," uttered Clay. "I gotta call Rachel. I gotta go. Bye."

"I think we surprised him," said Mick. Joelle smiled and nodded in agreement.

"What are you reading?" asked Joelle.

"Do you remember that book I picked up in Saint Malo?" asked Mick.

"The thunder something," said Joelle. "Yes, what about it"?

"It's called the *Thunder God's Gold*," said Mick, "and it's really interesting."

Joelle rolled her eyes at Mick and said, "I'm sure it is."

Mick moved out to the pool area to enjoy the February sunshine. Relaxing on a lounge chair by the water, he continued to read his book. A few minutes later, with his eyes closed, Mick began to drift off to sleep. "I wonder?" he thought to himself. "The Lost Dutchman's Mine. Maybe Lee and his wife Natasha would like to come to Arizona this summer to explore the Superstition Mountains?" Mick had drifted off to sleep.